BLATANTLY BLYTHE

#3 Ghost Falls

SARAH HEGGER

Sarah Hegger
Romance Writer

Dedication

If you were one of those readers who emailed me, texted me, messaged me or left me a comment asking for another Ghost Falls book, then this is one hundred percent for you.

Without you, I would never have sat down to write this book.

Acknowledgments

With this book, I'm launching into the scary world of self-publishing. When I started as a writer, I never saw myself doing this, but I'm equal parts thrilled and terrified I took the leap. I would also never have made this leap without my wonderful friends Tara Cromer and Kristi Rose cheering me on. I can't thank them enough for all their help and reassurance.

I'd also like to thank Deb Jones Diem for naming Pippa and Matt's new baby girl, Jasmine. You nailed it, woman!

Love and thanks also to Penny Barber for her kickass editing skills and Renee Rocco for taking my burbled emails and turning them into beautiful covers that make my writer's heart sing.

I also owe a debt of thanks to the Collective members who did a proofread for me—Debbie Fuller, Samantha Talarico, and Terry Hammoutene. Weeding out those oopsies and typos keeps me sane.

As always, I owe so much to my real life hero, Brent, who would like you to know that he took time out of his busy day to correct and improve the book. Let me reassure you that he did survive the experience, but only just.

Copyright

 Created with Vellum

Praise for Sarah Hegger

set in the small Utah town of Ghost Falls. This charming and fun-filled book has everything from passion and humor to betrayal and revenge." – Jill M Smith, RT Books Reviews 2017 – Contemporary Love and Laughter Nominee

Becoming Bella
"Hegger excels at depicting familial relationships and friendships of all kinds, including purely platonic friendships between women and men. Tears, laughter, and a dollop of suspense make a memorable story that readers will want to revisit time and again." Publisher's Weekly, Starred Review

"…you have a terrific new romance that Hegger fans are going to love. Don't miss out!" Jill M. Smith – RT Book Reviews

Nobody's Fool

"Hegger offers a breath of fresh air in the romance genre." – Terri Dukes, RT Book Reviews

Nobody's Princess

"Hegger continues to live up to her rapidly growing reputation for breathing fresh air into the romance genre." – Terri Dukes, RT Book Reviews

"I have read the entire Willow Park Series. I have loved each of the books … Nobody's Princess is my favorite of all time." Harlequin Junkie, Top Pick

BLATANTLY BLYTHE

Chapter One

Blythe Barrows loved Eric Evans. Every inch of him. Standing with his back to her, his attention on the awakening view outside his bedroom window, his towel white against the taut, tanned muscle of his back, just the sight of him filled her heart to overflowing.

Which made this morning the worst morning of her life.

As he raised his coffee mug to his mouth, the light caught the intricate tattoo work down one arm. She'd traced every swirl, dip and spike of his ink with her fingers, and her tongue. The taste of his skin lingered in her sense memory along with the musky scent that was all him.

Loving him had become a habit so long ingrained she no longer remembered when it had started.

Eric leaned one arm on the architrave above the window.

She loved his gorgeous body, his quick mind, his irreverent sense of humor and even his stubborn, heart-gouging inability to love her back.

Since she had doodled Blythe Evans all over her Algebra 2 exercise book until the entire cover had been so embarrassingly covered that she'd had to rip it off and stuff it into the bottom of her book bag, up to and including right now.

Clueless shit that he was, and she needed to keep it that way. Sooner or later those three words would slip out: I love you. Eric would never dump her—he was too awesome a guy for that—but he would slowly slip away from her and keep putting distance between them.

Blythe didn't blame him, couldn't even work up a decent head of angry steam. He'd never wanted what she did, and he still didn't. She had changed. She wanted the entire enchilada: love, marriage, children, family dog and picket fence. Eric just wanted things to stay as they were.

He looked over his shoulder and gave her his slow, satiated post-sex grin and a chin jerk. "What are you looking at?"

"I don't know but it's looking back." Not much had changed in eighteen years. Ghost Falls would die laughing if they knew how she felt about him. Right after they tarred and feathered her and ran her out of town for daring to touch one of the cherished Evans boys.

He sauntered over to the bed, muscle playing beneath his skin. "Look at you," he murmured. "All sleepy and sexy." He leaned over the bed toward her. "Come here, sweet thing."

"What for?" She gave him the pert response he expected. This time though, the words lacerated her heart.

He whispered against her mouth. "You'll find out when you get here."

Blythe pressed her mouth to his to hide the tears threatening to break free.

"Hmm." He sucked her bottom lip. "I wish I had time to stay and wake you right."

Blythe had counted on his early meeting giving her the escape she needed. After today she would never get to kiss that beautiful mouth again. Blythe tightened her grip on the silky dark hair at his nape and tugged him closer. Fastening her mouth to his, she poured everything into this one last kiss, all her heartbreak, all her pointless wishing and waiting, all the years of longing and those that would follow.

Eric groaned and took control of the kiss. His tongue slid into her mouth, owning her and demanding her response. His hands tightened on her face.

Blythe allowed herself this. Her body heated with their kiss, a kiss full of the promise of naked skin sliding against naked skin.

"Sweet thing." He pulled away with a soft laugh. "You don't play fair."

She let him go.

Stepping back from the bed, Eric dropped his towel and gave her a peepshow of the taut globes of his amazing ass. An ass she knew well enough to trace in her mind long after he'd left her. And he always stayed too little and stayed away too long.

"So." He hauled on his boxers and disappeared inside his closet. Muscle flexed in his arms as he reappeared, fastening his charcoal gray slacks. "I'm going to be a bit tied up for the next few days."

Blythe dropped to her back and stared at the high cathedral ceilings of Eric's bedroom. He'd built the house himself. A labor of love and dedication reflecting Eric in every elegant, powerful sweep of wood, steel, brick and mortar.

She stayed silent, waiting for what was sure to come next: the good excuse, the inarguable logic that put distance between them. She could end his efforts in two words—no problem—and give them both a break, but she couldn't quite summon the words. The pain, like two hard fists on either side of her ribcage, wouldn't let her speak yet. Instead she tucked the sheet over her breasts.

Subdued, tasteful lighting made macabre early morning shadows on the ceiling.

Eric shrugged into his crisp white shirt and did the buttons at the cuff first. Always the same order. Left cuff, flick of the wrist to settle the right cuff, and then those buttons. Next, his large hands fastened on either side of the front placket and jerked them neatly into place. Then he buttoned from the bottom up. "Do you need anything until we see each other again?"

Always the same question, and her answer remained unchanged. "Nope. Thank you anyway."

"You wouldn't tell me if you did." He gave her his wry half smile that she adored.

"Probably not." She couldn't force her facial muscles into the smile he expected. Not this morning. They'd been over and over the help thing. He didn't get it and now he never would. In Ghost Falls the freeloading Barrowses were legendary. She couldn't do anything about being a Barrows, but she could not and would not keep her hand held out.

Turning to the long mirror above the dressing table, Eric watched his reflection as he tied his bright red tie. "I'll give you a call when I get some time. See if you're free?"

It wasn't really a question, and they both knew it. He called, and she made herself free.

Except, not after today. Not anymore.

"Hey." She rolled to her side and propped her head on her palm. Despite the hammering of her heart, she kept her tone calm. "I need to talk to you."

A flicker of annoyance flit over the planes of his handsome face. "Now? Can it wait? I have a meeting."

"This won't take long." She sat up and dropped her legs over the side of the bed. After she got through saying what she had to, she needed a quick escape to the bathroom before she gave in and cried her river. "We can't do this anymore."

He stilled and cocked his head. His dark eyes studied her. "By this you mean us?"

"Yes." Dragging the sheet up with her, she stood. She felt stronger standing anyway. "I'm ending it. I'm ending this." She motioned from her to him. "This thing between us."

"Right." He raised his eyebrows and adjusted his tie. Annoyance flickered on his face as he met her gaze in the mirror. "I need to go. Help yourself to whatever you want. You know the way out."

He shoved his arms into his suit jacket in controlled, angry motions. In four long strides, he was out the door, his feet clopping along the hardwood floor.

And that was that.

Blythe stood with her feet stuck to the floor as he made the small sounds preceding his departure: grabbing his laptop from the dining room table, the rattle of small change in the bowl by the door as he dug out his car keys, and the awful finality of the door to the garage slamming behind him.

She'd done it. She'd broken up with Eric Evans. Like the moment before the pain registers when you cut yourself, when you watch with detachment as the blood oozes out of the wound, she calmly walked into the bathroom and turned on the shower.

Eric's wet towel hung in a haphazard bunch over the rack, and she straightened it. The citrus tang of his aftershave lingered in the humid air. Littered over the white marble countertop were his toothbrush and toothpaste, drops of foam from where he had shaved and tiny puddles of water.

This was all she had left of him, and it would have to be enough to last a lifetime.

Blythe Barrows loved Eric Evans with every fiber of her being, and because he'd be mortified if he knew—trapped between not wanting to hurt her, and not feeling the same—she needed to leave him, and this time she needed to stay gone.

ERIC BACKED his black Jaguar XJ out of his garage to the circular driveway outside his house. He repressed the desire to thrust his foot down on the gas and send the three hundred and forty supercharged horses beneath the hood roaring.

Blythe knew he had an important meeting this morning, and yet she'd chosen to break up with him anyway.

Again.

He nosed his car into the still, quiet street. Long morning shadows stretched out to stroke the car's hood.

Calling it a breakup gave whatever the hell it was between them too much credit. You could only break up if you were in a relationship, and he and Blythe were not now—nor had they ever been—in a relationship.

They hooked up from time to time. Fuck buddies. When the mood struck them, they gave each other a call. The mood struck them often enough, and the sex was good enough, that they had been doing this on and off for more years than he cared to count.

The sex was great to be honest, and it kept him coming back time and time again.

He didn't date. He didn't have time to date. He certainly didn't have the energy to date either. Dating led to expectations. Expectations he'd never fulfill.

Love and marriage were great. For other people. His brothers Matt and Nate had stumbled on to their happily ever afters with two great women. Eric loved his sisters-in-law and the nephews and nieces they would soon add to the one niece he already had.

Behind the hills ringing Ghost Falls, the sun painted the sky roseate. He liked to get to the office before anyone else and get his head together.

He needed to get his mind on his morning meeting. Evans Construction, which he ran with his older brother Matt, sat poised on the edge of do or die. He and Matt had built it up to this point, taking the town of Ghost Falls with them. They'd done their job well, too well. The growth happening in Ghost Falls had brought the big Denver and Salt Lake City companies out to play. They didn't give a shit about Ghost Falls or who they had to squeeze to make a buck.

Evans Construction needed to grow, and fast. The sort of growth a merger could make happen.

Still, visions of Blythe's huge green eyes nestled burr-like in the back of his brain. How a woman that tough could look so wounded was beyond him. Like he'd opened her main artery and left her bleeding to death.

That wasn't fair. He was probably one of the few people alive who knew Blythe wasn't half as tough as she pretended to be. She'd upset him enough this morning to bring out his inner asshole.

What they had might not be traditional but it was good. Blythe was special, and he knew that better than anyone. He hated the idea of there being no more them, and she deserved better from him.

Sure, they'd walked this path before. Any other time he'd have taken a seat beside her, held her close and talked it through. Then they would have made love and healed the hurt between them. It had only gotten to him this morning because of the importance of his upcoming meeting.

Some patience and caring on his part and her time and attention always put things back on track. And he and Blythe always got back on track. Always.

Chapter Two

By the time he nosed into his parking space outside the large brick building that housed Evans Construction, Eric had his A-game on. He thrived on the cut and thrust of negotiation. Pitting wills and wits against a worthy opponent got his blood up, gave him the high he craved.

He unlocked the glass front door and pushed it open. Always the first to get there in the morning, he flipped on the lights.

The receptionist, Mrs. Cameron, wouldn't arrive for another two hours. Matt had employed her when the school district had laid her off after many years of being the high school receptionist. She still made Eric want to check his shirt was tucked in. Despite her scary exterior, she did her job well. It had taken Eric weeks to soften her up, and now he was her favorite. It earned him first dibs on whatever cookies she brought in, and a constant supply of hot coffee.

Walking through the open-plan office, Eric flipped on lights as he went. Their dad had started the business before Matt had been born. Back then it had been only one floor of one building. Under Matt's guidance, the business had grown and swallowed up the two neighboring buildings.

A couple of years ago, he'd come back to Ghost Falls and talked Matt into expanding the traditional domestic construction business into real estate development with him. Matt had sacrificed enough for their family, and it had been way past time Eric stepped up and shared some of the responsibility of their mother, their younger siblings, and the business. As a tribute to Dad, they'd kept the name of his business, but they did way more than construction now.

Eric let himself into his office. Outside his window, the sun turned the horizon above the mountains into a gaudy painting. All the years he had lived in Denver, he hadn't known how much he'd missed Ghost Falls.

Fresh out of college, he hadn't been able to wait to shake Ghost Falls like a bad habit.

Being back had given him the chance to take his place as a member of the Evans family, and also to reconnect with his angry, heartbroken inner teen who he'd been running from for most of his adult life.

Blythe had been one of two who'd understood that broken boy. And he'd been a total dick to her this morning. They may not have been heading for love and marriage, but they had been lovers for enough years for her to deserve his respect and consideration.

He dug out his phone and pulled up her contact info listed under Sweet Thing.

She'd hated that name when he'd first come up with it. Eric chuckled at the memory of her horrified face. Over the years, it had become a joke they shared. Now the nickname was who she was to him, one of the sweetest parts of his day.

Sorry for being a dick, he typed. *Had a lot on my mind this morning.*

The message stayed dormant, without the three dots indicating she was typing a reply.

She was mad, and he didn't blame her. His meeting wasn't for another two and a half hours. He could have taken a few minutes to cajole her out of her mood. He should have taken the time to make love to her. Making love with Blythe only got better every time.

Let me make it up to you???? For insurance he added a series of emojis, and then laughed as he imagined her face when she saw them. Blythe loved emojis. A row of them appeared on any text she sent him. He teased her about it. About how sometimes her texts were more like deciphering hieroglyphics.

They had a history, and that history was made up of a series of great moments.

Still, she hadn't read the message.

So, she was really pissed. This would take an in-person intervention and some fancy footwork. Flowers were too meh. Only a clueless asshole sent flowers when he wanted to climb out of the hole he'd dug for himself. Same with chocolate, and Blythe didn't eat it anyway.

His libido hummed to life at the thought of Blythe's body. Genetics had been kind to Blythe, and she worked hard to keep it that way. He still got hard thinking of those long, toned legs that flowered into the full curve of her hips. A woman's hips, not the shape of a preadolescent boy. He could almost span her waist with his hands. The full curve of her breasts turned her into a pinup.

A man didn't let that kind of awesome stay mad at him for long,

Eric pulled out his laptop and fired it up. He would talk with Blythe later. Right now, he had the most important meeting of his life to get through. The Denver and SLC big boys had their coils around Ghost Falls and were snatching up any new contracts. The squeeze was on for smaller operations like theirs. Evans Construction needed to bulk up to take them on, and merging with Gunning Contracting offered a potential lifeline. But not at any cost. Relinquishing control of the company needed to be worth it.

Eric had been eighteen when Dad died. None of them

had had a clue how much trouble Evans Construction had been in. In a desperate silence, Dad had almost run it into the ground.

Eric got up and went to the kitchen in search of coffee.

Thinking about his dad always brought with it that anger so old it no longer flared, but the embers still smoldered.

In the kitchen, the coffeepot sat empty. He filled it with water and found the grounds but drew a blank on filters.

Matt had taken over the company at nineteen, turning down a full ride football scholarship to shoulder the burden. Eric would owe his older brother for that for the rest of his life. Matt had these touches of nostalgia around the office, and the ancient coffee filter machine was one of them.

He opened cupboard door after cupboard door. At this rate, he was going to have to make the trip to the coffee shop.

Screw it. When she got there, he was going to tell Mrs. Cameron to get a Keurig or something like it. This old school crap might make Matt happy, but it wasn't doing much for him that morning.

Footsteps pulled him out of his head.

"There you are." Grayson poked his head around the kitchen doorjamb. "I knew you had to be here already."

Eric smiled at his assistant. "What are you doing here so early?"

"If you're here"—Grayson spread his hand over his chest—"then my place is by your side."

Jerking his head at the coffee maker, he asked, "Can you?"

"I can do you one better." Grayson held up a takeout tray with two coffees on it. "You don't pay me enough, you know."

"Oh, I know." Eric grabbed the coffee and took a sip. Grayson had followed him from Denver. Despite Eric's attempts to promote him, Grayson resisted. He liked what he did, and Eric was painfully grateful he did. Over the years, Grayson had learned to read his mind. Like this morning. Grayson knew he would be keyed up about the meeting.

Grayson followed Eric into his office. "I did some more research on Gunning last night," he said and took the visitor's chair opposite Eric. "Personal stuff."

"And?" They'd done their due diligence on Gunning Contracting as soon as Gunning had approached them. Chase Gunning ran a rock-solid business. A business that lacked the flair Evans Construction brought to everything they did. Evans took more risks and sometimes that cost them.

The merger would work for both companies. Like a lot of people, Gunning was looking for an in at Ghost Falls. Evans understood the market. Hell, they'd almost created the market. Eric had first seen the potential for growth in the area and brought that proposal to Matt. But the bigger outside companies were winning bid after bid as investors saw the potential for safer returns. Bigger companies raised more capital, and could afford to take on higher project risk. Size meant using fewer subcontractors, which gave them better quality control. Gunning and Evans together had the assets and weight to keep the big dogs from eating them alive.

Grayson put his laptop on Eric's desk and flipped it open. "Gunning is a bit of a social media dinosaur," he said. "No surprise there. It fits everything we know about him." Grayson grinned at Eric. "Strictly LinkedIn and Facebook."

"Not even Twitter?" Eric played along.

"He has an account, but he barely uses it." Grayson tapped on his keyboard. "Three wives, last one Terri, now divorced. Seven kids." Nothing Eric didn't already know. "He likes blondes." Grayson slid the laptop around. "Several pictures of Chase with interchangeable blondes. He likes them young and hot and happy to selfie."

"The man has an ego." Eric shrugged. He had worked that out within minutes of meeting Gunning. Egos weren't a problem. Eric had a healthy one of his own. He looked at a picture of an early twenties hottie cuddled up to Gunning. "And a bit of a midlife crisis going on."

"Right!" Grayson raised his eyebrows. "He doesn't post pictures of his kids though. Not much of a family man. More of a trophy man."

Now that Eric could use. Once you understood the person across the boardroom table from you, it gave you that missing edge. Gunning had a reputation for being a hard-nosed businessman, a bit old school. He liked to wrestle for as much control as he could. Eric wasn't going to hand over controlling interest in Evans Construction, or allow Gunning to run operations. Evans Construction couldn't afford to walk away, but neither could they afford to roll over.

Game on. God, Eric lived for this shit.

MATT ARRIVED AN HOUR LATER, looking exhausted. He stumbled into Eric's office, sucked back a coffee, and then looked disconsolately into the bottom of the cup.

With a laugh, Grayson filled it up. "Late night?"

"Early morning." Matt grimaced. Both Eric and Matt had inherited their tall and dark genetic stamp from their father, but Matt's eyes were lighter. Nate, the next brother in line, was the pretty one. "Jasmine decided three a.m. was a great opportunity to spend time with her dad."

Eric adored his new niece. Six months, and with the lights just coming on behind her green eyes, an exact replica of her gorgeous mother's, Jasmine had them all wrapped around her chubby finger. "How's Pippa doing?"

"Great." Matt always got this part goofy, part smug smile on his face when he spoke of his wife. "She's been doing most of the nights. Last night she was so wiped she didn't even hear Jasmine." He took the seat beside Grayson. "Okay! Chase Gunning. What's the play?"

GUNNING ARRIVED five minutes before their meeting was due to start. Being late and making the other party wait for you was strictly for amateurs. Eric would have done the same as Gunning, which was a plus for this potential deal. They had similar values.

He and Matt went to reception to meet Gunning.

Fifty-one, about six one, two hundred pounds, Gunning was in great shape. He worked out every morning, didn't touch caffeine and only drank in moderation. Mostly martinis, but he would occasionally have an amber ale.

"Chase." Eric held out his hand and got a firm shake in return.

Gunning smiled at him, and then greeted Matt. "How are you?"

A young woman accompanied Gunning. In a severe black jacket and tight skirt, with sky high heels, she worked that whole clever, scary and fucking sexy thing.

Gunning motioned her. "This is Miranda Patel. She's working with me on this."

"Pleased to meet you." Her dark hair was pulled to her nape and highlighted the delicate precision of her cheekbones. Red lipstick drew attention to her full mouth.

Gunning had brought a secret weapon to the meeting.

Eric didn't need to look at him to know that Grayson would get right on the mystery of who, where and what concerning Miranda Patel. If another player entered the arena, they became fair game.

Patel was exactly the sort of woman Eric would have dated. Smart, successful and driven with a body that didn't quit. Clearly, Gunning had also done his homework.

Smiling, Eric shook her hand. "Pleased to meet you."

Her dark gaze did a lightning fast sweep of him, assessing him, rating him, deciding who he was. She smiled with a touch more warmth. "And you."

Ten minutes later, personal considerations had been shoved aside as negotiations began.

Matt sat back and let him take the lead. He and Matt worked well together. They understood and respected each other's strengths. Matt ran the operations side and did it damn well.

More comfortable in his construction boots than a suit, Matt had the normal guy touch on site that kept everyone working to budget and on schedule.

With Jasmine's birth and Pippa needing Matt around more while she recovered, Eric had been taking up the slack of Matt's role recently. But the boardroom was where Eric shone. This is what he brought to Evans Construction. Negotiation. Finessing the deal.

Gunning knew it too and addressed most of his remarks to Eric.

Next to Gunning, Miranda Patel was making the same assessment. Over the boardroom table, her dark gaze sent him the clear message: she liked what she saw.

Chapter Three

Blythe had picked her day to shatter her own heart carefully.

She'd deleted Eric's messages without reading them. He had that big meeting today about a possible merger and would be focused on that.

After leaving Eric's house, she climbed into her second-hand Prius and drove home. The house that would no longer be her home after today, that is.

She'd also chosen a day on which she would have enough distraction to keep the heartache at bay.

Today Blythe was moving out of the house she'd grown up in, and, despite the persistent tightness in her chest, that thought still gave her a thrill. She'd always be a Barrows, and in a town as tiny as Ghost Falls, that name stuck like dog shit to the bottom of her shoe and stank up anyone who heard it.

She accepted that it was too late for her to be anything else in the eyes of Ghost Falls. Blythe Barrows was no good, the town slut, just like her whore of a mother. No better than her petty criminal of a father, and those dreadful brothers.

Yeah, yeah, yeah. She got it. She'd heard it often enough for the sting to lessen, but there was still time for Will, and sweet little Kim. Blythe meant to make it that way. It had taken her far longer than she'd have liked to get where she could offer her youngest siblings the stability they deserved.

She passed the center of town with its quaint Victorian lampposts. Rumor had it Philomene St. Amor had decreed the old ones to be too ugly and upsetting to her artistic constitution. Blythe didn't know the diva well, but anyone who lived in Ghost Falls had heard of her. Will worked for her from time to time, and he really liked her. Of course, the diva like everyone else, still called Will that ridiculous name their father had saddled him with.

Out of his mind drunk, ostensibly celebrating the birth of another kid, Pat Barrows had thought it hilarious to call the new baby Wheeler. Hardy-har-har, with the joke on Will for the rest of his life.

God, Pat was a dick. He drifted in and out of their lives when it suited him. He'd been blessedly absent for eighteen months this time, but that didn't mean they'd seen the last of him. And, of course, Mom would take him right back again.

As much as Blythe resented the brush Ghost Falls had painted her with, her family had earned it.

As Blythe drove past, Bella Erikson, now Evans, was opening her high-end clothing store. Despite the gorgeous clothes, Bella's was the last place on earth Blythe would shop. Most of the town behaved like Bella was a cross between Mother Theresa and Tweety Bird. Only Blythe had seen the bitchy side of Bella.

Bella liked to stare down her nose at Blythe and do her best to make her feel like trash. It had worked all through elementary and then middle school. In high school Blythe had gotten her back by taking all the male attention away from Bella.

Of course, she had sacrificed her reputation for her efforts, but being a Barrows gave you a strike out in that department from birth.

Blythe took a left on Elm street. Neat patches of garden

SARAH HEGGER

fronted pretty homes on either side of her. One day she would
buy a little patch of paradise for herself along Elm street.
With her business taking off, getting new clients every day, it
was starting to look possible.

In one of the front yards, two kids were chasing each other
with piles of leaves and shrieking with delight.

The pain in her chest eased a mite as she watched them.
That could be Kim one day, playing with a kid from next
door.

Blythe didn't need one of the palatial houses on the top of
the hills surrounding Ghost Falls. The sort of homes Eric and
Matt built for people who often had more money than brains.
That sort of affluence didn't appeal to her. All she wanted was
there on Elm street. A nice, tidy little house behind a pretty
patch of green. A place she could plant some flowers and
maintain easily. A place in a good school district with lots of
families all around them where Kim could grow up away from
the Barrows stench. A place for Will to come home to between
his college semesters. A place they could all call home.

From Elm, she made her way farther from the town
center. The homes grew smaller, and the green grass gave way
to overgrown patches of weeds and dirt. The houses seemed
to glare at her, daring her to pass judgment on them.

She left the residential neighborhoods behind and followed
a rural road deeper into the patchy brush. Sherman's gas
station hadn't opened yet. As soon as Mandy had slept off her
hangover and crawled out of bed, it would open. As kids,
Blythe and Blake had walked down there when they could get
a few coins for candy and magazines. Most of the time, Brett
had been the source of those coins.

Pat didn't have any money and Mom kept what she had
for booze. Since she'd been old enough to earn money, Blythe
never brought it into the house if she could help it. Her
brothers regarded her money as theirs. For Kim and Will's

sake, however, she had been buying all the groceries and keeping the lights on. The free ride ended today.

Hanging drunkenly on the truncated remains of a dead tree was the number seven twenty-two. Home sweet home. She slowed over the rutted drive. Weeds grew so high in the front yard that she might have to fight her way out of her car.

A rusted-out car husk had found some friends, and they made a skeletal junkyard to the left of the house. The house itself didn't look so bad. Between her and Will, they'd managed to keep the worst of the decay at bay. Even managed to give it a coat or two of paint a couple of years ago. Keeping a decent house for Will and Kim was one reason it had taken so long to be able to afford her own place.

Blythe parked, took a deep breath and stepped out of her car.

Beneath some scrub oak, two motorbikes gleamed in the morning light. Two of her older brothers were home it seemed. It amazed her that they could take such care of those bikes and live like pigs.

A rambling old farmhouse, it might even have been a good-looking house if someone had given enough of a crap to make it so. A large, top loading washing machine with its mismatched dryer took up most of the front porch.

Raised voices came from inside the house as she eased open the door. The familiar stench of cigarettes and mildew welcomed her home.

Will sat on the bottom step of the staircase to the right of the door. He gave her a tight smile when he saw her. "Barron's here."

"Damn." She had hoped to get moved out early enough that they were either still out partying or hadn't recovered from the night before. "Anyone else?"

"He has some loser friend with him." Will kept his voice low as he glanced up the stairs. "They've been upstairs all morning. They haven't noticed the bags." He jerked his head to the pile of luggage in the doorway to the sitting room.

That was something at least. "Kim?"

"At St. Peter's." Will nodded. "I got her to kindergarten before they pitched up. I left my car at our new place." He jerked his head toward upstairs. "Don't want them to see it."

"Perfect." Blythe kept it cheerful. If her other brothers caught sight of Will's new car, they'd take it from him. "We can pick her up later."

"Motorcycle Man" pounded from Barron's room. Barron thought of it as his personal anthem and any time he was around, it was only a matter of time before it got played.

"Fuck yeah!" Barron yelled, and Blythe could almost see him up there, hands in the air, fingers working an air guitar as he headbanged.

She played it cool for Will. "You ready?"

"Yeah?" His sweet, shy smile warmed the cold place inside her. If she had to take on Barron, she'd do it to make sure Will smiled more often. "I got Kim's stuff all packed as well."

"Thank you." She touched his cheek. At nineteen, Will didn't yet have a full beard, and his skin was still baby soft. Of all her brothers, he looked the least like her. Dark haired like their father, with hazel eyes, he had inherited the more rugged bone structure that Brett and Barron shared. Will looked exactly like their father.

"You okay?" He cocked his head and studied her.

But his gentle, pure soul was all his own. God knows how he'd managed to shine through the genetic crapshoot of their parents. Bless him, he had, and done so with a determination to better himself that none of their other brothers came close to understanding.

"I'm good." Not even close, but she managed a smile.

"Little fucker?" Barron's voice rose over the music. "Bring us a beer."

Will's face tightened.

"Do it." Blythe nodded up the stairs. "Maybe it will keep him out of our hair while I get us all loaded up."

"Cool." Will dragged his feet toward the kitchen.

From now on Barron could buy his own beer. Once she got the kids out of there, she felt no obligation to the others.

Will had an odd assortment of backpacks, threadbare kit bags and trash bags stacked inside the front door. It took Blythe three trips to load up her car, all of them with her eyes on the stairs.

Not vicious like the oldest, Brett, had been, Barron still had an unpredictable temper.

After taking them beer and chips, Will helped her with the last few bags.

Despite her heartache, she felt lighter somehow, as if getting out of that house had lifted a burden. The burden of being a Barrows.

THE MASTER BEDROOM was situated on the ground floor to the right of the stairs. To the left was the sitting room that led into a dining room and kitchen. Blythe had given up on the kitchen years ago. The only things eating in that kitchen were the cockroaches.

Praying her mother was lucid, Blythe tapped on the door.

Carly Barrows must have been a knockout in her time. Some of that former beauty still clung to the delicate lines of her face. Time and being married to Pat had done a number on the rest of her though.

As Blythe stepped into the room, Carly turned bleary green eyes to her. "Baby girl."

"Hey, Mom. I came to say goodbye."

Carly's face crumpled. "You're still going to do this?"

"I have to."

At least Carly looked reasonably sober. Carly's lank, blond hair hung on either side of her drawn face. With a shaking hand she grabbed a pack of cigarettes and pulled one out. "You got a light?"

"No." Blythe wished her mother wouldn't smoke, but it wasn't a battle she had a hope of winning. "Will and I are leaving now."

"Taking my little girl with you." Carly's voice shook. She scrabbled in her bedside table and produced a hot pink lighter. "My pretty little Kyberlee. You were pretty as a baby but nothing on Kyberlee."

Not Kyberlee at all, but Kimberly, because Blythe had filled in the birth certificate before Carly's obsessions with the Kardashians had followed her baby sister around forever. Wheeler was bad enough. "You know why. We've spoken about this."

The flame turned the cigarette tip to a cherry as Carly sucked on it. "Talking." Carly made a face and pulled on her smoke. "You're always talking at me until my head hurts."

"You can come and see her." Under certain conditions, which Blythe had outlined painstakingly. No showing up drunk. No sloppy scenes. No smoking and no brothers. "And if you need anything, ask Dixie. She can let me know, and I'll come and see you when I can."

Carly didn't seem to hear her and stared past her. Through grubby net curtains, the view of the yard showcased an old bathtub leaned on its side, a dirty pool of rainwater stagnating inside it. "I didn't set out for things to be like this."

"I know, Mom." Nobody could have wished this existence on themselves. Mother to ten children, seven with up close and personal relationships with law enforcement, wife to a drunken lout who stayed only long enough to plant another baby in your belly. "You know I'll take care of her, and when you're back on your feet, I'll bring her right back to you."

"When I'm back on my feet." Mom really did want more for them. She smiled, showing gaps between her teeth. One for each baby they said, and Carly had brought ten full term and buried another three.

God, Blythe didn't want this to be her story. The walls pressed in on her and she stood. "I'll call you and let you know how we are."

"You do that." Carly stubbed her cigarette out in an overflowing ashtray and found a sixty-ounce bottle of rotgut vodka tucked in her bedclothes. Unscrewing the top, she paused with it halfway to her mouth. "Do better, baby girl. Be better."

Blythe left the room and paused in the clothing-littered hallway to breathe and remind herself that this was not her life, not her fate. Everything she'd done since she left high school had been about making sure she had choices, and that those choices extended to Will and now Kim.

Near the front door, Barron had Will by the nape, shaking him like a rat.

"Put him down, Barron." Blythe kept the fear out of her voice. Gut-deep feral, Barron fed on fear.

Barron turned bloodshot eyes her way and sneered. "After I teach him some manners." He shoved Will against the wall, and his skull made a dull thwack. "Mouthing off to me."

"He's sorry, Barron. I'm going to take him out of your hair now."

Will met her gaze, sending the silent message that had passed between them countless times: it's worse if you fight back.

Barron kept his grip on Will as he thought it over. His eyes were cunning in the harsh cruelty of his features. Dark unwashed hair hung halfway down his back. His heavily tattooed biceps strained his Motorhead T-shirt. "Where you going?"

"Out." No way she was sharing her plan with Barron. They'd told Kim as little as possible to avoid Barron knowing.

Smaller than Brett, Barron still had enough bulk to do some serious damage.

Fortunately, he wasn't as bright as Brett, and he let Will go. "We're out of beer. Make sure you bring some back."

Chapter Four

Negotiations had gone well. It had taken most of the day, but they'd finally hammered out a way to move forward. The high of his day made him feel like there was nothing he couldn't do.

Gunning invited them to dinner, but Matt begged off. Pippa needed him home, and whatever Pippa needed Matt made sure she got. Dad had been the same. Cressy demanded and Dad made sure she got it. That was where any similarity between Mom and Pippa ended.

Pippa loved Matt as much as he loved her. Just as Matt would bend himself backwards for her, there was nothing Pippa wouldn't do for Matt. Eric was glad Matt had found that sort of love in his life.

It didn't make him a believer, however.

He got back to his office for a brief five minutes before they went to dinner. Still no reply from Blythe. It could also be because she was busy. She'd taken possession of her new apartment today. He'd made sure she'd jumped the waiting list and gotten a good price. She'd kill him if she knew.

Talk to me, Sweet Thing, he texted. *Whatever it is, we can sort it out.*

He waited a few minutes for a response, and then joined Chase and Miranda in reception.

Chase had picked Eric's favorite restaurant in Ghost Falls, the Boulangerie. Great food, impeccable service, a huge wine list and prices to match, it was the place Eric would have chosen for the occasion. It said relaxed and business at the same time.

As the maitre d', Gerard, led them to their table, they moved through a dining room of similar people to their party. A few of them Eric knew, and he waved.

They arrived at their table, Gerard pulled out the table, and Miranda slid into the dark leather booth. Eric took his place opposite her.

Chase pulled his phone out of his pocket and checked it. "Damn." He indicated his phone. "I need to make a quick call. Get some drinks ordered, and I'll be back before the ice melts."

With a wry smile, Miranda unbuttoned her jacket and slipped it off her shoulders. Underneath she had a sleeveless silk blouse that gave Eric a hint of cleavage. It was the perfect transition from day into night.

For some reason it made him think about Blythe. Maybe because she'd been on his mind most of the day. Raised by a drunk mother on the wrong side of the tracks, she often complained of not knowing what was appropriate to wear. When he'd met her, she'd been all about too tight, too short and too low cut.

It used to embarrass him, and he never wanted to be seen out with her. He'd even tried to do the Pretty Woman thing with her, but Blythe hadn't wanted any of that. She made her own way through the world.

As he grew up more, he understood the way she dressed for the vulnerability it really was. She didn't know any better most of the time, and the rest she used her style like armor. If Ghost Falls was going to talk about her and call her names, and they did, then she wasn't going to show them who she really was.

Except with him. He always got the real Blythe.

"To a mutually beneficial future." Miranda raised her glass. Her honey and spice perfume twined around him. It suited her perfectly, sophisticated and exotic.

Eric clinked his glass with hers. He loosened the top button of his shirt and tugged his tie down. If she had shifted into relaxed mode so could he. "Patel? Is that Indian?"

"It is." She gave him a beautiful smile, her lipstick bright red against her amber skin and white teeth. "Have you ever been?"

"Regrettably not."

"Most of my extended family is still there." She toyed with the stem of her wineglass. Long, slender fingers topped with red nails stroked the glass. "Chase tells me you are originally from here."

"Born and raised." Eric added a little aw-shucks to his smile. She probably wouldn't buy him as a harmless local boy, but it was worth a try.

Chase rejoined them. "I'm really sorry about this." He grimaced. "The timing is horrible but I'm going to have to cut this evening short." He motioned the two of them. "But you two stay. Enjoy your dinner. On me."

And wasn't that convenient, leaving him alone with the beautiful Miranda.

She met his gaze and smiled. "You have to eat. I have to eat."

Eric returned her smile. Miranda was a beautiful woman, and there were worse things he could be doing with his time. Like waiting for his stubborn blonde to call him back.

The wine they shared took the sharp edges off the evening, and Eric enjoyed his dinner.

Smart, clever and surprisingly funny, Miranda made a great dinner companion. They had a lot in common as well, and the evening passed quickly. He liked her, and it had been a long time since he'd been out with anyone but Blythe.

He tried to calculate how long as Miranda told him about her college roommate. He managed to laugh in all the right places.

Blythe and he had never labeled their relationship, and she'd never demanded exclusivity from him. Or him from her, but the notion that she might not have been almost soured his gentle buzz. Still, he had never exercised the open hall pass. Those times he had been with Blythe, he had been with her alone. Until circumstances had pulled him somewhere else.

Despite Chase's instruction to have dinner on him, Eric picked up the bill when it came.

Gerard ordered a car for Miranda, and Eric walked her out.

As the car glided to a stop in front of them, she handed him her card with a sultry smile. "Call me if you want to do this again."

Eric accepted the card, as she'd known he would.

Miranda climbed into the car without looking back, a woman supremely confident in herself and her own appeal. She had no reason not to be. Any one of a dozen men eating in the restaurant tonight would have been happy to have her card.

Sliding it into his pocket, Eric strolled to his car. It was almost regrettable that Miranda was not the girl he wanted tonight.

It took him by surprise when Blythe answered his call. She sounded flat and weary. "Eric. It's late. Why are you calling?"

"How's the new apartment?" She had spent the day moving in and was probably tired. "I hope I didn't wake you."

"No." She sighed. "The apartment is fine. Listen, Eric I—"

"What do you say to me grabbing a bottle of red and bringing you a pizza? I can bring enough for Will and Kim.

We can have our own little housewarming." Her voice set a slow simmer snaking through his bloodstream. After Will and Kim went to bed, they could have a private celebration.

She didn't speak for a while, and Eric headed down the hill to Del Fino's. They made the best pizza in town and would still be open.

His headlights picked out the dark hulking shapes of the trees on either side of the road. In a couple of months, they would be covered in snow, and the entire area would be transformed in time for the chalet and ski crowd to move in. It made him proud that he and Matt had been a small part of bringing prosperity to Ghost Falls, and even more determined to make sure they stayed a part of it.

"That's very kind—"

"I know you like mushrooms and ham," he said. "What about Kim and Will? What will they have?"

"Stop it, Eric." She clipped his name like she did when she was pissed, and his mood crashed. In his pocket he had the card of a hot, smart, sophisticated woman, and he'd walked away from that because of Blythe. And she was still pissed at him. "I got your texts," Blythe said. "But I deleted them."

That jolted Eric and brought his full attention to the call. "Say what?"

"I deleted them." Her tone softened. "I meant what I said this morning and responding to them only drags this out." She took a deep breath. "The only reason I took this call was to ask you to stop."

"Stop?" Something close to anger slithered up his spine.

"Stop texting and stop calling," Blythe said. "We're done." She hung up.

"Fuck!" Eric pounded his steering wheel. Once, about six years ago, when he'd still been living in Denver, she'd hung up on him. That time, he'd thoroughly deserved it. Having left her behind in Ghost Falls, he'd not bothered to call until the next time he breezed into town. She'd refused to see him when

SARAH HEGGER

he'd called her looking for a booty call. But this wasn't that. He wanted to bring her pizza, celebrate that independence she'd been working so hard toward.

Next time he'd be better off calling Miranda Patel. There was a woman who understood the score, understood a man like him.

Chapter Five

Blythe needed to get up and get going. She had to get Kim ready for kindergarten and drop her off before she got herself to work. It was day three of being in her apartment, and she still woke with that sense of newness and contentment.

Other than the dull ache of missing Eric, she finally had turned her dreams into reality.

She took a few extra minutes to wallow in the pride of her space. Her space. Her bedroom she didn't have to share with anyone. Her bedroom in her apartment, with Will and Kim sleeping down the hall in their own rooms.

Three bedrooms had stretched her budget, and even with Will chipping in what he could, they'd had to stick to the seedier end of town. But it was a start.

She'd picked out and hung those white muslin curtains herself, like everything else in her apartment.

Hers.

Forcing herself out of bed, she grabbed her robe and headed for Kim's room.

Between Goodwill and Ikea, she'd managed to put together a pretty decent little girl's room. Pink curtains with big white and yellow daisies kept the morning sun on low. In her white big girl bed, Kim lay snuggled under her pink comforter.

"Hey." Blythe pushed a lock of Kim's vanilla hair off her face. "Time to wake up."

Kim grumbled and burrowed deeper. She really didn't like getting up in the morning. Yesterday she'd stopped asking if they had to go back to the old house that day.

"Come on, baby girl." Blythe gave her gentle shake. "I'll get your breakfast."

Heading to her kitchen, Blythe smiled at her open-plan sitting-dining set up. She even liked the ugly brown couches that she'd gotten for a steal. Throw blankets and pillows toned down their aggressive 70s vibe. She'd replace them in time.

She cracked enough eggs for Will and Kim. She could start them each morning with a good breakfast, a healthy breakfast that would help them through the day. Dropping the eggs in a pan to scramble, she popped whole-wheat bread into the toaster.

Once the eggs were ready, she put them on a plate next to the toast and placed a small bowl of fresh berries by both place settings. It was stupid how much she relished doing that.

"Looks good." Will pulled a barstool up to the counter, his hair still wet from the shower. "If you want to get going, I can get Kim to kindergarten."

"You driving for Uber today?"

Will nodded and ate his berries. "Last night was a bust. Made hardly anything. I'll start as soon I'm done with Katy."

Will worked too hard for a kid his age. Katy was his tutor and helped him bridge the gap between a crappy education and his college aspirations. They'd found her through St. Peter's, and she kept her rates way down for him. He never said where the car came from that he used as an Uber driver but Blythe had her suspicions.

Now that the apartment was livable, settling that debt was

top of her priorities. She, Will and Kim were going to make it, and without handouts and pity from the rest of this town.

Still looking sleepy, Kim wandered in and climbed onto the stool beside Will. She gave her eggs an unenthusiastic poke. "I'll have Lucky Charms."

"You'll have eggs and fruit." Blythe poured herself a cup of coffee and added milk. "Eggs make you grow and keep you smart."

"But I like Lucky Charms," Kim said.

Of course she did. They were a staple in the Barrowses' diet. "Soon you'll like eggs as well. Will is taking you to kindergarten today. I have to go to work."

No need to tell Kim that she had an informal appointment with social services first.

"Have breakfast." Will raised his eyebrow at her.

Not much got past him, and Blythe laughed. She got herself some plain Greek yoghurt and added berries and honey. If she told people to eat like this, then she needed to do the same. Nobody wanted a personal trainer who ate like a frat boy with the munchies.

Her phone buzzed a notification and she checked it.

Eric. *Sweet Thing, this is getting old. Let's talk.*

If only she could trust herself to talk to him, she wouldn't have to do this childish duck and weave thing. She couldn't talk to him. Being in the same room as Eric tested her resolve. She knew how this would go if she gave in because it had gone that way every other time she'd tried to end their...whatever it was.

Eric would be charming, sexy and funny. Then he'd give her a peek into the warm, caring sensitive heart of him. She'd see him, smell him, touch him, and that would be it. Straight back to them having sex as often as they could.

The erratic beat of her heart took a breath or two to calm. It could be that her inability to delete his name and contact from her phone showed a lack of commitment to this breakup, but she couldn't do it. No, she couldn't do it yet. There would come a day when Eric's name on the screen didn't make her want to drop everything and run to him. Or picture him and try and guess where he was and what he was doing.

Not today, however, and she put her phone down.

She saw Will and Kim out and then tidied the apartment. The social worker was dropping by to make sure everything was good for Kim.

The doorbell chimed, and she went to answer it, stopping first to peep through the spy hole.

Becker and Bo stood on her doorstep. Three years apart in age, yet they were often mistaken for twins. They shared her lighter hair and green eyes and were built slimmer. More like Carly than Pat.

Becker, the slightly taller of the two, stepped forward and faced the peephole. "Open the door, Blythe. We saw your car. We know you're in there."

Still, she hesitated. She didn't want them thinking they could barge into her apartment any time they wanted. Filling her home with their trash, destroying what she'd worked so hard for, and bringing their stolen crap here until they could fence it.

Becker raised his fist and pounded on the door. "Open the fucking door, Blythe, before we have to make friends with your nice new neighbors."

That did it. Blythe didn't want to start her time here becoming that person her neighbors wanted out of the building. She'd had a lifetime of that. Leaving the chain on, she opened the door and peered through the gap.

Becker pushed against the door, but the chain held. He scowled at her. "Let us in."

"No." Blythe kept an eye on the empty corridor, praying none of her neighbors came out and saw her brothers.

"Why not?" Bo peered over Becker's shoulders. "We're family."

Family they may be, but they looked like what they were: trouble. Dressed in filthy jeans, biker boots and T-shirts, they were both long past a shower. Bo's hair hung limp and filthy over his face and he hadn't shaved in days. Some men wore that look well. Bo wore it like he couldn't give a shit about himself or anyone else.

Blythe needed them to get it and get it well. "Because I don't want you here."

Bo looked taken aback.

"Bitch." Becker's scowl deepened and he kicked the door. "You remember where you came from before I bust down this fucking door and remind you."

"Brett'll do it for sure." Bo snickered and heaved up his sagging waistband. "He showed her before who's boss, and he'll do it again."

Brett, their older brother, was in prison, where he belonged. "Just a pity he's behind bars."

"Shows what you know." Becker's expression turned conniving. "He made parole, and you can bet your ass we'll be telling him all about you and your fancy apartment where none of us are welcome."

She knew she was staring at them like a rabbit in headlights, but she couldn't seem to stop it. Brett had made parole? The familiar nagging fear tightened around her belly. Her other brothers could be mean, but Brett had a streak of bone deep nasty that ran right through him.

At one time or another, every one of the siblings had felt Brett's temper. Normally communicated with his fists or his boots, and the last time she'd had the pleasure, by breaking her arm.

Her ulna gave a sympathetic twinge. She tried to bluff it out. "Bullshit. He's not due."

"Poor Blythe." Becker sneered. "All that education, and you still can't count. Brett's done his time."

Shit. Shit. *Shit.* She needed to move apartments. Towns. County. State.

"Everything all right here?" Sheriff Nate Evans strolled into view. Easily the best-looking man in Ghost Falls, and also Eric's younger brother, Blythe was both relieved and horrified to see him. Relieved about the backup, not thrilled about such a strong connection to Eric.

Becker and Bo felt no such ambivalence. They were equally unhappy to see him.

"No law against paying a visit to your sister." Bo looked sulky.

Nate approached them and put himself between the door and her brothers. "There is if your sister is asking you to leave. Are you?" He glanced over his shoulder at her. "Are you asking them to leave?"

"Yes." Blythe's voice came out a choked whisper. Brett had made parole, and Bo and Becker knew how to find her. Worse yet, they knew how to find Kim. Brett had never even met their youngest sister. It would be a cold day in hell before Blythe allowed him to either.

Becker threw her another glare before grabbing Bo by the shoulder and hauling him away.

Blythe stood by the door as they disappeared down the stairs and out of sight.

"Are you going to let me in?" Nate gave her that smile that had reduced most of the Ghost Falls female population to mush at one time or another. A good few members of their male population as well. Come to think of it, even dogs loved Nate. He'd never done it for her, though. Not in the way Eric did. Had.

She needed to remember that. Had.

"Sure." She fumbled the chain off the door and opened it.

"Not that I'm ungrateful for the save, but what are you doing here?"

"Myra asked me to come by." Nate stepped into her apartment and looked around.

Please don't let Myra not coming mean something bad. Was Nate here to take Kim back? "She's not coming?"

Myra was their social worker. In her late fifties now, Myra had inherited the Barrowses years ago and never managed to get rid of them. Blythe was pathetically grateful for her. Myra had been a lot of the reason Blythe had been determined to make the changes she had. It was Myra who had taught Blythe about her period and taken her to buy tampons. Later, Myra had taught her all about safe sex, and the importance of finishing school.

Nate shook his head. "Myra got caught up in something a ways out of town. She asked me to come by and have a look around."

"Go to it." Blythe held her arms out. She tried to appear casual, but her heart pounded in her chest.

Myra didn't always do things by the book, and Blythe thanked God for that. It was the reason she'd been allowed to take Kim with her. She had Myra's unofficial blessing and more than a few hints that if she ever chose to adopt Kim legally, Myra would put in a good word for her. However tempting that might be, Blythe couldn't do that to their mother.

Carly had few enough reasons to hang in there as it was. She just wished...except it was a stupid wish and Blythe knew it. She couldn't save Carly. Nobody could until Carly decided she wanted to save herself.

Nate did a thorough job. Blythe stood in the kitchen and let him look around. So much hinged on this visit. As much as she told herself she had nothing to be nervous about, Blythe would still be relieved when this was over. She'd consulted with Myra every step of the way, so today should be a formality. But the Barrowses had never had much luck, particularly not with authority.

"It looks great, Blythe." Nate came back in the room, and she got one of his killer smiles. "Myra said it would be, but you know how she likes to make sure."

"I do." And Blythe didn't blame her. Myra making sure had saved her often enough. Growing up, sometimes the only reason she had a meal was Myra making sure. "And tell her I won't let her down."

"I don't have to do that," Nate said. "She knows."

Their faith in her blindsided Blythe, and she had to look away before she embarrassed herself by crying. "Will took Kim to the kindergarten at St. Peter's. Could you tell Myra that I found a place for her?"

"I will," he said.

It sounded like everything was going to be all right. She should be celebrating, yet all she could do was stand there and wait for the bad news.

"Hey." Nate stepped in front of her. "You did good here, Blythe."

Her throat felt too tight for words, and she nodded. In his teens, before he'd joined the police force, Nate had nursed his own wild side. That wild side had sometimes brought him to her side of town. He understood her world. "How's your mom taking this?"

"When she's sober, she's okay with it." That didn't happen enough, unfortunately. "She understands that Kim will be better off with me. In her heart she wants Kim to have better; she just doesn't like it, and she misses her."

"Yeah." Nate nodded. He got what others didn't. Being unable to cope with her children didn't mean Carly didn't love them. Even the fact that she put booze before their welfare, still didn't mean she didn't love them. She just didn't love them enough. "I'll get someone to check in on her."

"Thank you." Blythe followed him to the door. "Pat hasn't

been around for a while, but if he's still breathing, he'll be back."

"You call me if he comes around here." Nate handed her his card. "And you call me if those two jokers show up again." Bending his knees, he forced her to meet his gaze. "I mean it, Blythe. You don't hesitate, and you don't try to deal with them yourself. You call me."

Eric used to say the same to her. "I'll call you."

"Good." He opened the door and took one last look around. "Damn, Blythe, I don't know how you did all this, but you did it. You should be very proud of yourself."

He made her want to bawl when he said things like that, so she changed the subject. "Can I ask you something?"

Turning in the door, Nate waited for her to ask.

"Brett." Blythe got her question out in a rush of breath. "Did he make parole?"

"Yeah." Nate took a step closer to her. "But you don't have to worry about it. If he even looks at you or Kim or Will in a way I don't like, I'll make sure he never sees the outside again."

Blythe managed a smile, but it was for Nate's benefit. The police didn't always get there in time. Both she and Carly were living proof of that. She was determined Kim wouldn't be.

ERIC SAT in his car and waited for Bo and Becker to drive away. There was no reason for him to stay, especially since Nate had pulled up as he was getting ready to interfere with Bo and Becker.

He'd had to do this a few times over the years he and Blythe had been seeing each other. She'd always bitched at him afterwards, but he wasn't about to let those assholes treat Blythe like shit. Not after the Brett thing.

After forty minutes, Nate left Blythe's apartment. He crossed the road and headed straight for Eric's car.

Lowering the window, Eric tried to keep it cool. "Hey. What's up?"

"That's what I'm here to ask you." Nate had his sheriff face on.

There was no way he could answer that without a whole lot of explanation, so he chose not to answer. "She okay?"

Nate studied him with an inscrutable expression. "She's fine. The apartment is great, and I told her to let me know if those jokers come around again." Nate stuck his thumbs in his utility belt. "Brett Barrows made parole this morning."

"Shit." Eric got out his car so fast, Nate had to leap out of the way.

Nate got in front of him storming toward Blythe's apartment. "What are you doing, Eric?"

"She can't stay here." Eric tried to duck around him. Nate didn't know the entire history. "If those other two jerks know where she lives, they'll tell Brett."

"I'm gonna need you to stand down." Nate put his hand on Eric's chest. "Nobody's broken any laws yet."

Eric suppressed the desire to punch his brother. They were way too old for that. "You don't understand."

"Oh, yeah?" Nate cocked his head. "Then why don't you explain it to me, Eric?"

Eric didn't know where to start explaining his involvement with Blythe. He had no right to be here, no right to take care of her and protect her, and he'd been the one who set it up that way.

Chapter Six

Blythe sat in her car outside St. Peter's Church on Friday night and replayed the message from Eric. The sexy rasp of his voice tugged on every part of her.

"Blythe." Not sweet thing anymore, which meant he was pissed. "I heard Bo and Becker were hanging around your new place the other day. Whatever is going on with you, don't let it make you stupid. Call if you need me."

Then his second message a few minutes later. "And I heard Brett made parole. Again, call if you need me. Or just call. What the hell, Blythe."

Eric cared about her, and he liked her. She'd never doubted that. In a way, if he saw her as nothing more than a convenient bed buddy this might have been easier. Whatever he felt for her was real, she knew that, but she also knew it wasn't enough.

For so many years, she'd lived and breathed for the times Eric rolled back into her life. Like a robot, she'd marked the months, and sometimes years, before he'd come back. Sure, she got on with her life. Her plan to move out had taken years to bring to fruition. There had even been boyfriends between one round of Eric and the next.

"I want more," she said to her phone, and then felt stupid for talking to a silent phone.

She climbed out of her car and grabbed her bag from the back. A man was raking leaves into piles on the church lawn.

Her first week in her new home had been uneventful. Nate might have said something to Bo and Becker because she had no more uninvited family banging on her front door. She tried calling her mother once or twice, but the first time Carly had been too drunk to make sense and the second time Barron had answered, so she'd hung up.

Pushing open the door, she stepped into the familiar comfort of St. Peter's recreation center. As a teen she'd always been able to come here and get away from her brothers. Parishioners there had helped her through high school, and then to get her qualification as a personal trainer.

Now they'd found a tutor for Will and given Kim a place in the kindergarten and aftercare for a ridiculously small rate. So on Friday and Tuesday nights she held an exercise class for whoever wanted to make it.

"Blythe." Reverend Michael greeted her with his huge smile, his big boots clumping on the polished floor.

When she had been a teen, Reverend Cummings had presided over St. Peter's. She'd for sure have been crushing on the tall, man mountain that was Reverend Michael Bradford if he'd been around in her time.

"Kim has been telling us all week about her new house. You did good."

Compliments made her want to squirm, so she nodded and motioned inside. "The usual suspects?

"Yup." Reverend Michael grimaced. "Although I hate to tell you that I still haven't talked Graham out of the white spandex cycling shorts."

Blythe made the same face and laughed. Eighty-seven-year-old Graham in his pale spandex with nothing underneath could give a girl nightmares for months. "I'll make sure he stays in the back."

"And away from the mirrors?"

"You got it." Blythe shouldered her tote and strode into the large central hall. When she had first started this class, she'd had only Gloria who worked in the church office and her sister-in-law.

Popping gum like a teen, Dixie waved her over. "You're late."

"No, I'm not. You're early."

Dressed in hot pink and neon yellow shorts that barely covered her ass and an exercise bra that defied the laws of physics and managed to keep her bounty concealed, Dixie was the best part of Blythe's brother Ben. Somehow, and God alone knew how, Ben had managed to land and marry that woman. As kind as she was stacked, Dixie had got Ben into a steady job and away from the rest of the family.

"How's the new place?" Dixie had always been a fan of Blythe getting out and taking Will and Kim with her.

Blythe made herself smile. Dixie didn't know anything about Eric. "It's good. Great."

"I'm proud of you, bitch." Dixie pulled her into a super-sweet-perfume scented hug. "And don't you worry about Carly. Ben and I will pop in and see her regular."

"Thank you." They'd all gotten lucky when Dixie had agreed to keep Ben around. "How's she doing?"

Waggling her head, Dixie pulled a face. "You know your mama. Some days are good, and some not so good."

Guilt clawed at Blythe. With her not being there, nobody would make sure Carly ate or showered.

"Oh, no." Dixie shook her head and set her chandelier earrings dangling so hard they threatened a black eye. "Don't give me that face. I know what you're thinking." She jabbed a sparkly black nail at Blythe. "You're not the mama here; Carly is."

"But—"

"Nope." Dixie crossed her arms. Her breasts heaved at the edge of her sports bra. "There is no but here. You got out and made a life for yourself, and when she's sober, that makes Carly real happy." She squeezed Blythe's arms. "Real happy and don't you forget it."

"We're ready for ya." Dixie's best friend, Ramona, shimmied into the room. She stopped and gave Blythe the onceover. "Damn, you're a hot bitch." Ramona stepped back and eyed her. "If I'd had your body, I'd be raking in the dough."

"Doing what exactly?" Gloria strolled over wearing her lemon-yellow tracksuit.

Ramona pumped her hips. "Working that pole, Glor. Working that pole."

"How are you, dear?" Gloria took Blythe's music from her and plugged it into the sound system.

"I'm good." Other than the huge lump she woke up with in her throat every morning. The same lump that lodged in her chest and refused to go away. Maybe she could talk to Dixie about Eric. No. Love her as she did, Dixie had loose lips, and she wouldn't understand Blythe's reasons for leaving. Dixie would assume Eric took care of her and didn't ask much in return other than the occasional hook up. And as the sex was off the charts good when he did come around, Eric was pretty much the perfect man in Dixie's book.

Blythe stripped off her sweatshirt.

Whistling, Ramona moved to the front of the class. "Work it, baby."

The class had grown to more than thirty. Men, women, boys and girls, all were welcome. Mostly she tried to have fun with them and do a bit of good for their health as she went.

The doors slammed open and Jo Evans ran in. Dark and tall like her brothers, she shared the Evans beautiful bone structure, only on her it was delicate. She clomped across the floor in her large boots. "Sorry I'm late."

And right back to Eric again, because they'd recently had a conversation about Jo. Eric worried about his sister. She worked too hard, wouldn't take any help and was fiercely independent. Blythe knew so much about Eric's family, and they had no idea of the role she'd played in his life all these years.

Blythe waved her to take a place. "No problem, we hadn't started yet."

According to Eric, Jo wouldn't take help from any of her brothers with her tuition or her living expenses. She refused to live with their mother, but that meant working two, sometimes three, jobs to keep her head above water. It drove Eric mad, and he'd sworn Blythe to secrecy, but he managed to bolster Jo's salary every now and again.

Jo had inherited the Evans stubbornness along with that bone structure, and she'd throw a fit if she caught wind of what Eric was up to.

One of the problems with having a secret lover was that he was secret. Nobody knew about Eric, so there was nobody to share her heartbreak with. Not that she had anybody anyway. Girls didn't like her. They never had, and she was through trying to impress them.

"Right." She clapped her hands for attention. "Let's get it started in here."

For the next hour there was no more time to talk as Blythe kept her class moving. She loved teaching classes like this, watching how others enjoyed them. The best part of teaching today's class was the pounding music and her ability to lose herself in it. For sixty awesome minutes it was her, the music, her class and an accelerating heartbeat.

And Graham's spandex situation, but she tried not to concentrate on that. Dear God, she tried not to concentrate on that.

After class, Dixie hung around. They both watched Graham walk away.

"Old man balls." Dixie shuddered. "How did those things end up near his knees?"

Blythe preferred not to speculate as she waved the rest of her class goodbye.

"Next week?" Gloria mopped her red, shiny face with a pale-lemon towel, which perfectly matched her sweat suit. She never took for granted Blythe would be there.

Blythe gave her a nod. "For sure. Good work today. You looked great."

"You're full of it." Gloria snorted and waved a hand at her.

"So." Dixie perched on a fold-up chair as Blythe packed up her music. "You finally did it. You moved out with Will and Kim."

"I finally did it." Blythe slipped into her sweatshirt. "Bo and Becker found me soon enough."

"Assholes." Dixie snorted. "They can't stand it when someone gets something better than what they have."

Blythe perched beside her and took a drink from her water bottle. "They told me about Brett."

"Speaking of assholes." Dixie rolled her eyes. "Your mama sure bred a tribe of dickheads."

True enough. "She had some help with that."

Dixie snorted again. "Anybody heard where your dad is?"

"Not that I know of." Blythe got to her feet. She had to get going. She'd left Will in charge of Kim, and he needed to get to work. "He'll wash up eventually when he needs money or a place to stay."

"Let's hope Carly can keep him out of her bed this time." Dixie stood with her and wriggled into a minuscule hoodie. "She can't be having any more babies. Somebody's got to tape her legs shut."

Kim needed to be the last. The message from the doctor

had been adamant. Dutifully, Blythe had passed it on, but with the sinking feeling that it would only be heeded for as long as Pat stayed away. "You know what she's like when he comes around."

"What are you going to do about Brett?" Dixie fell into step beside her.

Blythe shrugged and clamped down on the upswell of nerves. "I'm not really sure what I can do. Other than move to the far side of the moon."

"I hear the climate's good." Dixie shoulder bumped her. "I'll send Ben to have a talk with Brett, make sure he understands he's not to go near you."

If Dixie said it, Ben would do it. But Ben didn't stand a chance against Brett. "Don't do that. You know what Brett can be like. I don't want Ben getting hurt."

"Ben can take care of himself." Dixie shook her head. "How old were you when you last saw Brett?"

"In my twenties."

"And he broke your arm?" Dixie peered at her. "What the hell!"

Blythe stopped herself from reflexively rubbing her arm. Her arm and getting medical attention for it was one of those things she owed Myra. "I got up and in his face about him trying to use Will as a decoy while they jacked cars."

"Fucker!"

Blythe quite agreed, but a dangerous fucker as well, and they'd all do well to remember as much.

"Blythe." Reverend Michael strode down the corridor toward her. "You got a minute?"

"Ask me, Rev." Dixie stuck her hip out and batted her lashes. "I got all the time in the world for you."

"Dixie, you flirt." Michael grinned down at her. "You're just toying with me. You're happily married."

"Speaking of." Dixie kissed Blythe on the cheek. "I need to get home and kick his lazy ass."

"Why do I suspect that's exactly what she'll do?" Michael watched Dixie sashay away with a fond smile.

"Because she will." Blythe shared his grin. "Ben got so lucky when he got her. Fortunately, lazy as he is, he's smart enough to know a good thing when he sees one."

"Which gives me the neat segue I need." Michael's face grew more serious. "I don't want to make something out of nothing, but Will's been seen hanging around with the Flemming boys over on sixteenth."

Blythe bit back her f-bomb. Those Flemming boys were bad news. The drugs kind of bad news. Will had gone to school with them, and Blythe had always done her best to discourage their friendship. "I'll talk to him."

"Look, could be nothing." Michael spread his large hands wide. "It's entirely possible the whole thing is innocent, but I thought you might want to know."

"And I do." Blythe pressed his forearm. "Thanks for letting me know."

The door opened behind them and they both turned.

Jo Evans grinned at them. All the Evans kids had that smile. One side of their mouth tilted up more than the other and invited you to laugh with them. "Hey, Michael." She strode past. "Great class as always, Blythe."

Reverend Michael watched her go before he turned back to Blythe. "And you'll let me know if there's anything I can do to help."

It was easy to get lost in those beautiful sincere big blues of Reverend Michael's, and it amazed Blythe he was still single. However he did spend every hour he could between the center and the church, and it would take a special woman to put up with that. Also, the priest aspect probably kept the advances to a minimum.

"We'll be fine," she said.

He gave her his no bullshit look. "I'm sure, but you don't have to be, and we're here if you aren't."

Blythe parted from him at the building entrance. The long summer twilight wound down in a soft flush of peach across the sky. Only a few cars remained in the parking lot and she looked about her as she walked.

"Good night." Jo waved from where she sat perched on a fire hydrant.

Blythe stopped. The recreation center was not in the best part of town. "You okay?"

"Yeah." Jo waved her off. "My brother is coming to pick me up."

A sleek black car glided into the parking lot.

Blythe's heart stopped. There weren't too many Jaguars in Ghost Falls, and she knew who that one belonged to. Her heart pounded in her ears.

She couldn't see him. It was too soon. Like ten years too soon.

"Blythe," Eric called, as she ducked behind the dumpster and ran down the side of the recreation center. His voice lashed out again. "Blythe."

She slid into a narrow alley and pressed her back against the wall. How old was she exactly? Running and hiding like that. Still, she wasn't going out there until he was gone. Sometimes self-preservation looked a lot like childish, but it was still self-preservation.

ERIC WAS HALFWAY out his car to chase Blythe when Jo bounced up to him.

"Hey." She stood on her toes and kissed his cheek. "Thanks for coming to get me."

Still watching the direction Blythe had bolted, Eric said, "No problem."

"Did Blythe just run away from you?" Jo stared in the same direction as him.

Eric hauled on his blank face. "Why would she do that?"

"No reason." Jo shrugged and opened the car door. "Something has her in a huge hurry."

What the actual fuck was that about? Now they weren't even going to speak to each other? She'd taken one look at him and run for cover. That shit was going to end.

He turned his attention back to his sister. "What's wrong with your car?"

"Not much." Her face set in that stubborn expression that meant her car was toast, but she would walk over coals before she told him.

Eric had reached his quota for stubborn women for one month. "Just tell me what's wrong with your damn car, Jo."

Chapter Seven

Blythe parked in one of the two spots allotted to her apartment. The slot beside hers still held Will's car. He was waiting for her to come home before he went on his Uber run. That car had cost a lot more than Will could afford, and she knew who she owed.

This weekend, she was taking care of that. These three Barrowses refused to owe anyone anything.

Stepping out her car, the early fall chill made her shiver. Ghost Falls had a short fall season and galloped straight into winter. Up at Eric's place, the snow-white world looked magical in winter. This year, she wouldn't see it.

"Blythe." Tall and broad, Brett loomed out of the dark.

Heart pounding, she leaped away, and her back connected with her car. Her spine slid along the metal as she tried to put distance between them. "Stay back."

"Take it easy." He held out his hands so she could see him. Shadows hid most of his face.

Still, he stood between her and safety. "Step back or I'll scream."

She couldn't see his eyes for the darkening evening, but she and Brett stayed like that, frozen for long, tense minutes.

Then Brett stepped back. One large stride, and then two, and then three.

Finally she had enough of a gap and bolted for it.

"You can't hide from me forever, Blythe." Brett's voice followed her. "We need to have this out."

Blythe let herself into her apartment and locked the door behind her to the sound of *Finding Nemo*. She stood pressed against the door, her heart still hammering. Part of her expected Brett to come banging at the door any moment.

She pulled up Nate's contact card. She didn't want to waste his time, so she went to the kitchen window. The street outside her apartment was empty.

"Blythe?" Kim called from the other room. "Is that you?"

"It's me." She kept her voice upbeat. Nothing and nobody stirred in the night outside their apartment. Allowing herself a full breath, she went to greet Kim.

"Hey, sweet girl." She leaned down and kissed Kim's soft, pink cheek and drew in the bubblegum scent of little girl. "Did you have dinner?"

Kim didn't take her eyes off the screen. "Will made me fish sticks and peas."

"Did you eat all the peas?" Will did his best, but he didn't know how to cook.

"Y...es." Kim peered up at her. "I ate some of them."

Blythe let it go at that. Kim was already dressed for bed, so Will must have handled bath time as well. He was the best kid. Not many nineteen-year-olds would have been as mature. She really hoped Reverend Michael had seen nothing important.

"Hi." Will walked out of his bedroom, hair slicked back from the shower and dressed in pressed chinos and a white button down. "You're back."

"Thanks for feeding Kim and bath time."

"No worries." Will gave her his sweet smile and slipped past her.

"Will?" Blythe caught his arm. She almost told him about

Brett and then changed her mind. Brett's beef had always been with her. He'd more or less ignored Will. But her conversation with Michael, she couldn't ignore. Ignoring warning signs only led to more trouble. "Listen, I heard that you've been hanging out with those Flemming boys."

Irritation flashed across Will's face. "It was nothing, Blythe." For a moment he looked every inch a sulky teen, and then his expression cleared into one of affection. "Look, Blythe, I know all about the Flemmings. I'm not about to do something stupid."

"Good." She wanted to wrap him up and keep him from anything that could hurt him. She hated that she was already too late to prevent his past hurts. "Because I worry about you."

"I know you do." He kissed her cheek. "And I love you for it, but I know this is our chance Blythe. As much as you want me to take it, believe me, I want it as badly."

Blythe hugged him tight. Sometimes he felt more like her son than her little brother and she adored him.

Will hugged her back.

He was losing his boyish lankiness and would one day be as big as Barron. Maybe even as big as Brett. But Will would be nothing like his two older brothers. "We can be different, Will."

"We will be," he said and stepped back. "I made extra dinner for you. It's in the microwave. I'll be back later."

"Drive safely," Blythe called to the closing door.

She got a quick wave in reply. A piece of paper lay on the kitchen counter, and she picked it up. Addressed to Will, it came from a scholarship fund he'd talked about.

We thank you for your interest. Unfortunately…

She didn't need to read any more. As Will saved money for college, he'd been applying for scholarships and loans wherever he could. The answer kept coming back no. God, could her kid brother not catch a break?

After a quick shower, she changed into her pajamas and joined Kim in front of her movie. "Ten more minutes, Kim, and then bedtime."

Kim grunted that she'd heard, but this was her favorite part.

With one eye, Blythe watched Bruce the shark and his toothy grin. This was Blythe's favorite part as well.

Her phone rang, and Blythe checked it.

Eric.

She let it go to voicemail.

It rang again, and she let it go to voicemail.

Once her dinner was finished, she got Kim through teeth brushing and into bed.

When she got back to her phone, she had another three missed calls. As she watched, the screen lit up again. Eric was not going to give up. No chance he hadn't caught her duck and weave routine earlier tonight. She knew him well enough to know how much that would piss him off.

Calling up Eric's contact card, she hesitated for a moment. He'd been a part of her life for so long, it seemed crazy that she was even thinking this.

Maybe this would be easier if she could get angry with him, but Eric hadn't wronged her.

Eric had never lied to her, never promised her anything he couldn't deliver. He'd never said he loved her or ever showed one sign of having deeper feelings for her. He liked her a lot. They got along really well and were friends, of a sort. But Eric didn't love her.

Blythe didn't know when she'd fallen in love with him. It had been a gradual thing, and it wasn't like they'd seen each other all the time. Those years he'd lived in Denver, he'd only been home once in a while. It had been easy through those years to keep the fiction going about how they were only friends with benefits.

Then he'd started spending more time around Ghost Falls

when he and Matt had started growing Evans Construction together. What had been the occasional hookup every few months had grown into a weekly thing. She hadn't meant to fall in love with him, and in fairness, he would be horrified if he knew. She wanted to spare him that.

Like Will, she needed to make a clean break with her past. There would be no future for her until she did. No children of her own for as long as she kept waiting for one man to change his mind.

Blythe hit Block this Caller and then to make double sure, she deleted his contact card.

ERIC CLENCHED his phone in his fist, working against the desire to break the damn thing. He was so angry with Blythe right now, he wanted to storm over there and yell at her.

But Kim and Will were there and the whole situation had drifted into a childish farce. Refusing to take his calls was one thing, but running away and hiding in an alley?

Fresh and still sharp, his anger surged through him again. Blythe was behaving like a child. Christ, even Laura had behaved better all those years ago. Actually, that was a lie, but he had expected much better of Blythe.

His phone rang.

Righteous wrath surged through and died as he checked the caller ID. "Cooper?"

"Yeah, hi Eric." His construction manager on the Highgate development sounded weary and tense. "I hate to bother you this late, but we've got a situation developing here."

"Situation?" He and Matt had pumped a lot of money into Highgate, a luxury home development with incredible views and price tags to match. Interest in the development was high, but the outlay was higher, and it was part of the thinking behind wanting to expand their business. They couldn't afford any situations with Highgate. "What's going on?"

"We've got a crew up here working overtime, and they're not happy," Cooper said. "They want more overtime pay."

He really didn't need this. "Didn't we agree to that rate months ago with the subcontractor?"

"We did." Cooper sighed. "But they're not happy, and I don't think this is going away in a hurry."

"I'll be right there." It was just the sort of distraction he needed. Highgate hadn't been the smoothest project they'd put together. Supplies had been late getting to the site, which had ultimately resulted in the crew working overtime. Meanwhile, all around them, the construction sharks were throwing up crappy developments at the same price and finishing in half the time. "Is the subcontractor there?"

"Nah." Cooper grunted his irritation. "Asshole isn't answering his phone."

Not an unheard-of problem with this particular subcontractor. Nate would have him into the office in the morning. This shit couldn't go on.

He hung up from Cooper and jumped in his car. The Jag wasn't ideal for site visits, but he couldn't wake Matt up, and risk waking Pippa and Jasmine, to borrow his truck. Anyway, he was in the perfect mood to tussle with contractors.

As Eric parked, men were milling about the construction manager's trailer. About twenty of them, all wearing the gray overalls of the MIA electrical contractor. They had taken a chance working with this guy after he'd almost made them late on the last project, but with Ghost Falls booming, subs could pick and choose who they worked with.

With the Gunning deal looming, the timing couldn't be worse.

Cooper walked through the crowd toward him. "Thanks for coming up."

When the men saw him, their mood grew more alert.

"Who's their spokesman?"

With a grimace, Cooper pointed to a man leaning against the trailer. "Barrows!"

Just fucking great. Another Barrows to turn his night into a shit sandwich.

"Eric." Barron Barrows sauntered up to him. One of the nastiest of Blythe's brothers, Barron was a qualified electrician and could occasionally be persuaded to get off his ass and work.

They'd gone to high school together, so the use of his first name didn't annoy Eric as it was meant to. It didn't matter who fired the first shot; it was who fired the last that counted. "Barron." He nodded and stood his ground, making Barron come to him. "Wanna tell me what this is all about?"

"We need more money." Barron looked behind him to his crew.

An answering affirmative murmur rose from the men.

Eric glanced at the group. No doubt Barron was the ringleader and quite possibly the instigator. The rest were mostly sheep. "An overtime rate was agreed upon when your boss took this contract. If he wants to renegotiate, he can call me at the office, but I'm not having this shit on my site."

"Trouble is, the head office don't always speak for us." Barron smirked. "We're the ones on site doing the work."

"Tell your boss that." Eric saw where it was heading, and it was nowhere good. "I'm not the one who pays your wages, and neither is Cooper. If you've got an issue with what you're being paid, then take it up with who signs your paycheck." He looked at all the men in turn. "Until then, get off my site."

A few of the men glanced at each other and shifted. Not so sure now that somebody was playing hardball back. They had wives and children to support. Men like Barron thought only of themselves.

Barron wasn't stupid, and he picked up on their wavering. He stepped closer to Eric. "Or what?"

They were about the same size and evenly matched. Barron was making the mistake of thinking that someone who wore a suit wouldn't go there physically. But Barron had underestimated how much Eric wanted to hit something right then.

"Or I'm going to take your idiot head and shove it up your ass." Eric grabbed a fistful of overall and twisted.

"Eric," Cooper said, his tone warning that a physical confrontation was not the way to handle conflict. That was the sure-fire way for shit getting ugly.

Eric watched the idea of taking a swing at him rise in Barron's mind and dissipate again. Wrenching his overalls free, he stepped back. "You made a mistake here tonight, Evans. This isn't over." He motioned the other men to follow him.

Cooper let out a big breath. "Feeling feisty?"

"You have no idea." Eric kept his gaze on the men climbing into pickups. He'd relax when they were offsite.

"Hey, Evans!" Barron yelled from beside his bike. "I guess my sister couldn't do what it takes to keep you smiling. Bitch can't even fuck her way right."

A veil of rage descended over Eric. He went for Barron.

"No." Cooper got in front of him. A full head shorter than Eric, he was still built like a bull and stopped Eric's forward momentum. "Don't be stupid. You've won this round, but you take a swing at him and the whole thing shifts."

Across the dusty site, Barron smirked and threw his leg over his bike.

Cooper tightened his grip. "Shit! Eric, use your brain. He wants you to go for him. He's taunting you."

It was working as well but Eric forced air in and out of his lungs. He forced his desire to hurt Barron down again. "This is his last day on site," he said to Cooper. "Barron doesn't set foot on this site ever again. Or any other job I've got going in the future."

Chapter Eight

Blythe stayed alert as she took Kim to kindergarten the next day. She knew better than to believe Brett had given up, but this morning they had a reprieve. She dropped Kim off at the kindergarten and walked back to her car.

A redheaded woman wearing jeans and a linen shirt strode down the rec center's hallway toward her.

They recognized each other at the same time.

Laura stopped and blinked at her. She found her voice first. "Blythe."

"Laura." Blythe nodded. She'd heard that Laura had gone back to her maiden name, Turner, after her divorce. She didn't know the details, but it had something to do with Laura's grandmother, Diva Philomene, and gambling.

"You dropping off your sister?" Laura made a stunted motion toward the kindergarten.

This had to be the most awkward conversation in a long time. The air between her and Laura swirled viscous with all the secrets they kept between them. "Yes. You?"

"No, mine are older. At school." Laura smoothed her flawless shirt. "You look good."

"You too." Laura always looked good. She was one of

those women who always reminded Blythe of how trashy she dressed. Coming from this particular woman it was hard to swallow. "I need to get to work."

"Right." Stepping back as if she had been impeding Blythe's progress, Laura waved her on.

Blythe got to work without any further awkward encounters or visitations from violent older brothers. She'd been working out of the Body Works gym since she'd first started working toward her certification. It had everything she needed with none of the intimidating flash of some of the newer places in town.

One day she'd be able to have a space of her own, or work with her clients in their homes. But that was a dream for the future, when Will and Kim were settled. Today her eight thirty was due any second.

"Morning, Blythe." Huge, muscular arms leaning on the counter, Randy looked up from his body building magazine to greet her. He gave her a good-natured leer. "Looking fine this morning."

"You always say that." Blythe swiped her key card at the reader.

Randy winked at her. "That's because you always look fine."

She had a full morning of clients, and it kept her busy and out of her head.

The last thing Blythe expected to see during her 11:30 appointment was Eric, gaze locked on her, jaw tight, as he strode across Body Works toward her. Which may have been why it took her precious moments to react. Precious moments that enabled him to close the distance.

"Blythe." His voice could chill meat. He glanced at Joan Bayswater, her 11:30, and gave her a nod and a tight smile. "I apologize for interrupting, but I need Blythe for a moment."

"No problem." Joan blinked up at him, her cheeks going rosy. "I'll just finish my lunges."

Eric's smile warmed, ratcheting Joan's cheeks up to hot pink. "I appreciate this. I won't keep her for long."

Blythe found her voice and her desire to take control of the situation. "Eric—"

"No." He gripped her hand and strode across the gym toward her office, towing her along with him. "You don't want to speak to me, fine. Suits me perfectly, because right now you're going to listen."

A fellow trainer, Kurt, glanced up, took in the situation and stepped toward her. "You okay, Blythe?"

"Yes." She pulled Eric to a halt. "Could you keep an eye on Joan for me?"

"Sure." Kurt nodded but eyed Eric as if he'd rather be keeping an eye on him. When she had first started working here, she and Kurt had gone out a couple of times. It had ended, like most of her relationships, because of the man propelling her across the gym.

This was another reason she had to make a clean break. There never would be anyone else in her life for as long as she clung to the hope of Eric.

Eric tossed open her office door and nudged her inside.

The door snicked shut behind them, locking her in with a majorly pissed off Eric. God, he looked so beautiful that her starving gaze couldn't resist drinking every gorgeous inch of him in.

"Explain." Eric crossed his arms over his chest. His eyes had gone onyx with temper. "Explain why it's been over a week and you don't respond to a text, or a call. The last time you deigned to answer a call, you near enough hung up on me, and don't even get me started on your escape act yesterday."

Blythe's mouth dried around a truth she would rather not speak, and she licked her lips. "I can't talk about this now. I have a client."

"This won't take long," Eric said. "The sooner you give me an answer, the sooner you can get back to your client."

"I told you that morning. I don't want to do this anymore."

Eric shoved his fingers through his perfectly groomed dark hair. "What the hell, Blythe? You've said that so many times I can barely count them."

"I know that." His derision stung but she'd earned that much. Her own inability to break things off years ago had led to this point. "But I meant it this time. I do mean it."

"Blythe." Her name hissed from him on a low breath, and he closed his eyes. "I really don't get it. What makes this time different?" He took a step closer. "We're good together, sweet thing."

"It's not that." Sex had never been a problem, and she backed as far as her tiny office would allow. If he touched her now, she didn't trust her resolve.

Sensuality softened the hard planes of his face, warmed his eyes to molten. "You can't have forgotten how things are between us."

Not for a second had she forgotten. Even now her body was responding to him. "I haven't. I know. That part was never the problem." He didn't get it because she didn't want to spell it out for him. She played for more time. "I need more for myself, Eric. I need someone who wants to stick. Someone who wants me around all the time, not only when it suits them."

"Sweet thing." His voice went smooth and velvet. "It's not like that."

She knew that tone. It was the one that could talk her back into his bed time and time and time again. She hardened herself and put the desk between them. Just in case the spirit overpowered the flesh. "It's exactly like that." It took a piece of her to admit this much. "And it worked for me...until it didn't anymore."

He gazed at her for a long moment, as if judging his next angle of attack.

Blythe motioned to the door behind him. "I need to get back to Joan."

"And that's it for you. You're done, so I need to be a good boy and get the hell out of your life. After how many years, Blythe?"

Eighteen of them. Blythe had counted each one. "It doesn't make any difference." Eighteen of her best years waiting for something she knew would never be hers. "I need to move on with my life."

Shoving his hands in his pockets, he continued staring at her. "What am I missing?"

Through her office window, she saw Joan had finished her lunges. Kurt had taken over training her, and Joan looked happy enough about it.

Eric's determined expression made it clear she wasn't leaving until he got an explanation that made sense to him.

"Okay, I owe you the truth." Blood drained south, leaving her light headed. She could hardly believe she was going to out herself after all this time. "I'm not returning your calls or texts, and I don't want to see you because I need a clean break."

"But—"

She stopped him with an upheld hand. If she didn't get this out now, she'd lose courage. "I have to walk away from you, Eric, and keep walking..." This was getting harder. "Because I love you."

Eric flinched as if she'd sucker punched him. And there it was, right there. The reason she couldn't allow her heart to harbor the minutest morsel of hope.

"I love you." Her voice got stronger. "I'm not sure when it started or if maybe I always have. But I love you with that forever kind of love, and I want you to love me back."

His gaze boring into her, Eric opened his mouth and shut

it again. He stood frozen to the spot, and it hurt more than she could bear. No matter what people said, knowing a thing and seeing it confirmed were not the same. Seeing hurt way more.

She'd always known that if Eric knew she loved him, it would be the end of them. The real end of them. So perhaps she had been clinging to some tiny hope that he would look at her, have this huge epiphany about what he was missing out on, and suddenly give her everything she wanted.

It must be some kind of miracle that growing up as she had, she still believed in fairy tales.

"I want it all, Eric." She filled the silence as he stood there. "I want the house, the children, the happily ever after. Can you give me that?"

He looked tortured. "Blythe I…"

"Exactly." Blythe slipped around the desk and walked to the door. She stopped beside him, steeling herself against the scent of him. "If you ever cared for me, even a little, you'll let me go to find what I need with someone else. Don't call me. Don't text me, and please don't try to see me. Please."

Blythe left the office and joined Joan.

Glancing at her, Kurt raised an eyebrow in a silent question.

She managed a small smile in return. No, she wasn't all right, but she would be.

ERIC STOOD in her postage stamp office and stared at the space Blythe had occupied mere moments ago. He'd come charging into the gym all buoyed up on righteous indignation. Until this moment it hadn't sunk in that she meant it this time. There would be no charming her back into his bed and his life. Blythe had broken up with him, and they were going to stay broken up.

Boy, had she smashed the wind out of his sails.

Some part of him wanted to chase after her and demand she take it back. Tell her she didn't love him, couldn't love him. God, she of all women should know he was not the man a woman gave her heart to. He couldn't be trusted with anything that precious. Most of all he didn't want the responsibility.

The responsibility of his mother had slowly drained the life out of his father. It had almost killed every one of Matt's dreams as well. Eric wouldn't be dragged into that swamp.

Not that Blythe had ever been a swamp. He'd valued her honesty, adored her body and enjoyed her company.

It all made a sickening kind of sense. She couldn't stay in contact with him, not if what she said was true. As much as he wanted to deny it, the truth had been right there in those incredible green eyes.

Despite the way she'd grown up, Blythe's eyes always told the truth. She'd never been able to lie to him. All he had to do was look into those beautiful green eyes, and they would let the secret out.

How had he not seen it? How had a woman incapable of subterfuge kept this secret from him?

Across the gym her blond hair drew his gaze. She'd been his best kept secret. In his private self, he'd been so smug that he alone knew who Blythe Barrows really was. While the rest of Ghost Falls made their assumptions and jumped to their nasty conclusions, he had known the truth. Blythe Barrows was a woman of a steel spine and warm, gooey center. That she made love with her entire being and was incredibly picky about who she shared that gift with.

Now she would take all that wonderful to another man. A man who deserved it more. A man who could give her everything she deserved. And, fuck it, she deserved her forever dream, her white picket fence.

The least he could do is get out her way.

Chapter Nine

Blythe stumbled through the rest of Joan's appointment and the one after hers. Out of the corner of her eye, she'd seen Eric leave the gym.

He wouldn't be back, and he would honor her wishes. It was really over.

She'd known this when she left his house and his bed that morning, but it felt as fresh as that first cut.

After her last client for the day, she climbed in her car and got on with the next phase of her plan.

Since he'd first started working Will had been hired by Diva St. Amor. First for yard work, and then for more responsibility and money. The diva was known throughout Ghost Falls for her generosity, and she must be the source of Will's car.

As grateful as she was, Blythe hated how her family had survived on handouts for too long. Now with her new truncated family, the charity train had left the station.

Pulling down the long driveway, she wound through towering trees until she reached the house.

This was the first time Blythe had been this close to it, and it took a moment to take it all in. It looked like a gothic stage set. Gargoyles leering from the eaves made her slightly nervous as she parked her car and climbed out.

Flanked by oversized urns filled to the brim with a violent clash of orange, red and yellow, the steps led up to a wooden door. Blythe rang the bell, which sounded through the house on a hollow gong. She half expected Riff Raff to answer the door.

June, the diva's longtime housekeeper and probably the most miserable woman in Ghost Falls answered the door. She took one look at Blythe and sniffed. "Yes?"

"I'd like to see Mrs. St. Amor." The town should know by now how little she cared for their opinion of her. In her teens she'd done her best to stir them all up a bit. That had soon lost its appeal. It was just too easy.

"Ms." June jerked her dull yellow cardigan around her shoulders. "She doesn't like to be labeled by her association with a man."

Blythe kept a pleasant smile on her face but firmed her voice. "Right. I'd like to see Ms. St. Amor."

"You got an appointment?" June's dismissive gaze swept her from top to toe.

"No, but I—"

June eased the door shut. "If you want to see the diva, you got to make an appointment. She's an important lady."

Blythe could come back another day, but she wanted it over and done with. Moving into her new apartment, the break up with Eric, and now this. They were all stages of moving on with her life. The life she wanted to have. "Please, I—"

"Who is it that comes knocking at our door, dearest Junie?" In a nostril-searing waft of patchouli, the diva appeared and nudged her housekeeper out of the way. Her bright green velvet caftan bounced sunlight to the back of Blythe's eye balls. Ropes of gold chains and pearls dangled over her impressive bosom. "Why, it's *mon petite ange*." The diva sent bracelets crashing as she shooed June out of the doorway. "Make space for our guest, old woman."

With a snort, June took a few steps back and folded her arms. She glared at Blythe over the top of them.

"Run along and dust something." The diva waved her hands at June. She got hold of Blythe's arm in a firm grip. "And you will come with me. We will drink cocktails and have a little chat."

"Actually I don't—"

"La!" The diva trilled. "Wait until we are seated with a libation before you speak."

Feeling like it would be easier to stand in front of a speeding train, Blythe trailed her into the house.

The diva showed her into a lounge crammed with over-stuffed ornate furniture. It looked like she might slide right off those floral silk sofas. She assumed they were silk.

"Now." The diva shut the door behind her and turned to face Blythe. Her face grew serious, and her eyes so kind it hurt to look at her. "Now, you shall call me Phi and tell me what makes *mon petite ange* look so terribly sad."

"I'm not…"

Phi looked at her and looked some more.

Blythe dropped into a chair. "You said something about a cocktail?"

"Indeed." Phi turned and descended on a large globe bar. She tossed open the top and surveyed the contents. "I have been fortunate in my life to have only been acquainted with the agony of heartbreak once and it was many, many years ago." She grabbed a cocktail shaker and whipped the top off. "But I have not forgotten what it felt like. I see this look in your eyes."

"We've only ever met in passing." A part of Blythe goggled at the conversation, and another wanted to stay there forever. There was something about sitting there with Phi that felt like a different place and time.

Phi added gin to the shaker and gave her a meaningful stare. "We women do not have to know each other well to read each other's pain."

Blythe settled as best she could on the slippery sofa.

"I assume this has to do with the delectable Eric."

"Eh?" Shock straightened Blythe's spine.

Phi crashed bottles together and whipped a silver ice bucket out of the bar. She wrenched open the door and thrust it out. "We require ice, June, and you may stop listening at the door."

Nobody knew about her and Eric in Phi's family except Laura, and surely Laura would never have said anything. Divulging their relationship might lead to Laura having to share how it had come about, and Blythe was willing to bet she didn't want that to get out. Especially in light of her current troubles.

Blythe sat there beneath the endless patience and understanding of Phi's gaze, and the walls shoring up her broken heart crumbled. The depth of the pain staggered her and felt like there would never be a time when it was no longer there.

Phi turned and waggled her fingers at Blythe. "Come to Phi, my darling."

Blythe had no idea how Phi did it, but she was on her feet and wrapped deep in the best hug of her life before she could even form the desire.

"There now." Phi rubbed her back.

Somehow she was not only being hugged but she was sobbing like it was her last day on earth.

It took a while for the tears to come to an end, and Phi held her throughout, murmuring words in languages Blythe didn't understand, but they comforted her nonetheless.

Once she had calmed, Phi put her back down on the sofa with a rose bedecked box stuffed full of Kleenex. During her breakdown, June must have brought the ice bucket because Phi went back to the bar and got busy making cocktails.

"Tell me, *ange?*" Phi raised her voice over the clash of glassware. "How long have you been in love with our Eric?"

Some things you couldn't fight. "About eighteen years and eight months. How long have you known?"

"About eighteen years, seven months and two weeks." She widened her eyes. "Ask dear, dear Wheeler. I have my ways of knowing everything."

"Will." Blythe got busy mopping herself up. "I know he's christened Wheeler, but he prefers if we call him Will."

Phi snorted and tossed a hand. "I don't blame him. Ridiculous name. Wheeler." Another, louder snort. "What was your father thinking?"

"That it was funny," Blythe said. "It's amazing what amuses you when you're that deep into a bottle of rye whisky."

"Indeed." Phi's vibrato rumbled through the room. "Now William is a name I can work with. William."

Blythe blew her nose. "Actually, it's just Will."

"Wilhelm. I knew a wonderful flautist called Wilhelm once." She laughed like a tavern wench. "Marvelously talented lips, if you know what I mean."

Nodding, Blythe was very much afraid she did know.

Phi heaved a sigh big enough to raise her impressive bosom and catch light in all her necklaces. "Unfortunately, I had to leave Wilhelm in Vienna."

"Oh, dear." Blythe had no idea what else to say.

"Anyway." Phi took a sip of her drink and smacked her lips. "Let us speak of my darling Eric instead. Commitment issues are so passé, don't you find?"

"Um…"

"One would think such a delicious boy could come up with a more interesting dilemma." Phi shook her head.

Blythe felt like she was chasing a runaway train out the station. "He has his reasons, I suppose."

"He most certainly does." Phi's necklaces winked and danced. "I blame that silly cow, Cressy."

"His mother?"

"Pshaw."

Until that moment, Blythe had never actually heard someone say that.

"That woman is not a mother," Phi said. "She is no better than that Barr——" She snapped her mouth shut.

"Than my mother." Blythe finished for her. It stung but it was not exactly a surprise. "They both have their reasons for being the way they are."

Phi got up and grabbed the cocktail shaker again. "I apologize for that."

"No need." Blythe drained her glass. "I would protest but then we both know better."

Nodding Phi brought the cocktail shaker over and filled Blythe's glass. At this rate Blythe would be calling Will to come and fetch her. Except she had to pick up Kim in a bit, and she put her glass down.

"What reason did our Eric give for ending things?" Phi made herself comfortable.

It was almost a relief that Phi didn't know everything. "Actually, I ended things."

With an exaggerated gape, Phi sipped. "Oh, my." She chuckled. "That would not please our darling boy. Control." She leaned forward and winked. "He likes to have it. Needs it, really." Phi sat back. "After the death of his father, and his mother collapsing, Eric needs to feel as if he steers his own ship."

Blythe's heart still hurt for him. She remembered Mr. Evans dying. She had been in Nate's class and had seen the way the death had broken his children. All except Matt, who had put his shoulder to the harness and done what needed doing.

A year later she and Eric had stumbled into each other's lives.

"What did you say to him?" Phi watched her carefully.

There didn't seem any reason to lie. Having wept all over Phi, her dignity was a lost cause. "I told him I wanted more for myself. That I loved him and knew he didn't love me in return." The wobbly front of another crying jag swept toward her, and Blythe took a deep breath. "It's okay that he doesn't love me. He never said he did, and he never promised any more than what we had. But I need more. For me."

Phi studied her. "You sound awfully final about matters."

"I have to be." Blythe shrugged. "I have been avoiding his calls and not seeing him since the breakup. He cornered me today at work. He was angry."

"I bet he was." Phi chuckled again. She wagged a finger at Blythe. "You are a very clever and astute young thing, you know?"

"Thank you." Blythe didn't know what the glitter in Phi's eyes was all about.

"Phi?" a woman called.

"Ah." Phi gave an earsplitting trill and sprung to her feet. "Just the person we need."

The door opened, and Pippa came in carrying the most adorable baby.

Phi clapped her hands and descended on the baby. "You brought my darling baby girl."

"Well you threatened not to see me if I didn't," Pippa said with a fond smile at her grandmother. She handed the baby over, and then caught sight of Blythe. "Oh! Hello."

"Hi." Blythe always felt uncomfortable around Pippa, like she was in the presence of royalty, which Pippa kind of was Ghost Falls royalty. She had a successful television show, a wonderful husband, and now an adorable child. Plus Pippa was as close as Ghost Falls came to having a star, after Diva St. Amor that was. Then there was the way Pippa was always so effortlessly elegant. Blythe never missed an episode of Pippa's makeover show. She tried to pick up all the tips she could.

"How are you?" Pippa glanced from her to Phi as if sensing the atmosphere.

"Great." Blythe gestured the baby. "She's beautiful."

"Darling Blythe says she is great." Phi leaned closer to Pippa. "But I can see already that you suspect a lie."

"Uh, no." Pippa shook her head at Phi. "And even if I did suspect something, it's not my place to say something until she does." She turned back to Blythe. "And thank you." Pippa had the sort of blindingly beautiful smile that always made Blythe feel grubby by comparison. Her red hair shone and her green eyes danced with intelligence and humor. "She's not letting anyone get any sleep at the moment. Other than herself that is."

"Kim was like that," Blythe blurted. "My youngest sister, Kim. She woke up three or four times a night. I didn't get a full night's sleep until after she was two."

Pippa pulled a face. "Don't tell me that. I have hopes of getting there sooner."

The baby had hold of Phi's necklaces and was tugging on them enthusiastically.

"What's her name?" Eric had told her at some stage, but Blythe had forgotten. Plus she wasn't supposed to know.

"Jasmine." Pippa picked up the cocktail shaker and gave it a sniff. "God, I can't wait for cocktail hour with Phi again."

"Anyway." Blythe was acutely aware of her puffy eyes. She wasn't a pretty crier. "I should be going."

"I will see you soon, *mon petite ange*." Phi winked at her. "Pippa and I are going to help you."

"We are?"

"You are?" She and Pippa spoke at once.

"But of course." Phi looked smug.

"No. Thank you, but that's really not necessary." Blythe had horrible premonitions of her and Eric's long held secret becoming Ghost Falls gossip fodder. Oh hell, people would chew it over for months, their golden boy with the town whore.

"Of course it is." Phi dismissed her with wave.

Pippa studied her. "How are we going to help, Phi?"

Phi raised her arms and revealed the spangled diaphanous batwings of her caftan. "All will be revealed in the fullness of time."

Turning, Pippa fixed her with a look. "How long have you been practicing that?"

Phi gave her gutter laugh. "Months. But until now I have not had the opportunity to use it." She grinned and raised her batwings. "Want to see it again?"

Chapter Ten

Blythe picked up Kim and dropped by the grocery store on her way home. Will was working, so she'd see him later.

She started to pull into her parking space outside her condo to find Barron already occupying it. Apparently her day wasn't done having a crap on her.

Perched on his bike, he was sipping out of a paper bag as he glowered at her.

Kim sat in her car seat happily examining the painting she had done that morning.

As much as Blythe wished it was otherwise, she knew her family couldn't leave her alone. She represented all that they couldn't, or wouldn't, do with their lives.

"Kim." Blythe kept her attention on Barron. Barron had that Brett streak running through him, and he'd been drinking. "I want you to stay in the car. Okay, baby?"

"Is that Barron?" Kim peered through the windshield. She pulled a face. "I don't like Barron. I don't want to talk to him."

That made two of them. "That's okay." She kept the fear out of her voice. "You don't have to talk to him. I'll see what he wants, and then he'll go away."

"Okay." Kim's eyes were huge.

Blythe dug out her phone and got Nate's number up. She passed the phone to Kim. "If you see anything you don't like, you press the green button, baby girl. That's Sheriff Nate, and he'll come and help you."

Kim's voice went small and she held the phone to her chest. "Okay."

Only one thing would bring Barron here. He wanted money.

"Took you a while to get here." Barron sipped from his bag. "You been out there sucking dick?"

Blythe breathed deep, not about to rise to the bait. Barron was drunk and spoiling for a fight. If she gave it to him, it could very well end up in a Barrows-style crawl and brawl scene she really didn't want her new neighbors to see. She didn't want Kim to see it anymore either.

"What do you want, Barron?"

He sneered at her. "Is that any way to talk to your brother? Careful now, Blythe, or I might think you didn't miss me."

The sooner she let him get crap off his chest, the sooner he would leave. So she waited.

"I need money." Barron shook the bottle in his bag. "This shit doesn't come cheap, and your boyfriend got me canned."

She hadn't even known Barron worked for Eric, but she didn't blame Eric in the least.

Like hell she would say anything about Eric, however. Now came the tricky part. Her choices really sucked. If she gave Barron money, he would go away but then he'd be back and back again until she ran out of money or he got bored. If she didn't give him money, he would not be happy, and Barron wasn't shy about making his unhappiness known. She should have dialed Nate from inside the car.

Too late for that. She glanced over her shoulder

Kim was watching them both, her thumb in her mouth. She hadn't done that since they'd been living in the condo.

Blythe took a breath. "I'm not giving you money."

"Say what?" Barron laughed. "Because for a second there, it sounded like you said you weren't going to give me what you owe me."

"I don't owe you anything." She could only hope Kim would hit dial if things deteriorated. And how stupid was she to have left the responsibility in her baby sister's hands?

Barron climbed off his bike and advanced on her. "There's shit to eat in the house, and some dick came around the other day looking for his fucking payment. You gotta pay, Blythe."

"I don't live there anymore." Blythe kept her voice calm, but her heartbeat jacked up. "I'm not paying for you anymore."

A bottle smashing made her jump, but Blythe held her ground.

Grabbing her biceps, Barron tugged her closer. His breath stank of cheap bourbon. "I want money, Blythe, and you're going to get it for me."

"No." Blythe struggled against his punishing hold. "I'm not giving you anything."

"Bitch." Barron hit her.

Her head whipped to the side, and she tasted blood.

"Leave my sister alone!" Kim was outside the car, screaming, clutching the phone, her little body shaking. "Leave my sister. I told Sheriff Nate."

"What the fuck is she talking about?" Barron's other hand gripped her hair. "Tell the little brat to drop the phone or I'll give her a bit of what I gave you."

"Don't you touch her." Icy rage crawled through Blythe. She yanked free of Barron with strength she didn't know she had. Her voice shook as she blocked Kim from Barron's view. "You touch her, and I'll kill you."

A bike growled into the parking lot.

Barron glanced its way, and then grinned. "Just the man I need to show you bitches how to act."

Those massive shoulders and that bike belonged to only one man. Blythe snatched Kim and darted to the other side of the car.

"You better run, bitch." Barron made a mock lunge at her. "Because when Brett gets hold of you, you'll give me whatever the fuck I want."

Blythe grabbed her bag from the seat and fled with Kim in her arms.

Clinging like a monkey, Kim stayed eerily silent, her little back tense beneath Blythe's hands. "We'll get inside, baby girl. We'll get inside, and then they can't touch us."

"Brett." Barron sounded delighted as he greeted their older brother. "Come help me explain to Blythe why she needs to help her brothers out."

Brett's deep rumble echoed.

"Not far now." Blythe reached the stairs to her apartment. She had to take her hands from Kim to dig her house keys out of her bag.

Kim tightened her grip around Blythe's neck and waist.

"What the fuck!" Barron yelled from somewhere below them.

Blythe kept climbing. She reached the top with her breath coming ragged. Her hands shook but she inserted the key the first time and turned the lock.

Boots sounded on the stairs.

Blythe got the door open and sprang into the apartment. She locked the door, put the chain on and bolted it.

A fist hammered on the door. "Blythe?" Brett asked.

Kim whimpered and buried her face in Blythe's neck

"It's okay, baby girl." Blythe leaned her back against the solid door. Her knees gave, and she sank to the floor clutching Kim. She refused to crumble, and she kissed Kim's head. "We're safe now."

"Blythe," Brett called through the door.

Kim sniffed. "Make him go away."

"He will." Blythe tightened her arms around Kim. "If we stay very quiet. He will go away."

They stayed liked that, wrapped tightly together, barely daring to breathe.

Boots walked away from her door. A bike started up, and then another, and finally Blythe breathed again.

"Blythe?" Kim wriggled in her arms and looked up at her. She held up Blythe's phone. "I called Sheriff Nate. Like you said I should if I got scared."

"When, baby girl?" Blythe took her phone back. She had eight missed calls from Nate's number. She dialed from his last call.

"Blythe?" Nate sounded urgent. "Is that you?"

"It's me." The relief made her want to cry, and she hauled herself to her feet. "I'm okay."

"What the hell happened?" The hum of a car engine underpinned Nate's voice.

"Barron came around and wanted money." She smoothed Kim's hair back. Baby girl had done so well and kept her head. Blythe didn't remember being that smart and self-possessed at the same age. "I told Kim to call you if she got scared, and she did."

"Why did she get scared?" Nate didn't sound the least reassured.

For his and Kim's sake Blythe tried to downplay it. "Barron got a bit frustrated when I wouldn't give him any money."

"How frustrated?"

"I'm okay." She put as much reassurance as she had in her into those words. "Kim and I are in my apartment, and we're safe."

Nate grunted. "I want you to press charges."

How many times had she wished Carly would do the

same? "Can we talk about it in the morning?" Kim was still clinging to her leg. "I need to see to Kim."

"Fine," Nate bit out. "But we will be talking in the morning, Blythe."

She hung up and looked down at Kim.

Tears filled Kim's eyes. "Is Sheriff Nate mad at us. He sounded mad."

"He was mad." Blythe hugged Kim to her. "But he was mad for us. He doesn't want anybody to hurt us, because it isn't right."

"Barron hit you." Kim shivered and pressed closer. "I saw it."

Blythe forced herself to scoff. "Barron's a weenie." Maybe making light of things wasn't the best way to handle this, but Blythe was all out of ideas. "Let's make some dinner."

"The groceries are in the car." Kim stared at the door.

"Right." Blythe took a breath. "I'll go and get them."

Still they both stared at the door for a minute or so before she moved.

After checking through the keyhole, Blythe opened the door.

Her grocery sacks sat outside the door, and her car was in her parking place, doors closed. The car keys lay on top of the groceries. One of her neighbors had earned a huge thank you.

IT TOOK LONGER to get Kim to bed than normal. Given the crap evening they'd had, Blythe let her stay up thirty minutes later and read her one more story than normal. Truthfully, it helped her as well. Concentrating on Kim kept her from thinking about everything that had happened.

Eventually Kim went to sleep, and the apartment settled around her. She tried not to, but every noise posed a threat, the low growl of every engine sounded like her brothers' bikes returning.

She turned on the TV and played it louder than usual. Then she did what she always did when she was stressed; she cleaned.

It would have been better if she'd asked Nate to come around and make sure everything was fine, but it was too late for that now, and Nate was probably settled in with Bella by then.

How Bella had gotten a great guy like Nate amazed her. Everyone thought of Bella as sweetness and light, but they hadn't been on the judgmental side of Tinker Bell and her assumptions. When they had been in high school together, Blythe had made a game of seeing how outraged she could get Bella to look. With Bella's long-standing crush on Nate, it had been low hanging fruit to flirt with Nate and give Bella a helping of payback.

No, it hadn't been nice, and she wasn't proud of it, but neither was the way Bella had gossiped about her and looked at her as if she were lower than shark shit.

A knock on the door stopped her in the middle of shining the countertops. She stood in the kitchen, frozen by indecision. It could be either of her brothers, or it could be Nate.

The knock came again. "Blythe?" Eric called through the door.

That made her paralysis worse. Only that morning she'd told him she couldn't see him anymore.

Eric knocked a third time. "Blythe, I'm not going away until I see you."

Shit! He wouldn't either.

Blythe opened the door.

Both hands braced on the doorjamb, Eric looked up. He hissed out a breath and cupped her chin. "Did Barron or Brett do that?"

The slap must have left a bruise. "Barron."

Eric's gentle touch was the most dangerous thing of all. The temptation to stay still and bask in it rose and threatened to drag her under.

Blythe lifted her chin from his hold. "Nate called you?"

"Yeah." Eric shoved his hands in his pockets. "He thought I would want to know, and it's not like you were going to call, is it?"

Nate had no right to involve Eric. "Is that even allowed, with him being a cop and all? To call you and tell you someone else's business.

"Give me a break, Blythe." Eric's eyes flashed darker with irritation. "He's my brother, and he knows I care about you." He shrugged. "Besides he was not happy with not checking up on you. I said I'd do it."

"Oh." Nate hadn't really done anything bad, and he couldn't know how she felt about Eric. Being Nate though, he probably knew more than he let on. Behind his pretty face, Nate didn't miss much. "Well, you've checked, and I'm fine."

"Really?" Eric gave her a probing stare.

That sort of thing wasn't them. They'd always stayed on the periphery of each other's daily lives. Eric had offered to help her in the past, with money mostly, but she had always turned him down. Apart from her not wanting to feel like his side piece, she had always needed to do things on her own. If for no other reason than to prove to herself that she could.

Eric watched her, waiting for her answer.

He knew her too well for her to lie, so she went with the truth. "They scared me, and frightened Kim. Mostly I'm angry. They invaded my safe space."

He nodded. "Nate wants you to press charges." He raised a brow. "For what it's worth, I want you to as well."

"I'll think about it." Maybe if only to get a restraining order on Barron, but that didn't deal with Brett. Brett hadn't done anything to earn one. Yet. Her head felt heavy, and she leaned it against the doorjamb. "I just want to get on with my life, you know?"

"I know." He reached for her, stopped and jerked his hand back. "Sorry. Habit."

They both had habits they needed to break, and Blythe straightened. "It's okay that you came here tonight." More than that, and he hadn't done anything wrong. "Actually, it was sweet. A nice thing to do." She inched the door closed. "But it would be better for both of us if it didn't happen again."

Chapter Eleven

Since Eric had been spending more time in Ghost Falls, dinner with his siblings and their significant others had become a thing at least one Friday a month. They had tried including Cressy for the first few times but had abandoned that quickly. Cressy had spent dinner taking potshots at Pippa and then Bella.

As neither Matt nor Nate would tolerate having their wives at the end of Cressy's passive-aggressive cannon fire, the evenings had disintegrated fast. The others spent time with Cressy separately. Eric saw her as little as possible.

Matt might be okay with the way she had used him as a surrogate for her dead husband, but Eric still held that grudge. Cressy had clung to her children at a time when they needed her to be the parent. She still did, and Eric refused to get sucked into the same emotional vortex that had swallowed Dad whole.

Tonight's dinner was at Nate and Bella's house. A beautiful stone house with spectacular views on three sides that Nate was renovating bit by bit. Some weekends he and Matt would manage to muscle in and help him. But Nate was a stubborn bastard and liked doing everything himself.

"Eric." Bella opened the door and beamed at him. Small and blond, Pippa had nicknamed her Tinker Bell, and the name suited Bella.

"Hey, Tink." He leaned down and kissed her cheek.

"I hate that name." Bella twinkled up at him. She was all the right kind of sweet Nate needed in his life.

For his part, Eric liked his women a little more salty. Like...

Not anymore.

"How is work?" Bella got started on her interrogation. She was always like that with friends. She wanted to know everything about their life. Unlike a lot of people, Bella asked questions from a place of genuine interest. Like he said, all kinds of sweet.

Eric followed her into the large open-plan kitchen.

"Eric." Nate jerked his chin at him from the opposite side of a twelve-foot butcher block island. He knew the dimensions because it was one of the few things Nate had asked his help to source.

"Stairs look good." Eric jabbed his thumb at the wood and wrought iron staircase that had still been a hideous seventies throwback when he had last been there.

Pride showed on Nate's face. "Yeah, I finished them last weekend. They came out well."

Eric clapped Nate on the shoulder. "You do good work. Even Dad would have liked those."

"Is Eric here?" Pippa came through the French doors from the deck. She gave him a sultry wink. "How's my sexiest brother-in-law?"

"Hey!" Nate threw his hands out. "Standing right here."

"You're my prettiest brother-in-law." Pippa laughed at him. "Eric is the sexiest."

"Damn it, Agrippina." Matt sauntered in after his wife, Jasmine in his arms. "Now I'm going to have to beat the crap out of them. Again. And this is my favorite shirt. I don't want to get blood on it."

"Gimme." Eric motioned for his niece. Just because he didn't want children of his own didn't mean he didn't like them.

Matt handed him Jasmine, and he breathed in the sticky, sweet baby smell.

Jasmine gave him a huge sloppy grin.

"Every woman." Pippa rolled her eyes. "No matter what age."

Except one, apparently. Eric slapped a grin on his face. "It's my superpower."

"Hey! Hey! Hey!" Liz yelled from the door that she'd just flung open. Skinny, blond and always dressed like she'd strayed out of an episode of *The Real Housewives of Orange County*, Liz was good people. As was her short, unassuming husband, Noel, following in her wake as always and looking delighted to be there.

"Ugh!" Liz reached up and pinched his cheek. "Such a pity I didn't get to you before Noel got to me."

"You're too much woman for me, Liz." He nodded a greeting to Noel.

Liz waggled her head. "Damn straight I am."

Coming in behind them, and much quieter, was the only girl in the Evans family. Dressed in jeans and a baggy sweatshirt, Jo looked tired, but Eric knew better than to say anything.

Jo could be as stubborn as Nate. He greeted her, and then relinquished Jasmine to her.

Pippa studied him from the other side of the island. She cocked her head. "You okay?"

"Sure." He accepted a beer from Nate and twisted off the cap. Pippa's sharp gaze saw too much. "Just some stuff with the new project."

"Hmmm." She looked skeptical but accepted his explanation. For now.

Jasmine had the same dark hair as Jo and carried so much of the Evans genetics that she could have been Jo's daughter. Since her disastrous engagement, Jo hadn't mentioned anyone serious.

"What's news, Jo Jo?" He moved closer to her. The look of contentment as she cuddled Jasmine tugged at his heart. "When are you going to see about getting yourself one of those?"

Jo snorted and rolled her eyes. "What about you, old man?"

Eric opened his mouth to deliver his normal glib reply, but it got stuck. A child of his might look a lot like Jasmine. It could have been his baby being handed from one family member to another for a cuddle.

"Eric?" Jo raised her eyebrow at him. "Is there something you'd like to tell the class?"

He forced himself to snort and sip his beer. "You know how I feel about kids."

Or how he felt most of the time. All of the time. His conversation with Blythe had gotten under his skin more than he'd thought possible. Blythe had gotten under his skin more than he'd thought possible.

Maybe if he'd dated her, had a more traditional relationship with her, he could have brought her with him to family dinner. Where once he could never have pictured her there, he wasn't so sure anymore.

God, what a stupid thought. He dismissed it fast. The reason he had kept things with Blythe casual hadn't changed. When you brought a woman around your family, you raised expectations that he had no intention of fulfilling.

"Anyone heard from Isaac?" Matt started the conversation guaranteed to grab everyone's attention.

Eric heard from their youngest brother once a week, but

he kept that to himself. They had a deal: Isaac stayed in contact and promised to let him know if he was in trouble and to drop the occasional email to Jo, and Eric let him have the distance from the family he needed. Eric didn't entirely get it, but making sure Isaac had an open lifeline took precedence.

"I had an email from him a couple of weeks ago," Jo said. "He's gone fishing in the Bering Sea."

"What the fuck!" Nate slammed his beer down. He looked at Jasmine and started. "Sorry. But seriously?"

"Isn't that dangerous?" Bella shifted closer to Nate and slid beneath his arm.

"Yes." Nate's jaw tightened. He stared at Matt and then Eric. "How long is this shi—stuff going to go on?"

Matt shrugged. "As long as it needs to. Isaac feels he has some kind of point to prove. Until he decides he's proved it or he doesn't care anymore, he'll keep doing this stuff."

What a mess they all were. Matt had nearly let his chance of happiness go by letting Pippa walk right out of this life. After he'd already given up a full ride scholarship for his family. Then there was Nate who had almost lost Bella before he realized that he was worthy of the love she gave him so freely. Jo wouldn't accept any help from the family because she felt like a burden to all of them.

And then there was him.

Needing some air, he got another beer and slipped outside to the deck.

Matt appeared next to him. "Anything you want to talk about?"

"Nope."

"Fair enough." Matt squeezed his shoulder. "You know where I am if you change your mind."

Eric nodded, but he wouldn't change his mind. Keeping Blythe a secret had become a habit, and now one he never had to worry about again.

He tried to think why he'd always kept her a secret. Maybe

it had to do with the on-again, off-again nature of their relationship over the years. They'd gone months, and when he'd gone to college, years, without seeing each other, and always fell back into their twisted little arrangement.

Dinner was soon ready, and Bella called them all to the table.

Nate had found the old table and sanded it and repaired it himself. It seated all of them easily. Fortunately, Nate had done the cooking tonight. Bella couldn't cook for shit and was fair enough to admit it.

The wash of wine, good food and family carried him with it, and Eric felt some of the tightness in his shoulders ease.

He took a platter of meat from Nate and set it on the table.

"Did you go around and see Blythe?" Nate sat beside Bella.

Bella glanced at him in surprise. "Why would Eric see Blythe?" Then she pulled a face. "Why would anyone see Blythe Barrows?"

Eric had heard much the same from Blythe, but Bella's statement still bugged him. If she only got to know Blythe, she wouldn't say that. "I did, and she was fine."

Nate's focus narrowed in on him, all cop. "But?"

"But she's sporting a souvenir from Barron. He thought to make his unhappiness known." Eric had to breathe deep before he broke something. With the exception of Wheeler, Blythe's brothers were total assholes.

Bella gaped at them. "He hit her? Her own brother?"

"Yeah." Nate looked disgusted. "They're a bad bunch. Blythe is well out of that." He pinned Eric with a stare. "And you're going to leave it to the law to deal with Barron. Right, Eric?"

No way he was answering that, and he sipped his wine.

"It must have happened after I saw her." Pippa frowned

and took some salad and handed the bowl to Nate on her left. "At Phi's."

"She was at Phi's yesterday?" Eric felt like he'd been relegated to spectator in Blythe's life.

Bella wrinkled up her nose. "What was she doing at Phi's?"

"I'm not sure." Pippa shrugged and helped herself to Nate's slow-cooked lamb. "But she looked like she'd been crying."

Damn! That punched him straight in the gut. Fortunately, he managed to keep from spilling his wine. It sounded like Blythe had had a thoroughly crap day yesterday, which was now none of his business. And it bugged him.

Bella snorted. "That doesn't sound like Blythe. She's the one who makes other people cry."

A memory stirred. Blythe sitting cross-legged on his bed wearing one of his shirts. He had been asking why she didn't do something for her birthday. She had pulled a face at him and said, "Women don't like me very much. Especially not in this town."

Keeping his tone neutral, he looked at Bella. "What do you mean by that?"

"Uh-oh." Nate shook his head in warning. "Now you've done it."

"Blythe Barrows is a bitch," Bella said.

Seeing sweet Bella so bent out of shape made it all the more jarring. He couldn't leave it there. Blythe had some sharp edges, but for fuck's sake, she'd more than earned those. "In what way?"

"She's one of those women who delight in rubbing in your face exactly how hot they are." Bella dug into her dinner vengefully. "Always looking down her perfect nose at me."

That didn't sound like his Blythe. "Maybe she's shy."

"Blythe!" Now Pippa laughed. "Nobody in Ghost Falls would call that girl shy."

And suddenly he was caught in a time warp, back in high school. The ugly rumors and whispers that always surrounded Blythe. He knew, better than anyone, how false they were. After all, he'd been Blythe's first, and she'd been nineteen at the time. "Come on." Some of his frustration leaked into his voice. "Surely you can't believe any of that gossip about her."

"Oh, I believe it," Bella said. "You should see the way she sidles up to Nate whenever he's around."

"To be fair," Liz said, "the same could be said of every woman in this town."

Nate's cheeks went pink, and he ducked his head to his dinner.

"I thought you and she had a thing?" Pippa looked at Nate.

Nate shook his head. "Nope. I used to flirt with her at school." He shrugged. "Hell, everybody did; she was pretty and easy to flirt with."

Bella gave her husband a wrathful stare.

"What?" Nate looked confused. "This happened years ago. And it was never serious."

"I know." Bella frowned. "She just gets to me is all."

"I can see that." Eric knew he should let it go, but he couldn't. "But I'm not properly understanding why."

"Let me break it down for you," Liz said, eyes glittering wrathfully as she came to Bella's defense. "Blythe is a complete slut, and she likes nothing better than rubbing that in every other woman's face. She likes to remind you that she thinks she can take your man from you."

Bella nodded. "Exactly."

"That's a bit harsh," Pippa said. "But not untrue."

A cold, crystalline rage rose in Eric. He breathed in and out carefully and stood. Dropping his napkin on the table, he looked at his friends and family. "I love you girls, but you're full of shit." He needed to get away from them before he said worse. "I could write an entire book about what you don't know about Blythe Barrows."

"Eric!" Matt stopped him at the front door.

For a moment he nearly ignored him, but it wouldn't end there, so he stopped and waited.

"What the hell?" Matt came up behind him. "You want to explain what that was all about?"

"Not really."

Pippa came up behind Matt. "I'm sorry, Eric, I wouldn't have said anything if I knew you and Blythe were...close."

"We're not." Not anymore. "But I know her quite well, and before people judge her, they should first ask if their assumptions are true. And secondly, they should ask themselves if they're making those assumptions because of Blythe or her family."

Chapter Twelve

Blythe was catching up on some paperwork in her tiny office at the gym. Body Works wasn't as grand or upscale as the other gym in Ghost Falls, but she could use their equipment and facilities in exchange for teaching a few classes a week, and the atmosphere put even her most body-conscious client at ease.

"Hey there." Randy popped his head around her door. "You've got visitors."

"Me?" Blythe's heart jumped into her throat. Surely Eric had gotten the message the other night.

"It's three women." Randy seemed to read her thoughts. "One of them is that redhead from the television show."

That sounded like Pippa, but she had no idea what Pippa would be doing there.

Blythe got to her feet and checked her appearance in the tiny mirror in her desk drawer. There wasn't much she could do about the gym outfit and no makeup, but she could make sure her hair was neat. Meeting someone who ran a makeover show for a living intimidated her.

As she approached reception, she saw Bella Evans and her next-door neighbor and friend, Liz.

Blythe stiffened. That couldn't be good.

"Hi," she said as she approached them.

Bella still looked as if she would like to scrape Blythe off the bottom of her shoe, but Pippa gave her a careful smile. "I hope we haven't come at a bad time."

"No, that's fine." Blythe had no idea what they were doing there. "I've got twenty minutes before my next client comes."

Pippa nodded and shifted her feet. "I suppose you're wondering what we're doing here."

"A bit." Like a whole truckload.

"Phi has been asking about you," Pippa said. "She threatened to come down here herself, but I managed to head her off."

"Hi, Blythe," Bella said in that tight voice she reserved for her.

Blythe did what she always did and retreated inside. She wouldn't give people like Bella the satisfaction of knowing their derision hurt. "Hi."

"Actually I wanted to know if you had any openings," Pippa said. "I'm due to start shooting the next season of *Your Best You*," she said, "and I haven't quite lost all the baby weight from Jasmine."

Blythe took a good look at Pippa. "You seem to be doing great to me."

"Well, thank you." Pippa flushed. "But the camera can be brutal, and I was rather hoping you could help me get myself where I need to be."

Which didn't explain what the other two were doing there. Feeling a bit like she'd dropped through a wormhole, Blythe nodded. "I could do that." She pulled out her phone. "I will have to book you in for an assessment first, and then we can talk about the best way to achieve your goals."

"That sounds fair." Pippa checked her phone. She glanced at Liz and Bella. "Actually, could we do a session with all three of us?"

Now Blythe had dropped into a parallel dimension. Bella would rather chew nails than be trained by her. "What's this really about?"

"Getting to know you better." Pippa met her gaze squarely. "The baby weight is real, but something someone close to me said got me thinking."

Blythe waited. Pippa looked like she was being honest, but their conversation was still odd. "Why now?"

"That's a good question." Pippa grimaced. "And I wish I had a good answer for you, but this person asked me if I had made the mistake of tossing you in with the rest of your family." Pippa shrugged. "I love this person and value their opinion, so I hoped you and I could get to know each other."

This person had to be Phi, didn't it? She needed a moment to process, and she looked at Bella. "And you?"

Bella flushed. "I heard the same thing." She patted her hips. "And I wouldn't mind looking like you."

"You need to grow five inches first." Liz snorted, and then shrugged at Blythe. "I'm here to check out the hot bodies."

That dragged a laugh out of all of them and eased the tension somewhat.

Blythe motioned toward a small seating area to the left of the reception. "Why don't we have a seat?"

They all moved to the two couches and sat down.

Still not sure Bella meant any of it, Blythe perched next to Pippa. "So, to be clear, you're all here to get to know me better? Under the pretext of training?"

"The training is not a pretext," Pippa said. "The baby weight is real."

Bella pulled a face. "My butt has been steadily growing since my wedding. I can be thin or happy; apparently not both."

"Not me." Liz smirked. "I'm here to check you out, get the low down on you."

Blythe chuckled. "And the checking out hot bodies is a bonus?"

"You got it." Liz winked.

"How's that going?" Blythe couldn't resist. There was something about Liz that suggested she didn't judge.

"Meh." Liz waggled her hand. "I like you as much as I can like any woman with that insane body you have on you."

"Right." Pippa rolled her eyes, and then grinned at Blythe. "So, my number one goal is an ass like yours."

"Me too." Bella still looked sour about it though.

Blythe met her stare. "Are you sure you want to do this? With me?"

"Nope." Bella crossed her arms. "But I trust this person's opinion, and they got madder than I've ever seen them when I said you were a slut."

That kind of honesty took Blythe aback, and she blinked. "I'm not sure I can work with anyone who has a stick shoved so far up their ass."

"Guys." Pippa held out her hands, palms down like she was stroking troubled waters. "I think you could both do with getting to know each other better."

Liz nudged Bella. "You do sometimes have a stick up your ass about certain people."

Bella opened her mouth, looked at Liz, and snapped it shut. "You may have a point." She then looked at Blythe. "I can put aside whatever differences we've had in the past if you can."

"I can do that." Not with her last breath would she let Bella get the better of her.

"Great." Sounding overly enthusiastic for the occasion, Pippa stood. "So the three of us will get together and come up with some times that work for us, then we'll check those with you." She beamed at everybody. "I'm excited to get going."

Blythe stood with her. "Actually, I was hoping you'd be open to a trade of sorts."

"Trade?" Pippa cocked her head.

She really hated having to admit anything in front of Bella, but Blythe couldn't let the opportunity pass. "I don't know how to dress myself." The words came out in a rush, and heat spread over her face. "I mean, dress like you. I stick to gym gear because everything else makes me look trashy."

Pippa stared at her. "You mean you would like me to make you over?"

"I know you're busy and famous, and you must have people waiting for years to be on your show." Now that she'd asked, Blythe wanted to kick herself. Pippa didn't have time to help her. "I just meant a few tips."

"Oh, no." Pippa shook her head. "If we're doing a trade, then you're getting the full treatment."

"Great idea, Pippa." Liz rolled her eyes. "Let's make her better looking than she is now."

"It's what I do." Pippa looked her up and down, and then slowly circled her.

Blythe resisted the urge to fidget.

Stopping in front of her, Pippa grinned. "Oh, this is going to be fun."

"Really?" Excitement prickled through Blythe. Her look was either gym rat or town tart. She had no idea how to go about putting herself together in the effortless way Pippa did. Even Liz had toned her look down to run-of-the-mill cougar under Pippa's tutelage. "I need to create the right impression if I want to grow my business. Especially with those new women in the developments above town."

"For sure." Bella nodded. "That's why I revamped Bella's." Bella had inherited the shop from her grandmother. "They've got money to spend. Why shouldn't they spend it in Ghost Falls?"

"We have a deal." Pippa stuck her hand out.

Blythe took it and shook. "I told Phi that she needn't bother herself with me. I'm used to sorting my own life out."

Will had always told her how Phi was like a runaway truck when she got something in her head.

Pippa laughed. "You may as well save your breath. Phi is a law unto herself."

They exchanged numbers.

"I'll get back to you on a date for your makeover," Pippa said.

Bella took a deep breath. "I want to ask you something."

"Okay." Blythe braced for the worst.

Bella crossed her arms over her chest. "Why don't you like me?"

Blythe nearly swallowed her tongue.

Liz sidled up beside Bella looking like her skinny but mean henchman. "Bella's a wonderful person."

"To other people," Blythe said. The entire situation had caught her enough off guard to get the truth out of her. "Bella is always nice to other people. She's never liked me, not since Nate took me to prom."

"That's not true." Bella stopped and frowned. "Okay, that may be part of it, but the rest is that you always look at me like you think I'm stupid."

Stung, Blythe retorted, "And you always look at me as if I'm not good enough for you."

"Well, that escalated," Pippa said. "Do you think you might both have a point?"

Blythe glared at Bella.

Bella glared right back.

And suddenly Blythe saw the funny side. They were both well into their thirties and still behaving like tweens. She couldn't stop the smile creeping on to her face.

Bella's eyes widened, and then a smile spread over her face. "I was jealous of you. You were always so hot." Her gaze swept Blythe from top to toe. "You still have the most ridiculously banging body."

"And I was jealous because everybody always liked you.

You were sweet Bella and could do no wrong, and I was always that Barrows girl, as bad as her brothers."

Bella looked taken aback. "That is what people say about you."

"I know that." It didn't mean she had to be happy about it. "I could be standing right next to you, and you could do something bad, and it would be blamed on me."

Pulling a face, Bella had the grace to blush. "That actually happened a time or two."

"Damn right it did." Funny now that they were talking about it, the sting lessened a bit.

"But you're doing good now." Bella motioned the gym. "You have your own business, and everybody says you're the best. Nate says you even moved out and took your younger sister and Wheeler with you."

"Will," Blythe said. "He really hates being called Wheeler."

Liz snorted. "I can understand that for sure." She gave Bella a gentle elbow. "You know I love the hell outta you kid, but you do have a bit of judgmental thing going on. Think that might have happened here?"

"It's not entirely Bella's fault." Blythe couldn't in fairness allow the other woman to take all the blame. "I certainly did my part." She couldn't meet any of their gazes. "I used to make sure to be extra flirty with Nate when you were around."

"I knew it." Bella jabbed a finger at her. "I knew you did that."

"Yes, darling Tink." Pippa smiled at Bella. "But who is married to Nate now?"

"Me." Bella beamed as if she'd just remembered that fact. "I'm married to Nate."

"There you go." Blythe couldn't help but smile at the unbridled enthusiasm. "You won."

Liz eyed her. "Do you drink or are you one to those my-body-is-a-temple types?"

"I drink." Blythe went cautiously there. "But not a lot. Because of my dad."

"Right." Pippa gave her a look warm with empathy. "That makes perfect sense. I think what Liz is trying to ask is if you would like to come out for a drink with us some time?"

Blythe blinked at them, trying and failing to navigate the new territory. She'd never had a female friend. Now it looked as if three women were extending the hand of friendship, and probably the last three women she would have expected to do so.

They were all staring at her and waiting for her answer. Blythe got it together. "That would be fun."

"Good." Liz adjusted the strap of her purse on her shoulder. "And then you can tell us exactly what's going on with Eric, and why he tells his whole family to go to hell and jumps to your defense."

Chapter Thirteen

Eric spent until midmorning combing through Gunning Contracting's financials. He was sure Chase was doing much the same thing to theirs. Now they'd agreed to explore moving forward, it was time to peek beneath the drapes for both companies and start to put numbers to their intentions.

Something nagged at Eric, and he couldn't put his finger on it. Gunning's books were clean, no red flags, or not of the sort that might hint Chase was hiding anything. There were the usual weak areas, places that needed improvement, but Eric's doubt wouldn't go away.

He went next door to Matt's office and knocked.

Matt looked up and motioned him in. It had been Dad's office. Sentimental Matt still had the same oversize walnut desk and leather desk chair Dad had used. In Dad's day, the office had smelled of the pack a day that had eventually killed him.

"What's up?" Matt sat back in his chair.

Eric tried to put it into words. "I've been going through the Gunning books."

"Problem?" Matt linked his fingers behind his head. More

comfortable as a contractor than in a suit, he always wore a plain button-down over a white T-shirt.

"Nah." Eric stretched his legs in front of him to get comfortable. "The books look fine. I've got accounting going through them as well." He tried to express what the niggle was for him. "Do you think we're doing the right thing here?"

Matt raised his brow. "Didn't we have this conversation when Gunning first approached us?"

"I know." Eric had made his money being smart and doing his due diligence. But mostly he'd made his way by listening to his gut. The same gut that wouldn't shut up now. "We need this merger to stay in the game, but I'm hesitating."

"About the merger, or merging with Gunning?" Matt not dismissing him was one of the reasons they worked well together. Also, as brothers, they had no hesitation in getting honest and real with each other.

Eric shrugged. He wished he could articulate this better. "I'm not sure. Maybe it's giving up control of Dad's company."

"This hasn't been Dad's company for a long time," Matt said.

Matt had earned that right as well, giving up his young hopes and dreams to run Evans Construction.

His desk phone rang, and Matt picked it up. He listened for a moment, and then stilled.

That couldn't be good.

The grim look on Matt's face confirmed the bad feeling.

"We've got issues with Highgate again." Matt put the phone down. "We have men refusing to go on site."

Not this again. Eric swore under his breath. "I fired Barron Barrows last time I was up there."

"Okay." Matt sat forward. "Let's unpack that statement, shall we?" He counted the points on his fingers. "First, when were you last up there? And second, you fired Barron Barrows? Another entanglement with the Barrows family that you're keeping secret, and who the hell hired him in the first place?"

Just because Matt liked to play big brother from time to time, didn't mean Eric intended to let him. "Which question would you like answered first?"

"All your Barrows entanglements."

"Okay, so I was on site one evening last week. The electrical contractor's crew thought they could get more money out of us by refusing to work." He shrugged. "I set them straight, and mostly I set Barron Barrows straight."

"You threw him off site?"

"Yup."

Matt interlaced his fingers. "Was this before or after Barron hit Blythe, and you went rushing around there to check she was all right?"

"I'm going up to Highgate." Eric stood. Two reasons Matt could mind his own business: one, Eric really didn't want to talk about Blythe. Two, it drove Matt crazy when he didn't know shit.

Standing, Matt grabbed his truck keys from his desk. "Let's go."

"What's this we business?" Eric got in front of him,

Matt pushed impatient fingers through his hair. "As far as I know this is our company, and we do shit like this together."

Eric held his hand out for the truck keys. "Not when one of us has a wife and young baby at home, and things could get ugly."

"Cooper says it's already ugly." Matt didn't budge. "And I'm not letting you go up there alone. He says this thing is getting racial."

"Fuck!" Eric took the keys. "I better get up there and see what I can find out."

"I'm coming."

"No, you aren't." Eric put a hand up to stop Matt. "You'll stay right here, and later you'll go home to your beautiful wife and your gorgeous baby girl. If this is going to get worse, I'm in just the right sort of mood to deal with it."

Matt gave him a hard stare. "Yeah, about that…"

"I can't talk about it."

"Can't or won't?" Matt crossed his arms.

Eric didn't want to deal with this now. "It amounts to the same thing." Sometimes Matt didn't know when to back off. "Look, can you stop being my big brother for long enough for me to handle some stuff on my own? Maybe just trust me that I got this."

"Sure." Matt pulled a face. "Probably not, but I can try."

"That's good enough." Eric pulled his own car keys out his pocket and gave them to Matt. "You can take the Jag home."

ERIC ARRIVED on site in no mood to make more friends. The idle crane and drywall crew beside the construction office didn't improve his mood any.

Getting out of the truck, he gave the door a slam. Good thing Matt liked to buy his trucks sturdy.

"Where's Cooper?" he asked the drywall crew.

A middle-aged man stepped forward. He jerked his chin toward the cluster of walls and framing that would one day be expensive condos. If he could get the site running like it should. "He's up there."

"And the reason you're not up there?" He looked from man to man.

One or two met his gaze, but for the most part they averted their eyes and maintained a stubborn silence.

Fantastic! Suddenly everybody in his life felt like giving him the silent treatment.

Cooper's bright red hardhat bobbed in an area that would one day be a deck with a horizon swimming pool. He was facing a group of sullen looking men.

The big bastard in the front seemed to be doing most of the talking, using his arms and getting right in Cooper's personal space to make his point.

Eric grit his teeth. A bully really pissed him off.

Cooper was as tough as old boot leather. He'd been doing this job since before Eric's ass was cracked, but he was getting too old to deal with loudmouthed thugs.

Stalking across the site, Eric made note of a number of safety and site condition infractions. Used coffee cups and coke cans littered the floor. He stopped and picked up a cigarette butt. There was no smoking on his sites, and his crews knew that. They were also responsible for taking their garbage with them.

"Cooper." He joined his construction manager.

The big bastard stopped talking and stood trying to stare Eric down.

Good luck, dickhead. Eric was having a bad few weeks. He didn't feel inclined to play whipped dog. "Problem." He read the man's name tag. "Ray."

"Yeah I got a problem." Ray sized him up. "I got a right not to be on site with a bunch of Mexicans."

Eric wanted to shake his head to make sure he'd heard right. "Say again."

"I'm an American, I'm not going to work with a bunch of illegals who take work away from men like me." Ray warmed to his theme, his voice growing stronger as he spoke. A few murmurs of agreement rose from his group.

To the right of Ray's group, the rest of Eric's crew stood watching, ready to rush to the aid of the victor.

Their shit was costing him money every hour it went on. "This is a free country, Ray." He kept the rage out of his voice, but it was a close thing. "And right now you got a choice. You get back to work or you get off my site."

"Eric." Cooper shifted closer to him.

The men behind Eric stirred and looked to Ray.

"You can't do that." Ray folded his arms over his chest. "I got rights."

"So do I, and so do those men waiting by the construction trailer." Eric didn't let his gaze waver. Ray was like a feral dog; any sign of weakness and he would attack. Given the way he was feeling right now, Eric toyed with the idea of letting Ray come at him. It might be a great way to work off some of his frustration. "Need me to repeat your choices?"

Ray flushed and looked behind him. "If I walk, they all walk with me."

"That so?" Eric met the eyes of every man behind Ray. Most dropped his gaze. One or two stayed defiant. Fine by him. He didn't need their shit on his sites. Finally, he got back to Ray. "Make your choice?"

"Not gonna work with a bunch of wetbacks." Ray sneered.

Eric reached the end of his rope. "Get your racist fucking ass off my site." He raised his voice to make sure everyone heard him. "If any one of you agrees with this asshole, get the fuck out of here right now. Next time I'm going to do more than fire you. This is the only warning you get."

Ray stepped right up to him.

They were evenly matched in height. If it came to a fight, Eric judged it a close call. Adrenalin flooded his muscles.

"This isn't over." Ray smirked.

Eric silently dared him to take the swing he could see in Ray's eyes. "Bring it."

Shoving past him, Ray sauntered offsite. Only three men followed him. They all climbed into one truck and peeled out.

Doing a slow circle, Eric looked at the rest of the crew. "Anybody else got anything to say?" He made eye contact again. "Last chance."

"Your site, Evans." An elderly plumber Eric had worked with many times picked up a pair of cutters and climbed his ladder.

Beside him Cooper let out a long breath. "Any ideas how we're going to replace those men?"

"Nope." Eric managed a tight smile. "Fortunately, that's not my problem but yours."

"Gee, thanks." Cooper rolled his eyes.

A power drill started, and then a bandsaw, and conversation was at an end. "Keep your eye out for trouble," he said to Cooper as they walked back toward the construction office. "I'll arrange for some extra security for you."

"I hope we're not going to need it," Cooper said.

"Yeah, but I think we both know we are." Eric couldn't see Ray backing down easily. "And you need to tighten this site up. I see too much garbage and shit lying around. While we're at it, remind the crews that this is a no smoking site."

Cooper nodded. "Will do."

They went way back, he and Cooper, and they understood each other well. It was why Cooper was on this job. He was Matt's right hand man, and this project represented a massive investment for the company.

A man leaned on Matt's truck, a big man who straightened as Eric approached. About six-six and bristling with tattooed muscle, the guy had a shaved head.

He looked like trouble. As Eric drew near enough to recognize him, he knew he was trouble of the worst kind.

Everything in him went on high alert. "Brett."

"Eric." Brett's voice came from deep inside that huge chest. "How have you been?"

"Good enough." Ray was one thing. Brett Barrows belonged to a whole new definition of feral. It didn't matter how big he was, Eric wouldn't allow the guy to threaten Blythe. "When did you get out?"

"Couple of weeks." Brett pushed his hands into his back pockets.

Fuck, he was a big son of a bitch, and there was not an

ounce of fat on him. "Any reason you've been bothering Blythe?"

Something flickered in Brett's eyes. "She's my sister, and she has my baby sister with her."

"She doesn't want to see you." Only for Blythe would he stand there and compare dicks with Brett. The guy was as mean as he was big. Had he mentioned Brett was fucking huge? He'd gotten even bigger in prison.

Brett raised an eyebrow. "Way I hear it, she doesn't want to see you either."

Eric nodded to concede the point. "Why don't we both keep it that way? Did you come by to say hi, or is there something I can do for you?"

"You got balls, Evans." Brett chuckled. It made him look a mite less psycho, but not that much. "I heard you fired Barron."

"Yup." Now it made sense. Brett thought he could bully Barron back into a job. Eric silently dared him to try.

Brett nodded. "Good. He's a prick."

It took Eric a moment to catch on.

"Why would you hire him in the first place?" Brett smirked as if he could read Eric's thoughts.

Eric slapped on his poker face, the one he wore in boardrooms. "I didn't. One of my subs did, but I made it clear I wouldn't have him back on site." Eric stepped closer to Brett. There was only one language bullies understood. "We going to have a problem about that?"

Brett gaped at him. Then he threw back his head and laughed. "You are one crazy motherfucker." He shook his head. "You'd throw down about this, wouldn't you?"

"Yup." Eric met his stare. "And about Blythe. Stay away from her."

"I aim to." Brett stuck his hands in his back pockets. Muscle bulged along his shoulders and arms. How much could this guy bench press? "I'm not here about that. I'm here about a job."

All the breath left Eric in a rush. As far as he knew, and from what Blythe had told him, Brett hadn't worked a day in his life. Not legally anyway. "This is a legitimate work site," he said and locked gazes with Brett. "And it's going to stay that way."

"Didn't say it wouldn't." Brett shifted and rubbed the stubble on his head. "Look, let me be straight with you. I need a job. I got out of prison with the clothes I wore going in and about seven bucks and change. But I tell you now, I'm not going back there."

It took Eric a moment to realize it, and then it knocked him for a loop. Brett was apprehensive. The man was really asking for a job. "Why are you asking me? You have to know that Blythe told me what you did."

"I guessed as much." Brett pulled a face. An expression perilously close to regret ghosted over his hard features. "Blythe sure did take to you, and you took to her, which is why I'm coming to you."

"I don't follow."

"I don't need to tell you how many kinds of screwed up my family is. With Blythe gone that's only going to get worse." Brett shrugged. "I'm the oldest, and up until now I've been doing a damn fine job of avoiding that reality. They're fucked up, but they're my responsibility."

Eric tried to read Brett. His instinct screamed that the man standing in front of him was not the same one who'd been hauled away by four policemen. Still, the legend of Brett Barrows lived large and bright in Ghost Falls history. "You're saying you're going straight."

"I'm saying I'm going straight." Brett nodded. "And the rest of my brothers with me." He jerked his thumb in the direction Ray and his friends had disappeared. "Looks like you could do with a couple more men as well. You let me bring Bo and Becker up here, and I'll get them to work."

Eric couldn't help it; he laughed. "They're worse than Barron."

"Nah." Brett shook his head. "Barron is a mean piece of shit. Bo and Becker are more just lazy." He smirked. "But they're more scared of me than they are of work. If I tell them to work, they'll ask me how hard."

Eric wished like hell he could share their conversation with Blythe. "What makes you think I would trust you? Especially after what you did to Blythe."

Brett stilled, and his face hardened.

Eric braced.

"You're a fair man, Evans," he said after a while. "And that's why I'm gonna tell you this. If you were anyone else, I'd tell you to fuck off, and then take you apart."

Eric believed him, but that didn't mean he was going to back down. "Tell me what?"

"What I did to Blythe." Brett rubbed his shaved head. "I've done some fucked up shit in my time, but that ranks right up there with the worst. I have to fix things with her before she'll see me, and I get that."

"I'm not sure why you think I'd believe you." Eric didn't say it as a challenge. He genuinely didn't get it. His interactions with Brett before Brett went to prison had been limited.

"You don't judge," Brett said. "I know what they used to say about my sister. I also knew it was bullshit. You weren't like those other assholes. You stayed around long enough to find out the truth."

He hesitated for a moment, and then went with his gut. "Do you have any construction experience or skills?"

"No." Brett shook his head. "But Bo and Becker do. I thought I could work security. And it looks to me like you could do with a bit of extra security."

He had no reason to trust Brett, and about four hundred

reasons he shouldn't, but the man in front of him was not the man he remembered. All some people needed was a second chance. "See Cooper inside about your salary. You can start tomorrow."

"I can start tonight," Brett said. "That asshole has trouble on his mind, and he won't wait."

Eric nodded, still amazed at what had just happened.

"You won't regret this, Eric." Brett stepped away from the truck.

Eric met his gaze. "I better not, Brett."

Chapter Fourteen

Wednesday Blythe had a new client to assess. Her business was growing at a very satisfying rate. With moving into the apartment and the associated expenses, it would still be a while before she could breathe freely, but one step at a time.

With Pippa, Bella and Liz, that made four new clients that week. Living with Will was proving a blessing as they shared taking care of Kim. Next year when he finally had enough money to start college, Blythe would have to make another plan or revise her schedule.

That was a problem for another day.

A smile firmly on her face, she walked through to reception.

A tall, lean man in his fifties, already in gym shorts and a T-shirt, stood beside the desk.

From behind him Randy gave her the nod, confirming this was the new client.

"Chase Gunning?" She held out her hand. "I'm Blythe."

Chase looked taken aback but recovered and shook her hand. The smile he gave her nudged the too warm limit. "Hi. I asked around town for the best trainer, and your name came up."

"I'm flattered." Blythe kept it cool and professional. She had male clients, and none of them were a problem, but every now and again she had to remind someone that personal trainer wasn't a synonym for hooker. "Why don't we talk about your fitness goals?"

"I've been working with a trainer in Denver for a while, but I'll be spending a lot more time in Ghost Falls in the future."

"That makes this easier." Blythe led Chase into the gym.

After an hour session Chase signed with her for twenty more sessions. She liked him.

He listened to her, did as she said and worked hard. He was also in great shape.

She stood by the reception desk as Chase left the gym and waved him goodbye.

Randy jerked his chin. "Looks like you slayed another one."

"Nah." There had been that certain look in Chase's eye from time to time, but it had faded as the session wore on. As long as he kept it professional, they could work together.

Randy checked Chase's membership and raised his brow. "Platinum card. You should go for it."

"I'm not looking for that." Blythe ignored the pang Randy's suggestion caused. One day she would be ready to date someone else, but that for sure wasn't today. "And anyway, what does his platinum card have to do with whether I date him or not?"

Rolling his eyes, Randy leaned on the desk. "You know what your problem is?"

"I'm sure you're about to tell me." She leaned in to Randy.

"You're a romantic," Randy said. "And that makes it an awful waste of your hotness."

She couldn't wait to hear this. Randy had some good theories. "Meaning?"

"Meaning, someone who looks like you could get herself a nice little gig as arm candy." Randy gave her a lascivious wink.

"Wow." Blythe widened her eyes. "Really? You really think I could?"

Randy snorted. "But you are a romantic. You'd marry some loser because you love him and spend your life making excuses for him."

"Nope. I'm a hardened gold digger." Blythe hid her grimace and walked back to her office. Ouch! Randy had perfectly described her mother.

Carly, and God alone knew how, still loved Pat. When Pat came around, Carly walked straight into his arms. Then when he inevitably left again, she disappeared back into a bottle.

All that Blythe had done to establish her independence was about changing her script and not following along with Carly's. Breaking up with Eric had been a similar thing. She wanted more for herself. She wanted it all, and there was no reason to settle. Blythe didn't need to be Carly.

The rest of her day was full, and it was late before she left the gym. She checked on Will. He had picked up Kim, and all was good at home.

The gym sat in the divide between the good part of town and the bad. She had parked in clear view of the door, and Randy was watching from inside.

"Hey, bitch!" Barron's voice made her jump.

Concealed by the shadows to the side of the door, he slouched against the wall.

Blythe spun and headed back for the gym. The bruise from their last encounter had faded, and she wasn't keen to add another one to it.

"You don't need to run." Barron stepped into the light and raised his arms to his side. "I'm not coming near you."

Blythe stopped with her hand on the door. She could get inside before he came near her. Curiosity kept her there.

Barron wouldn't be here without a reason. "What do you want?"

"I'm here to do you a favor." Barron smirked. "I don't know why I bother with your ungrateful ass, but I guess I'm just that kind of person."

Refusing to even engage that errant piece of crap, Blythe waited.

Barron stopped about five feet from her. His left eye was swollen almost shut. A dark purple bruise surrounded it.

"This is your warning." Barron pointed to his black eye. "Brett did this to me, and he's coming for you, Blythe. He's coming for you, and he's a lot fucking madder at you than he was at me."

ERIC MET Miranda at a small Italian restaurant close to his office. She had called after his return from site. On the verge of turning her down, he had paused and considered that there really was no reason to turn her down.

Not anymore.

Miranda arrived ten minutes late, looking fantastic in a clingy black dress as she wound her way through the tables toward him. He was willing to bet she was late on purpose.

Miranda was a woman who made an entrance. She knew her value and how that dress clung to every toned curve of her body.

"Hi." He stood to greet her.

She leaned forward in a waft of exotic perfume and pressed a cool cheek to his. "Nice to see you."

"And you." Eric took his seat again. "Wine?"

"Please?" She flashed him her brilliant smile. "I wasn't sure you'd accept my invitation."

Neither had he been. He kept it light. "You know how work can get."

SARAH HEGGER

"Indeed I do." She sipped her wine and murmured her approval. Her dark eyes gleamed at him in the subdued light. "But I sense that is not the only reason you might have turned me down."

That would teach him to underestimate a woman like Miranda. "Ah, no. Until recently, there was a...situation." He couldn't even describe his thing with Blythe as a relationship.

"Sounds complicated." Miranda chuckled, a plush velvet huskiness that made a man wonder what noises she'd make in his bed.

A detached part of him wondered if she practiced that laugh. At the very least she knew its impact and employed it. It had been a long time since he'd dated a woman like Miranda. Smart, determined and assertive, Miranda valued herself and demanded the same from any man in her life.

When he had lived in Denver full time, the Mirandas of the world had been his preferred date. If asked, he would still have said the same, which did not explain why he'd been with Blythe since he'd moved back to Ghost Falls.

Did Blythe know they had been exclusive? Even more disturbing was the thought that she might not have thought so and acted on that. A surge of burning jealousy shot through him. Then reason prevailed. Blythe was a one man at a time woman. There had been occasions when she had been seeing someone else. She had either broken that off and been with him or turned him down. Come to think of it, he couldn't remember when Blythe had ever turned him down in favor of the other guy. Fuck! He'd known all along how she felt about him. At worst, he'd taken advantage of it, and at best remained willfully unaware. He managed a smile for Miranda. "It was complicated."

"Was?" She raised one sculpted brow. "As in over."

It shouldn't tear into him to reply, but it did. Somehow he forced the word out. "Yes."

"Good." Miranda smiled at him, slow and sultry. "Then there's no reason you and I can't get to know each other a bit better."

Chapter Fifteen

Every Thursday night, Blythe took Kim with her to St. Peters to help out at the soup kitchen. She wanted Kim to grow up with a commitment to give back. Will wasn't working, so he joined them.

Reverend Michael greeted them as they walked in. He roped Will into helping him set out tables and chairs.

Blythe went into the kitchen with Kim.

The woman running the kitchen waved her over to vegetable preparation.

Behind a mountain of potatoes and carrots, Bella and Liz worked their vegetable peelers.

They looked up when they saw her.

Blythe felt the old tension creep over her. Their discussion the other day was still so fresh she didn't entirely trust it.

"Blythe." Bella managed a shy smile. "I didn't realize you volunteered here."

"Every Thursday night." She lifted Kim onto the table. "My family owes a lot to this church."

"Normally we do Wednesdays," Liz said and handed Kim a peeled carrot. "Reverend Michael tells us you also do an exercise class here."

"That's right." Blythe picked up a potato.

Bella's smile widened. "It seems there really is an entire book of stuff I don't know about you."

Not knowing what that meant, Blythe returned her smile. "I could probably say the same."

"Probably not." Bella pulled a face. "My life has always been pretty much an open book." She held her hand out to Kim. "Hi, I'm Bella."

"I'm Kim." Kim crunched on her carrot. "I'm four."

"Four?" Bella made a show of thinking that over. "Are you sure, because I would have said six or seven?"

"That's because I'm tall for my age," Kim assured her.

They worked in silence for a bit.

Liz lasted about ten minutes before the silence got to her, and she chattered. Blythe half listened to her conversation with Bella. They were good friends and sometimes spoke in the sort of code that women who were close did. She didn't mind that she didn't understand everything they spoke about, because they still made her feel included in the conversation.

Kim got a bit bored, so Blythe showed her how to peel, keeping a sharp eye on little fingers. The way Kim mangled her potato meant it was probably never going to hit anyone's pot, but it did keep her happy.

Bella gave her a sweet smile and said, "An entire book of things."

Liz gestured with her knife. "Isn't that your brother?"

Will stood in the doorway between the kitchen and the dining room. He motioned her.

"You better go and see what he wants," Bella said. "He looks upset."

Blythe reached to take Kim off the table.

"You can leave her here if you like," Bella said. "I can keep an eye on her."

Kim grinned at her as if she liked Bella's idea a whole lot better

Drying her damp hands on a cloth, Blythe joined Will. "Everything okay?"

"Not really." Will glanced behind him. "I want to show you something…someone. But they haven't seen me or you yet."

She followed him behind some partitions stacked close to the wall. From there, they could see the dining room and the people gathering to eat.

"There." Will pointed to a table beside the far window. "Sitting with his back to the window."

A homeless man sat with his arms braced on the table. Blythe didn't see anything extraordinary about him. He wore a threadbare maroon woolen cap with a team logo on the front. Dirt and age had smudged it beyond recognition. His dark coat hung heavy on his slimmer frame. At first glance, she put him at mid forties, but a closer look placed him as much younger. Dirty and wearing the lines of fatigue earned by living on your wits, he couldn't be much older than her.

The man looked up to talk to someone opposite him, and Blythe got it. She grabbed the partitions for support and stared. "It can't be."

"Is it him?" Will pressed closer to her. "It is Blake, isn't it?"

Blake, the brother closest to her in age, only a year younger. Gentle, sweet Blake with his big heart and his passion for drawing animals. She still had a stack of faded sketches he'd made for her when they were younger. "What's he doing here?"

"We know why he's here," Will said. "He must be homeless."

Blake had left five years earlier to pursue his dream of being an artist. She wanted to march over there and demand to know what happened. She wanted to run over there and give him a hug. A bath first, but then a hug. She wanted to slip out the back of the kitchen and pretend she hadn't seen him.

"What are we going to do?"

The "we" added a greater level of complexity. She had Will and Kim to think of. True, Blake had been her favorite brother before Will was born, but he was still a Barrows and he was as capable of dishonesty and nastiness as the rest of them.

But he was still her brother. "I'm going to talk to him."

"Not alone, you're not." Will fell in behind her.

Will had also noticed the memento Barron had left on her cheek and wasn't happy about it. Always one to take too much on his young shoulders, Will had decided he could have somehow prevented it from happening. Blythe was happy Will hadn't been there. Barron would have been a lot worse with Will.

Will reminded her a bit of Blake, in his gentle soul. Blake had been her favorite brother growing up, but now that place in her heart he shared with Will. As much as she appreciated Will's support, it also made her angry that he'd had to grow up so much faster than he should. "He's not like the others. I'll be fine."

"I'm coming with you." Will's jaw firmed. Will also wanted her to press charges against Barron. Maybe there was more Carly in her than she had realized, but she didn't want to go that way. She wanted to get on with her life. At the same time, she'd promised Will if Barron came near her again, she would file those charges.

Yet, here she was, about to open the door on another brother entering her new life.

They approached the table, other people watching them as they went.

Blake looked up before they reached him and gaped. He stood and dragged the cap off his head. His dark blond hair stood up in all directions. "Blythe?" He blinked at Will. "Wheeler?"

"Will," Blythe said. "He prefers to be called Will."

"Will." Blake nodded. "You're a lot taller than when I last saw you."

The other men at his table followed the conversation avidly.

The small scar on his top lip was the same, but a newer scar higher on his cheekbone was new. His face was much thinner and his skin dull. "What are you doing here, Blake?"

"Thursday is roast night," one of the men at his table said. "Always come here for the meat on Thursday nights."

Blake gave her a helpless little shrug as if that answered everything.

She didn't understand why he was there and not at the house. "You're not staying at the house?"

"With Bo and Becker? Barron's there too most of the time now." Blake shook his head. "I'd prefer the streets and honestly, I'd be safer."

Barron used to bully Blake. She had forgotten that. And whatever Barron did, Bo and Becker soon jumped right on. "I hear Brett might be staying there too."

"He doesn't live there, but he pops in and out." Blake sniffed. "I went by there yesterday morning."

"Ah." That was not the news she wanted to hear. "How long have you been in town?"

"Since yesterday morning," Blake said. "I've been living in Denver for a while."

"Like this?" She indicated his clothes.

Blake nodded.

They stood there, the silence growing awkward between them.

Will cleared his throat and glanced at her expectantly. He wanted her to invite Blake to their house. It was the sisterly thing to do, but Will was younger than both of them and not nearly as jaded. Will remembered the Blake who had taught him to draw and made up stories for him at bedtime.

Blake may have been less violent than the others, but he'd

also done his share of petty thefts and carjacking. The others had often led him into their trouble.

She'd worked so hard to break away from all that, from the Barrows taint. She had refused to let Bo and Becker even into her apartment, only her past fondness for Blake had her even considering it. "They need me in the kitchen." She pointed as if nobody knew where the kitchen was. "I'll talk to you after dinner."

Will dogged her heels and barely waited until she'd cleared the doorway to the kitchen. "We can't leave him like this, Blythe."

"I know that." She really did know that. Her brother was homeless, a brother she actually loved. "I need some time to think."

Will shook his head at her. "What's there to think about? He's our brother, and he needs us."

But she'd done so much to make something new for her and Kim and Will. Every time Pat decided to drift back into their lives with sob stories and tears of remorse, her mother had let him back in again. Nobody had been more critical of that than Blythe. Yet, here she was contemplating making the same mistake.

Or was she? Blake wasn't Brett. He wasn't even Barron.

Damn her head hurt with all of this. Guilt twisted inside her. Blake lived on the streets, and winter was only a few weeks away. With Thanksgiving around the corner, she had been looking forward to celebrating her new version of family with Kim and Will. They would do it right, as well, with the turkey and all the fixings.

And while the three of them celebrated and gave thanks, the best Blake could hope for was a decent meal here.

"Everything okay?" Liz kept her voice low enough to keep it from Kim.

"Fine." Out of habit, Blythe produced a smile. Then she stopped. She'd heard this wasn't how female friendships worked. Apparently you went to your female friends to share a burden, voice a worry or ask for advice. "Actually, not fine at all."

"Kim, baby." Liz smiled at Kim. "Why don't you pop over there and see Celia." She pointed to the far side of the kitchen. "She has some brownies, and I'm sure if you tell her who you are, she'll find one for you."

Liz had Kim at brownies, and Blythe helped her off the counter.

"What's up?" Bella and Liz pressed closer.

"My brother is in there." She jerked her head toward the dining room. "And it looks like he's homeless."

Bella chewed her lip and frowned. "Which one?"

"Blake."

"Was he the one who stole the football team's equipment?" Bella asked it with no apparent judgment attached.

"No, that was Barron."

"The one who beat up Chris Tucker?"

"That was Brett." Blythe almost laughed. The Barrowses had gone out of their way to earn their stellar reputation. "Blake was in the class below me. He actually graduated. He was the one who liked to draw."

"Right." Bella waved her knife. "He was the nice one."

"He had his moments."

Liz propped one hip against the prep table. "I sense a but."

"But." Talking about her stuff was new to Blythe. "Blake was nice for a Barrows boy. Not nice in the sense of normal people."

"Normal?" Liz made a rude noise. "Who the hell is normal? Not me, and not even Tinker Bell over there."

Bella jammed her hands on her hips. "Hey!"

"Did you, or did you not, pine after the same man since first grade?" Liz fixed Bella with a look.

Bella crumpled with a giggle. "Okay, not everyone pines for the same man year after year."

"I'm the last one with room to talk there." Blythe only realized she'd spoken aloud when she saw the looks of avid interest Bella and Liz turned her way. "Back to Blake."

"I'd much rather talk about the other thing." Liz gave her a wicked grin. "I'm going to start a Ghost Falls dating service in which people who are hankering after each other actually man up and do something about it."

"You'd make a lot of money with that," Bella said.

"Or maybe not." Liz shrugged. "Sometimes the timing on these things has to be right."

"Or the little black dress sexy enough." Bella giggled. Then she got serious. "So, you're worried if you invite Blake to stay with you that he'll bring Barrows history to your new life?

She took the words right out of Blythe's mouth. Bella had just nailed it. "Yes. I'm working very hard to make something new here."

"You know we have the same issue," Bella said.

Blythe didn't bother keeping the skepticism off her face.

"Same but opposite." Bella waggled a carrot at her. "I was always the town good girl, and everybody treated me like that. I could never do anything wrong without incurring so much disappointment." She jabbed her carrot at Blythe. "Now you are the town bad girl, and everything you do is misjudged. See, same problem."

"Except Bella came tumbling out of her good girl closet last year," Liz said. "And now we're all wondering how the hell we misjudged her so badly."

Bella chuckled and boosted herself onto the table. "But we're not talking about me now."

"You know, having your brother to stay doesn't have to mean backsliding," Liz said. "You're not the same girl you were. You have changed, and you also don't have to let anyone drag you down."

"Everybody deserves a second chance." Bella shrugged. "And some of us need more than two chances."

"Besides which," Liz said. "I'm not sure you're going to be able to live with yourself if you don't at least try to help him."

Chapter Sixteen

Blythe woke the next morning to that strange sense of something having happened. Then it hit her. Blake had come home with them the night before.

There hadn't been a lot of time for conversation the night before, and she'd set him up on the sofa, but this morning they needed to talk. Based on her discussion with Bella and Liz, she intended to set some ground rules.

Ground rules were good. They let everyone know where they stood. She showered and dressed for work. Her first client was in ninety minutes, and she would drop Kim off on the way.

Blake's blanket and sheets sat neatly folded beneath his pillow at the end of the sofa. The smell of coffee lured her to the kitchen.

"Morning." Blake gave her a shy smile. "I was up, and I remembered you liked your coffee before you got to your conversing."

He had combed wet hair back, and his face was clean shaven. He wore a faded but clean T-Shirt and a tattered pair of jeans that hung on his narrow hips.

"Will gone already?"

"Yup." Blake stepped out of her way and stood by the island, looking so unsure of himself it almost broke her heart. "He said he works at Diva St. Amor's on Fridays."

"He does." Blythe poured her coffee and added caramel creamer to it. A food sin she kept secret from her clients. "Phi has been good to Will."

He raised his eyebrow. "Sounds like you know her well."

"She doesn't give you any other choice." Blythe had to chuckle, but this conversation reminded her that she'd gone around to pay back the money Phi had lent Will for his car, and the check was still in her purse. "She's larger than life."

"Right." Blake nodded. He took a breath. "Look, I'm grateful for last night. For the place to sleep but I want you to know that you don't need to feel obliged."

He surprised her into silence, and Blythe sipped her coffee.

"I'm used to living rough, and I can do it again. You didn't do anything that ended in me living on the streets. This isn't your problem to fix."

Her Carly impulse kicked hard, and she desperately wanted to believe him. "Will sees it differently. You have him to thank for last night."

"Will's still a kid." Blake shrugged. "He didn't really see all of what went on when we were kids. You protected him from a lot of it. A lot of Pat, and then Brett." Blake's coffee cup shook, and he put it down on the counter. "You more than anyone, don't owe any of us a damn thing."

"I know that, Blake." She needed to be as upfront with him. "But you're my brother, and it doesn't feel right to leave you on the streets."

He scoffed. "I got myself there."

"How?"

Sighing, he refilled his coffee and then hers. "Turns out that for all my grand talk, I'm not that much different from

Pat after all. Alcohol, drugs, I chased the high and screwed everything up in the process."

"Ah, Blake." The old sadness filled her. With all of them, they'd been born into a rigged game. It wasn't self-pity but at times it made her so mad, and at others, it felt like it could break her. "Are you still using?"

"No." Blake met her gaze. His was clear and lucid. "I've been clean and sober for about six months." He held up his hand. "I know that's not long but I'm working my program, Blythe. That's how I heard about the soup kitchen, from the AA meeting the night before at the church."

The Barrows family should move into St. Peter's at this rate. "What's the plan now?"

"Get a job." Blake shrugged. "I'm not fussy about what I do. Something that will get me on my feet and keep me out of prison. It's hard to get a job when you're living rough. Most of the time you can't find somewhere to wash and change so you don't look like you'll rob the register when you're applying for jobs. Or you don't have any way to get to where the jobs are offered."

Blake was saying all the right things, knocking down her misgivings one by one. But she'd seen this pattern all through her childhood. She couldn't afford to put her total trust in him.

"Okay." She made her decision. "You can stay here until you can get a place of your own. We can put an extra bed in with Will and you'll have to sleep with him."

Blake's face split into a grin of such obvious relief that she felt like a bitch for not throwing her home open to him sooner. "I can sleep on his floor or something."

"You need to sort that out with Will. It's his room, and I just got him clear of having to share." She kept her tone firm. "You can stay here as long as you're looking for a job and helping out. This is not a free ride."

"I wouldn't want it any other way," Blake said.

"Drugs are a hard no, as is alcohol in your case," she said. "If I even so much as suspect you're using or drinking, I'll kick you out."

Blake nodded. "I want to get myself back on track, start drawing again."

"I did most of this so Kim wouldn't have to grow up like we did," she said. "Not just the drinking, but the fights and the violence. The not respecting each other's stuff and the not respecting other people's stuff, I won't have that around Kim."

Blake stared down at his feet and when he looked up again, his eyes were damp. "You're a good woman, Blythe Barrows. God knows how you turned out like you did because you sure as shit didn't get any help from any of the rest of us. Kim is lucky to have you."

"Well, I don't know about that." She might not be good enough, probably was far from it, but she was here for Kim. "Listen, they all know where we live, and have all been around here. Including Brett."

"Damn." Blake scrubbed his hands over his face. "What do you think the chances are that Brett has changed?"

Blythe gave him a look. The suggestion didn't even deserve a response.

BLYTHE HAD enough time to swing by Phi's on the way to work. It felt weird leaving Blake alone in her apartment, but she didn't have any other choice. She'd made her decision when she invited him home with them last night.

Will was hosing down the yard outside the kitchen when she drove up. He stopped, turned off the hose and watched her. "What are you doing here?"

"I've got business with Phi." Will would hate it if he knew she was there to pay off his debt for the car, but the kid deserved a helping hand. He worked every hour he wasn't trying to get his grades up to scrape enough together for college tuition.

She let Kim out of her car seat.

Kim dashed up to Will. "Hey, Will. I'm going to school."

"Can you watch her for a minute?" If Blythe had anything to say about it, Will would have his dream come true, and be the first Barrows to go to college.

"Sure I can keep an eye on Kim." Will gave her a hard stare. "You've been here before."

"Why?" She didn't want to outright lie.

With an eye roll, Will said, "Because for years she's called me Wheeler." Then he did a surprisingly good imitation of Phi. "What an unfortunate name."

Blythe had to grin. "And now?"

"A couple of weeks back she starts calling me Wilhelm."

Blythe winced. "It beats Wheeler."

"Anything beats Wheeler." Will held his hand out for Kim. "Come on. I'll show you the horses."

Blythe tapped on the open top of the kitchen door and peered inside.

Phi sat at the kitchen table in a crimson velour jogging suit. She waved her hands at Blythe. *"Mon petite ange,* what a glorious surprise. Come in. Come in."

"Hello." Blythe obediently kissed Phi on both cheeks and greeted June.

With a sniff, June stalked out the kitchen.

"What an awful old woman." Phi watched June go with a fond smile. "If I did not love her to distraction, I would fire her scrawny, shriveled ass. Speaking of which." She gave Blythe a hard stare. "Are you losing weight?" She pressed a hand to her bosom. "Are you wasting away for love of Eric?"

Maybe her appetite had been a bit off lately, but still. "No."

"Good." Phi looked relieved. "Because going into a decline over a man is a colossal waste of time and energy. They don't even notice for a start."

"True that." Blythe settled at the kitchen table opposite Phi. The kitchen looked like an escapee from the middle ages, but it was cozy and welcoming at the same time. "Pippa came by to see me the other day. She said she wanted to get to know me."

"Oh." Phi's penciled eyebrows rose to her hairline. "She did not say anything to me."

"Really?" With all the drama going on it was hard to tell if Phi was lying or stretching the truth. "Anyway, I am always grateful for a new client, and Pippa and I made a trade. I'll train her and help her with her baby weight, and she's going to give me a makeover."

"Insist on lots of silver and gold." Phi rapped the table. "With your complexion it will be sublime."

Blythe wasn't at all sure about that. Besides which, she'd watched every episode of the show and had never seen Pippa dress anybody in silver and gold. "I'm sure she'll know what's right."

"Indeed." Phi beamed with pride. "Although I do often tell her to add a touch more pizzazz to her palette."

Whatever that meant, Blythe prayed Pippa didn't listen. "Actually I came here because the last time I came, we didn't get to the reason for my visit."

"You were quite clearly distraught." Phi took her hand across the table. "I could not ignore your pain."

"You were wonderful." Blythe wished everyone could experience a Phi in their life, just once. The over-the-top was amusing, but it was her warmth and capacity for love that made her truly special. "As you have been wonderful to Will for years."

"I like that boy," Phi said. "He reminds me a bit of me at that age."

This Blythe had to hear. "He does?"

"Oh, yes." Phi gave her dirty chuckle as if she read Blythe's mind. "Without the bosoms of course. But I had a dream to sing the opera, and I had this dream while living in the ass end of Nowhereville. I had to make my dream happen. Like Will has to make his dream happen."

Phi had a point. "About that," Blythe said. "I know you must have paid for the car he drives to Uber and taxi, and I also know he's trying to pay you back."

"Oh?" Phi looked imperious, every inch the diva.

It intimidated the hell out of Blythe, but she kept going. "Nobody in our family can or will help him, and he deserves a hand up." She pulled the check out and slid it across the table. "This is the first payment. I can pay you in four installments." She glanced behind her, suddenly nervous. "But I don't want Will to know."

"This—" Phi held the check up with her forefinger and thumb. "This is a gross impertinence." She sneered. "I acquit you on the grounds of loving your brother and being a wonderful girl." Phi ripped the check in half. "But whatever my financial dealings may or may not be with Wilhelm, they do not concern you."

Stunned, Blythe sat there and didn't know what to do. She felt ashamed and angry at the same time.

"My darling girl." Phi took both her hands. "I can see I have angered you, and I really do not care. Wilhelm is trying to make his own way in the world. You, more than most, know what that feels like and also what charity feels like."

"But he's my brother."

Phi shook her head. "But that does not give you the right to cut his balls off and carry them in your pocket."

Blythe was not sure she agreed, but it didn't look like Phi cared one way or the other. "I want to help him. He deserves it."

"You have helped him." Phi squeezed her hands. "You

have shown him love where there was none for him. You have believed in him when none other would. And you have shown him how to pursue a dream and bring it to fruition. No amount of money in the world can compete with that."

Chapter Seventeen

Another day PE, post-Eric, and still counting. Apparently a time would come when Blythe wouldn't count days by Eric's absence in them. Being new to this heartache thing, she'd have to rely on conventional wisdom for that, and also keep herself busy.

No worries there with the Barrows brothers crowding for space in her mind. Brett loomed on her horizon, a really large and really dark cloud with a chance of a heavy storm. Her older brother scared the shit out of her, and she was way past pretending he didn't. Last time she'd given that a try, she'd ended up with a broken arm. The time before that, she had made close personal contact with the wall. Enough said!

Blake occupied another portion of her mind and had her leaving work and heading for St. Peter's. Growing up Barrows gave you a front row seat into addiction. Regardless of what Blake said, he was going to need help to make his sobriety stick. Even then it was no guarantee.

She found Reverend Michael exactly where she expected him to be, shuttling in between the church and the rec center.

"Blythe." He gave her his broad, beautiful smile. "This is an unexpected surprise."

She got the feeling that most people got this greeting. "Do you have five minutes?"

"For you? Always." Behind the smile though, he looked tired. Not so much physically, but weary and drained. So many people wanted a piece of Reverend Michael, and no matter how broad those shoulders, that had to get exhausting.

"It's about Blake," she said as he led her into his small, cluttered office in the rec center. "I imagine you heard what happened on Thursday?"

Michael nodded slowly and settled himself behind his battered desk. Paper, books and posters covered every inch of faux wood. "I'm not going to lecture you about addiction," Michael said. "You've seen enough of it to know how this goes."

"You're worried about me taking in Blake," she said.

Michael nodded. "And the fact that you say that makes me feel a bit better."

"I do know addicts." Michael was one of those priests who invited the truth. Mainly because he never judged. "I'm trying to keep realistic about him. I also have to think of Kim."

With a rueful smile, Michael planted his massive boots on the edge of his desk. "You got it. Now how can I help you do that?"

It struck her how many people came to him for help, and she felt momentarily guilty for being another one. "I wanted to talk to you about his recovery. See what programs you offered here."

"You should talk to Daniel." Michael lurched forward and dropped his legs. "Daniel works in the teen program but he's also no stranger to addiction or prison."

Blythe took Daniel's details from Michael.

As she stood to leave, Laura poked her head around the door. "Just saying that I'm off now."

"Laura." Michael beamed and indicated Blythe. "Do you know Blythe Barrows?"

"Blythe." Laura looked taken aback. "I apologize, I didn't mean to interrupt."

With her perfectly groomed, shiny hair, immaculate makeup and tasteful clothing, Laura had created such a convincing mask, unless you knew what lay behind that fault-less exterior.

"Hi, Laura." Blythe hadn't really studied her when last they'd met. Laura had aged well. She looked better now than she had at nineteen.

"Good, you know each other." Michael stood and rubbed his hands together. He grinned at both of them, apparently clueless.

However, Blythe knew him better than that. A man this clever and intuitive had to be reading the atmosphere like a meteorologist.

"We know each other." Blythe let Laura know she still had her number.

Laura flushed. "We used to know each other. People change."

Wow, was this a dominant theme in her life right now.

"I was about to put Blythe in contact with Daniel," Michael said. "Perhaps you can help her out."

Minuscule as it was, Blythe still caught Laura's hesitation before she said, "Sure. He's actually wrapping up with his group in the other room."

Michael stormed for the door. "Great. I'll leave the two of you to it then."

Laura watched him go through narrowed eyes. She gave a short laugh. "Well, this is awkward. Again. Let me take you to meet Daniel."

Blythe followed her down the corridor and through the main room where she taught her class. Beyond were several smaller meeting rooms, and Laura went to one of these and peeked through the window in the door.

Actually, Laura had changed a bit. She now wore a pair of

well-loved jeans, but the cashmere sweater was still pure poison princess.

Laura dropped back onto her heels. "Looks like he might be a little bit. I could always give him a message for you." She looked pathetically hopeful.

"No, I'll wait." Poison princess could be contagious.

Laura's next question left Blythe gaping. "How's Eric?"

"Fine." The automatic answer left her mouth before she could stop it. Laura must be one of the few people in Ghost Falls who suspected what had been going on between Blythe and Eric. "We're not…" Blythe didn't want to define it any more than that. "Not anymore."

"Oh." Laura looked at her toes and nodded. "I'm sorry to hear that. You were good for him."

"What?" Their conversation had drifted into the weirdest place, and Blythe couldn't pretend. "I was never really anything to him. I was just around after you…when you…" The funny thing about keeping a secret for so many years was that keeping it became a habit, and even now, she didn't want to say it out loud.

"When I screwed him over," Laura said. "You were there for him when I trapped him into an engagement with a fake pregnancy."

"Holy crap!" Never in her wildest imaginings could she have pictured their conversation. Or Laura's blistering honestly. "You really want to talk about this."

"No." Laura shrugged. "But I've had a shitty couple of years. It makes you get honest with yourself."

"And everybody else apparently." Blythe shook her head, still trying to come to terms with it.

"You know, I don't to this day know why I did it." Rising on her toes again, Laura peered through the door. "I was nineteen and Eric was mine, but I knew enough to know he wasn't going to stay mine."

Blythe had always wanted to hear her answers, but Eric

didn't talk about that time a lot. Even though it had been the start of their friendship—or whatever the hell they'd had—he avoided the subject.

"You wouldn't be the first person to try that tactic," she said.

Laura grimaced. "And I chose my target well." She shook her head. "I played on his weak spot and I won."

"It could be worse." Blythe had come across a nineteen-year-old Eric, out of his mind drunk behind Cranks bar. Pat had spent a lot of his time and most of whatever money he could get his hands on there. The bar was a rough one and she'd only gone there to get Pat and bring him home.

She had spotted Eric sitting on a stack of empty beer crates outside the bar and stopped to talk to him. Drunk and frightened, Eric had unloaded the entire story on her. "At least you didn't keep it up until he married you."

"What a winner I am." Laura snorted. "I can't even take credit for that. Phi saw right through me and gave me a come-to-Jesus that left me reeling for days."

Now Phi knowing about her and Eric made more sense.

"I sulked around her for years." Laura chuckled. "There is nothing so humiliating as being called out on something and knowing you have no leg to stand on."

"I've been there a time or two," she said. "I heard you got divorced."

"You heard right." Laura saddened. "I hurt a good man. Another good man that is, because under that too cool for school charmer, Eric is a good man."

Blythe's heart gave that familiar pang. Things would be easier if she could consign Eric to asshole and walk way, but he wasn't. "But still allergic to being pinned down."

Laura gave her a long look, and then nodded. "I probably had a little something to do with that."

"Don't give yourself too much credit." Blythe smiled to soften her words. "Cressy did her thing long, long before you."

"Right." Laura rolled her eyes. Movement from the other side of the door caught her attention and she peered through again. "Here they come."

She and Blythe stepped back as the door flew open and ten or eleven teen boys tumbled out. They ranged in age from about fourteen to twenty, but they all carried their attitude like a backpack with them.

An attractive tall man in his thirties followed them out. Not strictly speaking good looking, he had brown hair flopping over a pair of hazel eyes. He caught sight of Blythe and smiled. "Hi."

Oh, yes, indeed, he had a little something-something going on. She held out her hand. "I'm Blythe, and Michael said I should speak with you."

"Remind me to thank Michael." His eyes twinkled. How anyone could deliver such a cheesy line and not sound lame she didn't know, but Daniel did it.

Laura shifted, and his attention swung that way.

"Hi." Laura's openness disappeared, and she looked tense.

Daniel's smile tightened. "Hi, Laura."

"I brought her along to meet you." Laura motioned Blythe. "Now I need to get going. Nice to see you again, Blythe."

"And you too." Surprisingly it had been.

She and Daniel watched Laura scuttle away. One of them may have checked out Laura's ass in those jeans, and it certainly wasn't her.

"So." Daniel flushed when he caught on that she'd busted him. "What can I do for you?"

Blythe told him about Blake.

"Here's my card." Daniel dug a card out of his back pocket. "Pass it on to Blake and tell him to give me a call." His expression gentled. "You know he has to make the call, right? About all of this."

"I know." She had learned the lesson the hard way. "But it doesn't mean I can't give him a hand."

"No, it doesn't." Daniel smiled, and that fizz pop came back again. She wondered if Laura had noticed it. Of course Laura had noticed it. You either ran from a man because you disliked him or because you really didn't.

"Are you ready to leave?" Daniel looked around them as he locked the meeting room door. "Because I'll walk you out if you are."

"I'm done." Blythe fell into step beside him. So much more done than she'd imagined when she came here today. The conversation with Laura still played in her mind. For years she'd hated Laura for what she'd done to Eric.

For years Blythe had held her fake pregnancy and miscarriage against Laura, and one conversation didn't take that all away. But Laura hadn't made any excuses for her behavior and hadn't tried to justify herself. That kind of honesty counted for something.

They reached the exterior door, and Daniel held it open for her.

Blythe waited while he locked it. Church recreation center or not, they were in a bad part of town.

Daniel waited by her car as she unlocked it. "Are you the same Blythe who does the exercise class?"

"I am." She tossed her purse into the passenger seat.

"Brett's sister?"

Blythe nodded. "You know Brett?"

"Yeah." Daniel rubbed his nape. "I was into some pretty bad stuff before I got sent to prison."

"Ah. That makes sense."

"Anyway." Daniel leaned on the open car door. "I'd like to chat to you about doing something aimed more specifically at my teen girls."

"Oh?"

"Yeah." He shrugged. "I wanted to explore the possibility

of exercise helping with their self-esteem issues. So many of them have them."

Blythe welcomed the chance. "It's called being a girl. Too many of us grow up with body issues and keep them even as adults."

"But not you?" Daniel's look of admiration was enough to soothe a girl's ego.

She laughed. "Nice line, but even me."

"I've got zero game." Daniel pulled a face. "But would you consider having coffee with me anyway?"

If she hadn't caught that look at Laura, Blythe would be all over his offer. Daniel was just the sort of guy to help someone over Eric Evans. At least he would be a step in the right direction.

"I'd love to have coffee," she said. "And put something together for your teen girls. But I don't think I'm the one you should be asking out for coffee."

He winced. "Caught that did you?"

Blythe had to laugh. "It was hard to miss."

Chapter Eighteen

Eric ignored his ringing phone and kept his gaze on the view outside his office window. Downtown Ghost Falls would never inspire creative greatness, but it made for better viewing than the growing pile of crap on his desk.

On top was his draft for the merger, mostly blank because he couldn't get his head in the game.

He checked his phone.

Miranda.

Their evening had ended pleasantly enough. He'd walked her back to her hotel and side stepped her offer to come in. He had given her a chaste kiss on the cheek and walked away.

She had told him she was going out of town for a few days and would be back. He guessed she was back and keen for a repeat of their last date.

There really was no reason for him not to, other than the growing realization that he didn't want to.

Outside her hotel room door, Miranda had looked up at him with her luminous espresso eyes and full, plum mouth, and it had done nothing for him other than send him running.

Cooper had also sent him a few messages, along with a sheath of incident reports.

Brett kept vigilant on the night shift. Thus far, he'd reported four incidents. None of them had amounted to anything, because Brett had chased the trouble away, but this kind of shit couldn't go on.

Also according to Cooper, Bo and Becker had pitched up, worked several full shifts and not bitched once. That must be some kind of record. His thumb was halfway to dialing Blythe and sharing with her before he stopped himself.

She was right and he owed her this much. If he didn't want the same things she wanted, then he had no business pursuing her. He had been keeping away from her, and any day now it would get easier. These reaches for his phone, or desire to share something with her would pass.

Four cars made their way down Main Street, constituting the extent of Ghost Fall's lunchtime rush. He'd given up a good life in Denver to be here closer to his family.

Right now, had he been in Denver, he would be making his way to Big Bites for a roast beef on whole wheat. Maybe, given his crappy day, he'd add a Fat Tire to his sandwich.

But no, here he was in swinging Ghost Falls, where apparently, the powers that be also felt the need to investigate his sites for health and safety procedures.

Their focus? Surprise, surprise, Highgate site. All of this crap hitting one site couldn't be coincidence.

Now he came to the truly troubling part. He really didn't give a shit. Not much of a shit at any rate. He'd rather stare out the window as Bets Schumaker bottlenecked what little traffic there was with her barge of a car.

"Hey," Nate's voice had him swinging his chair around.

Eric went back to his view. "Hey yourself."

"What are we looking at?" Nate joined him in staring out the window.

"Not much."

Bets was in the longwinded process executing a sixteen-point turn.

Nate sighed. "Damn, I wish I could get her to drive something else."

"Arrest her."

"For what?"

"I don't know." Eric got that he was being a dick but again, he didn't give that much of a shit. "Make something up. Isn't that what you cops do most of the time anyway?"

"Wow." Nate shoved his hands in his pockets. "Aren't you farting sunshine and rainbows today."

Eric had to suppress a smile. "I'm having an existential crisis."

"Is that what they're calling being an asshole now?"

He got his shit together. His brother was a nice guy. "I'm sorry, and you're right. I'm being a dick." He poked at the papers on his desk. "We seem to be getting hit by one load of shit after another."

"What's this?" Nate picked up the notice of a pending inspection. "When do they ever inspect anything?"

"Apparently, it's a brave new world." Eric took the notice away from Nate and put it back. "Don't worry about it. We're good with health and safety anyway."

"And this?" Nate didn't believe in personal boundaries and now had Brett's report in his hand.

"That's the report from my security detail at the Highgate site."

Nate frowned down at the paper. "Is this right?" He jabbed his finger at the name. "Brett Barrows is working security for you?"

"Yeah." Eric didn't feel ready to defend his position. He'd made the decision as more of a gut instinct than anything else. "He needed a job."

"You know his record." Nate raised an eyebrow. "Particularly the part where he roughed his sister up so badly that he broke her arm. And I know for sure that I told you he was

145

part of the reason Blythe freaked out that night you went to check on her."

"And just how is Barron?" A slow creep of anger tingled beneath his skin. "Knocked any more women about?"

Nate shook his head. "You know I can't do anything unless Blythe presses charges."

"Then you should have told me to handle it."

"Uh-huh." Nate folded his arms over his chest. "Because you going vigilante on me would make my day. Make no mistake, Eric, I will arrest you."

"I'm touched," he said but it lacked his former heat. Beating the shit out of Barron would be momentarily satisfying but not the solution. "Anyway, Brett's not the same. Not the same man they locked up this last time."

"Maybe." Nate shrugged. "But these guys who leave prison don't have much of a chance unless someone takes a leap of faith with them."

"Talk to him yourself," Eric said. Actually he had hit on a great idea. Nate had developed a cop's sense of people and could sniff out bullshit and looming trouble. "I'd really like to hear what you think."

Nate chuckled. "I'm sure you would."

"Meaning?" Eric didn't like the knowing look in Nate's eye.

"Really?" Nate met his gaze straight on. "We're still pretending that you don't know that I know that you have a vested interest in the Barrows family?"

"I don't." Which was the truth, because Blythe had carved him from her life. "Not anymore, anyway."

"When?"

"Just before that night Barron went around."

Nate grew thoughtful. "And before you ripped into Bella and the others."

"They weren't being fair." Eric would be fucked if he

backed down on this. "They don't know her and made judgments about her."

"They're trying to change that," Nate said. "After you left our place the other night, I talked to them about it."

Eric let him have the floor. Nate knew as much about the Barrowses' business as anyone, given that the call to do something about Barrows-made trouble often went through the sheriff.

"Blythe's good people," Nate said. "I don't know how the hell she managed to crawl out of that cesspit of a family, but she did. I've always liked her. Although, apparently not as much as you."

"Have you always known?"

"Nah." Nate shook his head. "I knew you two talked a bit after Laura, but I didn't realize it was more than that until a couple of years later."

"Well, it's over now." Eric went back to the view. The words burned like indigestion. "Apparently I don't like her enough."

Nate gave him a hard look, and then nodded. "I wondered when she'd wise up."

"What?" Eric stared at Nate. Nate had never said a word, not even murmured a suspicion that he knew what was going on with Blythe. "What are you talking about?"

"You and Blythe." Nate stared out the window. "Look at that." He clicked his tongue. "Damn Frank Wells is parking in the disabled spot. The only thing disabled about him is his common sense. "

Eric toyed with playing dumb, but for all his pretty face and his aw-shucks county sheriff spiel, Nate was sharp as a tack. "And here I thought I was being so discreet."

"You were." Nate continued to glare out the window. "God, I hate people who park in disabled spots when they're not. But this is my town, and I see shit."

"Huh."

"Plus." Nate slid him a sly smile. "You kind of gave the game away when you lost your shit the other night."

That might be coming a bit strong. "Would we say I lost my shit?"

Nate snorted. "I love you girls, but you're full of shit."

"Okay." Heat climbed his cheeks. "I might have lost a little of my shit there."

"Well, buckle up, brother." Nate rubbed his nape. "Because your lady is heading into another storm."

"She's not my lady." That hit him with serrated edges, and he had to take a moment and breathe deep. "What storm?"

Nate cocked his head. "What did she say? When she ended things."

"Hmm?"

A flat stare from Nate informed him his attempt to play dumb had failed.

"Are we going to eat ice cream and watch chick flicks or something?" He didn't want to talk about this. "What storm?"

"You know about Brett already." Nate let him off the hook. "But apparently Blake is back in town and has moved in with her."

"What the hell!" Eric stared at his brother, hoping like hell Nate was punking him.

Nate shook his head, dead serious. "Blake arrived at St. Peter's the other night for the Thursday dinner service. Blythe caught sight of him and took him home with her."

"She knows better than that." Eric reached for his phone, and then stopped.

Nate shook his head. "Yeah, she does. Bella said she was really conflicted about it."

"Bella?" The surprises kept coming. "What does Bella know about this?"

"Bella was the one who told me." Nate gave him a wry smile. "After your shit losing, the girls got curious. First they went to see Phi, and Phi is one hundred percent in Blythe's corner, and then they went to see Blythe."

Eric winced. He didn't want to think how that had gone over. "What happened?"

"They made friends." Nate shrugged. "They had a bit of a heart-to-heart and found common ground."

Of all the things he had expected Nate to say, that wasn't one of them. "Damn."

"And that's not all," Nate said. "Bella and Liz were also volunteering at the Thursday night dinner service. Apparently she asked them what she should do about Blake."

"Blythe asked Bella for advice?" The words sounded wrong even saying them out loud. Blythe had a big chip on her shoulder about Bella. Not altogether undeserved but there nonetheless. Or apparently, not there anymore. "That must have been some heart-to-heart."

"Bella is concerned about the Blake situation, but not worried. She said Blythe is not going into this blind."

"No, she isn't." Nobody who grew up a Barrows could take on a case like Blake blindly. Blythe had lost her innocent outlook many, many years before he'd even known her.

His phone had somehow found its way back into his hand, and he stared at it. He wanted to call her and ask if she was okay, if things with Blake were okay. He wanted to tell her she could count on him if things weren't okay.

That wasn't his right anymore. She'd taken that right from him.

Or perhaps he'd forfeited it by not being able to offer her more than they'd had. Along with forfeiting the right to sit beside her in his beautiful house and look out at the view and tell her about his shitty day. Forfeited the right to hear her laugh at something he said or tease him out of his crap mood. Lost the right to lose himself in her beautiful body.

Fuck.

"What are you going to do?" Nate indicated his phone.

Eric shoved it in his pocket. "I'm going to site to see if I can find out any more about what happened last night."

Nate eyed him speculatively. "You're not going to call her?"

"I can't." And that hurt like a son of a bitch. "She's not mine to call anymore."

ERIC TOOK Matt's truck again. With the amount of time they used each other's cars they may as well swap. Then again, Matt was heading the minivan route.

So weird to think of his brother making the school run and coaching little league. Matt had done his best to fill in for Dad when they were all younger, but this was different. Jasmine would grow, and Eric was willing to bet she'd have siblings before too long.

Fall leaves scattered beneath the wheels of his truck as he drove to site. Snow could come any day now, and they had been hoping to have the roofs on at Highgate before that happened. These delays were messing with his schedule big time, and it's not like Highgate was the only project they had going right now.

Cooper and Brett stood by the construction trailer as he drew up.

"Hey." Eric climbed out Matt's truck.

Cooper nodded. "Eric. Inspector is coming up tomorrow, but we got nothing to worry about there."

"I know," Eric said. Cooper ran a tight site. "It's just helluva coincidental that all this shit is coming at the same time."

"About that." Cooper jerked his head at Brett. "Brett and I were having a chat."

Everything in Eric went on alert. "Yeah?"

"I saw Barron at the house the other day," Brett said.

"Little fucker knows something about what's been going on up here."

"Meaning?" Eric would love to have answers.

Brett pulled a face. "Meaning there's no such thing as coincidence. All this trouble you're having, it seems to have a common source."

Eric had been coming to a similar conclusion. "And Barron knows who that source is?"

"He's too useless for that." Brett sniffed. "But he does have some information you should hear."

"We were about to head that way," Cooper said. "But now that you're here ..."

"I'll drive." Eric was already walking to the truck.

The cab shrunk as Brett shoehorned himself in the passenger side. If he didn't look so much like Pat Barrows in every other aspect but size, Eric would have some questions for Carly.

The silence in the truck thickened as Eric drove them down the mountain.

Brett tapped his fingertips on his knee and stared out the window.

When he spoke, Eric jumped.

"So, is Blythe okay?" Brett stared out his window. "Had a chat with Barron about harassing her."

"I don't know." If anything, admitting to her being out of his life had sharper hooks on it than ever. "I haven't seen her."

Brett grunted. "Probably for the best."

Like fucking hell it was.

They drove to Cranks, a biker bar just off the I-80 and Eric parked.

A few bikes stood outside, but it was early for the usual Cranks crowd.

Brett leaned forward and peered through the windshield. "This is Pat's old hangout."

None of the Barrows kids really spoke of Mom or Dad.

Probably because Pat and Carly had never stepped up to the name.

"Then it became mine." Brett opened his door. "I raised some hell in this place."

"I can believe it." Eric followed him across the parking lot and stopped. A service entrance ran alongside the right side of the squat, square gray building. Garbage cans and crates stood stacked against the wall.

He had been sitting there feeling sorry for himself when Blythe had first skipped into his life. Sure, he'd seen her at school, and what teen boy hadn't noticed the fuse to his hormones that was a teen Blythe Barrows? But he'd been sitting on a pile of crates getting wasted when she'd seen him and stopped to chat.

Brett turned and glared at him. "You coming or what?"

Inside, Cranks stank of spilled beer, cigarettes and weed. The owner was known not to give a shit about no-smoking policies and nobody was brave enough to question that. If you smoked and pissed off the person next to you, it would largely depend on how big and mean they were, and how much they objected to breathing your smoke.

A chair scraped and clattered over. Barron stood there, weaving on his feet and glowering at Brett. "What the fuck, man?"

"Not here for trouble." Brett held his hands up.

Barron paled.

Yeah, Eric got it. That gesture was about as reassuring as a mountain lion picking its teeth with a claw.

Glancing past Brett to Eric, Barron shook his head. "Nah man, Brett. I haven't been near that bitch."

Eric wished Brett would hit him anyway. Add a few more bruises to that fading black eye.

Barron's friends crouched low over their beers, staying out of Brett's eye line.

"This is not about Blythe." Brett motioned Barron closer. "You got some information I want you to share."

Dragging his feet, Barron moved closer. "About what?" Barron stopped out of Brett's reach but close enough to talk. "The dude with the S650?"

Brett jerked his head at Eric. "Tell him what you know."

Barron did a quick three-sixty glance and leaned in. "Most days the site guys come down the mountain for lunch," he said. "Places up there are too expensive. Nine bucks for a sandwich and a drink."

Brett growled.

"Okay." Barron licked his lips. "There's this food truck where most of the guys pick up lunch. Dude pulls up in this Mercedes-Maybach S650. Sweet fucking set of wheels, so I notice. He talks to Ray and leaves. Few days later people are talking about how there's money to be made to slow things down on your site."

"You didn't see who it was?"

Barron shook his head. "Nah. Only noticed the car."

Eric wanted to punch something. Hard. He also wanted to howl. At last he had some information about why things were happening, and information meant he could hunt.

Chapter Nineteen

Despite her misgivings, Blythe was feeling cautiously optimistic about Blake. As a houseguest, she couldn't fault him. He cleaned up after himself, was considerate and well behaved and did what he could around the house. He'd also been on one or two job interviews. Nothing solid had panned out but he bagged groceries at the local Safeway once or twice a week.

So far, he'd made all his meetings at St. Peter's and kept in close contact with Daniel.

Kim adored having another big brother around and made him her willing slave.

Blake read bedtime stories, played make believe, was a proficient finger painter and even allowed himself to be tied to the dining room chair.

As he had been most mornings since he'd arrived, Blake was up before her. The smell of coffee drew her to the kitchen, where Kim sat in front of a bowl of fruit and some eggs and toast.

"Good morning." Blake got her a cup and poured coffee.

Blythe watched it like a hawk until she got her hands on it. "Morning." She bent over and kissed Kim. "And good morning to you."

"Morning." Kim waved her toast in the air. "Blake makes the best eggs."

"Better than mine?"

Kim rolled her eyes. "Much."

Blake hid a smirk beneath his coffee cup.

"Is Will up?" Blythe looked for his keys on the hall table.

"Up and gone," Blake said. "He told me to tell you not to expect him for dinner."

"What?" Blythe lost her happy buzz. "He's supposed to pick up Kim today. I have a client." She hated canceling clients. She'd built her business on being reliable and good at what she did. And tonight was only her second session with Chase. She didn't want to look flakey.

Blake shrugged. "He said he had to work, and then he had a night class."

"Damn." She filled up her coffee. Maybe she could ask Kurt to take Chase.

"Um…Blythe." Blake looked sheepish. "You know, I could do it." He motioned Kim. "I could pick her up, if you like."

Sure Blake had been a model houseguest, but this was real responsibility. Kim couldn't be left at St. Peter's. Of course, the moms who ran the daycare would never leave a child alone but Blythe refused to be that parent that didn't arrive on time to fetch her child. The family reputation hung around her even at St. Peter's.

"Yeah." Kim grinned through a mouthful of strawberries. "Blake could pick me up. Then we could have ice cream."

The bid for ice cream was a constant in Kim's arsenal.

"I won't forget." Blake lowered his voice and looked at her earnestly. "It's close enough that I can walk there and fetch her. I can even take her to the park on the way home. If that's okay with you."

Kim's enthusiasm waned. "I don't like walking."

"Of course you do." Blake scoffed. "You're just scared that I'll walk faster than you."

"Am not." Kim beamed at him. "I can walk faster than anyone in my school."

"Yeah." Blake lowered his head until they were eyeball to eyeball. "But I'm not at your school."

Blythe didn't know what to do. It would certainly get her out of a bind to have Blake fetch Kim, and if their living arrangement was going to work, at some time, he would have to take on some responsibility. But this wasn't getting the groceries or paying a bill, this was Kim.

Blake pulled his cell phone out of his pocket, an old cell of hers that she paid for some airtime for him on. "You gave me this," he said. "Call me and remind me. Then I'll call you when I get to the school, and I'll call you when she's with me."

"And he'll call you from the ice cream place," Kim said.

Blake raised his eyebrows at Kim. "Or not."

"Can I speak to you?" Blythe motioned Blake to follow her.

They stopped out of earshot in the passage.

"I won't mess this up," Blake said, his expression sincere.

Blythe wanted so much to believe him. "I don't want her growing up like we did. I won't let her grow up that way."

"And you're not." Blake put his hand on her shoulder. "You may have been too busy doing to see, but she's nothing like us. That kid in there is as normal as any other kid. You did that, Blythe."

His words took her by surprise and made her want to cry. "I want to trust you, but…"

"I know, Blythe. I won't let you down." He tipped her chin up and made her look at him. "I double down swear on a stack of bibles, that I won't let you down." He gave her a gentle smile and finished their childhood vow. "Or you can rub fifty sticks of gum in my hair."

CHASE ARRIVED on time for his appointment. Dressed, as always, in top of the line workout gear. It wasn't showy or flashy, but it certainly beamed expensive to anyone around it.

Blythe put him on the treadmill to warm up. "So, what brings you to Ghost Falls, Chase?"

"Business." He increased his pace as she increased the pace on the machine. "I'm looking into a merger here."

"Really?" She used to find the client chit chat tough to do, feeling like people could tell when she opened her mouth that she was from the wrong side of the tracks. "What business are you in?"

"Construction." Chase smiled at her.

This has to be a coincidence. The world wasn't really that small. "What business are you merging with?"

"Well, it's far from final," Chase said. "And things are at a delicate phase in the negotiations, but Evans Construction."

There you had it. Blythe tried to hide feeling sucker punched

Chase frowned down at her. "Do you know them?"

"Matt and Eric?" She played it cool. "Small town. We all went to school together."

"Ah." Chase relaxed into a longer stride. "So you're the one I need to come to for all the dirt on them?"

So much more than he knew, or anyone knew for that matter. "I'd have to charge you for that."

She checked the clock. About now Blake should be going to get Kim.

Her phone buzzed with a message. Please don't let that be the kindergarten. "Excuse me, I have to check this," she said to Chase. "I'm checking my sister gets home safely from school."

"How old?" Chase motioned her to check her phone.

"Four." Apparently she didn't need to remind Blake at all. He'd texted to say he was on his way to fetch Kim.

Relief made her smile. "Let's get you started," she said to Chase.

"This wasn't started?" He mopped his brow with his sweat towel.

Blythe played along. "I think you'll survive."

"Everything okay with your sister?" Chase settled on a weight bench.

She loaded plates on the bar, assessed Chase and gave him a tiny bit more. "Yes. My brother is on his way to fetch her now."

"If you're worried, keep your phone out." Chase breathed in and pressed the bar up. "I really don't mind."

"It's not professional." Blythe tucked her phone into the hidden pocket in her yoga pants. She smiled at Chase. "Besides which, this may be your ploy to get me to allow you to take business calls while you work out. And that's not going to happen."

"Dang it!" Chase racked the bar. "And here I thought I was being so clever."

"Eight more." Blythe tapped the bar.

Chase went for the lift. "I have kids of my own, you know? I know how it feels."

"Yes? How many?" Chase had marked himself as single on his application. Perhaps there wasn't a Mrs. Gunning.

Breathing heavily, Chase finished his set before replying. "Seven."

"Wow." Blythe didn't know what to say to that.

"Three wives." Chase grimaced. "Took me three tries before I realized I wasn't the marrying kind."

Maybe his three wives would have been better off knowing that before he married them, but Blythe kept her thoughts behind a polite smile and asked him to do another set.

BLYTHE CHECKED her phone after saying goodbye to Chase. Blake had sent a picture of him and Kim at the park, and another of them at home with him and Kim waving crayons and settled in front of a coloring book.

Even knowing how silly she was being, Blythe couldn't be easy until she opened the door to her apartment that evening.

The smell of garlic, tomatoes, and onions made a welcome greeting.

"Hello." She dropped her bag into the tiny entrance hall and moved into the living room.

Without looking away from the TV, Kim waved at her.

Blythe crouched down and kissed the top of her head. "How was your day?"

"Fine." Kim kept her eyes glued on her program. "Blake said we couldn't have ice cream."

"Good for Blake." She stood up and faced Blake in the kitchen. She felt really stupid for her misgivings. Kim was fine and safe, and from the smell and the towel over his shoulder, it looked like Blake had dinner on the go.

Blake smiled at her. "How was your day?"

"Good." She perched herself on a stool at the kitchen island. "Is that dinner I smell?"

"You know it?" Blake went to the stove and stirred a pot. "Don't get too excited, it's only pasta, but I do make a good tomato sauce."

"This is something I thought I'd never see."

Blake grinned at her. "I acquired some domestic skills."

"So I've noticed." The apartment looked like he might have done some cleaning as well. "Did you clean?"

"I did. But I don't do windows." He went back to his pots and pans. "I did a job search this morning, but not much turned up." He leaned against the counter beside the stove. "There's not much of a market for someone with my impressive track record."

"You'll get there." The world was not that forgiving of

people like Blake. No matter how hard they tried to turn their lives around. "And in the meantime, you have somewhere to stay."

He grimaced. "I appreciate that, Blythe, really I do, so don't get me wrong. But I feel like a leach. I can't even contribute to groceries."

"You contribute." The tiny bit he could spare from his few days a week.

Blake made a rude noise and rolled his eyes. "Anyway, I'm just feeling sorry for myself." His face grew serious. "I think we might have an even bigger problem."

There were very few things that could bring that combination of concern and fear to Blake's face. Blythe hoped that this wasn't a case like Voldemort, whereby saying his name drew his attention. "Brett?"

"Yeah, Brett." Blake looked over to where Kim sat in front of the TV and lowered his voice. "When I went to fetch her, he was at the daycare."

"What?" All the air left her lungs in a rush. She should have thought about Brett going to Kim's daycare. Stupid, stupid her. Dixie was a treat, and Blythe really liked her, but she wouldn't be able to keep information from Brett if he asked. None of them would dare keep stuff from Brett. People didn't do so well who didn't give Brett what he wanted. "You saw him?"

Blake nodded. "He didn't go in, but he was standing outside at the time when the kids are let out."

"Did you speak to him?" Blythe pushed down the rush of panic. She didn't want Brett anywhere near Kim. He could be charming enough when he wanted to be. He could play harmless and trustworthy. It's part of what made him so dangerous. You didn't know what he was up to until his evil side put in an appearance.

"He approached me." Blake blew out a long breath. "Scared the crap out of me. I didn't see him until he stepped right in front of me." He shook his head. "As stupid as it sounds, I'd forgotten what a big bastard he was.

Brett would have loved that. He thrived on keeping people off balance. She hadn't forgotten anything about Brett. She could still remember exactly how big he was and how strong. "Did he get to Kim?"

"No." Blake shook his head. "He spoke to me before I went in. When I came out with Kim, he'd gone already."

There was that at least. "Do you think he's been hanging around the daycare?" Her mind went a mile a minute. "I should tell the teachers to watch out for him. That I don't want him near Kim."

"I asked them if they'd seen him hanging around." Blake shook his head. "Nobody has seen him before. I think we can safely assume this is the first time. He's not the sort of guy anyone would forget."

Once was one time too many for Blythe. "Did he tell you what he wanted?"

"He said he wanted to see Kim. That she was his little sister, and he'd never even seen her."

God, she'd been afraid of something like this. Brett liked to stamp his huge presence all over the family. It had nothing to do with Kim or even her. It was all about Brett making sure they knew he was around and in charge. "I don't want him near her."

"I know that." Blake squeezed her hand. "And I agree with you, but I don't think he's going to do anything that puts his parole at risk. Also he said he wouldn't try to see her without your approval."

"He said that?" That didn't sound like Brett at all. But then, Brett lied along with the best of them to get what he wanted.

Blake nodded. "He did, and I think he might even have meant it."

"Like hell." Brett did nothing that didn't suit Brett.

"Apparently, he has a job." Blake went back to stirring his sauce.

"A legal one?" She'd never known Brett to work anything that didn't have a get rich fast angle to it.

Blake chuckled. "Yeah, hard to believe as it is, he has a real job with a legitimate company."

"Then I feel sorry for them." Whoever Brett had conned into employing him would soon find out they'd been taken. "Which idiot had the stupidity to hire him?"

"The Evans brothers," Blake said, his back to her. "Brett says that Eric hired him to work security at one of his construction sites."

Chapter Twenty

Blythe parked on Main Street and made her way into the lobby of Evans Construction. A set of glass doors led into an elegant, understated lobby, all leather and wood with black and white construction photos on the walls.

She approached the reception desk and braced herself to deal with Mrs. Cameron. The woman still had the same tightly curled, chestnut hairstyle she'd had when she had worked as school secretary.

Eric had once confessed to her in bed that Mrs. Cameron still scared the crap out of him, but her husband had lost his job a couple of years back and the school board had let her go. Matt had hired her to help her out, and when she wasn't breathing fire, she was a good receptionist.

Mrs. Cameron's thin mouth disappeared into a purple painted purse of disapproval. "Blythe Barrows, what are you doing here?"

A question Blythe hadn't stopped asking herself since she'd decided to come. Nothing short of Brett would have brought her anywhere near Eric. Not when he still ached like a missing limb.

Despite her absolute obligation to tell them what Brett was

really like, to warn them, she'd still driven past the building and made sure Eric's car wasn't there before she'd come inside.

"I'd like to see Matt, please," she said to Mrs. Cameron. She had to fight the urge to give the woman a teenage sneer of rebellion. The arc of disapproval always brought that juvenile knee jerk out in her.

Mrs. Cameron peered over her glasses. "Mr. Evans is an extremely busy man, and unless you have an appointment, you can't see him."

Blythe got the impression that it would be a cold day in hell before Mrs. Cameron gave her that appointment. She took a deep breath. "I'll wait until he has a moment. It's extremely important that I see him."

"What about?" Mrs. Cameron glared at her.

Blythe met her look of disdain without flinching. She didn't need to let people make her feel not good enough. She had as much right to be here as anyone, and this was Mrs. Cameron's job. Although she had the feeling even a Pippa makeover wouldn't make Mrs. Cameron treat her any differently. "I'm afraid that's between Matt and me." She indicated a large leather sofa. "I'll sit here and wait for him."

Lips tightly compressed, Mrs. Cameron glowered at her as Blythe took a seat. "He's busy."

"I understand, and I'll wait. I'll only take two minutes of his time. This is important." She could back off and call Matt, but she'd be damned if she let Mrs. Cameron chase her away now. Similar incidents littered her childhood and teens, times they had chased her away and judged her. She didn't need to take that anymore.

Positioning herself with a view out the front door of Eric's empty parking spot, Blythe sat down to a long and stressful ten minutes.

Mrs. Cameron growled and glared at her. "Tell me what

this is about and maybe, and I mean maybe, I can find out if Mr. Evans has the time for you."

Time was ticking by, and she had a client in forty minutes. The longer she sat here, the greater the chance of an encounter of the Eric kind. "I need to see him about Brett."

"Your brother?" Mrs. Cameron frowned. Then she ruffled up like an angry goose and scowled. "Don't even think of coming here and asking the Evans boys to give that no-good thug a job. We don't want that kind in this company."

Wow! Did every person who walked in that lobby get treated like crap, or did Mrs. Cameron save something special for the Barrowses? It gave Blythe childish satisfaction to say, "They already did give him a job, and I need to change their minds."

Mrs. Cameron gaped. "Why didn't you say that in the beginning?"

Because generally receptionists didn't involve themselves in the content of the company's meetings, but what the hell. Blythe shrugged and went back to her parking watch.

With another growl, Mrs. Cameron snatched up her phone. "Good morning. Yes, hi Eric, I have that Blythe Barrows sitting here. She wanted to see Matt, but she needs to talk to one of you."

Everything in Blythe stilled, and Mrs. Cameron's words crept over her in slow motion. Oh, no, no, no. She didn't want to see Eric. She leaped to her feet and held her hands out. "No!"

Mrs. Cameron looked genuinely shocked. "What are you doing?"

"Eric's not here." She jabbed a finger at the parking lot. "Matt. I need to see Matt."

Standing, Mrs. Cameron glared over her glasses. "Blythe Barrows! Where do you think you're going?"

Blythe snatched up her bag. "I'll call Matt." She should have done that in the first place, instead of coming down and then getting into a standoff with Mrs. Cameron. She dashed for the door.

"Blythe?" Eric said from behind her. Had he run to reception from his office?

Hand on the door, Blythe wrestled with the childish desire to keep going and make a run for it. Except he might chase her. In front of that horrible, judgmental woman. Her nape prickled and she sensed him right behind her.

"What are you doing here?"

"I came to see Matt." Her car sat in the place she'd parked it, beckoning. She could be through those doors and in it before he could move.

No, she couldn't, and she was behaving like a complete idiot. This ranked way up there with hiding from him outside St. Peter's. Ghost Falls was a small town, and as much as she wanted to avoid contact, she could only ever be somewhat successful. Mentally hauling on her big girl panties, she turned and faced him. "But if he's not here, I can speak to you."

"How good of you?" His lips twitched.

God that expression hit her like a punch to the chest. Memories of their time together washed over her. Eric leaning over his kitchen counter as they made dinner together. Eric, firelight flickering across the aquiline lines of his face, as he handed her a glass of wine. Eric cradling her head between his palms as his big body pinned her to his bed. She loved that freaking expression. It rated as one of her top five. The way he laughed with his eyes and dared her not to smile.

She cleared the tightening in her throat and took a deep breath. "It won't take long."

Eric's twinkle blossomed into his heart-stopping grin. "Take as long as you need."

Blythe slammed the door on the memory vault because that grin also belonged in her top five favorite Eric looks. Top five? She nearly snorted aloud. Make that top fifty.

Dear God, she should never have come here. One look at

that face, the sound of his deep bass voice, the smell of his citrusy aftershave, and she wanted to crawl right back between the sheets with him.

Like most of her family, she was an addict, and Eric Evans was her drug of choice.

BLYTHE FOLLOWED his undeniably still fine ass through an open-plan office. There was no reason why his ass shouldn't still be fine. Although, she had been hoping her appreciation of it had diminished.

People looked up as she passed. Surprise and curiosity flickered over their faces. Coupled with the intense desire to obnoxiously chew and snap gum, Blythe had another flight reflex kick in.

As if reading her mind, Eric cupped her elbow and guided her into his office. The warmth of his hand penetrated her workout hoodie. Those large, laborer's hands, so at odds with the refined exterior and so capable of doing things to her that made her body sing his tune.

So much for all that progress she had allegedly made in getting over Eric. How stupid one woman could be really wasn't quantifiable.

He shut the door with a snick, and she jumped.

Alone in an office with Eric. All of Eric, smelling so good and looking even better. At least the office had glass walls, and they were in full view of the rest of the company. And the rest of the company had its eyes on them. Gazes running the gamut between hostile, curious and disdainful.

Eric lowered the blinds and closed them.

"What are you doing?" Her mouth went dry.

He glanced at her over his shoulder. "Are you kidding me? It's been ages since you would even speak to me, and now you're here. I don't want to share this with the rest of the office."

It would really help if he didn't say stuff like that either. "I'm not here about us."

"No?" He cocked his head. "I gathered as much when you asked for Matt at first." He gave her that devilish little half smile again. "Unless you were going to ask Matt to tell me that you wanted me to meet you after lunch behind the bicycle sheds."

And now he'd managed to make her laugh. He'd always been able to make her laugh. So much effortless charm had to be illegal. She stood a moment, struck dumb in the familiar dearness of his face. The tilt at the corner of his mouth, the gleam in his walnut eyes, the very hint of a raised eyebrow.

"Get over here, sweet thing."

"Why?"

"I'll show you when you get here."

She'd taken four steps toward him before she caught herself. He hadn't said a word. The echo of a memory was all it had been. "I hear you hired Brett."

He looked taken aback. "Yeah, I did. He—"

"You have to fire him." Holy crap she needed to say what needed saying and get out of here. Take a glacial shower and maybe pound her stupid head against a wall for an hour or two.

He lifted an eyebrow. "Why would I do that? So far we've had no problems with him. In fact, he's been great."

"You know what he's like." She couldn't believe she had to spell it out for him. "He's vicious and dangerous, and you should know better than to trust him."

Eric stepped toward her. "Calm down, Blythe."

Her temper simmered and spat into flame. Had anyone in the history of humanity ever calmed down when told to? Certainly not her, and not when Eric used that condescending tone on her. "I'm perfectly fucking calm."

His eyebrow rose higher.

Which flamed her temper. "I can't believe you're stupid enough to trust Brett. I should be having this conversation with Matt."

That got him. His eyes flashed return fire at her. "You'll damn well talk to me, instead of running away from me all the time. Unless you'd like to explain to Matt why I should know all about Brett."

"This isn't about you and me." The arrogance of the man amazed her, and it really shouldn't because this was not the first time she'd run headfirst into the giant block of man-conceit that was Eric Evans.

"Really?" His voice dropped into a silky drawl. "So you didn't come here asking for Matt because you wanted to avoid me?"

"You know why I would rather not...see you." He was missing the point. Deliberately. "And whether I came here to see you or Matt doesn't change the situation with Brett." Which brought up another point. "And let's not rewrite our history and say that sneaking around and pretending there was nothing between us for all these years was ever my idea."

He gaped at her. "You're telling me that if I'd said we take our relationship public, you'd have been up for that." He stepped into her space and glared down at her. "And I think Brett's changed."

"Don't be ridiculous." She stood her ground and refused to back down. "Brett doesn't change. God, you just have to look at the rest of my family to know that."

"I don't—"

"And don't even talk to me about you and I being anything more than your dirty little secret. You know damn well that was never going to happen."

"Well, now we'll never know."

God, he infuriated her with his bullshit. "I guess we won't."

"Fine."

"Fine."

They stood there a moment, scowling at each other, both of them breathing deep. She was too close to him. Being so close ate at the edges of her anger and twisted it into something much more dangerous. "Are you going to fire Brett?"

"No."

"Argh!" She ran out of words. She wanted to shove him, but she didn't believe in physical violence. "You are so goddamn stubborn."

"That's rich coming from you." A different type of fire lit his eyes now.

Blythe knew that look, she knew it well, and she forced herself to step back. A strategic retreat to save herself. "Don't look at me like that."

"Why not?" He closed the gap.

She put her hand up to stop him. Her voice dropped into a whisper that sounded less sure than she was trying to be. "You know why."

"I only know that you made a decision for both of us." His chest met her hand and still he kept coming. "A decision I don't agree with."

Mouth too dry to speak, her heart hammering in her throat, Blythe shook her head. "We can't."

"Why not, Blythe?" He curled his hand around her nape. "We're good together, sweet thing, you know we are."

God help her when his voice grew raspy like that. It chewed up her resistance and spat it out.

She made the mistake of looking into his eyes.

He wanted her. His look was all hot and needy. It strummed an answering chord inside her.

Her eyelids grew heavy. His mouth was so close and her body remembered the taste of him. The way he could kiss her into an aching frenzy. "Eric."

"Blythe." His kiss landed hard against her mouth. An uncontrolled thing of teeth and lips and tongues.

His grip on her nape tightened to keep her there.

Not that Blythe was going anywhere. The taste and feel of him rioted through her and set fire to the need she'd tried so hard to bury.

He groaned into her mouth and deepened the kiss. His other hand fastened on her hip and dragged her against him.

He was rock hard, pressing against her.

Blythe wanted to climb inside him. Sex had never been the problem for them. As often as they came together, it was always incredible.

But at the end of the day, it had only ever been sex.

Blythe ripped out of his kiss and staggered back to put some distance between them.

Her pulse still pounded.

He was breathing hard, his cheeks flushed. "I want you, Blythe. I still want you."

"No." She shook her head. He'd never know how much it cost her to ignore every screaming instinct that wanted to respond to their mutual passion and go back to what they had. Even if it hadn't been perfect, it had at least been something. A whisper in the back of her mind insisted that even that small piece of Eric was better than no Eric at all.

No, that wasn't true. For as long as she held on to that piece of Eric, she held on to the hope she would get all of him one day. For as long as there was hope for Eric, there could be nothing else in her life. She grabbed the door and yanked it open. "I can't, Eric. I want more. I want everything, and if I can't have it with you, then you need to let me go so I can have it with someone else."

Chapter Twenty-One

Fortunately, or maybe unfortunately, because it couldn't happen again—ever—Pippa called the next day with a massive distraction. They had a slot for Blythe's makeover.

Today.

Blake agreed to look after Kim, and Will would be around to help, so Blythe drove to the address Pippa had given her. *Your Best You* was filmed in a small studio in what passed for Ghost Falls' industrial district. A few auto parts dealers, a tombstone supplier and an industrial bakery crowded around the neat, cream building.

Inside a small reception area, Pippa, Bella and Liz waited for her.

"Hi." Pippa gave Blythe a big smile. "Thanks for coming at such short notice. You can blame me." She grimaced. "I was supposed to set this up days ago, but I forget to tell the production assistant, and then I got the date wrong." She rolled her eyes. "Honestly, pregnancy brain is a thing, and sleep deprivation makes it worse."

"Try menopause." Liz snorted.

Bella approached her tentatively. "I hope you don't mind. I mean, I can go if you're not comfort—"

"Stay!" Blythe needed as much support as she could get. That thought put a quick hitch in her stride. She and Bella Evans being supportive toward each other. Who'da thunk it.

Opening a door at the back of the reception area, Pippa motioned everyone through. "We decided to do it here because the team have all their stuff here."

"Team," Liz whispered. "If Blythe needs a goddamn team, they'd need a regiment for the rest of us."

Blythe snorted a laugh. Liz's flattery made her feel a bit more confident. She'd been told since she could understand that she was pretty, but she had never known what to wear or how to do her hair. She'd taught herself makeup from copying magazines, and later, YouTube tutorials.

Pippa's heels clicked on the floor, leading the way.

Blythe had no idea how she walked so confidently in four-inch heels. "We're going to try a few looks out on you, see what we like."

They reached the set, a dressing room floating in a pool of light at the far end of the studio. Lights, cables and cameras bristled on the outskirts as if daring her to step into the hot seat.

A beautiful blond woman dressed in a floaty skirt and a tank top approached. "Hi, I'm Bianca."

"You do the makeup," Blythe said. She never missed an episode.

Bianca smiled her bright, glorious smile.

"And this is Rory," Pippa said to the tall black man by her side.

Blythe knew who he was too. "Hair."

"Speaking of." Rory stepped closer and grabbed a handful of hers. "There is a lot here for me to work with."

"You're going to have to wait your turn." Bianca elbowed him out of the way. "I saw her first and I get to play first."

Liz tugged Bella over to a sofa. "We should have brought popcorn."

"I did." Bella dug in her huge purse and pulled out a bag of SkinnyPop.

"Really?" Pippa leveled a flat stare at them.

Bella blushed and looked abashed, but Liz grabbed a handful of SkinnyPop and grinned. "This is like sitting watching the show on television. Only better, because this way we get to add our two cents."

"Great." Pippa rolled her eyes, and then turned back to Bianca and Rory. "You'll get your chances, but both of you are going to have to wait."

Pippa walked her on set and over to a sand linen armchair, which Blythe recognized as the place they filmed all the interview and journal segments. "Phi had a really great idea and I want to see something." She faced the studio. "Bernie."

"Yo!" from the dark, a man called back.

Trying not to look as overawed as she felt, Blythe took a seat. "What am I doing here?"

"Phi said we should put you on screen." Pippa stepped back and eyed the setup critically. "Can we get started?"

"On it." A man popped up in front of Blythe with a light meter and gave her a naughty grin. "Don't mind me."

"I thought this was a makeover." Blythe looked to Liz and Bella for answers.

"Don't ask us." Bella shrugged. "But you look great."

Fat lot of help they were. "You haven't booked your assessment session yet."

"I will. Soon." Bella grimaced. "Pippa has been stalling."

"Me!" Pippa glared at her. "You said you—"

"Makeover!" Liz waved an arm between Bella and Pippa. "Focus on Blythe."

"Right." Pippa gave Bella one more hard look. "It absolutely is a makeover," she said and squeezed Blythe's hand. "But we want to get some film of you to see how you work."

"Now? I'm not wearing any makeup or anything."

Suddenly nervous she plucked at her workout hoodie. "I'm not dressed. Is this like an audition?"

"No." Pippa smiled and perched herself on a stool opposite Blythe. "This is you and me sitting here and having a chat."

"She's up to something," Liz called and jabbed a forefinger at Pippa. "That's the face she gets before she whips off your bedazzled track pants and puts you in a dress she says is age appropriate."

Pippa raised a brow at her. "What did we say about bedazzled things?"

"Can't remember." Liz dived back into the popcorn.

Bella winked at Blythe. "She totally remembers. She has more Juicy track pants than all of the Kardashians."

Someone moved behind one of the cameras. All Blythe could see was a pair of legs. Then a voice. "More light on Blythe."

Someone else shouted yes and bright light bounced off the back of her retinas. She had no idea what she was doing here. This all felt a bit unreal.

Pippa nodded to the camera, and then turned back to her. "I'm going to ask you a few questions, and I want you to answer as honestly as you can."

"Okay." This felt worse than that dream where you wake up naked, and everyone is looking at you.

"Why don't you start by telling us who you are, and how you got into training?"

"My name is Blythe Barrows." She stomped on the desire to nervous giggle. "I got into personal training because I used to be a cheerleader." No, that wasn't the whole story, and she shook her head. "Actually after I left school, I realized I didn't have that many options. I didn't do well enough in school to get any sort of college scholarship, and that was the only way I was going to stand a chance. Nobody in Ghost Falls was going to give a Barrows a student loan. Pat pretty much red-lined our credit rating."

Pippa made an encouraging noise. "Keep going."

"Well, there weren't a huge number of options open to me. As I said, I had been a cheerleader, and I always enjoyed exercise and being in shape. I started teaching one or two dance classes at my local gym." The next part of the story was not one she'd shared with many. "I got interested in the ladies in my class. What made them want to be there. Why some succeeded and some didn't. It made me want to do more for them."

Pippa leaned forward. "In what way."

"Well, we're all individuals, and it's the same when it comes to choosing exercise and diet. Or even what works for one person is different to what works for another." Blythe lost track of how long she spoke, but her nerves disappeared, and she spoke honestly about her passion for helping people do the best for themselves and take care of themselves.

When she'd run out of things to say, Pippa asked, "And what do you want, Blythe? When we make you over, what would you want to get from it?"

"To be taken seriously." Blythe didn't have to think about her answer. "For all my life I've allowed other people to tell me what I should look like. I was that Barrows girl, the slutty one with all the bad brothers, and I ended up dressing the part." She indicated her yoga pants and workout top. "Now I dress like this most of the time. Part of it is for work, and part of it is because I don't know any better."

"Really?" Pippa cocked her head. "I had no idea why you dressed like you did in high school. I always thought it was for attention."

Blythe couldn't tell a lie. "Oh, it was." She laughed. "And it certainly got me attention, but the wrong kind. Now I want to be treated like someone who has their crap together. Someone people can trust."

"I should have known that." Pippa shook her head. "I've been doing this job for long enough to know people hide all sorts of things behind appearance." She sighed. "I apologize, Blythe. I should have given you the same benefit of the doubt I give people who come on my show."

"It's okay." Blythe didn't know what to do with the apology. She really valued it but it made her want to squirm like a five-year-old.

Pippa huffed and stood. "No, it's not fine, but I will do better going forward." She looked at the camera and raised her eyebrow.

A short, dark haired man with thick glasses popped around it. "She's magic, Pips. Pure screen magic. The camera fucking loves her."

"Damn, Phi." Pippa laughed and shook her head. "When she's right, she's right. She said the camera would take to you."

Heat crept into Blythe cheeks, and she couldn't quite believe them. "Really? Me?"

"Yes, you." Pippa winked at her. "Bernie is never wrong, and if he says you're magic, then that's what you are."

"Now can we have her?" Rory stepped closer. "I know exactly what I'm going to do with that hair."

Bianca cupped her chin. "Hurry up because this face is begging for me."

The next hours passed in a blur of being tucked, primped, powdered, and coiffed.

Liz and Bella went off to get lunch for everyone and returned.

"Don't you have better things to do?" Blythe couldn't believe they wanted to sit there and watch.

"Nope." Liz brought wine with the sandwiches and handed it around.

Bella took a glass of wine. "And I sponsor some of the clothes for the show, so I have to be here."

Pippa took the glass of wine away from Blythe. "She can have this later. Now you two go and sit over there until we're done."

Pippa wove in between Bianca and Rory, having her try on a confusing array of clothes. She spoke to Blythe as she worked, explaining why certain things worked and others didn't. Bella piped up for a couple of these discussions. It made sense that Bella knew about clothes, what with her owning a high-end clothing store. But Blythe had never taken Bella seriously before. *Hello, Mrs. Kettle, this is Mr. Pot calling.*

As exhausting as the makeover was, Blythe loved it.

"I'll write this all down for you," Pippa said. "And we'll give you a binder when you leave with all our recommendations." She held up a pair of jeans and a shirt. "But for now, go and put these on, and we're done."

Ten minutes later, they all stood around her for her big reveal. Pippa insisted on her having the full makeover experience.

"Damn." Liz downed her wine. "I think I hate her."

"You look amazing." Bella teared up.

The curtain dropped from the mirror, and Blythe stared. Then she stared some more.

A tall woman with a movie star body stared back at her. She knew she was in good shape and had a lot of the right things in the right place, but not like this.

She stepped closer. "Is that me?"

"That's you." Pippa slipped an arm around her waist. "Do you like it?"

"I can't believe it." She tried to take it all in. The jeans made her hips look curvy and her legs long. The top hugged her tiny waist and accentuated the firm jut of her breasts.

Rory had put warm golds and caramels through her hair, and she no longer looked like a walking Barbie. Bianca's makeup was so subtle that all she noticed were her eyes, which looked bigger and greener than they ever had, and her full mouth.

"You look beautiful." Pippa hugged her. "You were beautiful before. We just gave you a chance to shine through."

"I can't..." Blythe's throat tightened, and she couldn't speak.

Bella waved her hands in front of her eyes. "I swear to God, if she cries, I'm going to."

"You already are." Liz dabbed at the corners of her eye with a Kleenex.

Blythe got it now, why women cried on their reveal. In the mirror was the embodiment of all she wanted to be and secretly dreamed she could be. A version of herself that was better than anything she could have imagined, and yet totally authentic. It was the best version of her.

Bianca hugged her from the other side. "You're going to knock 'em dead. In this studio and out there in the world."

"Well, hello, Blythe." Matt Evans strolled into the studio. He kissed Pippa first, and then turned to her with a low whistle of appreciation. "You were always hot stuff, Blythe, but this is...incendiary."

"That's a big word, Meat." Pippa slid her arms around his waist.

He looked down at her and grinned in a way that made Blythe's heart ache for a look just like it. "I know a lot of big words, Agrippina. I learned them from a book."

Pippa turned to the dim form that had followed Matt into the studio. "What do you think, Eric?"

WHAT DID HE THINK? A bellow of blinding rage climbed inside Eric and clamored to escape. "What do I think?"

That woman wasn't Blythe. Not his Blythe. It was like

they'd all conspired to take his Blythe away from him. All of them. Everyone in that studio, and Blythe herself

A kernel of rational deep in his brain tried to whisper caution. Blythe looked stunning. Breathtaking. A classy combination of beautiful and elegant and refined. The sort of woman any man would crow like a rooster to have on his arm.

Only she wasn't on his arm. That woman wasn't his Blythe, and what she represented was how much distance there was between him and his Blythe.

"She looks nothing like herself." He heard the words come out of his mouth before he could stop them.

Blythe blinked at him and took a reflexive step back. The hurt on her face gut-punched him.

Bella gasped and stared at him as if he'd lost his mind.

But some demon had him by the mouth, and it said, "I hate it. That's not Blythe. She looks like a dressed-up puppet."

"What the fuck?" Liz scowled at him.

"Eric." Pippa shook her head, giving him a look of astounded disappointment.

Matt gaped, and then scowled like he was going to kick his ass.

"You're a dick, man," Rory said. "She looks amazing."

And Blythe. His beautiful girl stared at him with the wound fresh in her eyes for about two seconds before the shutters came down.

Eric hated those shutters. They were her weapon to defend herself from the world around her. When people got cruel with her or treated her with contempt, she used the shutters to keep them out. Keep them away from that warm, huge heart and that pure gold center.

"Excuse me." She managed a tight, dismissive smile. "Apparently you can't please all of the people all of the time." Her brittle laugh carved right through him. "Who knew?"

Her heels clacked across the studio floor as she brushed past him and reached for her purse.

"Blythe," he whispered, not knowing what to say, how to fix it, make it right.

She stepped around him without looking at him. Her voice was so low that only he caught it. "I expect it from other people, but not you. Never you."

The door slammed behind her and reverberated through the tense stillness of the studio.

Matt's low growl hit him first. "What the fuck, Eric?"

He had no defense. Shame choked him, and he held up his hand. "I don't know why I said it. I didn't mean it."

"But you did say it." Pippa had never given him such a cold look. "And you hurt her. That's unforgivable."

"I know." He wanted to whimper like a child, but he'd done that, and there was no escape. Owning up was his only option. "I looked at her, and it terrified me."

Pippa folded her arms and frowned at him, but some of the frost left her tone. "Why terrified you? Are you going to tell us what's going on?"

"Nothing." He'd lost the right to lie to them. "Not anymore. She left me about a month back. She says she deserves more." The truth hit him like a pile driver. "And she does. She deserves it all. The man who'll stand by her side always. The children. The house. All that love and family. She deserves that and a whole lot more."

Matt punched his shoulder, but it wasn't the pound he deserved. "So, give it to her."

"I can't." And he felt like the lowest piece of shit saying it. "I can't."

"Then you need to let her go," Pippa said.

Eric wanted to smack his head against the wall. "I know that, but I can't seem to let her go either. And then I walked in here, and I looked at her, and she wasn't mine. I have to accept she's not mine and she's moving on with her life."

"Yes, you do." Pippa drew even with him. "But first you have to go and make this right with her. You were cruel, and that's not right. And then you have to wish her well and let her go."

"I—"

"Let her go, Eric."

Chapter Twenty-Two

Eric stood outside the door to Blythe's new apartment and peered at Blake through the gap allowed by the safety chain.

"She doesn't want to see you, dude." Blake looked a bit too smug about it for Eric's liking, but then he'd pretty much deserved whatever they were going to dish up.

What they didn't realize, but they would, is that he wasn't going away without seeing her. "I get that," he said. "And I really don't blame her, but I need to make it right. Tell her that I'm sorry."

"You made her cry." Blake's expression hardened. "And she didn't even cry when Brett broke her arm."

"Fuck." He couldn't believe what an unmitigated asshole he'd been to her. "Please, Blake." He would beg all night if he had to. "I know I don't deserve it but let me in to talk to her. I'll do anything to fix this."

Blake stared at him.

Eric let him see his intention.

"You gonna stay out there all night if I don't let you in?" Blake sniffed.

If that's what it took. "Yup."

"You're a dick."

"You're right, I am."

With a huge sigh Blake shut the door. The chain made a scraping noise as he disengaged it, and then opened the door properly. "She's gonna kill me but if what you've got to say will make her stop crying, it's worth it."

"Thank you." Eric shot through the gap into the apartment. He didn't want to take any chances with Blake changing his mind.

Will stood in the kitchen giving him an even dirtier look than the one Blake had bent on him. "What is he doing here?" he asked Blake.

"Says he needs to fix what he did."

"He's not what Blythe needs." Will looked Eric in the eye, the challenge clear. "He needs to leave Blythe alone, is what he needs to do."

People kept telling him that, and he didn't like it any more now than the first time he'd heard it. He liked it even less that they were right.

If he couldn't give Blythe what she wanted, deserved, then he needed to respect her and care for her enough to step aside. It's what any decent guy would do.

The apartment was on the small side with some of the ugliest furniture he'd ever seen. She'd rejected his overt offers of help, so he'd gone behind her back a little. Made sure she could afford the deposit and used influence with the landlord to keep her rent low.

Everything was neat and clean, and Blythe had added those little touches of hers. The fresh flowers on the kitchen island. The poster of her favorite Degas sketch on the wall. The big bright white wicker basket of toys in the corner.

His heart filled with pride in her. She'd worked years to make it so, but Blythe had made a home for herself, Will and Kim. Now it looked like she'd taken Blake under her wing as well.

One day she would make the same kind of home with a

man in it. A man who wouldn't be him. Somewhere inside him, he needed to find a better version of the selfish fuck he was currently being.

Blythe strode into the common living area. She still wore the outfit Pippa had put her in, and she looked incredible. Also, angry as hell. "Who let you in?"

"Blake." He and Will said at the same time.

Blythe turned her scowl on Blake. "What the hell?"

"He said he wanted to talk to you. Make it right." Blake looked sheepish. "I thought if he could make you feel better, it was worth a shot."

Her shoulders eased a bit, and her expression softened. "You're an idiot."

"Yeah, but you already knew that about me." Blake shrugged.

She turned back to Eric, and all the anger came back with her. "So talk."

Kim wandered into the living room and went to stand beside Blake.

Will watched him from the kitchen.

"Umm…maybe you could go and get a coffee or something?" Eric couldn't talk to her with her family watching on.

"We'll go out for a bit," Blake said.

Will snorted. "Like hell we will."

"It's okay, Will," Blythe said. "This conversation has probably been too long in coming anyway."

"I'm not leaving you here with this asshole," Will said.

Blythe scoffed. "I can handle this asshole. Give us about thirty minutes."

"Don't say asshole," Kim said, and then turned to Eric. "I like going out for ice cream."

Eric reached for his wallet.

"Don't." Will snatched up his car keys and sneered at Eric. "We didn't need your money before, and we certainly don't need it now."

Kim looked at him in horror. "For ice cream. We need it."

"I'll buy you ice cream." Will steered her out the door.

"Don't screw up," Blake said to him as he followed them out.

Being told by a Barrows brother not to screw up had to be some kind of poetic justice smacking into him.

The door shut behind them. And then there were two, and Eric couldn't think of a word to say. He started with the obvious. "I'm sorry about what I said." He wanted to close the distance between them, but her body language gave him the stop-right-there. "You look unbelievable, and that's what I should have said. Instead, I freaked out."

"You freaked out?" She looked at him askance. "Because I got a makeover. That doesn't make any sense."

"I know." God, he was never stuck for words. Why now? "You were standing there, looking so beautiful and so far away from me. And I suddenly couldn't pretend anymore. I've lost you."

"What?" All the tension rushed out of her on a breath and left a look of incredulity. "We broke up a month ago."

"That's the thing." And Eric needed to say this like he needed air. "We didn't break up. You broke up with me."

She frowned and made an I-don't-get-it hand toss.

Eric risked a few steps nearer. The need to touch her sparked through his nerve endings but his timing couldn't be worse. He had to make her understand. For both of their sakes. "I wasn't ready," he said. "For things between us to end. I walked out that morning expecting that I would give you a couple of days to cool off, then we'd talk, one thing would lead to another, and we'd be back in bed before the end of the week."

She winced and folded her arms. "Because that's what always happened."

"Right." He hadn't known this time would be different.

"I'm finding it hard to accept that you're not coming back this time."

"I'm not," she whispered. "I can't."

"I know." He came to within touching distance of her. The subtle floral note of her perfume teased him. "And when I'm not feeling sorry for myself, I understand, and I agree you deserve more." He couldn't stop himself, and he took her hand. "But, sweet thing, I miss you so much, and there's this big part of me that doesn't want to accept that I've lost you."

"Eric." She left her hand in his. "You don't love me. I don't get why this is so hard for you."

"Neither do I. But I miss it all." He tugged her close enough to rest his cheek against her head. If he didn't hold her now, he'd implode. "I miss the way you text me more emojis than words." His hand found the small of her back and rested there. He thanked God that she allowed him that. "I miss how you hate talking on the phone, and when you do, it's like speaking to a drill sergeant."

She huffed a soft laugh.

"I miss the way you can always make me see the funny side of my crappy day, and how you hate being held at night because you get too hot." He drew her into his arms and held her, light enough for her to break away if she chose. "I miss your beautiful body and how every time we make love, it's better than the time before. I miss it all, sweet thing, every tiny detail of our time together."

"But you don't want more." Her arms slid around his waist, beneath his jacket, just like she had always done.

The familiar way she tucked her head under his chin made him want to bawl like a fucking baby. "Jesus, sweet thing, I wish I did. I wish I could give you everything you want and make it worth your while to stay."

"I wish that too." Her soft sigh was filled with the same unbearable sadness inside him.

Eric tightened his hold on her. "I'm going to do better by

you, do right by you. For the record, I really, really can't tell you how much I don't fucking want to, but it's what you need. Let me just hold you for a few minutes and say goodbye."

Her breath hitched and his shirt grew damp where her cheek rested against him.

Damn, he'd made this brave, tough, incredible woman cry again.

"You found me at the lowest point of my life, Blythe." He had been nineteen, drunk and trying not to cry. Still reeling from the death of his father the year before and trying to deal with what had happened with Laura.

Then Blythe had tripped out of the bar in her tiny denim miniskirt, showing miles and miles of the most killer legs he'd ever seen. Through the gap between her shrink-wrapped T-shirt and her skirt, he had caught a mouthwatering glimpse of taut belly. At sixteen she had looked like his salvation.

Instead of offering sex, she had handed him a cup of coffee and perched beside him. Even drunk and hopped up on nineteen-year-old hormones, he had recognized the innocence in her, and despite everything he had heard about her, he had drunk his coffee and unburdened his soul.

First they had been friends of a sort. Both of them had acknowledged the staggering attraction but never acted on it. A few years later, they had run into each other again, and that time he'd been her first lover.

From there, they had drifted into a pattern. Whenever he had been in town, and they had both been single, they had found their way into the nearest bed together. The attraction had never gotten any less.

"You've been there for me too, when I needed you," she said. "You have been a big part of my life."

Her words slew him, and mostly because he really didn't deserve them. He'd been there for her at his own convenience. He had been part of her life because it suited him. "You're giving me credit I really don't deserve. I've been a selfish prick, and now I'm throwing a tantrum because someone took my favorite toy away."

She chuckled. "Maybe."

"Definitely."

"At least I was your favorite toy." She tried to make light of it, and that took another piece out of him. He was turning down all that warmth and generosity. Not because he thought he could find better somewhere else. He accepted that he was walking away from the best thing that had, and likely would, ever happen to him. But he couldn't be his dad. Even the thought of his dad's face and that baffled and bested look of utter despondency made Eric want to choke and loosen his collar for more air.

He put her at arm's length and looked down into her lovely face. "I'm here to say I'm sorry for all of it. Sorry I didn't do better when I had you, appreciate every incredible thing about you. Sorry for acting like a dick today and every other time I did, and mostly sorry that I'm not capable of giving you everything you deserve." He pressed his lips to her forehead. If he went near her mouth, he would kiss her with all the pent-up longing and lust inside him, not even ten seconds after he'd promised to do better. "So, this is goodbye to my lover, to my sweet thing."

Tears swum in her eyes. "Goodbye, Eric."

"Maybe you're not ready. Maybe I'm not ready, but I would hate to think that every part of us is over." Eric forced himself to drop his hands from her and stepped back. "There's no way to say this without sounding trite, but I'm hoping like hell there is enough of us left that we can one day be friends."

"Friends?" She gave a watery chuckle. "I don't think I was ever any good at being your friend." She shrugged. "But why the hell not? Let's try to be friends."

Chapter Twenty-Three

Eric wasn't much of a drinker, but leaving Blythe's apartment, he couldn't face being on his own.

Matt was probably still pissed at him. Pippa, Bella and Liz were probably rounding up the mob, and he didn't fancy one more person pointing out how much of an ass he'd been. That much was ringingly clear already.

Driving up the hill, he went into the bar Jo sometimes worked at. He wasn't sure if he was happy or not to see Jo behind the bar.

She looked at him with surprise. "Hey."

"Hey yourself." He pulled up a stool to the U-shaped sweep of mahogany, polished to a gleaming russet. "Got a drink back there for your brother?"

"Sure, if you got money." Jo leaned her elbows on the bar. "And you leave a huge tip."

"I can do that."

Not many people frequented the place tonight. They were in between the summer and winter seasons now, which affected the bars up here near the holiday cottages the most.

He used the term cottage very lightly. He and Matt had built a fair number of those cottages and tagged a price on them to match. Highgate was supposed to be the jewel in their crown. A month ago, he'd been riding high and feeling like he could take on the world and win. Now he watched his sister pour him a single-malt and wondered what took so long.

"What happened to your ink?" Her arms bared by her tank top seemed to have less ink than when last he'd seen her.

Jo grinned at him. "Some of them are temporary. I put them on just to see Matt almost swallow his tongue."

"Brat." Eric chuckled. Matt could never resist babying the rest of them. Especially Isaac and Jo. Eric reckoned it was why Isaac stayed on the run. The kid needed to find out who the hell he was without Matt looking out for him.

Eric didn't blame Matt. Matt had shouldered a huge burden at nineteen and putting it down couldn't be easy. Trying to single parent his teen brothers and sister made him due for a sainthood. Cressy had left all of that on her oldest son's shoulders.

She'd sucked Dad in, and then Matt, and slowly drained the life out of them. When Eric had seen how Matt felt about Pippa, and also that the dumb shit might let her get away, he had stepped in. Cressy hadn't won that round.

Jo served a couple of drinks at the far end of the bar.

Sipping his drink, Eric studied the view outside the large, plate glass windows. Yellows and oranges created colorful smudges amongst the browning scrub oak. The snow would bring the cottage crowd, and the bar would be standing room only.

"How's school going?" he asked Jo when she rejoined him.

She shrugged. She always shrugged, in case he got the mistaken impression that she needed his help.

Jesus, he was cursed by women who refused to take any kind of help, and he wanted to understand. He was sitting here drinking scotch on a Wednesday evening because he didn't get it.

"Let me ask you something." He finished his drink and

motioned Jo for another. He waited until she brought it before he spoke again. "Why are you so hell bent on taking no help?"

Jo stiffened and went squinty eyed.

"No, wait." That had come out wrong. "I'm not challenging that, I'm not even offering to help because I know you don't want that. I just want to understand why taking help is such a bad thing."

"It's not that it's a bad thing." Jo hunched her shoulders and folded her arms. She thought for a while. "It's for the same reasons as you wouldn't want to always be leaning on someone. Independence. A sense of pride in doing something yourself." She fiddled with her drying cloth on her shoulder. "And also it's about proving to yourself and other people that you can. Mostly to yourself actually."

"Huh."

"Well, hello there." Jo beamed at someone behind him.

Noel sidled up to the barstool beside him. "Eric." Noel gave him a nod and Jo a shy smile. "Miss Jo."

"I see we had the same idea." Eric motioned his drink. "What can I get you?"

"The same please, Jo." Noel was a soft-spoken man, short and ordinary looking. You had to know him to know the magic of Noel, and Eric was glad to say he did. "I'm supposed to lie and pretend I ran into you." Noel grimaced. "But I'm a horrible liar and Pippa sent me to find you. She said you probably needed somebody to talk to."

"Pippa?" Eric had to shake his head at that one. "And you lucked out on finding me here?"

"I texted him." Jo shrugged. "Pippa got to me too."

"Boy, do I feel loved." Eric wanted to get mad at Pippa for interfering, but even as she infuriated you, you had to love Pippa. She only meant the best. And she was right. Someone to talk to would be great. He couldn't have picked anyone better than Noel.

Jo smiled at him. "I'll leave you two alone to your man talk."

Noel sipped his drink.

Eric sipped his.

"Did you watch the game on Tuesday?" Noel broke the silence.

"No." Eric wasn't sure which game, but he knew he hadn't watched one.

Noel nodded. "It was a good game. Stone ended up getting his ass suspended."

"Really?"

"Yup, for twenty games."

"Damn." Eric welcomed the soft pedal Noel was doing. "That's gotta hurt the team."

"For sure." Noel grabbed the menu and scanned it. "I wouldn't want to be Sam Stone right now."

They both sipped their drinks.

"We got some issues on site." Eric opened another topic. "Got some of the crew agitating. Things could get nasty."

Noel shook his head. "You don't want that."

"Nope, but I think I've got it in hand now."

"Good."

Jo popped up in front of them. She glared at Eric and then Noel. "You're both pathetic. You know that?"

Noel nodded.

Not willing to give her the total win, Eric did a sort of head bob. A small enough gesture to give him plausible deniability.

"So, let me help you out." Jo put her elbows on the bar and leaned toward them. "We think Blythe and Eric have had a secret thing going, but nobody's sure for how long or how serious. Eric behaved like a horse's ass to Blythe, and we think it's because she dumped him." She straightened and motioned to them. "Think you can take it from here?"

Not a hope in hell, but Eric gave it his best. "You up for this?"

"I am if you are." Nodding, Noel smiled.

Talking about himself never sat well with Eric. Opening a vein and bleeding to another person felt like hell, but he also needed to share the conflicting mass of crap going on inside him. "You know, my dad. Well, you didn't know him, but my dad used to talk to me."

Noel sipped.

"Matt still believes he and our dad were the closest. Dad leaned on Matt, but he talked to me. I think it was because we were the most alike."

Noel nodded and motioned Jo for another round.

Now for the doozy. The thing he never spoke of and had made a vow not to. But his vow seemed pointless in light of the Blythe-induced shitstorm. "He didn't love my mother." The words hung out there like a newly stripped branch. "Oh, he did when he married her but not at the end."

"Cressy is an interesting woman," Noel said.

Interesting? Nah, his mother was a viper pit of need and manipulation. "Toward the end, he felt trapped. He stayed for us, but he felt trapped all the same. I think when he died, he was happy to be away from her."

Noel stared at him, unblinking. Those pale eyes could pierce right through bullshit into the truth. "Matt know this?"

"Nope. Nobody does but me. And maybe her, but she's sure as fuck not going to tell anyone." The weight of his betrayal to his father pressed down on Eric.

Noel nodded. "They won't hear it from me." He took a deep breath. "Your dad told you this?"

"Yeah." And there were days when Eric wished he hadn't.

"Helluva thing to tell your kid," Noel said. "Not sure a kid should know that about his old man."

Neither was Eric, but he did know, and there was no shutting that door when it had been thrust open. "The thing is, with being the most like him, I never wanted to be him. Trapped."

"Sure, you didn't." Noel pulled a face. "Nobody wants to be trapped."

Eric's third drink must have evaporated, but Jo was there with the bottle topping his glass up.

"I screwed around on Liz," Noel said. "Felt trapped and screwed around."

Most of them had heard Liz's side of the story because Liz tended to make sure you did. Not so much Noel. To hear Liz tell it, she'd been undergoing chemo for breast cancer when Noel had stepped out on her.

"I loved her, you know. Loved her more than I thought I could love another human being." Noel looked at him. "I'm not a looker like you or your brothers. Can't play a sport for crap. Don't even have a huge brain or anything." Looking down at his drink, Noel gave a soft laugh. "The only time I ever swung for the fences was with Liz. I couldn't believe she'd even look at me. Then she married me, and half the time I kept pinching myself to find out if it was real."

Talking about Noel was better than digging around in his crap, so Eric gave him a grunt of encouragement.

"Then she got sick." Noel's voice thickened. "And suddenly it was like I'd stumbled across a unicorn and it was dying. I panicked. Felt trapped by my own heart. Messed around and lost her."

Damn that felt a shade too familiar. Not the messing around part. He and Blythe had never talked about being exclusive but they both had been for those brief periods they'd been together.

He owed Miranda a call. There weren't going to be any more dinners.

"What did you do?" He knew the ending, but Eric wanted to hear the middle parts from Noel.

"Woke up one morning and found myself alone." Noel shrugged. "Not for sex. Sex isn't that hard to find."

According to Liz, and Eric really wished he didn't know this about the guy, but Noel had top of the line equipment and made it count.

"I missed her," Noel said. "Even her waking up beside me on Sunday morning with breath like a goat and making me get her coffee. I missed everything. Every crazy little detail that made up that woman."

They both sipped and contemplated the view.

Noel's story cut a little close to home.

"I convinced myself that I would be fine without her." Noel chuckled. "And ended up lonely as hell instead."

"What did you do?"

"I begged," Noel said. "I groveled, and I kept coming around and telling her I was here to stay, and I wouldn't screw up again."

Eric felt like such a whiner even voicing his question, but Noel wasn't the kind to judge. "What made you think you had the right to? What if you couldn't give her what she needed?"

"I'm still not sure that I can." Noel shook his head. "Don't think I ever will be. But here's what it came down to." He tapped his forefinger on the bar. "One day, another guy was going to step into the gap, and be the reason she smiled. You know that smile?" Noel glanced at Eric. "The one you know that you put on her face, and it makes your chest feel huge?"

Shit. Fuck. Damn.

Eric did know that smile. He'd given up his rights to that smile.

And why exactly was that?

"What if I can't give her what she needs?" He floated the question out there.

Noel laughed. "You have to ask yourself, firstly, why can't you, and secondly, if you can accept it and live with it when some other man does?"

They didn't say much more after that. They finished their drinks and paid Jo, not forgetting the huge tip she would have chased them into the parking lot for.

Not wanting to drive with four drinks under his belt, he decided to walk home. It was a long walk, but he needed to clear his head.

Here was the thing, the question had popped into his mind as Noel spoke and now wouldn't go away.

What if he tried?

At some point in his teens he'd made up his mind he wasn't the type who stayed. Desperate not to fulfill his father's legacy, he'd made a decision and stuck to it.

Now, here's where the issue got sticky. At about that point, Laura had done what she'd done to him and affirmed the decision. At the same time, however, an angel in a denim miniskirt and tiny shirt had also dropped right into his lap.

Angel in a denim miniskirt? Yeah, he wasn't much of a drinker.

However, the fact remained, that for as long as he'd been telling himself he would never settle down, there had been Blythe in his life. Sure she hung around on the periphery but she was always there.

Two young girls walked up the hill toward him. Dressed in jeans and band T-shirts for bands he'd bet his life they couldn't tell him one song of. Both girls looked at him as he passed, and then giggled as they walked away.

Girls about the same age as Blythe when she had walked into his life with a cup of coffee and a smile in her eyes that made him unburden his soul to her.

He turned and watched the two girls saunter away from him. So young and perched on the cusp of so much to come.

Had he robbed Blythe of those years?

"Get over here, sweet thing."

"Why?"

"I'll show you when you get here."

She said she loved him, and on some level, he'd known that, but it had been more convenient to pretend she didn't and avoid making the decision to end things. His cowardice taunted him. He'd not wanted to face the way she felt because he liked having her around too much.

And now she was gone, and he sure as hell didn't like that. Despite what he'd said to her earlier, he wasn't reconciled to letting her walk away from him. Then there was what Noel had said.

He'd given Blythe the all-clear to go out there and find some dickhead to marry her, see her beautiful smile, slide into bed beside her every night, make her laugh. Make love to her.

Not a fucking chance.

And here was the big question, the big what if.

What if he could be that dickhead?

Chapter Twenty-Four

Even with Dixie's assurances that Brett didn't live at the house and would be at work now, Blythe's hand still slipped, slick with sweat, on the steering wheel, and her heart beat uncomfortably hard. But it had been weeks since she'd seen Carly. Her brothers wouldn't check that Carly ate or care if she didn't. God alone knew what had happened to her personal hygiene.

As Carly didn't leave the house for anything, Blythe had to come to her.

Dixie stood in the yard, waiting for her. The old bathtub had been hauled away, along with the rusted out relics of cars that someone planned to fix someday.

Someone had mowed the grass and cleared the weeds from the walkway.

Dixie caught sight of her and whistled. "Well now, lookee there at you, Miss Thang."

"Hey Dixie." Blythe still kept an eye out for Brett.

"You look amazing." Dixie picked up a tendril of her hair. "Ah-maze-ing. Where did you get all this done?"

"Pippa St. Amor gave me a bit of a makeover." She walked onto the porch.

The clothes washer was working, rocking the porch as it did. Judging from her life there, she had believed herself the only one who ever did laundry.

"Brett." Dixie jerked her head.

Blythe's heart stopped and she swung around.

"Not here." Dixie snorted and nudged her. "I wouldn't do that to you, but he told Bo and Becker to get on with the laundry."

Blythe's eyebrows hit her hairline. "And did he make them clear up the yard as well?"

"You know it." Dixie laughed. "You could hear them bitching about it from our place."

Following Dixie into the house, Blythe looked about her.

The house looked like it had been cleaned. Not perfect, but coats actually hung on the rack, and several pairs of large motorcycle boots were neatly lined up beneath them.

"Wow!" The kitchen looked cleaner than when she had lived there. "Brett again?"

"Yup."

"That doesn't sound like Brett."

"You'd be surprised." Dixie filled the coffee maker and started it.

Blythe pointed to it. "Is that new?"

"Yup." She spooned grounds into the top. "Brett threatened to break Barron's legs if he came anywhere near it."

"What did Barron do?" Blythe pictured a throw down of epic proportions.

"Screwed if I know." Dixie shrugged, flipped the switch, and then leaned her back against the scrubbed counter. "He gave Brett a bit of lip about that and the tidying, and Brett threw him out."

Blythe gaped. She couldn't help it. Barron had been Brett's mini-me, then later his sidekick. The only reason Barron hadn't followed Brett into prison was because Brett had taken the fall for both of them, and then had made Barron swear not to speak up.

"Right?" Dixie shook her head. "Never would have thought I saw that coming. Barron tried to throw down as well, but Brett wasn't having none of that. He lit right into him." She pulled a face. "I'm sorry, honey, but they broke your grandma's bureau in the fight that followed."

"That's okay." When you had history like she did, you didn't get sentimentally attached to stuff. Plus, she still couldn't make sense of Barron and Brett falling out.

"Look who's here." Bo slouched in the doorway and sneered at her. "Aren't you all fancy. Sure you want to be here and risk getting your new duds dirty?"

Blythe knew better than to flinch or back down. "Hi Bo. You look just the same."

"Then you aren't paying close enough attention." Dixie chuckled. "Brett lined him and Becker up outside and hosed them down. Said they couldn't come back in this house until they didn't stink no more."

Bo flushed. "Watch yourself, Dixie. Ben ain't here right now, and he wouldn't do shit if I taught you some manners anyhow."

"Nah." Dixie sashayed up to Bo and poked him in the chest with one silver acrylic nail. "You watch yourself, Bo Barrows, because your mean big brother has his eye on you, and he won't like the way you're speaking to me or our Blythie."

In Blythe's case, Brett would probably ask her other brothers to hold her while he did the manner teaching, but Brett had had a soft spot for Dixie. Blythe had once overheard him tell Carly that Dixie would be the making of Ben. Even at his most violent, Brett had been smarter than the rest, and with moments of kindness that made him impossible to read from one day to the next.

"Brett was real interested to hear where you live now." Bo

looked sly. "Wanted to hear all about that new, fancy place you got yourself, and how you and Wheeler and Kim was living there now. Like the three of you was better than the rest of us."

"I don't think that," she said. Bo didn't scare her. He was a loudmouth and a jerk but he lacked the streak of pure mean that Brett and Barron shared. "I pretty much know it."

"Bitch." Bo curled his lip up.

Blythe didn't break the stare down. "And Brett has already been 'round my place, so you got nothing."

"Shouldn't you be running along?" Dixie shooed him with her hands. "I would hate to be you telling Brett how you spent another day lying around the house when you should be doing that job he got for you."

"I got the day off." Bo sneered at Dixie. "Shows how much you know about it."

Blythe gaped at Dixie, for the second time today. "Brett got them jobs?"

"He sure did." Dixie fetched coffee cups out and set them on a tray. "Told them they couldn't live here unless they started chipping in for food and stuff. Get this." Dixie leaned in with mischief dancing in her eyes. "Brett has them working construction at the same site where he works security." Dixie chuckled. "Same place Barron was fired from the week before."

Blythe's belly twisted. Eric had himself embroiled in all her brothers it seemed. The only one missing was Bart and he was serving time still.

She had warned him, or tried to. That hadn't gone as planned at all, and she couldn't risk a repeat.

"Blythe?" Carly appeared behind Bo and peered at her through surprisingly lucid eyes. "Is that you?"

"Hi, Mom."

Bo shifted to the side and Carly walked into the kitchen.

Her bathrobe was clean, and her hair brushed. She had

more color in her face but was still desperately thin. There was something else different about her that Blythe couldn't put her finger on.

"I'm okay." Carly slunk over to the table and sat. "You know I get all these headaches, but I live with them. I don't like to complain." She leaned over the coffee cups. "Is there one for me?"

"Sure, Ma." Dixie gave her a smile. She was always kind to Carly, which is one of the reasons Blythe had always liked Dixie. "I even brought some of those cookies you like so much."

"I'm not sure I can eat." Carly grimaced. "I don't know if my stomach can take it."

Dixie put a plate of cookies on the table in front of her. "Well, you think about it and if you decide you might be up to it, give one a try."

Bo leaned in.

"There's a cup here for you too," Dixie said. "And you're welcome to join us as soon as you stop acting like a jackass to Blythe."

He muttered but flung himself over to the table and took a chair.

"Is Brett here?" Carly perked up and looked about her.

Blythe certainly hoped not.

"No, Ma. He's at work," Dixie said. "He'll be home later, and he promised to take you for a drive."

"I don't know." Carly chewed her lip. Her glance bounced around the kitchen. "I don't feel right leaving this house. What if I have a fit or something?"

Bo snorted. "You won't have a fit. Not unless he drives you past a liquor store."

"Hey." Dixie cracked him across the head. "She's trying."

It hit Blythe what was different about her mother. The constant smell of cigarettes and alcohol wasn't clinging to Carly.

"Like that's going to stick," Bo said.

"Don't be a dick." Dixie snatched the cookies away from Bo. "Your ma is trying and that's a lot more than I can say for you."

"Dixie," Bo whined. "I don't mean nothing by it. Just trying to be funny is all."

"How is Kim?" Carly's hands shook so badly, she could barely lift the coffee mug. The desperation to know in her eyes twisted Blythe's heart.

"She's really good, Mom." Blythe steadied the cup so Carly could sip her coffee. "She's going to a regular kindergarten, and she loves it. They tell me she's one of the smartest in her class."

Carly's eyes filled with tears. In a drunken doldrum, Carly had once confessed her fears to Blythe about Kim and fetal alcohol syndrome.

"She looks just like you." Blythe tucked a piece of hair behind Carly's ear and helped her put her mug down. "She has your exact hair. So pretty, and your eyes."

"Brett said if I work real hard on not drinking, he would talk to you about letting me see her."

The plea in Carly's eyes yanked Blythe's heart out. She really hadn't taken Kim from the house to hurt her mother. Incompetent mother though she was, Carly still loved all her children. "If you work hard on your not drinking, of course you can see her. She misses you."

"She does?"

God help her, but surely a little white lie couldn't hurt. Maybe it would give Carly a life raft to cling to, because despite their history, deep inside Blythe was a little girl who desperately wanted to see her mother recover. "Of course she does. You're her mama, aren't you?"

"Yes, I am." Carly sniffed and drew strength from a hidden reservoir and sat up straighter. "I am her mother, and a girl needs her mother. I'm gonna make sure I come right for my little girl."

Not for your other little girl, though. Blythe didn't tolerate self-pity but there were times when it snuck up on her. "That's right, Mom. A girl needs her mother."

She didn't stay much longer. Carly drank her coffee, ate a couple of cookies and went back to bed. Bo managed to be silently belligerent, which she took as a win.

Dixie walked her out. "You doing okay?"

"Yes." Blythe managed a big smile. "I'm not a big fan of coming back here."

"I get that." Dixie snorted. "You look great, no doubt about that but you feel…sad."

Blythe had never told anyone in her family about Eric. "I'm fine."

Dixie studied her, as if debating whether to push the matter or not. She nodded. "If you say so."

Becker rode in as she reached her car.

He passed her without even a wave, which was fine by Blythe.

"Listen, about Brett." Dixie leaned on Blythe's open car door. "I know how you feel about him, and I know why. Don't blame you one bit. But he does seem different."

"Really?" Blythe didn't bother to hide her skepticism. Just like the Pats of this world, the Bretts didn't change. He might be getting everyone in the house moving and shaking, but she'd lay money on him having an ulterior motive.

Dixie grinned as if she read Blythe's mind. "I don't blame you for thinking I'm talking shit. Like you, I grew up around here, and there's only so many times you can trust that people turn over a new leaf. Only so many times that new leaf slaps you in the face before you wise up."

"I can't take that chance around Kim," Blythe said. "So far, she's had a Brett-free life, and that's a good thing."

Dixie nodded and stepped back. "You know best what

you're doing, and I'm not going to argue with you. I'm only telling you what I've seen."

Blythe kissed her cheek. "You're a sweetheart, Dixie. Ben is lucky to have you."

"Don't I know it." Dixie snorted. "And I remind him of that fact every chance I can."

Laughing, Blythe started her car and drove away. She would be on time to fetch Kim, and she left Will a message to say as much.

A red pickup headed down the road toward her. An older model, it looked like it needed some love and attention.

The pickup drew level with her, and the driver turned his head.

They recognized each other instantly.

Brett's head whipped around, and he stared.

Blythe froze and snapped her eyes away. Her heart jumped into her throat.

In her rearview mirror, the pickup slowed and pulled to the shoulder.

She grabbed her phone and went for Eric's number. Shit! She'd deleted it days ago. Will would be no good.

The pickup sat by the side of the road, and then pulled back into its lane and carried on its way.

Blythe's breath rushed out of her mouth. Shit, that had been close. Too close.

As soon as she could, she pulled into a strip mall parking lot and stopped her car. She took a few deep breaths to regain her composure.

A knock on her car window made her shriek.

Chase Gunning stared back at her. "Blythe?"

She rolled her window down, relief making her giddy. "Chase, you scared me."

"Are you okay?" Chase frowned at her. "You're sheet white."

"I got a fright." She managed to string words together. "It

was something on the road that scared me." A six-six, two hundred pound something with a bad attitude. The strip mall she had pulled into didn't seem Chase's sort of place. "What are you doing here?"

"Rescuing you." He gave her a disarming grin, and then he said, "No, I have a few associates I was seeing."

"Around here?" Blythe knew what sort of people hung around there, and Chase didn't belong.

He waved a dismissive hand. "From way back. More of a social thing."

"Okay." Blythe's pulse headed for normal. "Thanks for checking on me. I need to get going."

"It's time to pick up your sister, isn't it?" Chase checked his watch.

"Yes." It surprised her that he'd remembered that detail. "I'll see you tomorrow evening."

"Right." Chase stepped back and shoved his hands in his pockets. "I was…um…wondering if you have a no fraternization rule with your clients."

"Sorry?" She hadn't seen that coming. "Um, no, I mean yes, I do have a rule about that. I don't fraternize."

"That's what I thought." Chase gave a curt nod. "But if you did…"

She needed to shut him down. Even if she didn't date her clients, she was far from ready. Keeping her tone firm but gentle, she said, "But I don't, Chase."

Chapter Twenty-Five

It took Blythe three days to stop checking over her shoulder all the time, and another two to be comfortable leaving her house without fearing Brett lurking in the shadows. She spoke to the kindergarten about him and left clear instructions that Kim was not to be entrusted to him.

By the next week, she had relaxed as much as she could with Brett out of prison. It probably wouldn't be long before he landed himself in trouble again. He may have Dixie fooled but Blythe had seen right into his cold, black heart, and she really didn't want another peek.

She arrived at the gym to train one of her favorite clients. Bonnie had come to her severely overweight with a number of related health problems. Two years later Bonnie was off her blood pressure medication and was no longer heading for diabetes.

Clients like Bonnie made Blythe love her job.

She walked over to the treadmill where Bonnie was already warming up. "Good morning."

"Good morning." Bonnie beamed at her. "Down another two pounds this morning."

Blythe held her hand up. "Congratulations. You're killing

it."

"Thought I'd get myself a box of donuts to celebrate." Bonnie winked at her.

"Agrippina." Phi's unmistakable voice vibrated across the gym. "Why, this place is a veritable smorgasbord of delicious young flesh."

Bonnie almost missed her step on the treadmill. "Who is that?"

"That's one of the best ladies in the world." Blythe didn't want to modulate the huge grin that spread over her face.

Phi sailed through the gym with Pippa in her wake. "If I'd only known." She winked at Randy, who almost dropped a forty-pound weight on his foot. "All this time, and I have remained in ignorance. I knew there had to be a reason people came to these places."

"They come here to stay in shape, Phi." Pippa had Jasmine in her arms. "Not to be gawped at."

"If they do not want to be gawped at, they should wear more clothing." Phi stopped to study Connor, who was busy training for an upcoming fight. "Well, aren't you a sight for sore eyes."

Connor blushed, and Blythe took pity on the rest of the gym.

"I'll be right back," she said to Bonnie and approached Phi and Pippa. "Were you looking for me?"

"Blythe, darling." Phi threw open her arms and enveloped her in patchouli. "How lovely to see you." She put Blythe at arm's length. "You look fabulous. Doesn't she look fabulous, Agrippina?"

"She looked fabulous before." Pippa leaned over and kissed Blythe on the cheek. "I have no idea why I thought bringing her here would be a good idea."

"I can hear you." Phi breathed a deep, happy sigh. "I do so love it here." She waggled her fingers at a group of college students working on their quads. "Keep it up, boys."

"That's what she said." Pippa snickered.

Phi whirled around, her purple, pleated caftan belling out around her in a jingle of tiny bells sewn along the bottom. "Did you tell her?"

"Not yet." Pippa handed Jasmine over to Phi. "Keep your great grandmother out of trouble," she said to her daughter.

"Tell her." Phi shifted from foot to foot. "We came all this way to tell her." She raised her voice. "Into this place, which although is filled with lovely looking boys, is also a touch malodorous."

Pippa rolled her eyes. "I'll apologize to the management."

"No need." Blythe enjoyed the Phi show too much to take offense, and she had the feeling everyone else did as well. "He needs to get stronger extractor fans."

Pippa's green eyes sparkled. "It turns out Bernie, the cameraman, got a mite carried away taking footage of you." She lowered her voice. "We suspect he might have a bit of a crush."

Heat climbed Blythe's cheeks.

"And Chris Germaine saw the footage of you."

Everybody who owned a television knew who Chris Germaine was, the first lady of talk show television. She was also the power behind Pippa's show, *Your Best You.*

"Chris loved everything about you," Pippa said, and Blythe forgot to breathe for a second. "And she's never wrong about who is going to work on the small screen and who isn't."

Blythe was sure she looked all kinds of stupid with a goofy grin all over her face. "Thanks for letting me know. That's very flattering."

"That's not the best part." Phi poked Pippa. "Tell her the best part."

"I was getting to that." Pippa threw her grandmother a fond, exasperated glance. "Chris wants you to take a regular role in the new season."

The words entered Blythe's brain and sat there like

discombobulated goo. "She wants what?"

"She wants you to be part of the show. A feature."

"Oh." Bonnie breathed from beside her. "Blythe would be wonderful at that."

She had no idea when Bonnie had arrived, but she must have heard most of the conversation. "On television?"

"I know." Phi grimaced. "Vulgar little box that it is, but it's what answers for the glory of the stage in this new world."

"It's strange that its vulgarity doesn't stop you from spending hours watching your soaps," Pippa said.

Phi looked at her with bemusement. "I must stay current, Agrippina."

"God, that name." Pippa rolled her eyes. "Anyway, here's the name of my agent." She handed Blythe a card. "If you want to go forward with this, then you need someone to negotiate good terms for you."

Feeling floored, Blythe stared at the card. The letters danced in front of her and made no sense. She didn't have the first idea of how much money to ask for. "Thank you."

"Will you do it?" Bonnie leaned into her. "I really think you should do it."

Pippa gave her a kind smile and squeezed her arm. "Look, I know this is all rather sudden, but I wanted you to know before Phi broadcast the news everywhere."

"I'll have you know I'm the very model of discretion," Phi said, and then collapsed into her raunchy laugh. "No, I am not. Not even the tiniest bit."

They left shortly after, and Blythe put the conversation in a tiny box in the back of her mind to be taken out later and pored over.

She got through her session with Bonnie, and then she shut herself in her office and let the excitement ooze out. Pippa had offered her a great opportunity. If it worked out, who knew where she would be a year from now.

She wanted to share the news, and there was only one

person she could think of sharing it with. Before she could overthink it, she found an old business card of Eric's and dialed his cell.

Sharing goods news was part of being friends, right?

"Sweet…sorry. Hey, Blythe." His voice poured over her like warm honey. "How are you?"

"Is now a good time?"

He paused. "Now is always a good time for you."

She didn't know what to make of the hesitation, so she told him her news quickly.

Eric's delight was unfettered and made the whole thing seem more real. "Call Pippa's agent," he said. "Make sure she gets you a good deal."

"I will."

"You'll be fantastic, Blythe. I know you will."

Tears prickled behind her lids. His faith in her was humbling. "You think?"

"I know." He sounded so certain, and Blythe was glad she'd given in to the instinct to call him. "Look, sweet thing." He sounded distracted now. "I'm delighted for you, I really am, but can I call you back later?"

Blythe needed to unblock his number for that to happen. "Sure."

BLYTHE'S CALL couldn't have come at a worse time, but after interminable radio silence, she'd finally called, and it would have taken an act of God—and a hefty one—to stop him from taking her call.

The angry group of men facing him ran a close second to that.

"Interesting time to take a call," Brett said from beside him. "I take it that was my sister?"

Eric wasn't going to answer Brett's questions about Blythe.

He'd given the man a job, and so far, Brett had been doing it really well. He would not, however, betray Blythe's determination to keep her new life as separate from Brett as she could.

He jerked his head at the tight knot of workers. "What's the problem?"

Brett had called him to site because the workers had all downed tools.

"Our friends from the other day have been making trouble," Brett said. "They've been issuing threats to anyone who turns up for work."

"Shit!" This damn job had a curse on it. "Any sign they're following through on those threats?"

"For sure." Brett looked grim. "They beat up Angel last night. He spent the night in hospital, and it'll be a while before he can get back to work."

Angel's wife had just had a new baby. Eric would make sure the family was cared for while Angel recovered. "And these guys are scared?"

"Yup." Brett folded his arms. "These are the ones who showed up, and they want more money for doing it."

Eric didn't know an expletive bad enough for what he felt. "I can't do that. It's not in the budget."

"Then I really hope you're great with a hammer," Brett said. "Because nobody is going to risk working on this site without you making it worth their while."

He and Matt had to get to the bottom of this. Someone was pulling the strings here and making this job as difficult as possible. "Let me talk to my brother, see what he says."

Brett grunted. "What do you want me to do about these guys?"

"We'll pay them for the day, the normal rate and let them know our decision." Eric turned away from the workers and approached his truck.

He needed to get his head out his ass and deal with this situation. He'd taken his eye off the ball, and someone was taking advantage of that. He also needed to speak to Matt about what was going on. Shielding him while he dealt with his new baby wasn't working out.

"Eric." Brett jogged his way. "Wait up."

Eric opened his door and waited.

"I don't think you're coming to site right now is helping," Brett said.

It might be true but it pissed him off. "This is my site."

"Yeah." Brett didn't look even a bit impressed by that. "But you're going to get your ass beat if you keep coming here like this. The situation is getting ugly, and I'm not enough protection for you."

"I don't need anyone's protection." Eric might not have spent his adult life in prison, but that didn't make him some kind of bantam weight.

Eric stared at him. "Look. I've been hearing things. It's not about you. It's about what's going to go down here is only going to get worse before it gets better." Brett rubbed his nape and sighed. "I'm on parole, Eric. There's a limit to what I can do without violating the terms of that parole."

"What are you suggesting then?" Eric forced his temper back. "I can't walk away from this job."

"Let me handle this," Brett said. "Let me talk to the principle players in this thing and sort out what's what."

Eric really didn't know if he could trust Brett that far. So far, he'd been great but Brett was talking about a whole other level of trust here. "I'm not sure that's a good idea."

"And I get that." Brett didn't take offense. "And I understand why you would say that. You have no reason to trust me, but you might not have a choice."

Motioning him to carry on, Eric tried to keep an open mind.

"Nobody is going to talk to you. You're the suit in this situation. I'm like them. In the trenches with them, and they'll be far more likely to talk to me."

Brett made sense. "To what end?"

"So we can find out who is fucking with us like this," Brett said. "With all due respect to them, these are working men. Men who need their paycheck to feed their families. What happened here the other day didn't make sense."

Eric had been having much the same thought.

"Ray Gallagher is a dickhead." Brett mentioned the chief agitator from the other day. "But he also has three kids and a wife. He's also not the sort to create hell because he can." Brett gave a rueful chuckle. "And believe me when I tell you I know the sort. I've been locked up with them for the last few years."

Eric didn't hire the crews, Cooper did, but Cooper didn't have a history of hiring troublemakers. "You're thinking Ray and his buddies are getting money from somewhere?"

"That's what I'm thinking." Brett nodded. "Give me a chance to ask around and see if anything floats to the surface."

He didn't have to like it, or even fully trust Brett, but Eric was out of options. "How long will you need?"

"I'll know in a day or two if I'm going to find anything," Brett said.

"Okay." Eric held out his hand. "Do it."

Brett nodded and grabbed Eric's open door. "She okay?"

It took Eric a moment, and then he got it. "You know she doesn't want anything to do with you, and that extends to me not telling you anything."

"I hear she doesn't want much to do with you either," Brett said, his eyes going steely. "You make sure you do right by her."

Eric found that almost too much to take, and he held Brett's angry gaze. "It seems to me that if anyone needs to do right by Blythe, it's you."

"I'm trying," Brett said.

Eric almost laughed. "Me too."

Chapter Twenty-Six

A phone ringing at 2 am is rarely a good thing. Eric rolled over and snatched his cell from the bedside table. "Yup."

"Eric." Cooper sounded tense, and Eric's lingering sleep fog cleared. "We've got trouble."

"Tell me." He'd already figured as much.

"The Highgate site is on fire. Someone saw it from the road and called me."

Eric leaped out of bed and grabbed the nearest pair of pants. "Did you call 911?"

"Right before I called you," Cooper said. "They're on their way, but you know how far away they are and we don't have the hook up for that fire hydrant yet."

"Fuck!" Eric grabbed his shoes and a shirt and ran. Ghost Falls moved slowly, and they'd put in the permitting months ago. "I'm on my way."

"Eric, what good do you think—?"

"I'm on my way." That was his money catching fire on the hillside above town. "Call Matt and let him know."

From the car he called Nate.

"Eric." Nate answered immediately, sounding alert. "The call already came through, but I'm about forty minutes away."

"Get there when you can." Because he had the feeling Nate's services were going to be needed before this was done.

Breaking more than a few traffic laws, he gunned the Jag through town and up into the hills. He tried the number Brett had given him, but it rang and rang, and went to voicemail.

The smell of smoke reached him first, and then the orange smudge on the horizon as he approached the site. He climbed out of his car and could only stare for a moment.

The entire project was ablaze. All six new builds and the model home. The fire truck would arrive in time to make sure the blaze didn't spread, but with bare open ground all around, that didn't seem to be an immediate danger.

Eric walked closer to the roaring beast that had been the Highgate project. He felt numb inside, helpless to do anything but stare.

A dark form lurched into his path. "Eric?"

"Yes."

"It's him!"

More figures coalesced around him in the night broken up by macabre orange and black shadows.

Two of them grabbed his arms.

Eric kicked out and hit flesh. With a grunt, one of his arms was released.

He swung and hit the other guy restraining him.

The man in front connected a fist to his jaw.

Eric tasted blood and punched. In the fractured dark he couldn't make out much but limbs swinging and solid parts, which he aimed for.

His fist hit something, and someone swore.

A heavy weight pounded his back and drove him to his knees. Rocks bit into his knees as he fell but the others were on him, fists and boots swinging. He took a blow to the ribs that winded him.

He kicked and connected.

A man grunted.

A punch to his kidneys had him collapsing. Then a blow to the back of his head that exploded his vision in starbursts of light.

There were too many of them. This was going to be bad, but he'd leave them something to remember him by.

Blows and kicks came from all sides. One explosion of pain gave way to another. His nose cartilage crunched, broken for sure.

A face hovered in front of his. Lips drawn back in a snarl.

Eric braced.

The guy disappeared and another set of legs joined the melee.

Suddenly, there was an opening in the bodies around him, and Eric crawled to his feet. His body screamed its objections, but he kept hitting, fighting free.

A large form stood side by side with him, handing out the punishment and clearing a space for Eric to stand.

"You okay?" Brett asked.

"Nope." Eric spat blood. "But I sure am glad to see you."

Brett swung his fist, bone crunched, and someone shrieked. "Told you not to come here." He punctuated each word with a blow.

"Fuck that." Eric kicked a knee, and then a shot to the groin. "That's my money burning."

"You've got fucking insurance." Brett pounded on a man until he went to his knees. "Haven't you?"

"I've got insurance." Eric grabbed someone by the back of the head and brought his knee up. A satisfying crunch and groan followed.

His ribs screamed at him, and his legs shook. He didn't have much more in him.

A siren wailed.

"Fuck this. Let's blow." Eric recognized Ray's voice. Big surprise!

Then he and Brett were free. Three figures scurried away, dragging two more with them.

Eric jackknifed over and vomited.

Brett tapped his shoulder and handed him a bottle of water. "This will help. Only take a small sip."

Not wanting to humiliate himself further, Eric did as he was told.

The firetruck slid to a stop in a cloud of dust, and firemen hopped off.

"Anyone inside?" A fireman appeared in front of them.

Brett shook his head. "Nah, but my buddy needs medical attention."

"I'm good." If Brett Barrows could tough it out so could he.

"For fuck's sake." Brett shook his head and spoke to the fireman. "He was jumped by five guys. He needs medical attention."

Matt shouldered his way through. "Eric! Jesus." He turned to Brett. "What happened?"

"I'm guessing the fire was set on purpose to get him up here," Brett said. "I was over the far side of the site trying to clear some brush away so it wouldn't spread."

"And you just happened to be around." A path cleared through the bodies to admit Nate. Flashing red and blue lights played over faces.

"I hired him to work security here." Eric might cry if he didn't sit down soon, and he didn't put up too much resistance when an EMT slid his shoulder beneath his arm.

"Can you walk?" the EMT asked.

Eric nodded, not at all sure he could but determined not to wimp out in front of Brett.

Nate followed them to the ambulance. "Brett was here as security?"

"Sure." He lowered his aching body onto the open back of

the ambulance. "I would say he's something of a security expert."

Someone snorted a laugh, he thought it might be Brett.

"I'll need a statement from you." Nate evil-eyed Brett.

Brett nodded. "Just what I always wanted, more time in a police station."

This time Nate cracked a smile. "We give you coffee on this side of the bars."

"Bet you keep the donuts for yourself though," Brett said.

If his ribs weren't yelling at him, Eric might have laughed.

Matt hovered by his side. "Let's get a doctor to check you out."

"Nah, I'm—"

"You should go," Brett said. "You were holding your own when I got here, but five guys can do a lot of damage." His grin turned evil. "Most of which you won't feel until later and tomorrow."

"Swell!" Ego aside, seeing a doctor right now was not a bad idea.

Nate watched him stand with a grim expression. "Any idea who did this and why?"

"I recognized one voice, but not their faces." Eric took a moment to catch his breath before attempting to climb into the ambulance. "I've been working on why for a while now."

"Anything to do with you?" Nate swung his gaze to Brett.

"The trouble started before Brett got here." Eric didn't want Nate blaming Brett. "In fact, I might not be standing here if Brett hadn't come along when he did."

"Which is another thing." Nate rested his fists on his hips. "What were you doing here in the middle of the night?"

Eric wondered the same, but he couldn't let Brett take any more shit. "I told you, he worked security."

"All night?" Nate frowned. "With no place to sit or get a cup of coffee."

Brett took a deep breath. "I've been sleeping in the model home."

"What?" Matt stared at him. "Why would you do that?"

"Couple of reasons." Brett shrugged.

When Nate spoke, it was not a request. "Care to share them?"

"First off, the trouble has been growing on site," Brett said. "I've been hearing rumors that made me guess they might try something. I wanted to be here to stop it."

"And?"

"And I'm an ex-con." Brett met Nate's hard stare. "You've been sheriff for long enough to know how hard it is to get back on your feet. Especially in this town. You also know what my family is like." Brett shook his head. "Sometimes I need to get out of that house and get my head right."

Nobody argued with him about that, and Eric sank onto the ambulance stretcher bed with a whimper of relief.

An EMT bustled around him with an oxygen mask.

"I don't need that." Eric moved it away from him.

"Stop being a baby." Matt climbed up beside him and took the mask. He placed it over Eric's mouth. "Now let's see if you've got something to cry about."

Matt waited until they were moving before he asked his next question. "You gonna tell me what's really going on?"

"The trouble on site has been escalating." Eric tried to keep it light but the look in Matt's eye said he didn't believe it.

What the hell. His brother deserved to know and this protecting him from the truth thing had gotten old. He had once accused Matt of not sharing the family burdens, and now he was doing the same thing. Also he owed Brett Barrows big, like his life big.

BLYTHE PLAYED it cool and professional as she met Chase in the lobby for his session the next night. It wasn't the first time a client had asked her out, and she wanted to dispel any awkwardness.

"Blythe." Chase met her by his treadmill and climbed on. He motioned between them. "Is this going to be awkward?"

Clearly they'd been on the same page and she laughed. "Not for me."

"Not for me either." He smiled ruefully. "It's not the first time I've been shot down." He grimaced and started up with the machine. "Probably won't be the last either."

"Somehow, I don't think you get turned down that often." Chase has a lot to offer and maybe if she'd had one small part of herself to share with someone else, she might have considered it. Client or no client.

Chase grunted and laughed. "That's not always a good thing. Ask any of my exes."

They finished on the treadmill and went to the weights section before Chase spoke again. "I didn't ask you what you were doing in that part of town last night."

Funny, she'd had much the same thought. "I live there. At least, I used to live there. I was raised there. So I went to visit my mother last night." Overshare, much!

Giving her a long look, Chase completed his set before he spoke. "And yet you ended up here."

"I didn't get that far," she said, and not nearly as far as she wanted to get.

Chase shook his head and took a sip of water. "Don't knock what you've achieved. I know from personal experience that breaking away from your past take guts and determination. It isn't easy."

"You came from the wrong side of the tracks? I would never have guessed." Blythe showed him what she wanted him to do next.

"I go out of my way to hide it," Chase said. "My mother was a good woman, but she had me at fifteen without my father in sight. When she did marry, she chose badly. He used to get drunk and beat the crap out of her." Chase racked the weights. "I swore I would get us out of there. I was only partially successful."

"What happened?" This side of Chase opened up a totally different man.

His expression softened. "She didn't make it. She got sick before I could make enough money to get her away from that bastard." He smiled. "But at least by then I'd made enough money to make sure she could see good doctors and that she was comfortable in the end." Looking away from her he cleared his throat. "Cancer took her."

"I'm sorry." Most of the time Blythe kept a strict physical distance between her and her clients, but his story touched her, and she squeezed Chase's shoulder. "Thank you for telling me."

"Not really sure why I did." Chase picked up a set of weights. "It's just when you said where you were from it made me think about Ma."

"Mine is housebound," Blythe said. "And she has a drinking problem, so I have to go and see her."

"You mentioned brothers the other day," Chase said.

"I have eight of them." She laughed at Chase's horrified expression. "And one little sister, as you know."

He nodded and carried on with his weight set.

Something about knowing they shared a similar past made it easier to talk to him. "Most of my brothers take after our father, which is not a good thing. But Will, the youngest brother, is going somewhere. He's been saving up for college since he was thirteen."

Chase looked taken with that.

Blythe found herself telling him more. "He's part of how I managed to get out. Partly, he inspired me to change what I didn't like, and partly because I wanted to get him out with me."

"And you took the little sister with you too?"

Blythe nodded.

"You're quite a woman, Blythe Barrows." Chase's look warmed her deep down. His admiration had nothing to do with her looks or being attracted to her. "It seems we had more in common than I thought."

They worked in silence for a while.

"Look." Chase stopped and put his weights down. "I'm gonna put my cards on the table here."

Blythe tensed at his direction and the renewed interest in Chase's expression. "I'm sorry, Chase, but I—"

"You don't date your clients." He held his hands up. "I know that, but I also sense there's something more behind the no dating than just me being a client."

He was right but Blythe wasn't going to talk about Eric. Especially not since Chase had business dealings with Eric.

"I'm older than you," Chase said. "But hopefully not old enough to be creepy. And I really like you." He grinned. "For more than the fact that you're about the most beautiful girl I've ever met. If whatever this other thing is that's influencing your decision goes away, or you change your mind, let me know."

"I don't think that's going to happen." She didn't feel threatened or cornered. Chase kept it honest and straight-forward.

"But if it does." Chased picked up his weights. "You let me know. I think we could be good together. I understand where you came from, Blythe. I can understand what you want out of life."

He made some pretty bold claims, but they didn't sound outrageous. She couldn't give him false hope. "It's not going to change for a long time."

"And I'm not going to wait," Chase said. "I'm too much

of a realist for that. I just want you to know that I'm interested. Very interested, and if the timing gets right, I would like to explore this thing."

Calling what they had between them a thing seemed a little presumptuous to Blythe. They were client and trainer and had discovered a common history. Still, Chase's interest made her think. There would be life after Eric, and for the first time she could consider that future having a man in it.

Chapter Twenty-Seven

Blythe took a call from an unknown number the next morning. "Hello."

"Hi, Blythe. It's Bella. Bella Evans." She took a breath. "I used to be Bella Erikson."

As if she knew any other Bellas. "How are you?"

"I'm good." Bella warmed up. "I didn't know if you'd recognize my voice."

Blythe laughed. "Even though we went to school together for most of our lives?"

"Fair point." Bella laughed with her, but it sounded a bit strained. "Listen, I wasn't sure whether to call you or not, but Liz said I should."

"Damn straight I did." Liz yelled from Bella's side of the call. "Girl needs to know what happened to her man."

"What man? What happened?" Blythe's pulse jumped and kick started her heart beat into an erratic rhythm. She mentally sifted through the men in her life. She might not like her brothers but that didn't mean she wanted them hurt. No it couldn't be them. Dixie would have called, which meant it could only be one person. "Eric! Is he all right?"

"He's out of hospital now," Bella said.

"Out of hospital." Heads whipped around in the gym, and Blythe tried for an inside voice. A nearly impossible task when she wanted to reach down the line and drag the details out of Bella.

Eric had been hurt. Hurt enough to be in a hospital. She was going to throw up. Or pass out.

Bella was speaking but she'd missed most of it. "What fight? Where?"

"On one of his building sites," Bella spoke slowly and clearly. "There was a fire there last night, and Eric went to check it out. Nate said he was jumped by five men—"

"Five men!" More looks snapped her way. They could stare all they liked. She didn't give a crap. "Who? What? I'll break their goddamn heads open."

Randy met her gaze across the gym, all wide eyed and shocked. Well, he could just suck it up. You didn't grow up with eight brothers like hers and not know how to inflict some hurt.

"That's our girl," Liz yelled.

Bella chuckled. "Nate's got that in hand. I called to let you know Eric had been hurt but he was all right."

"Thank you." Blythe hung up a few seconds later.

Her client stood waiting for her at the weight benches.

Last night Eric had gotten beaten up so badly they'd taken him to hospital. She felt hollow and jittery and not with him.

Screw it.

"Gerald, I'm sorry," she said to her client. "I have a family emergency. I'm going to have to reschedule or make it up to you somehow."

Gerald murmured something she didn't catch, because Blythe was already out the door.

She tried Will first and got voicemail.

"Will, it's Blythe. There's something I need to do. You and Blake need to take care of Kim." Both her brothers had proven themselves more than capable.

As she drove to Eric's house something Bella had said penetrated the brain fog. That Brett had been there and saved Eric. She needed time to get her head around that, but that was time she didn't want to spare right now.

Eric's house key was still on her chain with her car keys. Funny, she'd forgotten she still had it. Or maybe she'd had another of those convenient memory lapses that happened where Eric was concerned.

She let herself in through the oversize, dark wood front door and called, "Eric."

She stepped into the silent house. God, she loved this house. In her days with Eric, she might have had a fantasy or two about living here. Dark wood floors, pale walls and high cathedral ceilings crisscrossed with thick dark wood beams, the house had been built to maximize the impact of the incredible views of the mountains.

"Eric." She didn't want to scare the crap out of him, and her workout shoes made very little noise.

The house brought back a flood of memories, and for once, she allowed them to come.

One of the things they'd loved to do was cook together in that beautiful creamy marble kitchen with its state-of-the-art appliances. Or she'd cooked, and Eric had poured them a glass of wine.

Those memories were what made being with Eric so confusing. They behaved like a couple but weren't a couple.

She walked down the hallway beyond the kitchen to the master bedroom and peeped through the ajar door.

Eric lay on his side on the big bed, fast asleep.

Blythe tiptoed closer and stopped.

His lip was puffy and split on the side she could see. He also sported an enormous black eye on that side. His breathing rasped through his nose, and she'd heard her brothers make that noise enough to know it had probably been broken.

Not wanting to wake him, she crept back out to the

kitchen. She stood and pressed her fingers into the marble island top and tried to push back the tears. It didn't do any good because they refused to be denied.

Eric had been hurt, and part of her hurt for him. An even bigger part wept with relief that he was battered and bruised but basically okay.

ERIC KEPT his kitchen remarkably well stocked for someone who didn't cook, and she was able to scrounge up the ingredients for a curried chicken soup that he used to love. While she cooked, she let the peace of the house settle around her.

His house in Denver had been spectacular, but this one felt like more of a home with less glass and steel and more wood and natural stone.

She got the fire going in the lounge to keep the room warm and cozy.

A key turned in the front door lock, and Matt let himself in, his hands full of grocery bags.

They blinked at each other.

"Hi, I didn't—"

"I'm sorry I thought—"

Matt laughed and walked into the kitchen. "You go first." He put the groceries on the counter and sniffed her soup. "Smells good."

"Thanks."

"Or are we still pretending you and Eric haven't been having a...whatever you call it for the past however many years?" Matt winked and put a carton of milk in the fridge.

"Bella told me what happened." Blythe joined him in the kitchen and helped with the groceries. "I wanted to make sure he was all right."

"Yeah." Matt's face tightened into anger. "When we find out who is behind this, there'll be hell to pay."

Blythe gave the soup a stir. "He doesn't know I'm here." She jerked her head toward the bedroom. "I let myself in while he was sleeping."

"With a key you don't have because there's nothing between you and Eric?"

The twinkle in his eye made her chuckle. "Something like that."

"You're not going to give me any details?" Matt frowned. "Even though Pippa is going to be all over me once this gets out."

"It doesn't have to get out."

Matt laughed. "Then you don't know my wife. Of course it'll get out." He carried on with the groceries.

She shouldn't have given in to her need to see Eric and come here because now she felt foolish. Eric had a family who adored him. Plenty of people to take care of him. She gathered up her bag. "Now I know he's okay, I'll be going."

Matt stilled and studied her. "Why?"

"You're here now." She picked up her sweatshirt. "The soup will only take another ten minutes or so. You can turn—"

"Blythe." Matt took her by the shoulders. "I'm going home to my wife and my daughter. Now that I know Eric is in good hands, I can leave him. I'll let Nate and Jo know that he's taken care of."

"But—"

Matt rolled right over her. "There is no doubt in my mind that Eric would much rather see you than any of us when he wakes up." He opened the front door and dropped his key on the table beside it. "Call if you need anything. Eric has all our numbers."

"But—"

The door shut behind him.

"Blythe?" Eric stood in the passageway from the bedroom, wearing only a pair of boxers and swaying like a stiff wind would blow him over. He blinked and looked bleary. "Are you here or am I dreaming?"

"I'm here." Blythe put her arm around his waist and steered him back to his bedroom. "And I'll still be here when you wake up."

"Stay." He let her position him back in bed, then caught her hand. His dark eyes stared at her, naked and vulnerable in his need. "Stay with me."

"I will." Because her heart hadn't really given her much choice.

He closed his eyes and she turned to leave.

"Here." His eyes popped open again. "Stay here."

He meant beside him in that bed. "Eric, I—"

"Please." He winced. "You're totally safe from me."

It certainly looked that way. "Okay," she said. "I'll get us some soup, and I'll be back."

"Don't take too long." He yawned, groaned and closed his eyes.

Blythe surrendered the fight she didn't want to win. Here was where she wanted to be, right beside him, as close beside him as she could get.

She brought them both some soup and helped him to eat.

His swollen lip made the entire thing look horribly painful.

Afterwards, she made a few calls to check on Kim and move some clients. She settled on the bed beside Eric and turned the television on low.

Eric's breathing deepened into the heavy sleep rhythms and she got up and went into the other room.

Will answered her call. "Where are you?"

"I'm with Eric. He got hurt."

The silence from Will shrieked, and then he said, "You shouldn't be there, Blythe. You know it's not good for you."

"I can't leave him." It sounded weak.

"Yes, you can." Will grew more insistent. "He has family

who love and will care for him. Like you have family who need you here."

"Is Kim okay?"

Will sighed. "She's fine, Blythe. I'm fine and Blake's fine. And we'll even be fine if you decide to stay, but I'm worried about you. It took you long enough to get out of that relationship."

"I'm not getting back into it." She meant every word. At least her brain did. "I'll be fine. I'll take care of him until he's back on his feet, and then I'll come home."

Will took a long pause. "Okay," he said. "You know what I think, but you're a big girl and you get to make your own decisions."

"You'll take care of Kim?"

"Of course."

"Call me if she needs me. Or you need me." The guilt at being there and not home tugged at her. Maybe she should go home and care for her family and let Eric's care for him. She had no reason, nor right, to be there.

"Blythe?" Eric called from the bedroom.

"Just a minute." Then she spoke to Will. "I'll come home. I'll call his brother to come and care for him and come home."

"Blythe." Will loaded her name with meaning. "You want to be there, so stay. I've got everything under control here and Blake is helping me out."

Will hung up.

"Blythe?"

She moved to the bedroom.

Eric had woken and was struggling into a sitting position. "I thought you'd gone."

"No." She should go, she really should, but she wasn't going to. "I called Will to make sure he and Kim were all right."

Eric nodded. "Are they?"

"Yes." She leaned against the doorjamb. His color looked better and some of the swelling had gone down. Of course the bruising would get truly colorful in a day or two. "Are you hungry?"

"I am." He nodded.

She turned for the kitchen. "I'll get you something and those pills Matt left for you."

"Blythe." His voice made her turn. "I'm glad you're here," he said. "I know it's not easy for you to be here, with things like they are between us. But I'm glad you're here."

"Me too." She was, but that didn't mean she wasn't dreading the fallout when she left. It was temporary, and she needed to remember that. Once Eric felt better, she would leave again and leave him behind. Because Eric was still Eric, and she wanted more of him than he was willing to give. "I'll get you some dinner."

Chapter Twenty-Eight

Eric woke and lay very still.

Beside him, Blythe was sleeping deeply, and he didn't want to disturb her. It had been too long since he'd woken with her beside him, even if he hurt too much to do anything about it.

"You're awake." She rolled to face him.

He couldn't be sure, but this might be his favorite Blythe. Early in the morning, her face still soft from sleep and bare of makeup. Her long blond hair tangled across his pillows like someone had been running their hands through it all night. That someone used to be him.

His lip hurt too much to smile. "I'm awake."

"Any pain?"

Not if you thought a fifteen on the scale of one to ten counted. "A little."

"A little?" She grinned at him, the same grin that had been lighting up his day since she was sixteen. She didn't look much older than that right now. "You mean a lot."

"Yeah, but that's not manly to say."

Winking at him, she sat up. "I won't tell."

"Is that mine?" She must have found one of his T-Shirts to sleep in.

"Yup." She climbed out of bed and stretched.

Dear God, it was a cruel, cruel thing to do to a man in his condition. Miles of long, toned leg ended in her pert, round ass. She was tall, and his T-shirt barely covered her butt cheeks. He may have whimpered in protest when she grabbed his robe from behind the door and slipped it on.

"I'll be right back with juice and medication," she said.

"And coffee," he called after her. "Don't forget the coffee."

"Like I could." Laughter filled her voice. "As if I didn't know that about you already."

They ate breakfast together, after which she used his shower and emerged from his bathroom dressed for the day. "I need to swing past my apartment and check on things," she said as she brushed her hair into a ponytail. "I've already moved my clients for today. I also need to pick up a couple of things."

Feeling like he was one ball away from the magic lottery number he dared to ask, "Does that mean you're staying for the day?"

"If you need me to."

Bingo! He managed a feeble smile. "That would be great."

While she was gone, he managed to haul his ass into the bathroom and turn the shower on. Thank God he had one of those shelves in his shower because he spent most of the shower sitting there like a jellyfish.

It seemed to take years and plenty of stops before he got his teeth brushed and struggled into a fresh pair of boxers. His torso looked like a stained-glass window going from red, to blue, to purple to yellow. They had worked him over good.

His lip looked less swollen this morning but his shiner had matured into a beauty. Nope, he wouldn't be winning any best in show contests any time soon.

He got back into bed and called Nate.

There was no progress on who was behind the attack, but Brett had been incredibly helpful.

Next he checked in with Matt. They got past the how-are-yous and talked a little shop before Matt caved.

"So." Matt dragged the word out. "How is Blythe treating you?"

Matt would be dead and buried before he stopped interfering in the rest of their lives. "Blythe and I are not up for discussion."

"But there is a Blythe and you?"

It hurt his ribs to laugh. "Bye, Matt."

Waiting for Blythe to return, he must have dropped off to sleep.

When he woke, he knew she was there. He couldn't say why, but the sense of her occupied his space.

She peeped around his bedroom door before coming in. "Hey there. You were sleeping before, and I didn't want to wake you."

"How long have you been back?" Dressed in her yoga pants and a tank top, she made his mouth water. He didn't want to miss a moment of time with her.

She climbed onto his bed and crossed her legs. "Not long." She picked up the remote. "Anything you want to watch?"

You. All day, every day. "You choose."

"Don't say that." She laughed at him. "You always hate what I pick."

"Let me guess." Them together like this felt so right. "We'll be watching reality TV for the rest of the day?"

"Yup." She scooted up the bed and propped her head and shoulders up beside his on the headboard. Green eyes dancing beneath her raised brows, she said, "Speak now or forever hold your peace."

"Let the *90 Day Fiancé* marathon commence."

IT WASN'T REAL, this time out of time she spent with Eric. Blythe knew that but she wanted it anyway. She wanted it enough not to question but to spend the day with him and enjoy it.

There hadn't been many days like this in their relationship. Mostly, they met up at night or in secret. Time spent together had been more of a prelude to sex than getting to know each other.

This, what they had today, was what she had wanted from him.

Despite the way things stood between them, neither of them allowed any awkwardness to creep in. They watched television, ate, laughed and even read together.

By the time night fell, Eric was moving around the house much more comfortably, and she had run out of reasons to stay. She loaded their dinner dishes in the dishwasher and finished her glass of wine.

Her magical day of make believe had come to an end and it was time for sensible Blythe to save the day and get her out of here.

She rinsed her wineglass and stared out into the night behind the kitchen window. In the absence of streetlights, the dark was so much more intense out here. It wrapped them in a black cocoon and made it too easy to pretend the rest of the world wasn't waiting for her.

Eric came up behind her and put his hands on either side of her hips. His front pressed against her back. "Deep thoughts?"

"I'm thinking it's time to go."

He tensed and shifted closer. "I was afraid that's what you were thinking."

"We both know it's for the best."

He gave a wry laugh. "We both know that, do we?"

"Eric." One of them had to be sensible. "We've been

down this road too many times, you and I. It doesn't lead anywhere. At least, nowhere I want to go."

"What if it did?" His breathing rasped in her ear and sent miniature shock waves rippling down her spine. "I miss you, sweet thing. I don't want us to be over."

"We don't want the same things." Everything in her wanted to melt back into his heat and his strength.

"I want to try, Blythe." He feathered her neck with his lips, and then found the sweet spot where her neck and shoulder connected. He bit lightly. "Give me a chance to give you what you want."

"You don't mean that." Her heart heard his words and rejoiced but her head stayed stubbornly cautious. "You don't want commitment or to settle down."

"I don't want to be like my dad." He tightened his arms around her. "But I also don't want to be without you."

She believed him, that he meant every word. But not wanting to be without her didn't add up to her happily ever after. Still, the physical connection between them pulsed stronger than ever.

Coming here had been careless. Staying with him through last night and day had been reckless. She was in so deep it didn't seem to matter if she stepped off the precipice. "I'll stay the night, but it doesn't change anything between us. When I leave here in the morning, we won't be together."

"I don't agree, but I'll take tonight and work on changing your mind about the other thing." He turned her to face him. The familiar heat in his gaze lit the slow burn inside her. He dipped his head and stopped. "You know what will happen if you stay?"

Blythe walked to the bedroom and held out her hand. "Get over here, Eric."

"Why?" He smirked.

"I'll show you when you get here."

Eric took her hand and tugged her to a halt. He cupped her face between his palms. "I missed these beautiful eyes."

"You need to stop saying things like that." She closed the distance between them and kissed him. Because she needed to stop hearing them.

She kissed him gently, careful of his sore lip.

His arms dropped to her waist and pressed her closer to him.

The familiar feel and taste of Eric rushed through her and tangled in the knot of sadness that always sat over her heart. It reminded her of everything she had been without these past weeks. It reminded her of everything she couldn't have. It reminded her how much she wanted those things.

"Blythe," he whispered. He wiped his thumbs over the tears she hadn't realized she was shedding. His dark gaze searched deep inside her, looking for something. "You should never cry, my sweet Blythe. Never."

She couldn't hold the intimacy of his gaze, and she pressed her mouth to his.

Eric put a small distance between them. "I'm going to make it up to you. I'm going to make it so you never cry again."

"You can't say things like that." There are some words that should never be said. Once they were said, they were out there, and she might never be able to forget she'd heard them. "Just give me tonight."

"If I was a better man, I'd stop this right now." He bent and hoisted her into his arms. "But I'm not that man, and I fucking want you so badly."

"Eric." This couldn't be good for him. "You need to put me down."

"Screw that." He carried her through to the bedroom and laid her on the bed.

Forearms on either side of her head, he came down over her. His weight pressed her into the mattress, warm and hard.

239

Blythe wrapped her legs around his hips, bringing his erection to right where she wanted it.

Eric groaned and pressed into her.

His mouth came down over hers.

She tried to be careful of his lip, but Eric wasn't having any of it. He deepened the kiss, his tongue sweeping into her mouth and demanding she kiss him back. His mouth owned hers. His body pressed her deep into the mattress.

She slid her hands under his T-shirt and found the silky, hot muscle of his back. Just like she knew he liked, she pressed her nails into his flesh.

His groan was her reward as his mouth traveled down her throat, finding the sweet spots at her pulse and further down where her shoulder and neck met.

His body was so familiar, but the wanting him never got any less intense.

Arching her back, Blythe pressed her breasts into his chest. Her erect nipples scraped against her shirt fabric, so sensitive they made her moan.

Eric pushed himself up to straddle her, fisted his shirt and dragged it over his head.

Blythe frowned at the colorful collection of bruises over his ribs.

"Right now I'm feeling no pain." The heat in his gaze reached out to an answering heat in her. Fisting the bottom of her T-Shirt he tugged it up. "Off."

She wriggled to help him, and he tossed her T-shirt into the dimly lit space around the bed.

Eric's gaze fastened on her breasts, and he hissed in a breath. "Even better than I remember, and I remember everything, Blythe. Everything."

He palmed the weight of her breasts, stroking her nipples with his thumbs.

Impatient to have his hands on her bare skin, Blythe arched her back and released the clasp of her bra.

Eric peeled it off her and hummed his approval. "So fucking beautiful." He cupped her bare breasts, his touch more urgent now. He ducked his head and took a nipple gently between his teeth. He rolled it between his teeth before sucking it deep into the heated chasm of his mouth.

He knew exactly how she liked to be touched and where she liked his mouth. His caresses grew bolder. His mouth drifted down her rib cage and to her belly. Grabbing her yoga pants in both hands he tugged them down her legs.

"Eric." Blythe writhed beneath him. "Come here. I want to touch you."

"Later." He spread his hand over her panties, the heel of his hand pressing her clitoris lightly. "First I get to play. Next time you can touch as much as you want."

Blythe opened her thighs.

"Tell me what you want." Eric slid a finger beneath the leg elastic of her panties.

"Touch me." Blythe wriggled closer to his fingers.

"Like this, baby?" He slid his finger into the seam of her body. Closing his eyes, he grimaced and groaned. "You're so wet. Wet for me."

Bracing her feet on the bed, Blythe pushed her pelvis into his touch. "I need you."

"What do you need?" He slid a finger inside her, and then another. He pumped into her slowly and deep. "Do you need my fingers? Or maybe my mouth?"

"Mouth." Blythe panted and writhed as he stroked inside her, his thumb playing her clitoris.

Eric took his hand away, and then whipped her panties off.

Opening her thighs wider, he spread her for him. He wedged his shoulders between her thighs and pressed her legs open even wider. "So sweet." He lapped her. "Mine."

He opened his mouth over her and sucked.

She almost came right then. "Eric!"

He settled into driving her out of her mind, licking and

sucking, fast and then slowing down, drawing her into his mouth and feasting on her.

It had been too long, and he knew exactly what she liked. Blythe's orgasm uncurled from deep inside her and crashed over her.

Eric kissed his way back up her body, taking a moment to reacquaint his mouth with her nipples.

"You're too good at that." Blythe stretched beneath him, feeling sated and boneless.

Eric's grin was pure cockiness. "We aim to please."

"And we do." She wrapped her arms around his head and drew him down to kiss her.

His cock pressed against her entrance. Eric thrust his hips against her. "You still on the pill?"

"Yes." She tilted to have him slide closer to where she wanted him most. "There's been nobody else."

"For me either." Eric fisted his cock and positioned himself at her entrance. He closed his eyes and thrust, slow and steady.

Her flesh parted around his invasion, encasing him inside her.

"Jesus." Eric pressed his forehead to hers. "So perfect. Every fucking time. Perfect."

She wrapped her legs around his hips and tilted to take him deeper. "I'm going to need you to do more than lie there."

He raised himself onto his forearms and stared down at her. "So bossy."

"Get to it." She tightened her vaginal walls around him.

"Yes ma'am." Eric withdrew and thrust, harder, driving her up the bed. "Like that."

Heat blossomed deep where they connected and ripened with each determined stroke of his cock. "Just like that."

Reaching over her head, Blythe grabbed the headboard to anchor herself. Her breasts brushed his chest with each thrust.

Sweat slicked their skin into a slap and slide against each other.

Eric's face grew intent and tight above her. Perspiration beaded his forehead and slid down the sides of his face as he pushed them both closer and closer to where they wanted to be.

His dark gaze found hers and stuck.

He worked his cock deep inside her.

Blythe rose to meet each drive.

The pace between them quickened. His expression darkened as he held himself back until she came. The tendons in his neck stood out with the control he exerted.

She knew this man, intimately. He wouldn't come before she did, no matter the effort it cost him.

Her vaginal walls tightened around him as her orgasm built. "Eric."

"Take me with you, baby." His gaze stuck on hers. "Take us both there."

Blythe came with a shout. Her body bowed off the bed and took him deeper.

Above her, Eric grunted and gave a hoarse cry as he emptied himself inside her.

Collapsing on her, Eric's weight pressed her deep into the mattress.

Their breathing panted together in the rise and fall of where her breasts pressed against his chest. His heart beat strong and fast against hers.

Blythe wrapped her arms around his back and held him to her. Dear God, she loved this man. Tears blurred her vision, and she pressed her face into his neck to hide them.

With Eric it had never, ever, not even once for her, been only sex. It could never be that way with him.

She'd given him her virginity because of this love she had for him.

Blythe Barrows loved Eric Evans, and she was very much afraid she always would.

Chapter Twenty-Nine

As she knew he would, Eric fell asleep shortly after. She waited for his breathing to drop into a sleep pattern before she slid out of his loose hold. She eased her feet onto the floor and stood.

If she stayed much longer, it wouldn't be long before he picked up on her emotions. They boiled too close to the surface and she had to get away from him and try to tuck them back into place.

She grabbed whatever clothes she could find without the risk of waking him and crept into the kitchen. She hadn't been able to find her panties or her shirt, so she slipped into her yoga pants and a hoodie of Eric's he'd left on a kitchen stool earlier today.

Her shoes were by the door with her bag, and she grabbed them and slid them on. Staring at his key on her keyring she almost didn't take it off. In the end, she forced herself to remove it and leave it on the table by the door. She didn't have the right to let herself in and out of Eric's house anymore.

The drive home was quiet and uneventful. Letting herself into her quiet apartment, she crept into her bedroom and got ready for bed. She showered the scent of Eric off her and brushed her teeth.

Once she was safely beneath her duvet, she let the harsh control over her emotions go. She rolled over, buried her face in her pillow and sobbed. She had known before she'd made love with Eric that there would be a price to pay and she was paying it.

She didn't know how long she sobbed silently into her pillow, but she must have fallen asleep because she came to with Will shaking her.

"Blythe." His face hovered over her. "You need to wake up. You're going to be late."

"Shit!" She rolled over and grabbed her phone. She was more than a little late. "Shit, shit, shit!"

Hopping out of bed, she dialed her first client and canceled. She threw herself into the shower and got dressed. Thank God her gym clothes were interchangeable because she barely paid any attention as she grabbed yoga pants and a shirt and wriggled into them.

She arrived in the kitchen to find Kim already eating her breakfast.

Blythe pressed a kiss on the top of her head. "Hey, Kim. How are you?"

"Good." Kim chewed peanut butter and toast. "I made a new painting."

"I'd love to see that, baby girl, but I'm running late." Blythe smiled her thanks to Blake and sipped the coffee he had handed her.

Kim giggled. "You slept too late. Will didn't know you were here. He told me you had a sleepover." She cocked her head. "What happened to your sleepover?"

"I needed to get back to you guys." She tried to keep it light, but a tremor snuck into her voice.

Blake crossed his arms and gave her a flat stare. "You okay?"

"I will be." She snatched up the things she needed and shoved them into her bag.

"Go." Will shooed her with his hands. "We'll get Kim to kindergarten. You get yourself to work."

"I'll bring her home," Blake said and handed her a piece of toast. "Go and make sure you put food in the bottomless pit that is Kim's belly."

"Hey." Kim giggled. "You eat more than me."

Blythe let herself out of the apartment to the sound of their good-natured argument. That small piece of normal gave her something to hang on to.

Her rush to work was a mixed blessing. As much as she hated being late, it also prevented her from having to think about the stone lodged in the center of her chest.

Beth, her client, arrived at the same time as her, and they went straight into their session.

A text came in halfway through Beth's time, but she didn't check it until she had said goodbye to Beth.

Eric's name on her phone made her heart stutter. Yesterday he had discovered his contact deleted from her phone and insisted on putting it back. He had laughingly refused to let her delete it again.

Morning. I woke up to no Sweet Thing?????

Blythe closed the text and turned her phone off. It would be too easy to reply, too easy to slip back into what they'd had before, too easy to take what she could get and keep wishing for what she would never have.

⚬

ERIC STARED at his phone and swore. She'd read the text. He could see she had. Yet she didn't reply.

When he had woken up and found her gone, it had been worse than a kick in the nuts.

He made himself coffee and took a few of the pain tablets.

As good as last night had been, his body was still reminding him of the pounding it had taken.

"Fuck." He sipped his coffee.

Blythe was back on the run again. He really should have know better than to assume he'd managed to slide beneath those gargantuan walls of titanium she had built between them.

It didn't help that she'd built those goddamn walls because of him. If he'd realized sooner what he had, and what she meant to him, she would never feel the need to protect herself from him.

Well, he was going to have to sack up and channel his inner Noel. Blythe was worth fighting for and he was up for the fight. The alternative, as in not having her in his life, he wouldn't even consider.

He pulled out his computer and got a bit of work done from home. By lunchtime she still hadn't called or texted back and it looked like he might have to take more direct action.

Feeling like a wimp, he took a nap and woke up starving around four.

There was a whole pot of Blythe's soup left and he put it on the stove to reheat. Tomorrow he could get back to work and see what he could find out about whoever had done this to him.

A knock on the door interrupted him and he went to answer.

Brett stood on his doorstep, hands shoved into his pockets.

"Hey." Eric opened the door and motioned him inside.

Brett stepped into his house and stopped. Taking a slow circle, he whistled. "I really should have spent more time in school and less time learning how to jack cars."

"But the carjacking did give you an intensive course in street fighting." Eric led the way into his kitchen. "A course I am very grateful for, by the way."

"You didn't do so badly." Brett smirked. "For a suit."

Eric shook his head but took the shit. Brett had saved his ass. "Want a beer?"

"Sure." Brett perched on a barstool looking like he was afraid he might break something.

"I'm glad you're here." Eric put a beer in front of Brett. "I don't know if I got around to thanking you. For the other night." He raised his own beer to Brett. "Let me know if there are any consequences from saving my ass, in terms of your parole."

"Nah." Brett sipped and looked about him. "Your brother sorted it out. Sheriff Evans is okay. For a cop."

Eric stirred the soup. "You had dinner yet?"

"It's four thirty." Brett raised his eyebrow.

"Then let's call it an early bird special and eat," Eric said.

Brett leaned over the counter and looked at the soup. "That looks like a soup Blythe used to make."

"Huh." Eric sipped his beer. "Weird."

"Actually there is something you can do for me," Brett said. "If you were feeling grateful that I saved your life."

"Saved my life, huh?" Eric suppressed a grin. "I'm not sure I'd go so far as to say saved my life."

"I would." Brett grinned and sipped his beer. "They were totally kicking your ass."

"True that." Eric nodded to concede the point. "What do you need?"

Brett jerked a thumb at the soup. "Blythe," he said. "I want to talk to her."

"Why?" Eric's protective instincts roared to the surface.

Stilling, Brett stared at him. "What's it to you?"

"I think you know the answer to that." He held Brett's flat stare.

On an exhale, Brett dropped his gaze and shrugged. "I just want to talk to her. Nothing else. Want her to know that I regret what I did to her, and that I won't hurt her again. She doesn't need to be scared of me."

Despite every horror story Blythe had told him about Brett, Eric believed him. The man sitting in front of him now showed true remorse.

"I'll try," he said and grabbed two soup bowls. "But in the interest of full disclosure, you should know that she's not taking my calls right now either."

"What did you do?" Brett's head snapped up.

If only it were that simple. Eric huffed a laugh. "She doesn't trust me."

Brett grunted and dug into his soup. "That's not exactly surprising. This may totally blow your mind, but our Blythe hasn't exactly had the best male role models in her life."

"You don't say." If it had been about anyone else but Blythe, Eric might have laughed.

"She's scared shitless she's going to end up like our ma." Brett tore the bread roll Eric had given him into pieces and popped one into his mouth. "Ma has basically hung about in a shit marriage to an abusive man for her entire life."

"I guessed as much." Not that guessing had taken any genius. Most of Ghost Falls knew how it went with Mrs. Barrows. "Blythe thinks I can't commit."

"Can you?" Brett stopped eating and stared at him.

Eric owed him the honest truth. "If you'd have asked me that a month ago, I would have said no. But she left me, and suddenly being committed seemed a whole lot better than being without her."

Nodding, Brett got back to his soup. "You'll do, Eric Evans."

"Like you've any right to judge."

It took him a moment to realize the gravelly sound was Brett laughing. "You see it's real simple for me. I look at a guy and compare him to me. If he's even close, then I break him before I let him anywhere near my sisters."

"You've met Kim?" Eric found Brett's statement unbelievably sad.

Pushing back his empty bowl, Brett shook his head. "Nah. Blythe doesn't want me anywhere near her. I've been by the church kindergarten a couple of times to see her. She's a dead ringer for Blythe at that age." He gave a wry laugh. "Reminds me of how fucking sweet she was."

"She still is." Eric finished his soup and loaded the dishwasher. Thinking about Blythe's sweetness set up a dull ache in his chest. She'd left his house only that morning, and already he felt her absence. "She just keeps it well hidden."

"You think?" Brett's face was deadly earnest, his gaze intense as if he needed to believe what Eric said more than he needed his next breath.

"Yeah." Eric nodded. "I know. The trick is getting her to let you near enough to see it."

"It eats me up. The thought that maybe I've killed that in her," Brett said. "When I look at Kim, I see a chance to do better. To do right by her."

Looking at Brett Barrows nobody would believe this conversation. Brett looked every inch the ex-con and thug, the man who had grown up dirt poor and scrabbling to get ahead.

Eric remembered Brett from before his last prison stint. That must have been quite some fucking epiphany.

His phone rang, and Eric picked it up. "Evans."

"Eric," a man said. "This is Michael from St. Peter's here. I got your number from Bella."

"Yeah." Eric's sense of bad news prickled. "What can I do for you?"

"Listen, I can't get hold of Blythe or Will, or even Blake," Michael said.

Eric looked at Brett. "Is something wrong with Kim?"

Brett shot up.

"No, she's fine," Michael said. "It's just that they're wanting to shut the aftercare for the day, and Kim is still here."

Chapter Thirty

Blythe thought she might lose her shit when Eric strode into the gym as she wrapped up her last appointment for the day.

He caught sight of her and made a beeline.

She should have known better than to think he would take the hint of her not answering his text. Knowing he would follow, she turned and walked into her office.

"Blythe—"

"No." She shut the door behind him. "You need to listen to me. You can't keep showing up—"

"Blythe." He stepped right into her space and forced her to look at him.

His serious expression stopped her, and she got the nasty sense that all was not well. "What is it? What's wrong?"

"Not—"

"Is it Kim?" She grabbed his arm. "Will?"

"Listen." He grabbed her hands and held them. "Everybody's fine but I got a call from Reverend Michael."

The room lurched around her. "Oh God, it's Kim."

"Kim is fine." Eric cupped her face. "She's fine, now breathe. Michael called me and said nobody has been to pick her up and they want to shut the daycare center."

Blythe dug out her phone. "Why didn't he call?" Because she'd had her phone turned off all afternoon. She grabbed her bag and her hoodie. "Thanks for telling me. I'll go and get her."

"I'll drive you." Eric took her bag.

She had to run to keep up with his long strides. "My car is just outside."

"Either I follow you or drive you." Eric turned and looked at her.

He meant it as well, and Blythe didn't have time to argue. She needed to get to St. Peter's.

As a child, she'd never known if someone would pick her up or she would have to make her own way home. But Kim wasn't her. Kim didn't know how to walk home on her own.

When she saw her brothers, she would bang their damn heads together. They knew how she felt about Kim growing up with the sort of uncertainty they had.

They knew. They should have picked her up, or called or made a damn plan, but Kim came first.

While Eric drove, she called Will first. His phone went straight to voicemail. The same with Blake.

"I don't understand." She tried Will again. "Will and Blake said they would sort out who picked her up."

"I'm sure there's a logical explanation." Eric kept his gaze on the road.

Blythe called Dixie. "Hey," she said as soon as Dixie answered. "Have you heard from Blake or Will this afternoon?"

"No," Dixie said. "What's up?"

"One of them was supposed to pick up Kim from kindergarten and they haven't."

"Assholes," Dixie said. "They probably forgot."

"Probably." Doubt crept around the edges of her anger. She hung up and stared out the windshield. She could maybe believe Blake forgot. "It's not like Will."

"Let's get Kim first and then we can find out what happened to your brothers." Eric took her hand and kissed it before placing it back on her thigh.

"Sure." He was right and she needed to fetch Kim. She had plenty of time afterwards to fight with Eric about his high-handed take charge attitude. Beside which, it felt nice to have him by her side. And, no, she was not going to pick that apart.

When they reached St. Peter's, Blythe hopped out the car and made her way around back to the kindergarten.

First she saw Kim, perfectly fine and chatting to the big man by her side.

Brett stood next to Kim.

Blythe froze and then she ran. "Get away from her!" She grabbed Kim by the hand and pulled her away from Brett. "Don't you come near her."

Raising his hands Brett stepped back. "It's okay, Blythe. I'm just talking to her."

"Take it down." Eric came up beside her. "You're frightening Kim."

Kim blinked up at her, huge eyes in a pale face. "I'm sorry, Blythe. I was only talking to him."

Blythe had to breathe in and out several times before she got her heartbeat under control. She could still not look at Brett. "I'm not angry at you, Kim." She pushed Kim's hair away from her face. "Can you wait for me by the swings?"

She waited until Kim did as she was told before she turned on Brett. Only her fear for Kim was greater than her fear of Brett. "You stay away from her." She hated that her voice shook. "You stay away from her or I'll get a restraining order."

"Blythe." Brett looked so sad, but she knew better than to fall for that. "I would never—"

"Hurt her?" Blythe took a step away from him. She marched over to Kim and took her hand. "I've heard that one before, Brett."

They stood by Eric's car waiting for him.

Eric went up to Brett and spoke to him. Blythe couldn't believe her eyes. She couldn't believe Eric was falling for Brett's bullshit. She had known how this would go the second she'd heard that Eric had given Brett a job.

Brett was a con man, a liar, just like their dad. Only Brett was a fuckuva lot better at it than Pat.

Clapping Brett on the shoulder, Eric turned back to them and opened the car.

The drive back to the gym and her car happened in a silence so tense that even Kim didn't chatter.

Blythe put Kim into her car and closed the door before she confronted Eric. "You knew he would be there."

"I was with him when Michael called." Eric didn't look in the least apologetic.

The shock of seeing Brett still pounded through her system, and she wanted to hit Eric and scream at him all at the same time. The depth of his betrayal also made her want to cry.

She kept a grip on it for Kim's sake. No child deserved to witness the adults around her losing their shit. The world was a scary place for a kid when you didn't trust the adults in charge to guide you through it. "How could you?" So trite but all she could manage. "You know how I feel about him."

"I know, sweet thing." Eric gripped her shoulders. "But you need to listen to me—"

"No, I don't." Blythe managed to keep her voice down, but she shrugged his hands off her. "You need to listen to me. Brett is a vicious bastard. He's a criminal and a psychopath, and he's really good at hiding both those things."

Eric rubbed his nape and grimaced. "I really don't want to fight with you about this. I know how much he triggers you, but I think you're wrong about Brett."

"You think I'm wrong?" Her voice rose to a shriek. "You think I'm wrong? Because you know him so well? You grew up with him and saw him in action every day until the police pulled him off you and took him away?"

"Blythe." Eric reached for her again. "If I thought he would hurt you or Kim, I would never let him near you."

"You don't know him." Blythe had to get away from there and calm the fuck down. "Brett is like some kind of Svengali, and as long as you're drinking his Kool-Aid, I don't want you anywhere near me or Kim."

Eric's expression tightened into anger and his dark gaze bored into her. "That's not going to happen either, sweet thing. You spent last night in my bed and that tells me you still want what I want, which is for us to work this thing out between us." He gestured between them. "I'm going now because you're upset, and you need to settle Kim, but I'm not going far."

ALL THE WAY HOME, Blythe sensed Kim sitting in her car seat and wanting to ask questions. Fortunately, Kim was smart enough to know to leave her alone for the duration of the drive.

They arrived back home and got into the apartment in silence.

"Will?" Blythe dropped her bag inside the door and waited.

Kim followed her in and took off her shoes at the door, without being asked. A sure sign her sister was on best behavior.

Walking into the lounge, Blythe called again. "Will? Blake?"

"Where are they?" Kim wrapped her arm around Blythe's thigh.

Stroking her hair, Blythe smiled down at her. "I'm not sure, but we'll find them. Are you hungry?"

"A little." Kim's eyes were huge.

"A little?" Blythe managed a grin to let Kim know she wasn't mad at her.

Kim grinned back, and the tension leaked out of her. "Maybe a lot."

"Take a seat, short stuff." Blythe lifted her onto one of the stools and got busy making her a snack.

"Blythe?" The tone was warning enough.

"Yup."

"Is Brett my brother?"

She cut Kim's apple into slices before she turned. "Yes, he is our oldest brother."

"One of the ones who went to prison?"

Blythe no longer questioned how Kim found stuff out. Children always seemed to know the family secrets. "Yes, Brett went to prison, but they let him out now."

Kim accepted her snack with a small thank you. She picked up an apple slice, chewed and swallowed. "Is he a bad man, Blythe?"

Yes! She wanted to yell the word loud enough for the world to hear. Something stopped her, however, and it was more than Kim looking at her apprehensively.

Brett had looked—she couldn't find the right word. Regretful? But that couldn't be. Brett charged through life, going over and through anyone who stood in his way. Yet, something had been different about him.

"I really don't know how to answer that." She sat down next to Kim. Now that she had calmed down enough to process the earlier scene, the fear and fury had vanished. "What did you think of him?"

"He was nice." Kim ate another slice. "He came to see me and told me he was Brett, and he was my big brother."

Blythe nodded.

"He said that you were coming to get me and that I mustn't worry."

"Were you worried?" Will and Blake would hear from her when they arrived home. Assholes were probably lying low somewhere waiting for her to calm down.

Kim shrugged. "A bit, but I knew you would come for me."

That hit her where she lived, and Blythe ducked her head. She didn't want Kim to see her cry like a baby. All she'd done, every damn thing, had been to know her sister felt safe. That Kim always knew someone would come for her.

Blythe got up and fussed with the kettle. She didn't want tea, but it had been an emotional hour or so, and she needed time to compose herself.

"I don't know if Brett is a good man or a bad man," she said when she had it under control. "I know he wasn't a good man before he went to prison. I haven't seen him since he got back."

"Maybe he learned his lesson," Kim said.

Wouldn't it be great to live in Disney's version of the world? She smiled and ruffled Kim's hair. "Maybe."

Chapter Thirty-One

Blythe drove Kim to kindergarten the next morning.

She had woken up this morning convinced her brothers would be home, but both their beds hadn't been slept in.

After dropping Kim at her classroom, she went to find Reverend Michael.

He was in the kitchen listening to one of the women who helped with the soup kitchen. Catching sight of her he smiled and held up his hand to indicate five minutes.

"Blythe." It was only a shade past five minutes when he joined her in the hallway outside the kitchen. "Hope everything was all right yesterday?"

"Um...yes." Reverend Michael didn't miss much, and if he hadn't witnessed her freak out yesterday, there was a damn good chance someone else had informed him. "About Brett."

"Ah." Michael motioned her to precede him. "I think this might need my office."

Blythe wasn't sure it would, but she followed him.

Michael indicated for her to take a seat. "Do you mind if I call Daniel in for this?"

"Why?" Blythe hated having her family dirty laundry hung out to dry on the town grapevine.

"Daniel is an ex-con." Michael had the sort of voice that could be endlessly patient. "I know he's been working with Brett since his release."

"He has?" Blythe sat back in her chair and let that sink in. On his past prison releases, Brett had never worked with anyone. He'd gone straight back to doing whatever it was that had landed him in prison in the first place. "Sure. Let's see what Daniel has to say."

Michael made a call, and then sat back to wait. "Kim okay?"

"Yeah." Kim hadn't spoken about yesterday this morning, so Blythe was hopeful it was forgotten. "She wanted to know who Brett was."

"What did you tell her?" Along with that voice, Michael had soulful eyes that looked like they had seen the worst the world had to offer and come out the other side even more accepting of all they saw.

"She asked if he really was our brother, and I told her he was. Somehow she knew he'd been in prison."

Michael gave a rueful chuckle. "Kids know so much more than we give them credit for."

"Then she wanted to know if he was a bad man."

A knock sounded, and Daniel poked his head around the door. "You wanted to chat?"

"Come on in." Michael waved him in. "Blythe is here to talk about Brett."

Daniel looked at her, his expression empathetic. "Is this about yesterday?"

"You know about that?" Blythe looked at Michael, but he shook his head.

Daniel took the seat beside her. "Brett told me. He said you were really upset about it."

"I was. I am." The ground beneath her convictions didn't feel as firm as it had when she'd arrived. The Brett she knew ran his own ship, headlong into trouble, not stopping for anything. "I don't trust him."

"That's understandable." Daniel's expression softened. "He also told me what happened, what he did to you."

Now she understood what people meant when they said they were dumbstruck. All she could do was stare at Daniel. "What did he tell you?"

"About beating you up," Daniel said. "About beating you so badly that he broke your arm."

"He broke her arm?' Michael frowned. "I didn't know it was that bad."

"It was." Daniel found the words that had escaped her. "Brett got himself tangled up in drugs. He was into some pretty bad people for a lot of money. It's not an excuse." Daniel shrugged. "There are no excuses, and he knows that."

"We're still talking about, Brett, right?" She knew it sounded like she was being a smart ass, but the question was genuine.

Daniel actually laughed. "He said you would say something like that."

"Blythe?" Michael looked at her, no judgment, no expectations just that endlessly patient look of a man who'd seen it all and a whole lot worse.

"I don't know what to say." She caught herself bringing her hand to her mouth to bite her nails, an old childhood habit when she was anxious. "I'm not sure what to think either."

"Why don't you tell us what's going through your mind?" Daniel leaned his elbow on his knees. "Just talk. No right or wrong."

"Well." She took a breath and tried to order her thoughts. "I hear what you're saying, and I know neither of you have any reason to lie to me. I even see Eric with him. Eric gave him a job and tells me he's changed. But this is not the Brett I know."

"You don't think people can change?" Michael watched her.

"Do you?"

He chuckled and shook his head. "I really don't have a definitive answer for that. I think it's hard for people to change. And I think the temptation to resort to old patterns of behavior is always there."

Boy, did she know a little something about that. One look at Brett near Kim, and she'd been the old Blythe. The one who reacted without thought, the Blythe who lived her life in fear and struck out before she could get struck down. "You're saying Brett has changed?"

"Daniel?" Michael glanced his way.

Daniel nodded. "I'm saying that I believe Brett has had a long hard look at himself and didn't like what he saw."

That didn't surprise her at all. Not many people liked what they saw when they looked at Brett.

"But he respects that you are not obligated to forgive and forget," Daniel said. "Part of owning his mistakes is Brett knowing he's not entitled to forgiveness because he is feeling repentant."

"He wants me to forgive him?" The knowledge twisted inside her with razor sharp edges. Forgiveness. A word people threw around with trite expressions like *I'm sorry*. Pat liked to toss that one around like confetti. Whatever he did, or whatever his sins of omission and neglect, he would scatter apologies and pleas for forgiveness, and then assume all was forgiven. "I'm not sure I can."

"And that's fine." Daniel didn't look disappointed or sound it, but Blythe sensed he would have liked her to answer differently.

Michael smiled at her. "What if we started smaller than that?"

"How small?"

Daniel glanced at Michael as if looking for permission to

proceed. "Would you agree to meet with Brett? I could be present, Michael too. Even Eric if you wanted him there."

Blythe wanted to give them that. It really didn't sound like too much to ask, but she couldn't. "I'm sorry. I'm not ready."

"That's fine." Daniel took her hand. "You are under no obligation here."

Then why did she feel so guilty?

BY THAT EVENING, Brett and even Eric were the least of her worries. Neither Will nor Blake had gotten in contact with her. She'd run by the apartment between clients and still, no sign of them.

She stopped for groceries on the way home from fetching Kim.

"Sorry, declined." The checkout clerk handed her card to her with a long-suffering look.

Blythe stared at her, and then at the box of pasta, the jar of sauce and the bag of salad greens. "Pardon."

"Your card." The clerk spoke slowly as if Blythe was simple. "It's been declined. Do you have another?"

She didn't, because she hated living on credit, but she had enough cash to cover the few items. There had to be mistake, she had more than enough money in her account to cover her one bag of groceries.

She drove home with a sick churning in her gut.

One of the problems with being a Barrows is that her mind always went to worst-case scenario. The bank was already closed but she would call the number on the back of her card when she got home.

Barrowses' cards weren't declined because the bank had made a mistake. They were declined because the account had been emptied, or they were stolen cards.

Now, she knew her card wasn't stolen.

Another problem with being a Barrows is that you didn't believe in coincidence anymore. Blake was missing, and her card had been declined.

She couldn't, wouldn't, believe Will capable of stealing from her. But he was also missing, and that worried her. Focusing on Will held the rising wave of panic at bay. Every penny she had was in that one bank account. Every penny she'd scrimped and saved to put between her and Kim and destitution.

It wasn't much, because their move into the apartment had depleted her saving. Right now, she was getting by pay check to pay check, until she could build those reserves up again.

By compartmentalizing she got through dinner with Kim. When Kim was sitting watching her TV show, Blythe tried the bank.

"I'm sorry, Miss Barrows," the sweet voiced girl on the other side of the call said. "Would you like to report your card stolen?"

"Yes." The steady drum of her escalating heart rate pounded in her ears. She stood in her apartment with her phone in her hand and tried to get her brain to slow down enough to enable her to think this through.

Bella. She dialed before she could think better of the idea.

"Blythe." Bella answered with a laugh in her voice. "Are you calling about that girls' night we keep promising each other?"

"Um...no." Her thoughts wouldn't arrange themselves into words,

Bella's tone changed instantly. "What is it?"

So many things, she started with one. "Will is missing, and I don't know where he is."

"Let me get Nate."

"No..." But Bella had already moved out of hearing distance.

The next voice on the line belonged to Nate. "Blythe? Bella tells me Will is missing."

"Hi Nate." The awful soul sucking tide of her suspicions rushed over her and suddenly she was crying, sobbing and trying desperately not to.

"Blythe, sweetie," Nate said calmly and so kindly that it made her cry even harder. "Where are you?"

"H-home." God, it sounded like Will was dead. "It's okay. I'm just being stupid."

"I'm on my way," Nate said.

"N-no." But the line was already dead, and Blythe was secretly relieved because she didn't want to be alone. She wanted someone to lean on right now.

She wanted Eric with every fiber of her being. She dug her nails into her palms to stop her stupid, needy self from calling him. From the lounge, canned laughter drifted over from Kim's cartoon.

Blythe's legs felt like noodles, and she slid down the wall and sat next to the front door. Her world was flipped upside down. Brett was suddenly the good guy. Blake had disappeared. Will was missing. She didn't have any money. And now asking for help didn't feel like ripping off a limb.

She must have sat there for longer than she knew, because the doorbell rang.

Clambering to her feet, Blythe opened the door to a sea of faces. But she only saw one.

Split lip, black eye and all, he was the most beautiful thing she'd ever seen.

"Sweet thing, get over here." Eric opened his arms.

Safe. Blythe breathed him, felt the hard strength of him and stayed right where she was. Her heartbeat slowed, her thoughts calmed, and she knew she would find her way through this.

"Now you're freaking me out." Eric's arms tightened around her. "You never come to me for anything."

Because she tried her best not to. Right now, however, he felt too good and held her too tightly for her to want to let go. "Put it down to stress."

"Gonna share what's causing that stress?" Pressing his temple against hers, Eric whispered in her ear.

"Are we still pretending they're not a thing?" That sounded like Liz.

People filed into her tiny apartment. She stayed where she was as they went past her, most with a nod and smile. Matt and Pippa, holding Jasmine. Noel followed in Liz's wake. Bella slipped past with a finger waggle and then Nate with a firm nod.

Nate shrugged. "We couldn't stop them." He winked at her. "I will admit to calling Eric."

"Thank God Phi is a firm believer in beauty sleep, or she'd be here," Pippa said. "She's talking about calling the coastguard."

"We're on land." Nate looked at Bella, who shrugged.

Pippa laughed. "She doesn't care, she likes the uniform."

And from somewhere Blythe found her sense of humor, and she laughed.

Another person appeared in the doorway.

Daniel slipped past her and Eric, and then Laura.

"Eric." Laura nodded to them. "Blythe."

"Laura." Eric tensed.

"I made some calls," Nate said.

"And then I made some calls." Daniel nodded. "I brought Laura along because she knows where Will is."

The look on Laura's face didn't auger well. At all.

All amusement fled from the faces in her apartment.

Then Laura pulled a face full of regret, and Blythe knew she wasn't going to like what she heard next.

Chapter Thirty-Two

Blythe stepped away from Eric. "Where is he?"

When you saw them together, it was clear that Laura and Pippa were sisters. Same red hair, same green eyes and the same flawless sense of style.

Laura sent Daniel a loaded glance, and then said, "Will's been seen. Earlier today in fact."

Daniel stood by Laura's side. "I called Laura because she has a great ear to the ground with the kids Will's age."

"Do you know where he is?" Another twist in her life. Not so long ago, Blythe would not have been in the same room with Laura, and now here she was, waiting for Laura to help her find Will.

"The crackhouse on Eighteenth."

"Fuck." Nate jammed his hands in his pockets.

Her knees went iffy, and Blythe's legs weakened.

Eric was there, his arm around her, holding her up, giving her support, being with her. "I take it that's not good," he said.

Nate's jaw muscles bunched. "It's not good."

"I didn't think Will did drugs." Laura looked at Blythe "At least I've never heard that he does. I've seen him with some kids who do, but never seen or heard anything to suggest he uses."

"He doesn't." At least he hadn't up until this point. Blythe would swear to that. "But something else happened, and it might have affected him."

All eyes turned her way, and Blythe took a deep breath. Sharing her family shame, telling her secrets terrified her. It was like stepping into a huge chasm filled with unknown threats.

"Will has been having a hard time lately. He's doing all he can to get into college. Tutoring for his grades, working to save up the tuition, helping me out." Had she put too much pressure on Will? She'd deal with that later. "He might have reached the end of his rope."

All gazes stayed on her.

"Blake is missing as well."

Liz cocked her head. "That's the brother we saw at the church soup kitchen?"

"Yup." She'd known right then Blake would be trouble, but she'd allowed Will's eternal optimism to sway her. "He moved in a couple of weeks ago. He's being doing fine as far as I could tell."

"We saw him at the church a few times," Daniel said. "He seemed to be working his program."

"Yes, well that's what I thought too." If she wasn't still panicked about the missing money, she might have managed a bitter laugh. But there was nothing funny about rent, especially when you were short. "He was helping around the house, taking care of Kim. He even contributed when he could."

She found Eric's gaze, needing the connection to get through the recitation of her new stupidity. Fool her once, shame on them, fool her every day for most of her life, and the shame came home to roost. "My card's been maxed out. Blake is missing. I don't believe in coincidence."

Bella looked distressed. "Maybe he—"

"Babe." Nate put his arm around her. "Given everything I know about Blake, and Blythe's instincts on this, I think we need to consider strongly that she's right."

"How much did he take?" Eric's jaw tightened.

No way would she give him numbers. "Not everything. He only had access to my credit limit, which I keep on the low side." Still, Blake had taken enough to hurt.

Nate took out his phone. "How long has Blake been missing?"

"The last time I saw him was yesterday morning when I went to work," Blythe said.

Kim pushed through the throng of adults and stopped at Blythe. "Are you talking about Blake?"

"Yes." She touched her sister's cheek. After all they had tried to do to shelter Kim from the worst of the Barrows, it was still reaching its sickly tentacles toward her. "We think he might have gone away."

"He has." Kim nodded. "He told me goodbye when he took me to school yesterday."

Blythe hadn't thought to ask Kim about any of this. "Did he say anything else?"

"He gave me a message. An important message." Kim preened under the intense adult focus on her. "He said that you might be cross with him." Kim took her hand. "But that I was to say he was sorry, and he would make it right."

Surprising as it was, Blythe must have been holding some tiny slither of hope that she was wrong about Blake, because Kim's words punched straight into her gut.

"That was a big message." Matt held his hand out to Kim. "You did a great job remembering all that. Why don't we find Jasmine something to drink?"

Kim took his hand and followed him. "I'm thirsty too."

"Really?" Matt took Jasmine from Pippa. "What do you think we should do about that?"

Kim giggled. "We would get me some juice or some chocolate milk?"

"Hmm." Matt disappeared into the kitchen. "Or a glass of water."

"Blythe." Eric stepped closer to her. "What do you want to do?"

"Will." She was good at compartmentalizing, so she shoved Blake in the To Be Worried About Later pile. "I need to get him out of there." The next bit might be tricky, and she looked at Eric and then Nate. "Will doesn't have a criminal record. He's the only one…"

"He still doesn't have a criminal record." Nate gave her a flat look. "And he won't unless I happen to see him either taking or dealing drugs." He shrugged. "For instance, if I was in the front with the cruiser, and somebody else got there five minutes before me and slipped somebody out the back, I wouldn't see them."

FOR ONCE, Blythe didn't put up a fight about his help as Eric loaded her in Matt's pickup and followed Laura's car. The neighborhood they were going to, his Jag would scream its presence.

Pippa, Bella and Liz had stayed at the apartment with Matt. They still didn't know Blake wouldn't put in an appearance. Eric didn't think it likely, but Matt would never leave Pippa and Jasmine alone in a situation he judged as even a little hazardous.

Eric wasn't hella thrilled his lady was sitting in the truck beside him and driving to a crackhouse. But he didn't even try and dissuade Blythe from going.

They drove through the center of town and past the church.

Laura's Volvo station wagon couldn't have been more out

of place as she wound her way deeper and deeper into the underbelly of Ghost Falls. He was glad Daniel was with her, and made a mental note to ask someone if Laura made that drive often. She needed some protection if she did.

He'd been so angry with Laura for so many years, and it took too much effort now. The spoiled, selfish girl, desperate for the attention her younger sister garnered so effortlessly was long gone. This new Laura he didn't know at all, but she looked like a much more interesting woman than the girl had been.

She'd recently gotten divorced, and rumor had it her ex had won the majority of custody of their children. He couldn't be glad about that happening to anyone.

Blythe stared out the window, tension radiating from her. As they wound their way through the oldest part of town, he knew he had to come clean. She wasn't going to be happy about what he had to say.

"I called Brett," he said.

She sucked in a breath and threw him a look loaded with reproach. "What the hell, Eric?"

"I know how you feel about him, sweet thing."

"Don't call me that. Especially when you're about to twist the knife in my back."

Shit! But there was no going back now. "He's worried about you and Kim. He wanted me to tell him if you two ever needed anything."

"And you couldn't wait to spill, could you?" She closed her eyes and put her head back on the rest. "I really don't get this little bromance you have going with my brother."

"Bromance?" He almost chuckled but she looked bone weary, and he wanted to hold her and tell her to trust him, and that everything would be all right. But Blythe had learned the hard way, over and over again, that trusting people ended in her getting flayed alive. "I really think he's changed, sweet…Blythe. So do Daniel and Reverend Michael. He only wants five minutes to speak to you."

"You have no idea what Brett can do in five minutes." But it lacked her normal heat.

Laura slowed and edged her car into a space behind a bright purple pimpmobile with under-lighting and lightning bolts splashed down the side.

"I think we're here." He touched her hand.

Blythe moved her hand away and leaned forward to peer through the windshield. "Dammit, Will," she whispered to the derelict building. "Once I get your ass out of there, I'm going to kick it."

"I'll help you do that." The building's windows had been boarded up. Vegetation pushed through cracked concrete at the foundation. Someone called Monsta566 had tagged all over the front.

Laura climbed out her car. Daniel hit the sidewalk a split second behind her and got between her and the building's disintegrating walk way.

Folding her arms, Laura stuck her chin out in a way he recognized as Laura digging her heels in. In this case, Eric couldn't agree with Daniel more, and he climbed out the truck.

"Laura." He approached the arguing pair. "Don't even think about going in there."

She rolled her eyes at him and looked past him.

"You can't stop us." Blythe had joined him and wore an identical expression to Laura.

Daniel stared at both women. "No. Not a fucking chance."

"I'll make sure they stay in the truck." Brett materialized from behind a large scrub oak in the garden.

Blythe tensed and shrunk closer to him in a move Eric was fairly sure she didn't even know she'd made.

"I can't go in there." Brett jerked his head at the building. "I'm not breaking my parole for that little idiot."

"He's not an idiot."

Eric could have scripted Blythe's response. "I'll go," he said.

"No offence, Suit Boy." Brett looked him up and down. "But you'll stick out like a set of dog balls in there."

No offence taken, Eric had no desire to blend in this particular environment.

"Which is why I'm going with him." Daniel stepped up beside him.

Concern flickered over Laura's face. "Aren't you on parole as well?"

"Yeah." Daniel winked at her. "But the sheriff likes me, and I know shit about him."

Laura snorted but a small smile played around her mouth.

Daniel and Nate went way, way back, to a time Nate didn't like to talk about much.

"Let's do this." Eric checked his watch. "Nate gave us five minutes, and we're already three minutes down."

Daniel looked up at the building and took a deep breath. "This is going to suck so hard."

"True that." Eric joined him. Before he turned to go, he glanced at Brett. "Make sure she stays put."

"Don't tell me how to look after my sister." Brett folded his arms and scowled at him. "You haven't earned that right until she tells me you have."

BLYTHE STARED AT BRETT, not sure she'd heard right.

He looked back at her and raised his eyebrow. "How are we gonna play this, Blythe?" He glanced at Laura to include her in the conversation. "I swore to myself I'd never put my hands on you again, but you gotta get into that truck and stay there."

"This is bullshit." Laura tried to get past him. "I work with these kids every day. I'm not going to stand out here while you all indulge in some outdated form of chivalry."

"Ma'am." Brett stepped in front of her. Big as a barn, he barred her way. "Same thing I said to Blythe. You're getting into that truck and staying put. The only choice you have is how you get there."

Brett's expression was impassive as stone, and Blythe knew that expression. She touched Laura's elbow. "He means it."

With a nod, Brett walked forward and herded them toward the truck. "Smart girl, Blythe."

The words sent fear snaking down her spine. Words Brett used as a warning not to test his explosive temper. She turned and climbed into the truck cab.

Laura joined her and they sat for a moment and stared at the building. "So." Laura huffed. "Interesting brothers you have."

A chuckle snorted out of Blythe. She couldn't help it. The stress of the situation got to her and she laughed. "You have no idea."

Brett looked at the two of them and rolled his eyes. He leaned his back against the truck hood near Blythe's door and watched the building.

"How did you turn out so well?" Laura shook her head.

Nobody ever said that to her, and that it came from a woman she'd resented for so many years made it even stranger. "I'm not sure I did."

"You turned out great," Brett said and stared at her through the windshield. "But you got some hairy trust issues there."

Blythe snapped her mouth shut. "What the hell would you know?"

"A lot." Brett snorted. "I'm the one who gave most of them to you."

Laura stared at her and mouthed, "Wow."

Not knowing what to do with Brett's statement, Blythe sat

there and stared at the building. If Will was in there, Eric would find him.

Then she thought of what Brett had said to Eric earlier, and the images flipping through her brain made her smile. "At least he didn't go in there wearing Armani."

With a quick glance, Laura threw back her head and laughed. "Him being in there does stretch the imagination."

Brett's deep bass chuckle underscored their laughter. "Suit Boy in a crackhouse."

"He really must love you," Laura said as she chuckled.

God, wouldn't the world be a nicer place if her hairy trust issues allowed her to believe that for a second.

Chapter Thirty-Three

Blythe stared at Will. He swayed between Eric and Daniel, blinking her into focus. She wanted to check him for damage and hug him because she'd been so worried about him. At the same time, she wanted to smack him for being so stupid and messing with drugs.

All that he'd done to escape that fate, and now it had caught up with him anyway. And Will had stood still and let it corner him.

How could she not have seen it coming? The pressure he'd been under. She should have known.

"He okay?" Brett took over.

She never would have thought she'd be grateful to Brett for taking charge, but she felt numb and powerless.

Daniel shrugged. "He's pretty out of it, but as far as I can tell, he'll be okay when he dries out."

"Hey, kid." Brett cupped Will's nape and made him look at him.

Blythe stepped forward to protect Will.

Brett glanced at her but turned his attention back to Will. "We're going to get you straightened out. Hear me?"

Will blinked at him, his eyes unfocussed. His gaze lurched to her, and he winced. "Blythe."

"Will." She had so much she wanted to say to him, but it was all pointless while he was this out of it. Focusing on the practical seemed easier, and she looked at Daniel. "What do I do with him?"

Laura stepped up beside Will. "Let me take him. I know a place where we can get him seeing straight again." She looked at Daniel. "Crack?"

Daniel shook his head. "Meth."

"It's going to take a while." Laura sighed. "We need to make sure he's not going to go right back there."

"Do it." Brett nodded, and then looked at Blythe. "Okay with you?"

"Yup." She might resent his manner, but Brett was doing exactly what she would have done. "When can I speak to him?"

"I'll call you," Laura said. "You say he's not an habitual user, but we need to make sure. We won't know anything until we can get him clean again."

Blythe managed a tight nod. Addicts lied.

Will looked so young in the glare of the streetlights. A police cruiser rounded the corner and Daniel looked at her. "Time to get him out of here."

"I know." She hugged Will. "I love you. Don't you forget it."

"Blythe?" He looked confused.

Eric put his arm around her shoulders. "Let me get you home. Daniel and Laura will take good care of him."

"I know." She allowed Eric to turn her to the car.

"Blythe?" Brett stopped her. "It's going to be all right, Grub. You're not doing this alone."

She didn't know what to do with Brett. His behavior had her thoroughly confused but she couldn't think about that right now. Her head was too full of Will. She managed some sort of nod in Brett's direction.

Eric shut the car door behind her and got in the other side.

Brett stood on the sidewalk as they drove away, a large, sinister shape that blended with the seedy neighborhood.

As they passed the cruiser, Nate waved to her. In the side mirror she saw Nate get out and talk to Brett for a bit before moving into the house with a couple of deputies flanking him.

She stared out the window, but she still had to ask. "How bad was it?"

"Not good," Eric said. He kept his grim stare on the road. "But he hadn't been there long, and we'll get him the best help."

"We?" Blythe wanted to laugh until she cried. "There is no we in this scenario, Eric. Only me and my sister, and my now junkie brother."

"That's not true, sweet thing." Despite the endearment, Eric's voice carried an edge to it. "Tonight must have showed you that."

"Maybe." Her head hurt, her heart hurt worse and she wanted to crawl into bed and stay there until they stopped.

Eric glanced away from the road at her. "Come on, Blythe. I understand you're upset about Will, but we were all there for you. Nate, Bella, Pippa, Matt, Liz, Noel, Daniel, even Laura and Brett. These people showed up for you. They showed up because they care about you."

"You're right, you don't really understand." She was so grateful to all those people, even Brett in this moment, but tonight wasn't about that for her. "Your family wasn't perfect. Nobody's is. But there's not perfect and there's being a Barrows." The throb in her chest intensified. "He was my hope. As bad as the others got, I could always look at Will and know there was a way out."

"Blythe." Eric took her hand.

She moved it away from him. "He did everything right." She wanted to beat against the unfairness of life. "Since he turned thirteen, he's been working at this and that, putting away money. Planning to go to college. That was Will. He was my fucking hope."

"What about you?" Eric stopped in front of her apartment and faced her. "Will isn't the only one who changed their path. You got out, you took Kim with you."

She laughed and laughed, because if she started crying now, she wouldn't stop. "I didn't get out, Eric. I'm still trapped in that fucking house. Trapped by my rage and my fears and my despair. I'm still there. I'll never get out."

ERIC MADE it through getting Blythe back into her apartment and settled for the night. She didn't speak much after the last outburst, and he didn't know what to say to her. He didn't entirely get it, but he understood she needed some time to process tonight. As much as he wanted to stay, he sensed she needed the solitude more.

"You not staying?" Matt stopped him before he got in his car.

Eric shook his head. Blythe didn't want him there, and it made him so angry he could barely speak. Angry at himself mostly, because he'd created this dynamic between them. Also angry at her for her compulsive knee jerk to keep the rest of the world out. He needed to take his anger where she couldn't see it. Right now she didn't need another damn thing on her plate.

"You okay?" Matt watched him.

"Nope." Eric needed to punch something and punch it hard. "But I don't want to talk about it."

Matt nodded.

A sleeping Jasmine in her arms, Pippa joined them outside Blythe's apartment.

Standing on the sidewalk, Eric watched Matt's taillights shrink. The light in Blythe's kitchen still shone. She must be up there, maybe making herself a cup of that herbal tea she liked. Maybe Kim was awake, and Blythe was settling her for the night. Or maybe Blythe was sitting in her kitchen staring at nothing with that hollow look in her eyes. He didn't know because she'd shut him out.

He wanted to climb those stairs and pound on her door, demand that she open up.

Insist that she let him in.

And wasn't that a fucking metaphor.

Dad had killed himself trying to make a woman happy who could never be satisfied. Slowly Dad had been ground under the hell of the knowledge that whatever he did, it would never be enough.

All his life Eric had fought that fate, and now here he stood looking up at the darkened apartment of a woman who needed more than he was able to give her.

Large and scary, Brett loomed out of night. "They alright?"

"Sleeping. I think."

Brett nodded. "So what has you standing out here like a creep?"

"You're also standing here." The complete lack of sympathy was exactly what he needed.

Brett shrugged. "I come by most nights." He thrust his hands in his pockets. "I don't trust Barron further than I can throw him, and when I found out Blake had talked his way inside, I wanted to make sure she was okay."

Christ, she had them baying at the moon.

"Feel like a drink?" He threw at Brett over his shoulder as he opened his car door.

Brett strode to the passenger side. "Only if you're buying."

"If I'm buying then I'm not going to one of your dive bars."

Brett laughed. "Fair enough."

They drove in silence for a while until Eric snapped on the radio before his own head made him want to scream.

"You know." Brett tapped the dash. "The last time I was in one of these was when I lifted it."

Eric snort laughed. "If you get the urge to do that again, just ask, and I'll give you the key."

"Where's the challenge in that?" Brett threw him a flat look.

Eric took Brett to one of the bars on the hilltop.

Stepping out the car, Brett rubbed the back of his head. "This should be interesting."

"They make good wings, and I want some." Eric walked ahead.

Brett dropped into place beside him, his big boots crunching the gravel in the parking lot. "Is that a Suit Boy equivalent of ice cream and a chick flick?"

"Fuck you."

"No thank you, Suit Boy." Brett clapped him on the shoulder. "You're really not my type."

The bouncer gave Brett a hard look.

Brett gave it right back.

Dropping his head, the bouncer took off to the other side of the bar.

At the bar, Eric ordered wings and a beer with a whisky chaser for both of them.

His elbows propped on the bar, Brett looked around him with interest. The guy reeked bad assery, and Eric had a momentary twinge of envy. Then again, you had to live Brett's life to earn that degree of hard, and Eric would rather give that a pass.

A group of women had locked eyes on Brett.

Brett glanced their way and turned his back. He shook his head. "Rich girls."

"What do you have against them?" Eric glanced at the group.

A brunette had noticed him and gave him the nonverbal green light. It had been a long time since he'd picked someone up, had a meaningless hookup.

Brett glanced back at the women. "They don't know I'm an ex-con, but they know I'm not like the other men in here." He jerked his head. "They like to play with rough every now and again, but in the end, they go back to their own kind."

There was a whole wealth of information to mine in that one statement. "What—"

Brett growled. "Drop it."

All right then. Eric went back to his beer.

Blythe had dumped him over a month ago, and he hadn't even thought about another woman. In fact, he'd ended things with Miranda before they could get started. Maybe he was one of those guys who only wanted what they couldn't have. It was a humbling realization that he and his issues might not be all that unique.

"I can feel you thinking." Brett shot his whiskey. "Drink instead."

The whisky burned all the way down, hit Eric's stomach and radiated warmth. "She speak to you tonight?"

"Nope." Brett didn't need him to explain what he meant. "She sat in the truck and glared at me."

"Fuck." Eric motioned the barman for another round. He was glad Jo wasn't working tonight. "Blythe is never going to let either of us near her."

"Maybe not." Brett leaned one elbow on the bar and stared at him. "So what."

Eric choked on a mouthful of beer. "So what? Why do you keep trying if you don't even give a shit if she gives you a chance or not?"

"Oh, we're going to pretend that we're talking about me, are we?"

"Screw you."

Brett jerked his head at the women. "Them first. Wait your turn, Tiger."

Shit, the laughter felt good.

"It's like this." Brett tapped his forefinger on the bar. "Just because I want her forgiveness and I want her to give me a second chance, doesn't mean she has to."

That made a certain sense. "But you and I are not asking for the same thing."

"Really?" Gaze hard as granite, Brett raised his eyebrows. "You gonna tell me you have always done right by my sister?"

"I...no, I'm not going to tell you that."

"Right." Brett sipped his beer. "Which is why I don't break your face for using my sister as your booty call for all these years."

That cut too close to the bone, and Eric suddenly wanted to take a swing at Brett and see where that led.

"Don't." Brett gave his bunched fist a pointed stare. "I'm not going to fight you back, but if you want me to join your pity party, you're delusional. You got what you set in motion, Evans, no more and no less."

All the fight bled out of Eric, which was probably a good thing because Brett could mop the bar with him. "It was right there in front of me all this time, and I didn't see it."

"Which makes you a dumb shit," Brett said. "But I'm no different." He pressed his palms into his eyes. "She was the sweetest kid you've ever seen. She used to follow me around, always asking what this was or what that was. She saw Pat for the asshole he was, but she never looked at me like that. She always saw a better version of me than there was. I was her hero big brother."

Whelp! That sounded disturbingly familiar. Not the big brother part but the part about Blythe seeing him as better than he really was. She could look at him and make him feel ten foot tall.

"Decide if she's worth it." Brett shrugged. "Otherwise save both of you the aggravation and walk away now."

That was easy enough. "She's worth it."

Brett looked at him. "I've made the decision that I'll stick by her, whether she wants me to or not. She might never want anything to do with me, but she's always going to be my baby sister, and I will break anyone who hurts her. That includes you."

"What about you?"

Brett gave a bitter laugh. "That goes double for me."

Chapter Thirty-Four

The next morning, Blythe woke feeling bruised on the inside.

The news from the bank was bad but not dire. She would make rent this month, and if she cut their expenses, next month as well. By which time the bank promised to settle her claim. Plus she had the offer from Pippa to look forward to. She made a note to call Pippa's agent that afternoon.

Over breakfast she talked to Kim about Blake not coming back and Will going away for a while.

It broke her heart that Kim took the news about her brothers' fall from grace with a calm nod of acceptance. Even this young, people drifting in and out of her life had become the norm. People failing and falling didn't surprise her.

"Will is coming back." Blythe brushed Kim's hair into a ponytail. They had the same thick, wavy hair that got tangled easily.

Kim nodded. "Blake did something bad, didn't he?"

"Yes." Protecting Kim meant preventing things like this happening. It didn't include lying to her when they did. "He stole and ran away with the money."

Eating her cereal, Kim didn't speak for a while. "Why?"

"I really don't know." Blythe didn't have a better answer

for Kim. Why did any of her family do what they did? At a certain point you couldn't keep blaming it on a shitty set of genetics. You had to accept responsibility for yourself.

Her phone rang, and she recognized the number now. "Hi, Laura."

"How are you holding up?" Laura said.

"Okay." For now she and Kim still had the apartment, and they were still on the other side of town from the rest of the family.

"Can you make a meeting this morning?" Laura said. "We have some more information on Will and Blake, and I think you need to hear it."

Blythe really didn't like the sound of that. A headache whispered behind her eyes and threatened to bloom into something more substantial. "Sure."

She got Kim ready and drove them to kindergarten.

Laura was waiting for her with Daniel and Michael when she left the kindergarten after dropping Kim.

They moved to Michael's office.

Brett stood near the window, and with him stood Eric.

"What are you doing here?" Either of them was welcome to answer her question.

Eric looked at Brett.

Brett shrugged. "I asked Daniel to keep me up to date."

"I called him." Daniel walked into the office and shut the door. He motioned Laura and Blythe to take the two visitor's chairs. "Laura's people managed to get some more information out of Will last night."

Blythe dragged her attention away from Eric and Brett. This was about Will and she needed to pay attention. "And?"

Laura glanced at Daniel before she continued. The sort of look that told Blythe she was really going to hate what they had to say.

"Blake didn't just steal from you," Laura said. "Apparently he cleared out Will's college fund when he left."

"What?" The blood drained from her head and the room swam around Blythe. She couldn't find the right words.

Eric crouched beside her chair with a bottle of water. "Breathe."

If she hadn't needed the water so badly, she might have hit him with the bottle. Fuck breathing, she needed to hear this. "But how did he get access to it?"

"Apparently he discovered where Will kept his account number and password." Laura shrugged. "Will wasn't very coherent on the how. But the theft sent him into a spiral."

"Fuck." Brett thumped the window ledge beneath his hips. "That little shit was always a sneaky bastard."

"Not always." Blythe didn't know why she argued with Brett, other than force of habit. Except some part of her needed to believe there had been some goodness in Blake. That she hadn't been that wrong about him.

God, he'd taken Will's college money. She looked at Laura. "All of it?"

"Blake cleaned out the account."

"Oh, my God." For some reason she spoke to Brett. "He's been working since his freshman year in high school. Doing whatever he could and putting the money away."

"I'll get it back for him, Grub." Brett approached her and crouched at her feet. He held out his hand. "I swear to you, Grub. I'll get him every cent. He'll go to college."

"Grub?" Laura raised an eyebrow.

Blythe's choked laugh sounded more like a sob. "He's always called me that."

"She liked to play with mud." Brett's gaze held hers, and she saw the big brother she used to adore looking back at her. "She would make mud pies around the side of the house and invite me to tea parties."

"You remember that?" Blythe couldn't seem to find her voice without the wobble.

Brett lifted his hand.

Blythe flinched.

An unbearable sadness filled his eyes, eyes so like Pat's. Slowly he brought his hand to her face and brushed a tear away. "I remember it all, Grub. I remember all the good and all the bad. Even the things I'd tear out my brain to forget." His voice grew rough. "I remember everything."

"I… can't." It all felt like too much to get her head around. She'd spent too much time in fear for her life from this man.

Brett stood. "Let's concentrate on Will for now." He turned to Laura. "Did he say anything else?"

Laura spoke as if the words hurt her. "Just that he didn't see any point in continuing to believe things could be different."

THOSE WORDS STUCK with Blythe as she left the office and walked to her car.

"Blythe?" Eric followed her out. "He's going to be all right."

"Will he?" She really didn't need the lies about a happily ever after she hadn't believed in since she was a small girl. "Nobody can know that for sure."

Eric looked taken aback. "I'm saying that because I believe it. We'll make sure he doesn't go through this alone." He took her hand. "That neither of you go through this alone."

"Could you do something for me?"

"Anything," Eric said, and she could see in his face that he meant it.

"Could you make sure Kim gets home from school?"

He frowned at her. "Where are you going?"

"Where I need to."

After a hesitation, he nodded. "I'll take care of Kim. You

go and do what you need to." He touched her cheek. "But remember while you're doing it that you're not alone."

Blythe almost laughed at that, but he would only worry if she did, so she managed a nod. "It's okay if Brett wants to spend time with Kim," she said. "As long as you're there."

Eric nodded. "I won't let anything happen that you wouldn't want to happen."

Except it already had, and Blythe got into her car and drove.

The changes Brett had made to the house were still in place. In fact, the washer and dryer had been moved from the porch and new boards shone of new wood where they had been.

The inside of the house was as tidy as last time she'd been here.

Carly sat in the kitchen, a bottle of vodka in front of her. Another Barrows doing what they did best, screwing up.

Carly puffed on a cigarette and turned bloodshot eyes to Blythe. "Baby." Her words were slurred and her face was flushed with alcohol. "My beautiful baby girl."

"Hey, Mom." Blythe took the seat opposite her mother. Sitting across from her was what Blythe would look like in thirty years, if she spent the next thirty years smoking and drinking herself into premature aging. "I thought you were trying not to drink."

"What?" Carly's expression turned belligerent. "Now you sound just like Brett." She thumped her fist on the table. "I'm the mother. Don't need to be talking about what's wrong with me and what I need to do better."

So, Brett hadn't managed to pull that miracle off. "Did you know Blake has skipped town?"

Carly wheezed out a laugh and pointed at her. "Sure he did. Only person who is surprised is you. Always was a slimy little shit." She threw herself back in her chair. "Only person who never knew that was you." Carly opened her eyes and cackled at her. "Stung you good, did he?"

Blythe sat there and let the blame come home to roost where it belonged. She had invited Blake into their home. Despite all she knew and all she had learned growing up in that house, she'd let him into their lives and given him the gap he needed to do what he'd done.

"Serves you right." Carly glared at her. "Uppity little bitch, thinking you're so much better than the rest of us." She lurched forward across the table. "Don't you get it by now, you stupid slut. This is what you are." She waved her hand at the kitchen. "This is all you'll ever be, and it don't matter what clothes you wear or who you fuck." Carly cackled at her. "You're trash, baby girl, just like your mama. Nothing can change that."

Chapter Thirty-Five

Blythe drove past Cranks on her way home from seeing Carly. On a whim, she pulled into the rutted dirt parking lot.

So much of her life had taken part in and around that bar. There, she'd first learned what an alcoholic was, dragging Pat out and getting him home. There she'd also learned how liquor made some men violent. Her fight with Brett that day had started in this parking lot.

She'd spoken to Eric there for the first time.

Was Cranks where she really belonged? Maybe she was kidding herself with her new apartment and her new life.

Opening the door, she stepped into the dim, dusty interior. As always, it smelled of stale beer and cigarettes, marijuana, and urine from the permanently leaking bathrooms. Gazes swung her way as she walked up to the bar.

Pat had always sat in this exact place. Damn, even the barstool with its definitive Africa-shaped crack looked the same. She had thought she'd traveled so far, but here she was again.

All her pretending to be someone else had gotten her a gut load of pain. She got to the bar and rapped her knuckles on it for attention.

"Hey, Blythe." The bartender gave her a toothy grin. "Haven't seen you in a while."

His name popped into her head. "Hey, Slade."

"What's your pleasure?" Slade sidled closer to her and leaned both elbows on the bar. "Say me and I'm yours."

See there, Slade knew where she belonged. The only person who had forgotten was her. "Why don't we start with a beer?"

He winked. "You got it."

She sipped her beer and surveyed the bar. To the left of the battered dartboard was the table Barron always sat at, and before him, Brett had held court there. The Barrowses must have sunk a good portion of their income into Cranks.

When she'd found Eric outside, and he'd not only acknowledged her but spent most of the afternoon confiding in her, it had felt like confirmation that she could be different. That maybe her dreams of a different future were not so outlandish.

What a joke.

A tall man sidled up next to her. Most of his face was covered in a thick, dark beard, and he wore an MC cut. He looked like exactly what he was: trouble. The sort of trouble she attracted. The sort of trouble that was Carly's legacy to her.

She'd been all kinds of stupid to ever think she could have Eric. She'd always known that. It had just taken her all this time to cut ties. She wasn't that different from Carly when it came down to it. The only difference between them was their drug of choice. Carly hit the sauce and couldn't shake her Pat Barrows habit. Blythe's drug of choice was Eric Evans.

Good old Mom was right. You couldn't change who you were. Barrows mud always rose up and sucked you back down again.

"Hi." She smiled at the man next to her.

He leered down at her, his gaze eating up every inch of her. "Aren't you just a sweet thing?"

She almost winced. Eric had started calling her that as a joke, when she'd said she hated men who called girls babe.

The man jerked his head at the bartender. "Buy you a drink?"

"Sure." She shoved aside her misgivings. This was her. There really was no point in trying to change the way things were. It hurt too much to keep trying. "Whatever you're having."

He ran a forefinger over her bare shoulder. "What's your name, baby?"

"Blythe." She shifted away from his touch. "Blythe Barrows."

"Barron's sister?" Her new friend's eyebrow rose. "Damn, girl." He ogled her. "How come Barron never told us he had a smoking sister like you?"

The bartender delivered two beers with Jack Daniels chasers.

The man lifted his beer and toasted her. "Name's Razor."

"Nice to meet you, Razor." She clinked her beer against his, then turned to survey the bar.

Razor's was not the only attention she'd captured.

Across the bar, a guy playing pool rested his weight on his cue and stared at her. Heavily tattooed and wearing a muscle shirt, he rivaled Brett for size.

She'd been punching above her weight class with Eric. This was her division.

The big guy strolled over to the jukebox and keyed in a selection. "Pour Some Sugar On Me" pounded out of the bar's speakers. His gaze met hers, and Blythe smiled.

Beside her, Razor stiffened. "You looking for trouble, baby?"

"I'm just looking." She let her gaze wander over him. The

beer tasted bitter, and she suppressed a wince. "Step back if you don't like it."

A large shadow loomed over her.

"You play pool?" The big guy had a raspy voice, and she had to look up at him to maintain eye contact.

Blythe stamped on the warning sounding in her mind. "Depends who's asking."

"Fuck off, Griff." Razor shifted. "I saw her first."

Griff's gray gaze turned harder. "And?"

"And you can both step back." Liz shoved her way between the two men.

Looking bemused, Griff stared down at her. "Who the fuck are you?"

"I'm the one who's going to tell you to go and sell it somewhere else." Liz went toe to toe with the behemoth.

Blythe didn't know what she was doing there, but she couldn't let Liz get hurt. "It's fine, Liz. We were only talking."

"Right." Liz sneered up at Razor. She took Blythe by the arm. "And we're out of here."

"What's your hurry?" Razor took hold of her other arm. "You haven't finished your drink yet."

Griff's gaze focused on Razor's hand on her arm. "Get your hands off her."

"I bought her a drink." Razor led with his chin.

"Here." Bella appeared beside Liz and thrust a handful of bills at Razor. "And now she's paid for her own drink."

Razor stepped back as if he'd been stung. "Sorry Miz Evans. I don't want no trouble."

"Evans?" Griff scowled.

"Sheriff's woman," Razor said and pushed the money back at Bella. "You tell your man that Razor took care of your girl and even bought her a drink."

"Holy Crap!" Liz looked impressed. "You're useful to have around."

Bella made a face. "It could have gone the other way too."

"True that." Liz picked up Blythe's shooter, downed it, and then made a face. "I saved you." She shuddered as she looked at Blythe. "You can thank me later."

Pippa arrived, out of breath. "What did I miss?"

"Blythe's swains." Bella giggled. "I scared them off."

"Good thing, too." Pippa looked at Razor and Griff standing at the other end of the bar and swallowed. "Can we leave now? This place makes me nervous."

"You shouldn't be here." Blythe finally found her voice. She had no idea what they were doing there but they were completely out of place.

"Neither should you." Bella cocked her head.

Pippa studied her. "What are you doing here?"

"It's where I belong." Blythe stared forward. She didn't want to see the disappointment in their faces.

"Like hell you do." Liz snorted. "What made you decide you did?"

She couldn't explain it and they probably wouldn't get it, so Blythe waved a hand dismissively. "It doesn't matter."

"It certainly does matter." Pippa turned Blythe to face her, and her expression softened. "I don't know who this person is, but she's not the woman I know and respect."

"This is where I belong." Blythe stayed right where she was.

Pippa stared at her, and then sighed. "Right." She dug out a wet wipe and cleaned a stool before she perched on it. "If this is where you're staying, then we're staying with you."

"What's going on?" Bella climbed onto a barstool beside her and grimaced down the bar. "I don't suppose they do cranberry martinis here."

Liz snorted. "I doubt it." She motioned the bartender over and ordered beer for all of them.

Blythe looked at the three women as they settled them-selves in. "What are you doing here?"

"Brett called and told us you were here." Bella took a tentative sip of her beer and shuddered.

Still no clearer, Blythe asked, "How did Brett know I was here?"

"Oh." Bella wrinkled her nose and fluttered a hand. "A friend of Brett's called to tell him you were in here. Then Brett called Eric, who called Nate. I was standing there, and I called the girls."

"And what?" Blythe looked at each of them in turn. "You decided to come slumming it for a drink?"

"No." Pippa cleaned the rim of her beer glass before taking a cautious sip. "We came to find out why you felt the need to slum it."

"Pippa thought you might be punishing yourself for what happened to Will." Liz swigged her beer with a sigh of relish. "I really like beer. If it wasn't so fattening, I'd drink more of it."

"Like you have to worry about that." Bella gave her a hard side glance.

"This isn't half bad. But that could just be because I've been nursing for so long I'm in withdrawal." Pippa took another, longer sip of her beer. "Are you punishing yourself for Will?"

Blythe's mouth opened to utter a hot denial, but no words came out. Was she? "I don't know. I went to see my mother."

"What did she say?" Bella edged closer to her.

"Pretty much what I was thinking." Blythe tried to shrug it off. "That no matter what we do, or try to do, nothing much changes. This is what I was born to." She motioned at the bar. "I was driving by and something made me come in. It struck me while I was sitting here that there really is no point in continuing to try to escape my reality. I might as well embrace it."

"Bullshit." Liz sniffed. "What?" She gave them all an unrepentant look. "She's had a crappy couple of days and her

brothers are mostly assholes. But that doesn't have to be you."
She looked at Blythe for the last part. "Because if this is you,
then it's Kim as well."

Everything in Blythe rejected that notion. She hadn't been
thinking of Kim when she came in.

"Kim was born to the same thing you were." Liz sipped
her beer and looked about the bar. "This is as much her
reality as it is yours."

"I want more for Kim."

"I know you do." Liz tucked her arm into Blythe's. "She
deserves more, and so do you. So did I."

"You?" Pippa looked at Liz.

"Yup." Liz finished her beer. "My childhood wasn't that
different from Blythe's. Nobody was all happy and fulfilled
when I was born. I was one more mouth to feed in a family
that already had too many mouths."

Bella stared at Liz. "How come I am only now finding this
out about you?"

"Because it's my past." Liz shrugged. "Like breast cancer
is my past and splitting up with Noel is my past. We can't keep
groveling around in there if we want to move on."

Pippa smiled at Liz. "You're an amazing woman, Liz
Gunn."

"I am." Liz nodded. "But that doesn't mean I'm perfect or
that my life is perfect. I go through my shit, same as everyone.
Sometimes I handle it brilliantly, and sometimes I screw things
up all the ways to next Sunday."

She knew all about that, and Blythe nodded. "It seemed
like a good idea to come here at the time."

"Really?" Pippa looked about her. "Not even Brett
thought it was a good idea to set foot in this place."

"He was not happy about you being here," Bella said. "He
was all for marching in here and dragging you out, but we
persuaded him that you needed a bit of girl time more."

"And then Eric got on his case as well." Liz looked at her

meaningfully. "Apparently he regards it as his right to drag you out of here."

"Speak of the devil," Pippa murmured.

Eric walked into Cranks and made straight for her. Several hostile gazes swung his way.

He reached her side and nodded to the three women. "You ready to go?" he asked her.

"What are you doing here?"

"I'm here for you," Eric said.

"Evans." A man had stood up near the door and approached them. Two of his friends flanked him. "You shouldn't be here."

Eric stiffened. "Why Ray? You three going to attack me without your buddies this time?"

These were the men who had attacked Eric, and part of Blythe wanted to break bottles over their heads. A more sensible part of her recognized the need to get Eric out of there.

The man shifted and stared down at his feet. "About that."

"What?" Eric tensed. His hands curled into fists by his side.

"I'm ready to go." She tugged Eric's arm, but he remained in a stare-down with the stranger. "Come on, Eric. Let's get out of here."

"We've been talking." Ray motioned his buddies. "We got stuff to tell you. If you want to hear it."

Eric growled. "And let me guess. In exchange for this information, I don't file charges against you."

Griff approached them and stood behind Eric. But his gaze locked on Ray. "Problem?"

"No, Griff." Ray backed up with his hands raised. "I just wanted to clear the air."

"How about you clear the air without conditions attached?" Eric said. "And then we can talk about pressing charges."

Griff stood beside him, arms crossed. "And how about you try coming at my man here one at a time, or even two next time." He nodded at Eric. "I'll hear what Ray and those pricks have got to say. I'll let you know."

"Who are you?" Blythe looked up at Griff, and up some more.

Griff's mouth tipped up in one corner in what was very nearly a smile. "I'm Brett's friend. The one who called him to let him know his kid sister was about to get her pretty ass in a whole heap of trouble."

"Thanks." Eric held out his hand to Griff. "But don't make a habit of checking out her ass."

Chapter Thirty-Six

Eric drove her home in silence, which she didn't break. Exhaustion slammed her and all she wanted was to take a hot bath and get into bed.

She didn't fit into her old world either. Liz was right. There was no going back.

Without asking, Eric followed her into the apartment.

Brett sat on her couch, dwarfing it with his sheer size. He stood when he saw her. "Kim had pizza for dinner and now she's sleeping."

"Thanks." Brett in her space would still take some getting used to. The part of her still stuck in the past would take a bit longer to learn to trust him. Unfortunately Blake had made that part of her even more alert for any sign of betrayal.

Brett folded his arms and scowled at her. "And what the hell, Blythe?"

"What?" The parental look of disapproval on his face made her want to smack him. It also made her want to act out like a rebellious teen. "What does any of this have to do with you?"

"It has to do with me because I chose to make it that way," Brett said. "You've got no business going to Cranks."

"And you do?"

"Do you see me there now?"

"Enough." Eric cut through their stare down. "It's been a shitty couple of days, and we could all do with some time out."

For a moment Brett looked like he wanted to carry on arguing and then he nodded and walked to the door. "I'll see you around." He opened the door and looked at her. "But you can be damn sure we're going to talk about your choice of drinking buddies."

Blythe suppressed her super mature desire to stick her tongue out at him.

That left her alone with Eric. He moved about her kitchen, finding a bottle of wine and opening it. She hadn't bought that, so it must have come with him.

"This seems to be getting to be a habit," she said when the silence felt too long for her.

Eric glanced at her. "Me being around?"

"More like you being around when things are imploding for me." She wanted to wash the stench of Cranks from her skin. "You aren't going to ask me what I was doing there?"

"Does it matter?" He brought her a glass of wine. "You're here now, and that's what matters most."

She didn't know what to say to that, and she didn't want him seeing her like this. "I'm going to take a bath. You should go."

"You can take your bath." Eric shook his head. "But I'm not going anywhere."

"Even if I don't want you here?" She really didn't have the energy to fight him.

Eric walked past her to the bathroom and turned on the bathwater. "You keep saying that." He glanced at her as she stood in the doorway. "And I don't believe you any more than I did the first time I heard you say it."

"What the hell does that mean?" She put her glass beside the bath.

Eric poured some of Kim's bubbles into the water. Lavender scented the steamy air. "It means I'm tired of standing back and waiting for you to wise up."

Words escaped her and she gaped at him.

"I've listened to everything you've had to say." Eric tested the temperature of the water. "I've stood aside and let you call the plays because I thought you needed space."

Blythe stared at him. "I told you what I needed."

"You said you wanted a forever kind of thing." Eric motioned to the bath. "Get in."

"With you standing there?" Blythe crossed her arms over her middle.

"Get used to it." Eric folded back the sleeves on his shirt. "I intend to stand right here for the rest of your life."

She knew that look on his face.

Eric wouldn't be moving from the stand he'd taken.

"You don't mean that." She dropped her hoodie on the closed toilet seat. What the hell, he'd seen it all before. So many times that one more could hardly hurt, and that bath was calling her name. "You've spent all these years telling me how you're not into commitment."

Eric's gaze dropped to her breasts, and she pulled her workout top over her head. "I've changed my mind."

"So what happens when you change it back again?" Blythe wriggled out of her yoga pants.

"Damn, sweet thing." Eric's gaze ate her up and he shook his head. "You still take my breath away."

Her own breathing went a bit awry. Hot enough to incinerate her and laser focused, that look melted her every time. She locked eyes with him and shimmied out of her panties.

Eric leaned his shoulder against the tile beside the bath. "You've got about ten seconds to get in that bath or get over here."

Blythe climbed into the bath and lowered herself into the water.

With a wry look, Eric handed her the wine. "Not the choice I would have gone with, but at least this way we can talk."

"I'm so tired of talking." Blythe rested her head on the bath.

Eric stretched out on the floor beside the bath and sipped his wine. "I'm staying here until you wake up to the fact that I'm not going away."

"Eric." The warm water did amazing things to the tension in her muscles. "That's never going to happen."

"Why not?" He didn't sound pissed off, just curious.

"Because nothing you say will convince me that this is what you really want." The wine eased some more of her stress. "Say what you like about Blake, but I knew I couldn't trust him."

"You're comparing me to Blake?" Now Eric looked pissed off. "Nice, Blythe."

Suddenly she didn't want to fight anymore or argue. "Can we not do this tonight?"

Eric looked at her for a long moment. "All right. We can defer this little chat." His jaw tightened. "But I'm staying the night."

"I can't exactly throw you out." And the apartment felt lonely without Will. "You can sleep in Will's room or take the sofa."

Eric's gaze touched her like flame. "Maybe."

IN THE END, she didn't even argue about their sleeping arrangements. Eric stripped and crawled into bed next to Blythe.

She let him pull her into his embrace.

SARAH HEGGER

Damn but she smelled so good and so familiar. The glide of her soft, silken skin against his tormented him, but he let her sleep.

Even in sleep, the tense grooves on either side of her mouth didn't completely relax. He texted Laura for an update on Will, and so far, the news on that front looked like it might have a positive outcome.

Will had come through the first phases of withdrawal. Not having been a habitual user, the come down wasn't too bad. They had gotten him to eat something, and now he was sleeping. Much like his older sister.

Eric stared at the message from Laura and allowed himself a wry smile. He was texting a woman who he had never wanted anything to do with ever again. A woman who had come as close to breaking his heart as anyone could get.

Until Blythe. He pushed a tendril of hair off her face.

Oddly, he had been terrified when Laura told him she was pregnant. He hadn't wanted to be a father at nineteen. Scratch that. He had never wanted to be a father at all. Then Laura had told him about the miscarriage, and he'd been gutted.

Enter the sweetest handful in a skintight denim mini and a crop top that showed all those luscious inches of silky skin. Things with Laura had ended about as sour as they could. And the universe had served him up a dose of pure honey, which being the dumb dickhead he was, he hadn't appreciated until he'd lost it.

Well, screw that. He wasn't going to let it go without the fight of his life.

Once Laura's name on his phone would have brought the anger. Now...

He hit the icon to call her.

Laura answered almost immediately and sounded surprised. "Eric?"

"Hey, Laura." They'd spent so many years dancing

304

around each other. Once he'd finished being butt hurt, he'd gotten a huge charge out of tormenting Laura. "I thought we might talk."

"Really." He could almost see the way she would crinkle her forehead and chew on the outer corner of her lip. "Okay."

"Want me to go first?"

She drew a deep breath and let it out in a crackle down the line. "No, I suppose that particular joy belongs to me. I was never pregnant."

"No?" He appreciated that she didn't play for time but got straight to the point. Laura really had changed. The girl he had dated had a hit-and-miss relationship with the truth. He guessed they'd all grown up. "I wondered about that."

"But you never asked." She gave a dry little laugh. "Not that I would have told you the truth anyway."

"Why, Lo?"

She gasped. "Wow! It's been a long time since someone called me that."

"It's been a long time since I felt like calling you that."

"What changed?" Her voice softened.

"I got tired of reading from the same worn out script," he said, and because the moment demanded it, he kept it real. "Seeing you the last few days has brought a lot of stuff up for me. Mostly, I'm not angry anymore, and I don't want to be enemies."

"Oh, Eric." A soft sob broke over the line. "I really don't deserve that."

"You got it anyway." He reckoned her divorce and lack of access to her children made for enough punishment.

"You asked me why," Laura said. "I'll try to explain it, but I'm not even sure I entirely understand what went on." She paused, and Eric gave her the space to find the words. "I wish I could say that love drove me," she said. "It sounds better than what I suspect was the real reason."

"Being?"

"I wanted to hang on to you," Laura said. "I could sense you slipping away, and I wanted to make sure you couldn't leave. I never felt like I belonged anywhere, or that I had anyone of mine. I was jealous as hell of Pippa. She got to be exactly who she wanted, and everyone loved her." She took a breath. "Whereas for me, there seemed to be a whole ton of conditions attached to that love. And then this hot boy swaggered into my life."

Eric had to laugh at her description. "More like a cocky little shit."

"Whatever." Laura chuckled. "It worked for me, and I couldn't let it go."

Laura had been possessive. That possessiveness had strangled his young love. "So you tried to bind me to you."

"Yup." She sighed. "And then I realized how wrong that was and turned you loose. I was too ashamed of myself to come right out and confess that I'd lied, so I invented a miscarriage."

"Huh." Beside him, Blythe was sleeping deeply. "That's what Blythe always said."

"Blythe's a very perceptive woman," Laura said. "I used to hate her. Hate her for how free I thought she was. Blythe didn't have to measure up to anyone's standards of perfect. The way I saw it, Blythe got to flip the bird at the world and do exactly what she wanted."

A murmur escaped Blythe, and she shifted in her sleep. "She would argue she was as trapped as you in everyone's perception of her."

"Right." Laura chuckled. "And then I hated her for the way you looked at her."

"You knew?"

"I knew." Laura cleared her throat. "I knew as only the jealous ex-girlfriend with mild stalking issues could know."

"I guess Blythe and I were never as secret as we thought

we were." He shook his head at himself. It didn't matter anymore because there would be no more sneaking around and pretending.

Laura laughed. "You were still pretty good at hiding it."

At nineteen he had been too scared to tell everyone he was dating Blythe Barrows. Like her, he had feared the way Ghost Falls would judge that. Particularly he had feared how his mother would react. In short, he had been a sniveling coward. Too afraid to claim the love this woman had given him.

As the years slid by and they drifted in and out of each other's lives, he'd convinced himself that she wanted the same thing as him. It had made a convenient excuse to hide the truth behind. The truth he now saw laid out before him like a prize to be won. He had always loved Blythe. On some level, his fucked-up commitment-phobe self had never been able to walk away from her totally. Only get far enough away to soothe the scared little boy inside him.

"We good now, Lo?"

She took a breath. "Yeah, we're good, Eric. And thank you."

BLYTHE LAY AS STILL as she could and listened to the deep rumble of Eric's voice as he spoke to Laura. She'd woken sometime in the middle of their conversation. Some of what Laura said she'd managed to hear. Funny how they'd both been so jealous of each other, and so far from understanding that they were both in pain.

Beside her, Eric's warmth drew her. Despite what he'd said earlier, she knew how things would go. He would put his careful barriers between them again, and they'd drift back into their part-time, no-strings arrangement.

Tonight though, she didn't care. He was here and he was warm, and she wanted him.

Turning, she slid her arm over the taut skin of his waist and pressed a kiss to his chest.

"Blythe." His breath hitched.

His skin beneath her lips felt hot and smooth, and she pressed wet kisses down his chest.

Eric's stomach tightened beneath her mouth. "Babe." His voice grew raspy. "You've had a shitty night. This is not a great idea."

No it really wasn't, but Blythe didn't give a shit. She licked and kissed her way down his stomach, pushing the sheet down as she went.

Eric always slept naked and his erection jutted hard and strong.

She took him in her mouth and Eric hissed. His muscles tightened and his back bowed as she sucked him deep. The slightly salt-soap combination of his flavor made her crave more.

"Baby." His fingers speared into her hair. "I—" He groaned as she took him deeper still, cupping his balls in the way she knew he loved.

His hands tightened around her scalp as his hips bucked. He kept his thrusts gentle and shallow, but Blythe hummed around him, encouraging him to give her more.

In her hands, his balls tightened. His stomach muscles clenched as he held back his orgasm.

Blythe ran her tongue down the underside of his cock, pressing slightly in a way that would drive him over the edge.

On a grunt, Eric arched his back and came. He fisted her hair as she stayed with him through his orgasm.

He dropped back onto her bed with a soft sigh, and Blythe crawled up to snuggle beside him. Large, lazy hands stroked her back, down over her ass and up again. "That was…" He chuckled. "An unexpected surprise."

Blythe still craved more from him, and she pressed her mouth to his neck.

Cupping her ass, Eric drew her on top of him. He lifted her head up and kissed her. Beneath her, he hardened again, and Blythe writhed against him. She needed him inside her, joined with her as she blanked out all that had happened in the last few days.

Tightening his grip on her ass, Eric ground her against him. His kiss grew deeper, wilder, all consuming.

She pushed herself up and lifted up enough to stroke his cock. Fitting him to where she needed him, Blythe took him inside her.

Eric dug his fingers into her hips and groaned. "Move on me, sweet thing. Let me get you there."

His cock pulsed inside her, strong and hard, and she wanted all of him. Blythe took over their rhythm, driving herself to release.

The tendons in Eric's neck stood out as he held on to control.

Sweat bloomed on their skin and turned their slow grind into a slick slide.

Blythe's orgasm started deep in her core, radiating out along her nerve endings. She quickened the pace, her body screaming for release. Everything tightened in her and she gripped Eric's cock as she came.

Beneath her, he cried out and joined her.

Spent and sated, Blythe slumped onto him.

His heartbeat pounded in her ear. His chest rose and fell with his breathing.

With her muscles perfectly relaxed, sleep crept through Blythe, and she closed her eyes.

Eric pressed a kiss to the top of her head. "I love you, sweet thing."

Chapter Thirty-Seven

Blythe slept deeply, and the sun streamed through the window when she woke. The indentation in the pillow beside her was the only sign of Eric. That and the pleasant ache between her legs. He'd made love to her once more last night. She hadn't been aware of him leaving, but it was better this way.

They didn't want the same things and after all this time together, she didn't believe they ever would.

She pulled on a robe and peeped in on Kim.

Tangled in her bedding, Kim was still sleeping, her sweet baby face flushed, her breath coming deep through pouty lips.

Blythe smoothed a strand of vanilla hair off Kim's face. She loved this baby girl with all her heart. Last night she'd almost given up on both of them. Good friends had saved her. Friends who loved her enough to go grubbing into the belly of her beast and haul her ass out.

A knock sounded on the door as she was putting the coffee on.

Speaking of those friends. Pippa, Bella, Liz and Phi stood on her doorstep.

"Darling." Phi got to her first and enveloped her in a patchouli-drenched embrace.

Blythe took a moment to wallow in the endless comfort Phi offered. "I'm okay now."

"Indeed." Phi set her back and examined her. "I will say this once because I do not believe in repeating myself. We are all worth being the best versions of ourselves."

Resisting the urge to fidget under that keen scrutiny, Blythe managed a nod.

"I was a nobody from a nothing town in the middle of nowhere," Phi said. She tapped her chest with a beringed hand. "But I had a light inside me, and I was determined it would shine where most of the world could see it. I still believe in that light of mine." She pressed her hand to Blythe's chest. "And I see the same unquenchable light in you."

God it was too early to start crying but Blythe's lids prickled with unshed tears.

"Now." Phi floated past her. "Pippa has brought cake and I smell coffee." She looked at them all hopefully. "Is it too early for mimosas?"

"Yes. And some of us are still nursing." Pippa winked at Blythe and put a pink bakery box on the counter. "Matt has taken Jasmine for the morning. I'm free as a bird."

Bella gave her a kiss and a hug as she followed Pippa into the apartment.

"I picked up a couple of crates of beer," Liz whispered as she hugged her. "Let me know when you want to slum it again. Better yet, invite your big brother and his bigger friend."

Pippa shook her head. "Do you think Noel will agree to that?"

"It keeps Noel on his toes." Liz winked. "And I can still look, can't I?"

Laughing, Blythe followed her into the kitchen.

Bella pulled cups from the cupboard and gave her a supportive smile. "We came by to make sure you were all right." She arranged cups on the counter. "Just know that we're here to talk whenever you're ready."

"What the hell?" Liz gaped at her. "I want all the deets." She rapped the counter. "And I want them now." She glared at Blythe. "Spill! Everything about our yummy Eric."

"Indeed." Phi gave a happy wriggle on her stool. "Leave no detail, however small, out."

Having girlfriends was a new experience for Blythe. She would have to get used to their insatiable desire for all the details, and then their need to pick each nugget of information over.

About an hour after they had arrived, Kim wandered into the kitchen. She was kissed and cuddled and seated in front of an enormous muffin.

Kim watched Phi with huge eyes.

Yeah, it was a lot to take in.

"And what is your name, Precious Princess?" Phi got eye to eye with Kim.

"K-Kim."

"Nonsense." Phi looked affronted. "Only one syllable for a morsel of golden loveliness such as yourself?"

Giggling, Kim chewed her muffin.

"Surely there is a name by which you would adore to be known?" Phi leaned forward.

Swallowing her muffin, Kim gave it some thought. "My friend is called Maddison, and I like it when people call her Maddy."

"Maddison?" Phi shuddered. "That is a county. Not a person. You shall be a Maddy, but I shall call you Madelaine."

"Cool." Kim gaped at her.

"Go with it." Pippa winked at Kim. "It makes no difference if you do or not. That's what she'll keep calling you anyway."

Phi moved closer to Blythe. "Darling." She looked uneasy. "As crass as this is, allow me to talk money for a moment."

"No." Blythe took her hand and squeezed it. "I have an idea of what you're going to say next, and I can't tell you how much I appreciate your generosity."

Phi frowned. "But?"

"But I don't want to take any more charity, and I'm fairly sure I speak for Will when I say that." Blythe needed to sit down and think things through, but she refused to let one setback beat her and Will. She hadn't spent all that time fighting for her independence to let her family drag her back down into the morass again. "We'll find our way out of this."

"And with what the show will pay you, you'll be out of this hole in no time." Pippa winked at her. "I put a word in my agent's ear this morning. You're not going to be cheap."

Blythe didn't know all of the hows yet, but sitting here, surrounded by support, she could believe it would happen.

Someone knocked on the door.

"More people." Kim's eyes sparkled. "We have lots of people coming to see us."

For this alone Blythe would be forever grateful. On the morning Kim would have spent missing her brothers, she was having a lovely time.

Blythe let her open the door and Daniel walked in. He took in the women and grinned. "All my favorite girls in one place."

Brett stood in the doorway and looked at Blythe for permission.

She nodded, and he stepped into the apartment.

"Brett." Kim stood and looked up at him. "Blythe says you are my brother."

"Blythe is right. I'm your oldest brother. I'm her oldest brother too."

Kim thought this over. "She says she's not sure if you're a good man or not."

"Me neither." Brett winked at her. "But what about we see if we can work that one out together."

"Okay." She held out her arms, and Brett picked her up.

Kim wrapped an arm around his thick neck. "Blake went away."

Blythe's heart lodged in her throat. Her instinctive fear still leaped to attention when Brett was around Kim. At the same time seeing her sister so tenderly held by her big brother touched her. The way he spoke to Kim made her want to forgive and forget everything.

"Blake does that from time to time," Brett said and walked into the kitchen with Kim. "I'm going to see if I can find him for you."

"Brett?" Blythe stared at him. She didn't want him making promises to Kim he couldn't keep.

"Hey, Grub." He winked at her.

"Grub?" Kim shrieked and giggled. "You call her Grub?"

"That's right." Brett grinned at Kim. "Because when she was your size, she used to be one."

"Brett asked me to come with him." Daniel kept his voice for her ears only. "He thought you would be more comfortable."

"I appreciate that." And she really did, but something else worried her. "He's not seriously going after Blake, is he?"

A muscle jumped in Daniel's jaw. "I can't talk the stubborn shit out of it."

"But his parole." Blythe glanced at Brett.

He was looking bemused by Phi, who was in full flirt mode and had both hands around one of his biceps.

Daniel shook his head. "He says this is more important."

"Brett." Blythe motioned her brother. "I need to talk to you."

Brett raised an eyebrow at her tone but put Kim on the floor. "I'll be right back, and we can work on a nickname for you."

"I am Madelaine," Kim said with a regal wave.

Blythe led Brett into Kim's room and shut the door. It had

been a long time since she'd gone toe to toe with Brett and it still scared her. "Daniel says you're going after Blake."

"That's right." He folded his arms.

"You can't."

Up went his eyebrow. "Says who?"

"Says me." She put as much starch in her voice as she could manage. "You will violate the conditions of your parole, and that will land your ass right back in prison. They will throw the key away this time."

"Grub." His expression softened. "This shit is partially my fault."

"How do you work that one out?" Blythe couldn't let him go down that road. In his own way, Brett was as much a victim as the rest of them. "You're going to take Pat's crimes as well as your own on your shoulders?"

"I was the oldest." His face tightened.

Blythe stepped closer. "But you were still the child in his scenario. You caused enough shit in your own right. No need to burden yourself with Pat's as well."

"We're gonna have to agree to disagree on that, Grub." He wore his stonewall expression.

She wanted to smack him until he saw sense. "You're really going to do this?"

"I'm really going to do this." He nodded. "And I'm going to drag that useless goat fucker back here."

"He will have spent the money by then." Blythe tried again.

"I'd bet my life on it," Brett said. "But he still has to come back here and face the consequences of his actions." He raised his hand as if to take her hand, and then dropped it again. "And when I get back here, we will find a way to send Will to college. You don't have to do this alone anymore, Grub."

"I will if you get sent back to prison." Blythe stepped closer and touched his wrist.

315

"It's going to be fine." He opened his arms, inviting the hug but not moving to take what she didn't want. "I know the sheriff, who has as much as told me that he has a massive blind spot I can slip through."

Heart pounding, Blythe stepped into his hug. "Don't screw this up, Brett."

"I won't." He brought his arms around her and kept the hold light. "I wish I could tell you how fucking sorry I am, Grub. For all of it. For what I did to you, and for what you've had to go through while I was locked up. I will make it up to you."

"Just don't screw up." Trusting again hurt like growing a missing limb.

"You have the biggest heart, Grub. And I'm an asshole because I know that, and I bet everything on it coming through for me. Betting that big heart would find a way to give me a second chance." He tightened the hug. "How about you send some of that to my boy Eric?"

"Brett?"

"Hmm?"

"Too soon for that sort of interference."

"Noted."

Chapter Thirty-Eight

The last thing Eric felt like tonight was this fucking business dinner, but a night away from Blythe might be good for him.

What the hell was he saying? The only reason he wasn't camped out on her doorstep was because he suspected he'd pushed her about as far as he could, and her next step might be a slammed door in his face.

"Mr. Evans." The maitre d' at the Boulangerie hurried over to him the moment Eric stepped into the restaurant. "How lovely to see you. We haven't seen much of you in the last few weeks."

No, they hadn't, because he'd been spending every waking moment away from the office trying to persuade the woman he loved to give him another chance. "I'd tell you I've been gainfully employed but you know me better than that, Gerard."

"You can't fool me, Mr. Evans." Gerard gave him an eye twinkle. "You need someone to remind you not to work too hard."

"I'm working on it." He managed a smile that may or may not have looked a bit grim, because Gerard's flawless smile faltered.

"Mr. Gunning is already here." Gerard motioned Eric to follow him. "I put him at your regular table."

Eric shot his cuffs and did a discreet check in the smoky amber mirror behind Gerard's station. Showtime. This was what he did best. Somehow despite the cluster fuck of Highgate, he could salvage the deal with Chase.

Following Gerard through the restaurant it struck him that other than the first dinner with Chase and Miranda he really hadn't been here in a while. When he had first moved back to Ghost Falls the bar attached to the Boulangerie had been his hunting ground. The sort of women he liked to pick up frequented it. Women who would make him feel like a man who had made it.

Then, in a moment of weakness, he had called up Blythe and the Boulangerie's single scene had been without him since then.

"Eric." A gorgeous brunette held out her red-tipped hand to him as he passed. "Where have you been, darling?"

Gerard stopped and waited.

"Kendra." He leaned down and brushed her cheek with a kiss, ignoring the way she pressed into the caress, inviting him to linger. "You look well."

Kendra preened and sent him a sultry smile. "I should be furious with you for not calling."

"Yes, you really should be." He and Kendra had enjoyed a couple of nights before he'd reconnected with Blythe this last time. "I apologize for being an asshole."

"You can make it up to me." Kendra bit her full, plum-painted mouth between her straight white teeth. "Maybe we can get together later."

"Unfortunately, I'll be busy later." He re-appropriated his hand. "It was nice to see you, but my associate is waiting for me."

"Rain check?" Kendra cocked her head and studied him like a hungry bird would a worm.

"Off the market," Eric said, and sent a quick prayer to whoever might be listening he had that right. "Permanently."

Arms spread over the back of the dark green leather booth, Chase watched him as Eric approached the table. As per usual, his hawkish features gave none of his thoughts away.

Eric knew he'd schooled his features into a similar expression as he held out his hand. "Chase."

"Eric." Chase shook his hand. "Matt not joining us?"

"Not tonight." Eric spread the crisp white napkin over his lap. "Jasmine is still ruling her Daddy's life with an iron fist."

"Mr. Gunning." A waiter approached with two glasses on a tray and put one in front of each of them.

Chase nodded his thanks to the waiter, before turning to Eric. "I hope you don't mind, but I took the liberty."

So, Chase was in control mode. Eric's inner alarm light flickered on. Chase in control mode meant Chase feeling very sure of himself. The martini was the least of Eric's battles tonight, so he raised his glass in a toast. "To a mutually beneficial future."

Chase sipped and looked smug. "Actually, that's what I wanted to talk about."

A siren joined the blinking alarm light, but Eric played it cool and stared at Chase, giving him the silence to fill.

Managing to hold his ground for three minutes, Chase eventually gave. This couldn't be good.

"I'm hearing some disturbing rumors around the Highgate contract."

Eric would pay good money to know who whispered in Chase's ear all the time. Again, he let the other man fill the silence. If Chase wanted information from him, Eric was going to make him work for it.

Across the restaurant, a blonde caught his eyes and smiled. Eric sent her a polite smile that would let her know he wouldn't be taking up her invitation.

"I hear the job is behind schedule after a fire leveled most of it." Annoyance bracketed Chase's tone. "And that the budget is in free fall."

"You hear a lot." Eric forced a cool smile to his lips. Fuck it! If Chase knew the extent, their entire deal would fall apart, and Eric couldn't blame him if it did. He wouldn't get into a business drowning in shit either. He sipped his martini. "And as per usual, there's a bit of truth in every rumor."

Chase's hazel eyes narrowed. "How much truth?"

"Enough to make it my priority." Eric met and held his gaze. "We had some trouble. It's under control now."

"Right." Chase looked skeptical but dropped the subject.

They ordered and ate with Eric having very little recollection of the food. Chase was in a Machiavellian mood and kept him tap dancing throughout. Subtle jabs here and there. Fancy verbal footwork to gain the upper hand and elicit more information than he was willing to give. Eric met him at every twist and turn. Evans Construction needed this deal to stay in the game and Matt was counting on him.

He dropped his credit card on the bill when it came. Not so long ago, this sort of evening would have fired his adrenaline. Skating the fine edge of disaster had always been his crack. Tonight, all he wanted to do was beg Blythe to let him into her apartment and sit there and watch one of her pain in the ass reality shows with her.

Sprawling back in his seat, Chase looked smug. "Let's cut the shit, Eric."

Eric nodded. He had been ready to cut the shit hours ago.

"Get this situation under control." Chase raised a hand to forestall anything Eric might say. "I hear what you say, but frankly, Eric, I don't believe you." His smirked. "I think you're twisting the truth to keep this deal together, and I don't blame you. I would do the same in your position." He sat forward, gaze like a hungry shark. "But there won't be any partnership if your house is not in order."

Given the way the evening had gone, Eric wasn't surprised. "I hear you. There won't be any reason for this deal not to go forward."

Chase dug in his pockets and pulled out a slip of paper. He pushed it over the table to Eric. "I've taken the liberty of calculating your company's worth. Given recent events."

"That should make interesting reading." Eric slipped the paper into his pocket. Chase was threatening him with a total buyout, and he didn't need to read the figures on the paper to know they would be insultingly low. He'd have done the same thing as Chase if their roles were reversed. "I'll chat to Matt and we'll get back to you."

"I'm glad we understand each other." Chase stood and preceded Eric out the restaurant. The power game was so subtle, but Chase felt confident enough to take top dog position and leave Eric following him.

They didn't speak as they waited for the valet to bring their cars around.

A black sedan glided to a stop in front of them and the valet held the door open for Chase.

"Let me know when you're ready to deal," Chase said as he climbed behind the wheel of his Mercedes-Maybach S650.

"Mr. Evans?" A second valet watched him, waiting for him to get behind the wheel.

Eric dialed Brett from his car.

"Yo!" Brett rasped over the Bluetooth.

Mind reeling, wanting to punch himself in the stupid face, Eric said, "Can you get hold of Barron for me?"

"Why?" Brett's voice hardened. "Want me to break the little fucker?"

It surprised a laugh out of Eric. "No, I need information from him."

"He's here. We're at my mom's house," Brett said. "We can meet you."

"No, I'm on my way." As the shock faded, Eric wanted to

throw back his head and laugh. He should have seen it from the get go. Chase had played him like a violin, all the time driving for the merger, while he worked to break them behind their backs. "Don't let him leave."

"Barron isn't going anywhere."

Eric hung up. Both he and Matt had been distracted and hadn't noticed what they should have. He needed Barron to verify this and then Chase Gunning would pay the price for fucking with the Evans brothers.

Eric stopped outside the house and stared through the windshield. "Shit!"

This was where Blythe had grown up and it was so much worse than he had imagined. She had told him bits and pieces over the years. What words couldn't convey was the sense of despondency that clung to the house, like this was the black-hole down which all hope vanished.

The front door opened, and light limned a figure in the doorway. Judging by sheer size, it had to be Brett.

Eric climbed out of his car and suppressed the desire to activate the locks. They'd only steal his hubcaps if he did.

The stairs creaked beneath him as he climbed them.

Brett threw an arm out. "Welcome to the family estate."

The inside of the house was neat at least, but stank of cigarettes and beer. Eric walked into a sitting room to the left of the front door.

Bo and Becker lounged in eighties style floral sofas. They straightened when they saw him and stood.

"Boss?" Becker's gaze flickered from him to Brett and back again.

"Barron," Brett called from the hallway. "Get your ass down here."

"What the fuck for?" Barron responded from somewhere up the bare wooden stairs.

Hands on his hips, Brett shook his head. "You gonna make me come up there?"

A moment's silence was followed by footsteps stomping overhead and then Barron appeared at the top of the stairs. "What?"

Brett motioned Eric. "Wants to ask you something?"

"I know fuck all." Barron scowled at Brett, but it looked more petulant than anything else. Like a toddler making a token protest that they knew they would lose.

"The guy you told me about." Eric stepped back into the hall. "The one in the S650. You sure about that car?"

"Yeah." Barron shrugged and stomped down the stairs.

"He won't forget a car," Brett said with a smirk. "They're something of a family passion."

Eric needed to be sure. "But you never saw the driver?"

"Nah." Barron scratched his left armpit. "Dude kept the windows up mostly. Tinted. Ray did though. He said he wanted to speak to you about him."

"An S650?" Bo sauntered into the hallway. "Black?"

All gazes swung his way.

Brett stepped closer to Bo. "You know something about this?"

"I might." Bo looked nervous and put some distance between himself and Brett. "S650 pulled up to the Burger King drive thru when I was getting lunch."

"You're sure?" Eric's blood stirred as the hunt began again.

"Yeah, I'm fucking sure." Bo sneered at him. "Aren't that many of them on the road, and especially in Ghost Falls."

Eric thumbed a picture up on his phone. "This guy?"

Bo peered at the image. "Yup."

He had the fucker now.

"This the guy who's been stirring up shit?" Brett peered over Eric's shoulder at the phone.

Eric wanted to howl his triumph. "Yes."

"Want us to take care of it for you?" Brett motioned his brothers. "My favorite T-shirt got torn in that fight."

323

"Oh, no." Eric smiled. "I'll take care of this myself."

Brett took a step away from him. "You're one scary motherfucker, Evans. You know that?"

Yeah, he did know that, and soon Chase Gunning would know it too.

Chapter Thirty-Nine

Eric grabbed coffee and muffins on his way to see Chase the next morning. He'd spent the night making calls and now he was ready.

Chase's temporary offices occupied a small space above the new coffee shop, Mugged, not too far from Bella's. He'd been using the space since he first came to Ghost Falls.

Looking up as he opened the door, Miranda smiled. "Eric. Were we expecting you?"

He didn't know what, if any, part Miranda had had in Chase's strategy.

"You weren't expecting me." He put a coffee on her desk. "Nonfat chai latte, if I remember correctly."

Her smile broadened. "You remembered perfectly."

"Is Chase in?" Eric held up a second cup. "Black, plain."

Miranda nodded and sipped her latte. "He's on his way now. It shouldn't be too much longer."

"May I?" Eric indicated the sand colored sofa against the wall.

"Please." Miranda gestured.

He sat and put the muffins on Miranda's desk. He'd be

surprised if she ate one. She had the look of a woman who watched everything she ate.

Cup in her hand, Miranda sat back and studied him. "Chase said your meeting went well last night."

"Yes." That was one way of putting it. "Very informative."

The look in her onyx eyes sharpened as she sipped her latte. "Why am I getting the impression you're here for something other than accepting our offer?"

"Our?" He raised an eyebrow. "I'm still trying to ascertain exactly what your involvement in this has been."

"Involvement?" She put her cup on her blotter and adjusted it to fit in the corner. "Why don't you ask what you came here to ask?"

Eric cut to the chase. "Did you know Chase was behind all the trouble we've been having on Highgate?"

Her expression didn't change. She sat perfectly still and looked at him. "That's a fairly large accusation you're making there, Eric."

No shock and no outraged protestations of innocence. Either she had a great poker face, or she must have known, suspected at the very least.

"Of course, if I handed my proof to my brother he'd be here instead of me." Eric sipped his coffee and sat back in the sofa. He crossed his ankle over one knee. "My brother, the sheriff, that is."

"Ah." Her lips twitched as if she was enjoying the game they were playing. He found it hard to believe that there had been a time when women like Miranda did it for him.

Not anymore. Now he wanted someone who didn't see relationships as a battleground. A woman who knew how to love. A home that wrapped comfort around him when he went there.

Miranda wiped her thumb across the lipstick stain on her coffee cup and then used a tissue on her thumb. "Would you believe me if I protested my innocence?"

"I'm not sure." He shrugged. "I'm also not sure it really matters any more."

"Blythe Barrows." Miranda cocked her head. "I never stood a chance did I?"

"No." He saw no reason to sugarcoat this. Miranda was a big girl, and she could take care of herself. "At the time I didn't realize it if that helps."

"Not really." She pulled a face. "But you needn't concern yourself with me. Merely a bruised ego. No permanent damage done." She glanced to the door. "Chase has just arrived."

"Good." Eric looked forward to this. "Just for the record, how aware were you?"

"You don't expect me to answer that." She smirked. "At least not honestly."

No, he hadn't, and he sipped his coffee as Chase opened the door.

He caught sight of Eric and stopped. "Eric? We didn't have a meeting today." He checked his watch. "I really wish you'd called first because I don't have time for this."

"You'll make time." Eric stood. "Do you want to do this in front of Miranda or not?"

Chase did an almost adorable confused look. "I'm not sure I understand? What are we doing?"

"Yes, Eric." Miranda leaned back in her chair. "What are we doing?"

They were cool customers. Eric would give them that. "I believe this is the part where I lay down all my accusations and you protest your innocence. I then point out that I have witnesses. Let you know that Ray and his buddies have rolled over on you."

"I've no idea what you're talking about." Chase pointed to the coffee. "Is that for me?"

"My treat." Eric smiled. "We both know me standing here and accusing you is going to get nowhere. Frankly, I'm too busy to bother." He stood and straightened the crease of his suit pants. "You tried to reduce the value of Evans Construction so you could step in and rescue it for chump change." Eric dropped the piece of paper into a crumpled ball on Miranda's desk. "There's no point to my reading that." He held up his hand to stop Chase from speaking. "I know. You're innocent. How dare I. You'll sue."

Chase went still and scrutinized him. Here, at last, was the real Chase Gunning. The ruthless predator and not bothering to hide it. "Let's assume for a minute you're right." He sipped his coffee. "Accusations that I categorically deny, but let's assume. What are you going to do about it? You sunk all your available capital into Highgate and now it's gone belly up."

"I have people ready to swear they took your dollar to disrupt my site." Eric let that sink in. "I did my homework on you too, Gunning. You're arrogant and that has always been your downfall. You should have sent someone else to do your dirty work."

Chase chuckled. "Again, I have no idea what you're talking about. But I was going to send around a document by courier this morning with a fair offer for Evans Construction. What it's worth today. In light of all the trouble you've had."

"That's your arrogance again." Eric wagged a finger at him. "Did you really think one project would break us?"

Chase's confidence faltered and he glanced at Miranda.

Ah well, it was too much to hope that she hadn't known all along.

He turned to Miranda. "You should have dug a little deeper."

"Clearly." The woman was still enjoying this. Eric didn't envy Chase that.

"Now, we both know this could tie us both up for months," Eric said. "So, here's what's going to happen. You're going to give me the labor and raw materials, at your expense to fix the Highgate site."

"You're insured," Miranda said, looking more intrigued than concerned.

Eric shrugged. "Yeah but I'm losing my no-claims bonus and my premiums are going sky high after this." He tried to look apologetic, but he'd spent all night setting up and he wanted his moment too much. "As I was saying, you're going to fix what you broke, but you're also going to do it where you came from. As in not close enough for me to catch sight of either of you."

"Or what?" Chase sneered.

"Great question." Eric beamed at him. "Or your loans are getting called in"—he checked his watch—"in about ten minutes if I don't call first. You will also lose the Patterson and Beaulieu contracts you're about to sign." He shrugged. "And all this after I take my proof to the authorities."

Chase glanced at Miranda.

She was watching Eric as if she found him fascinating. "You sound very confident that you can do all this."

He pushed his hands out, palms up. "I am, and I can do all these things because this is what happens when you spend your career not screwing people over."

BLYTHE WAITED for Chase to arrive for his regular appointment. He was late, which he never had been before, but clients were often late, and she didn't let it stress her. There was only so much she could do and if they chose to cut their time short, the loss was theirs.

Chase arrived, dressed in a suit. He gave her a tight smile. "Sorry I'm late. Is there somewhere we can talk?"

Randy raised his eyebrows behind Chase's back.

Blythe shrugged. She had no idea either. "In my office." Blythe led the way.

Following her, Chase closed the door behind them.

Blythe indicated his suit and tie. "I assume you're not training today?"

"No." He shoved his hands in his pockets, looking uneasy for the first time since she'd known him. "Actually, I'm not going to be able to train with you any longer."

"I see." Damn, she really didn't like losing clients. Particularly with things as they stood at the moment. Still these things happened, and she needed to move forward. After all she'd done, she was not going to let Blake break her. She'd come too far. Kim needed her, and when he got better, Will was going to need her more than ever. "I'm sorry to hear that."

"Listen, this is not my place, but I like you Blythe. I feel a connection with you, and I don't want to see you get hurt," he said.

Nothing good could come of a conversation that started like that. "Okay."

"I'm gonna level with you." He sighed. "I know you and Eric Evans are a thing. I've known about it since I first came here."

Chase needed to update his information. "We're not a thing."

"Really?" Chase frowned. "Because my information indicates otherwise."

She wasn't going to argue with him. It was none of his business. "I'm not really sure where you're going with this, Chase."

"Right." He refocused. "It's just that if you and Eric were a thing, you should know not to trust him."

Now she really didn't like where it was going, but she'd spent eighteen years keeping the details of her and Eric's relationship to herself, and she and Chase were not close enough for her to share any of that with him.

Frustration tightened his features, and he broke the silence. "Eric has been seeing my associate Miranda Patel." He thumbed up a picture on his phone and showed it to her. "They've been an item since we arrived in Ghost Falls."

The woman in the picture with Eric looked perfect for him. Beautiful, sophisticated, elegant and classy, she was Eric's female match. Except for one thing. The woman in the picture looked cold and contained.

As much as Eric appeared to be the same, he wasn't. Eric burned molten gold at his core. He loved his family, and he loved his friends. He gave of himself freely and he needed that warmth around him.

Blythe handed Chase's phone back to him. Chase was after something. He had the same look in his eyes Pat got when he thought he had the upper hand. Only her desire to find out Chase's endgame kept the conversation going. "She's beautiful."

"Yes, she is." Chase watched her as if trying to find the chink in her armor. "Eric certainly thinks so."

Chase had a good game face, but he was pushing too hard, and he had from the beginning. Pat would never have made such a rookie error. The way Chase had tried to ingratiate himself with her, provide that manly shoulder for her to lean on. Then the way he'd seen a gap and tried to forge that connection between them.

He stared at her expectantly.

Blythe held his gaze, but gave him nothing.

Chase smoothed down his tie and cleared his throat. He shoved his hands in his pockets. "I do my research on my business partners and that includes anyone associated with them." He produced his charming smile but it was looking a bit forced and worn around the edges. "I wanted to see who you were and what Eric saw in you. After I met you, I came because I liked you, wanted to be near to you. I still want that."

In much the same way as a rattlesnake cozied up to a mongoose. "Huh."

He stepped closer to her. "I know you're having some trouble right now, too." He spread his hands in a manner that was meant to be disarming.

"And?" Blythe kept her anger off her face. Pat and her brothers had given her a lifetime of experience in dealing with scumbags. You never showed your hand first. Part of her was also curious as hell where he was going.

Chase gave her a charming smile. "I'm a man in a position to help you." His gaze crawled over her in an unmistakable message that made her want to shower. "I'm known to be generous with my…friends."

As long as his friends dropped neatly into line. "We're not friends."

"Eh?" He blinked at her. "Of course we are. I'm here to warn you Eric is messing around on you. There's no reason for you to hang around for a man who's making a fool of you."

"Really." She almost laughed.

"I'm here to save you." His perma-smile faltered. "If revenge is your thing, then I can make sure Eric never stops regretting the day he let you go."

"If I sleep with you."

Chase's face tightened in anger. "I was talking about something more permanent than sex."

"Get out." She didn't bother hiding her contempt.

Chase scowled at her. "I came here because I care about you. To save you from yourself. Eric Evans is laughing at you behind your back with Miranda."

No, Eric wasn't and the truth hit Blythe like a ton of bricks. She trusted Eric. Trusted him that he would never see anyone behind her back. Trusted him with her family. Trusted him with her pain and her vulnerabilities. Trusted him with every part of her.

Blythe grabbed her bag, brushed past Chase and opened her office door. She walked into the gym, not caring if Chase followed or crawled back under his rock. She had somewhere she needed to be.

Chase had come there with that stupid picture, so sure she would gobble up his lies.

Randy looked up as she approached. "You okay, Blythe?"

"I'm more than okay." For the first time since that awful day she'd left Eric, she felt wonderful. Goddamn incredible. "I'm leaving. And I won't be back for the rest of the day."

Chase yelled after her, "I'm not done talking to you, Blythe."

"What do you want me to do with that?" Randy jerked his head at Chase.

Blythe glanced back at him. "I really don't care."

Truth be told, Chase had done her a favor. If he hadn't shown her that stupid picture, she might have gone on floundering in uncertainty. She'd like to think that eventually she would have gotten there on her own, but that didn't matter now. None of that mattered. Joy bubbled up and she laughed aloud. Not for one second had she considered Chase might be telling her the truth.

Blythe Barrows loved Eric Evans and trusted that Eric Evans loved her right back.

Chapter Forty

Eric poured himself a single malt and stood looking out at the view from his sitting room. Like he'd done in Denver, he'd built his house himself. Unlike the Denver house, the space cried out for love and laughter, family and warmth. It cried out for Blythe and a beginning to all those things.

Matt had taken the news about Gunning remarkably well.

"You always felt like something wasn't right," he'd said. "As always your instincts were spot on. We'll get through this."

Eric's calls to outflank Chase had unearthed a couple of promising leads. He and Matt wouldn't consider another merger, but there were some interesting financing options out there for them. Like he'd said to Chase, you do business honestly and people wanted to do it with you. Evans Construction would fight on, grow bigger and better from here, because together the Evans brothers could do anything.

He checked his phone, but Blythe hadn't called. When he'd left her place the other morning, he'd been hoping she would call him first and give him some indication that she might change her mind.

The single malt created a pleasant simmer in his belly. It was probably still too soon, but Eric didn't intend to give up on her. She'd made huge strides toward forgiving Brett and that gave him hope.

The doorbell rang and he went to the door.

Blythe stood on his doorstep with a cup of coffee. She handed it to him. "You look like you need this."

It was the same thing she'd said to him that night outside Cranks.

She brushed past him, took his single malt and sauntered into the house.

Not sure what she was up to, but thrilled to have her there, he followed. "What's going on?"

"Chase Gunning came to see me." She took a sip of his single malt.

Eric put the coffee down on the kitchen island and reached for another scotch glass. If he had to talk about that prick, he wasn't going to do it on coffee. Besides she didn't look like she intended to give him back his original glass anytime soon.

"He tried to tell me that you were messing around behind my back." She faced the view, her back to him.

Eric gripped the bottle tightly and reined in his temper. "That's bullshit and you know it."

"Yes, I do know it." She turned to him and her smile was blindingly beautiful. Not a trace of reserve or caution dimmed the edge of her loveliness. "I know."

"And?" Hope stirred in his chest.

Blythe laughed. "And I know because I trust you. I trust that you won't hurt me. I trust that you mean what you say when you tell me you love me."

"I do mean what I say." Eric couldn't help himself and he reached for her.

"Wait." She ducked away from him and shot the rest of the single malt. Eric almost winced for his sixteen-year-old Lagavulin but she could gargle with the stuff, mix it with Coke for all he cared, just as long as she always looked this happy.

She stood outside his reach. "I need to finish this before you touch me." She rolled her eyes. "Because we both know what happens then."

"And this is a problem how?" He sipped his drink and waited. Please God, let him not be hearing her wrong.

She giggled. "Let me say this because it's been too long in coming. You know how hard it is for me to trust."

He nodded, his throat too constricted for words. He coveted her trust like a rare jewel but felt almost unworthy of it.

"I'm giving you my trust," she said.

Eric inched closer, his heart crashing against his chest wall. "Do you trust me now when I say I want to give you everything? And to be clear, by this I mean marriage." He motioned the house. "You, me and Kim living here and when he's better, maybe Will as well. Marriage, the picket fence, the whole deal. Even the dog."

"The whole deal." She grinned. "And along with me, you get all of my hefty baggage as well."

"I'd like to help you carry that." Not Barron's though; that asshole still needed to pay for hitting her.

She laughed, her face awash in delight. "You see! I know that and I want you to help me carry it." She stopped laughing and frowned. "To a point, because I don't care what we are to each other, I don't like handouts."

She would be the death of him with that pride. "I love you."

"I know." She beamed. "And I love you."

"I know." He was grinning like a loon, but he didn't care. "Get over here, sweet thing."

She lifted her chin. "What for?"

"Everything. I have everything for you, over here, and waiting for you to take it."

What Happens Next in Ghost Falls...

Laura Turner was the good girl of Ghost Falls, until she came tumbling off her pedestal. Now she must piece together her broken life as she wrestles with the guilt of her fall from grace. She is certainly in no place for big, bad Brett Barrows to leave her breathless and wanting things she has no right yearning for. It's taken a miracle, and a lot of jail time, but Brett Barrows is on the straight and narrow. He's there for his family, the infamous Barrow's clan, and stepping into the shoes his deplorable father never bothered to occupy. But all-class and way out of his league, Laura Turner, sneaks beneath his guard and makes him want what a boy from the wrong side of the tracks has no business even thinking about. As they both struggle for footing in their new realities, can these two wrongs make a right?

The Ghost Falls series

For Pippa Turner there's only one place to go when
her life self-destructs on national TV—home to
Ghost Falls, and her heavily perfumed, overly
dramatic, but supremely loving grandmother,
Philomene. If anyone will understand how Pippa's hit
makeover show was sabotaged by her vengeful ex,
it's Phi. But she's not the only one who's happy to
see her—and Pippa can't help but wonder if Matt
Evans, her gorgeous high-school crush turned Phi's
contractor, is game for a steamy close-up... Matt
owes his whole career to Phi and her constant
demands to embellish the gothically ridiculous house
he built for her. Getting to see red-headed, red-hot
Pippa is a bonus, especially now that she's no longer
the troublesome teenager he remembers. He's
willing to stay behind the scenes while she gives her
own life a much-needed makeover, but not forever.
As far as he's concerned, their connection is too
electric to ignore. And the chance to build something
lasting between them—before she can high-tail it
back to Hollywood—is going to the top of his to-do
list...

This Christmas, a good reputation can really get in a girlâ€™s way . . . As long as she can remember, Bella Eriksonâ€™s been the unofficial sweetheart of Ghost Falls, Utah. And ever since Nate Evans dipped her braids in purple paint in the first grade, heâ€™s been her dream guy. Not that she minds the attention, but sometimes she wishes people saw more in her than just the girl who still has a crush on Sheriff Evans. She has a life after all, a new bridal shop to run, and more mature relationships to pursue . . . Nate knows heâ€™s not good enough for sweet Bella. But heâ€™s pretty sure the new guy sending her heart emojis and giant bouquets isnâ€™t either. And when Bellaâ€™s suitor turns stalker, protecting Bella isnâ€™t just Nateâ€™s instinctâ€"itâ€™s his duty. Crammed together for safety and really talking for the first time in years, Bella and Nate canâ€™t fight the moment their chemistry turns into pyrotechnics. Whether it will burn them out or light up the sky, only time will tell . .

.

About the Author

Born British and raised in South Africa, Sarah Hegger suffers from an incurable case of wanderlust. Her match? A hot Canadian engineer, whose marriage proposal she accepted six short weeks after they first met. Together they've made homes in seven different cities across three different continents (and back again once or twice). If only it made her multilingual, but the best she can manage is idiosyncratic English, fluent Afrikaans, conversant Russian, pigeon Portuguese, even worse Zulu and enough French to get herself into trouble.

Mimicking her globe trotting adventures, Sarah's career path began as a gainfully employed actress, drifted into public relations, settled a moment in advertising, and eventually took root in the fertile soil of her first love, writing. She also moonlights as a wife and mother. She currently lives in Ottawa, Canada, with aforementioned husband, filling their empty nest with fur babies. Part footloose buccaneer, part quixotic observer of life, Sarah's restless heart is most content when reading or writing books.

f

Stay in Contact

Keep a closer eye on me by signing up to receive the @Home Collective
http://sarahhegger.com/newsletter-sign-up/

Or join the Sarah Hegger Collective on Facebook
https://www.facebook.com/groups/808770372512991/

Everything you need to know and more
Website: http://sarahhegger.com

Also by Sarah Hegger

Urban Fantasy
The Cré-Witch Chronicles
Prequel: Cast In Stone
Vol l: Born In Water
Vol ll: Purged In Fire

Sports Romance
Ottawa Titans Series
Roughing

Contemporary Romance
Passing Through Series
Drove All Night
Ticket To Ride
Walk On By

Ghost Falls Series
Positively Pippa
Becoming Bella
Blatantly Blythe
Loving Laura

Willow Park Romances
Nobody's Angel
Nobody's Fool
Nobody's Princess

Medieval Romance

Sir Arthur's Legacy Series

Sweet Bea

My Lady Faye

Conquering William

Roger's Bride

Releasing Henry

Love & War Series

The Marriage Parley

The Betrothal Melee

Western Historical Romance

The Soiled Dove Series

Sugar Ellie

Standalone

The Bride Gift

Bad Wolfe On The Rise

Wild Honey

www.ingramcontent.com/pod-product-compliance
Lightning Source LLC
Chambersburg PA
CBHW071151100726
47908CB00002B/335